AMISH CHRISTMAS
at North Star

FOUR STORIES *of* LOVE & FAMILY

CINDY WOODSMALL,
MINDY STARNS CLARK
AND EMILY CLARK,
AMANDA FLOWER, AND KATIE GANSHERT

WATERBROOK
PRESS

Amish Christmas at North Star
Published by WaterBrook Press
12265 Oracle Boulevard, Suite 200
Colorado Springs, Colorado 80921

Trade Paperback ISBN 978-1-60142-814-1
eBook ISBN 978-1-60142-815-8

Cover design by Mark D. Ford; cover photo by Doyle Yoder

Published in the United States by WaterBrook Multnomah, an imprint of the Crown Publishing Group, a division of Penguin Random House LLC, New York.

WaterBrook and its deer colophon are registered trademarks of Penguin Random House LLC.

Library of Congress Cataloging-in-Publication Data
Amish Christmas at North Star : four stories of love and family / Cindy Woodsmall... [et al.].
Mindy Starns Clark and Emily Clark, Katie Ganshert, and Amanda Flower. — First edition
     pages cm
   ISBN 978-1-60142-814-1 (paperback) — ISBN 978-1-60142-815-8 (electronic) 1. Amish—
Fiction. 2. Christian fiction, American. 3. Christmas stories. I. Ganshert, Katie. Guiding star.
II. Flower, Amanda. Mourning star. III. Woodsmall, Cindy. In the stars. IV. Clark, Mindy Starns.
Star of grace.
   PS648.A45A33 2015
   813'.01083823—dc23

                                                    2015023716

Printed in the United States of America
2015—First Edition

10 9 8 7 6 5 4 3 2 1

Prologue

by Katie Ganshert

*R*ebekah Schlabach was accustomed to young women looking a little scared. She was well acquainted with the anxious expression, the painful grimace, the sweaty brow. She could close her eyes at any given moment throughout the day and see the look of dogged determination that often crossed a woman's face when it came time to push, the exhaustion that followed when the baby tarried. As a midwife for going on twenty years, Rebekah had helped countless women bring new life into the world. This was the first time, however, that she could remember a mother-to-be looking so terribly haunted.

"Will my *Mudder* come?" the young woman asked, her face pale and drawn, the dark circles beneath her big blue eyes so pronounced they could almost be mistaken for bruises.

"I'm not sure." A gust of wind rattled the windowpane, calling Rebekah's attention to the thick flurry of snow swirling outside. Not more than an hour earlier that snow had floated peacefully from the sky. It was alarming how quickly some things could change. She wiped the young woman's brow with a damp cloth, worry knotting her stomach.

No matter how many babies she helped birth, the nervousness never went away, though she had grown adept at hiding it. This, however, called for so much more than nerves. The full weight of the situation was settling on her shoulders. Ruth Hershberger was not the only woman in Rebekah's care today. Down the hall, Lydia Beiler rested in

bed, her stomach every bit as swollen. And earlier that morning, before
the unexpected snow began, Glen Danner had come to the house to cut
firewood and had mentioned that his wife, who should have already
had her baby by now, woke up feeling uncomfortable. The very real
possibility that Rebekah might be attending to three women at once in
the midst of a snowstorm pressed an anxious hand against her heart.

"Do you think the gentleman was able to get my parents the message before the snow picked up?" Ruth asked.

Rebekah gave her hand a reassuring pat. An *Englischer* had dropped
Ruth off twenty minutes earlier. Apparently she had been out for a walk
nearby when her water broke. Rebekah had jotted down the address of
Ruth's parents and asked the gentleman to let them know their daughter was safe. "His tires looked nice and big, *ya*?"

Ruth smiled, but the gesture came without any spirit. Something
more than childbirth was troubling this young woman.

Normally Rebekah would sit by her side between contractions and
coax the trouble out. Normally she would ask why a smart girl like
Ruth had been walking in the snow so far from home when she was
heavy with child. Today, however, did not lend her that luxury.

"I know this isn't what you had planned," Rebekah said. Ruth had
returned to North Star, Pennsylvania, to have her first child at home
with her mother and eldest sister. She had never intended to be here, at
the birthing center. "But I promise you're in good hands. Now I want
you to focus on taking deep, soothing breaths, and I will be right back."

Rebekah slipped out into the drafty hallway, torn between stoking
the fire and checking on Lydia, who had arrived two hours ago. Her
husband, James, had dropped her off before being sent back home by
his wife to look after their other children. James had hesitated until
Lydia reminded him that this was their sixth child. She could deliver
the baby all by herself at this point.

Rebekah had agreed. James was needed at home and would be little help to them here. Even if Glen Danner arrived with Rose, Rebekah was confident, especially with a veteran like Lydia, that she could deliver two babies at once. But then the Englischer had come with Ruth. And now . . .

Now Rebekah found herself wishing she could take back her words.

She washed her hands in the bathroom sink and scurried into the room down the hall. Lydia rested in bed, the few loose tendrils of hair sticking to her neck the only sign of her hard work. Rebekah checked to see how Lydia was progressing and then made a quick decision.

She had to get a message to Glen. He and Rose were new parents, and nervous ones at that. They wanted the competency of an experienced midwife and the comfort of their own home, so Rebekah had agreed from the beginning to make a house call when the time came. If that time happened to be today, as she suspected, she needed to get word to Glen that he would have to bring Rose here. Rebekah could no more make a house call tonight than she could make the wind stop howling outside.

After feeding the ravenous stove some more firewood, she put on her winter cape, a matching black bonnet, and a pair of snow boots and headed out into the gale. Snow assaulted her cheeks. Wind whipped her skirt. Gray sky gave way to darkness, making visibility next to nothing. Thankfully, Rebekah could find the phone shanty with her eyes closed.

By the time she arrived, her fingers had turned to ice. Shivering, she was reaching for the receiver to call the phone in the Danners' barn when she saw the blinking light on the answering machine. The message was from Glen, saying that Rose's discomfort continued to worsen and that, with the weather so bad, he was going to hitch up the buggy and drive over.

The knots in Rebekah's stomach pulled tighter.

Another gust of wind pushed against the shanty, so strong Rebekah was sure it would tumble right over. She hung up the phone and hurried back to the house, snow well above her ankles. When she reached the front porch, she made out the vague image of a horse and buggy parked nearby. She waited for Glen to appear through the flurry of white, supporting his wife.

But Glen and Rose did not materialize. Mary Hochstetler and her eldest son, Luke, did. He held one of his mother's arms while she supported her bulging abdomen with the other.

"I'm sorry, Rebekah, but this *Bobbeli* will not wait," Mary said.

She wasn't due for another two weeks at least.

"I had Luke drive me here while we could still make it."

"Yes, *kumm* out of the cold." Rebekah waved mother and son inside, ignoring the frantic butterflies flapping about where her dinner should be. "Kumm."

Before she closed the door, the faint *clippety-clop* of horse hoofs was carried on the wind. That would be Glen and Rose.

Rebekah asked Luke to go outside and help them. She settled Mary in a room and then hurried back to greet Rose, whom she settled in the last remaining room—her own. She checked on Ruth and Lydia, then went to the living room to speak with her inadequate team. The young men didn't know a lick about bringing babies into the world, but they could keep the fire stoked and melt snow should the pipes freeze. Both seemed very glad to have something to do and went to work at once.

Down the hall one of the women groaned.

Rebekah rushed toward the sound, praying for strength and courage as she went. Praying that God would protect each heartbeat and guide her hands.

She didn't stop until the last baby arrived at two minutes before midnight, greeting the world with a gusty wail. Rebekah, totally depleted, finally took a breath of her own.

Four babies in one night. All healthy and whole.

A miracle of God.

When all was clean and calm, Rebekah stepped outside, kneading the taut muscles in her neck. The storm had ceased, leaving behind a crystallized blanket of white that draped itself over the landscape. It covered every rooftop, every tree branch for as far as her eyes could see. The town of North Star had turned into one of those snow globes she saw in the Christmas aisle at the local grocery store. And inside that globe, on her front porch, the world had gone quiet.

Rebekah inhaled cold air deep into her lungs, then exhaled—her frozen breath forming a cloud around her lips.

A star shone up above—a bright beacon in the night.

It was officially December first. Advent had begun. Christmas was on the way.

Rebekah wrapped a shawl around her shoulders and smiled, her thoughts turning to another baby, born to a virgin millenniums ago and laid in a manger while angels sang to the shepherds on a hilltop. Light had come into the world at last, and the darkness would not overcome it.

Closing her eyes, she prayed over each child in her home. Three precious baby girls and one handsome baby boy. She prayed that no matter where they went or who they became, each one would grow up to know this light all the days of their lives.

Guiding Star

KATIE GANSHERT

*F*loorboards creaked beneath Chase Wellington's work boots as he set another labeled box near the open hatch in the floor, stirring up a host of dust motes. They floated like glitter in the stream of light pouring in through the attic window.

"Be careful not to break anything!" his mother called from below.

"Don't worry, Ma. I'm being extra careful."

Brooke poked her head up through the trapdoor, a bright smile on her face. "You know how Mom is about her stuff. Telling her not to worry is like telling the sun to cool off."

"Good point." He lifted another box from one of the shelves with a grunt. Their mother was an infamous pack rat. Chase often joked that she could star in an episode of *Hoarders,* to which she always scoffed and said her house looked nothing like a hoarder's, thank you very much. But that was only because she and Doug had plenty of storage and Mom was highly organized. Now that they were moving into one of the new town houses a few neighborhoods away, she might have to get things under control.

He set the box next to Brooke. A week ago his kid sister had turned thirteen. And she had a boyfriend. Last night over dinner, she said they were "going out." But they were thirteen, for crying out loud. Where in the world were they going to go? He expected Mom or Doug to disapprove. Instead, Doug teased Brooke about the kid's haircut. Brooke insisted it was cool. And Mom used the conversation to pry into Chase's love life.

When was he going to "go out"?

"Chase has ADHD when it comes to the women in North Star, Ma," Brooke had said matter-of-factly. *"None of them can hold his attention for very long."*

He'd lobbed a roll at her.

Brooke climbed a few more rungs of the ladder and read the box's label. "Why doesn't Mom let Gage deal with storing his trophies?"

"Because Gage would throw them away."

Brooke peered down the ladder. "Mom, we aren't going to have room for this stuff, you know."

"We'll find room. And if we can't, your father promised he'd rent me a storage unit."

Brooke rolled her eyes.

"I heard that," Mom called.

"But I didn't say anything!" Brooke turned her exasperation on Chase. "How does she hear an eye roll?"

"I'm your mother, that's how."

Chuckling, he grabbed another box. It was filled to the brim with old newspapers. He wouldn't put it past Mom to have kept every single article he'd ever written. He was a construction manager by trade, but he also wrote for the *North Star Tribune* on the side. He'd been doing so ever since he graduated from college with a random minor in journalism.

He peeked inside, but instead of finding his work, he found old copies of *The Budget.* Mom had been a subscriber to the Amish newspaper for as long as Chase could remember. Every time one came in the mail, she'd brew a pot of coffee and read it beginning to end. Growing up in Lancaster County, he was no stranger to the Plain life. Growing up with a mother so intrigued by that life made him extra familiar.

"I'm supposed to tell you that lunch is ready," Brooke said.

"I'll be down in a bit."

"Don't wait too long. You know how Mom gets." She shot him a wink before climbing down the ladder.

Chase set the box next to the others. Yes, he did know. Mom was perpetually concerned with his thinness even though he was perfectly healthy and fit. It didn't matter what the BMI charts said. Mom wouldn't be happy until he settled down with a nice wife who fed him home-cooked meals for breakfast, lunch, and dinner and he had a Santa belly. Chase wasn't sure that breed of woman existed anymore, at least outside the Plain community, and as much as he admired the lifestyle, he wasn't about to marry into it. Or marry at all, for that matter. It hadn't worked out for his brother the first time around or for his mom. So unless Chase met a girl who could convince him it was worth the risk, he was happy being a bachelor.

He glanced at the faded newspaper on top. The headline caught his attention.

Unable to resist a special-interest story, he put the box by the others and read the article all the way through. On November 30, 1990, a record-setting blizzard slammed Lancaster County. And in the midst of that blizzard, right here in his hometown of North Star, Pennsylvania, an Amish midwife named Rebekah Schlabach delivered not one, not two, not three, but *four* babies all in the same night—three girls and one boy.

Wow. Talk about a pressure situation.

As Chase spent the next thirty minutes carting boxes down the ladder into the hallway, his intrigue grew. Special-interest stories had a way of doing this to him—grabbing and not letting go. When he was no more than three years old, while wind gusted and snow swirled outside, while power and telephone lines failed, a woman delivered four babies in a single night not more than a few miles away.

"Chase, honey?"

He blinked away the scene unfolding in his mind.

Mom stood at the top of the ladder, her bottle-brown hair pulled up into a messy bun, gray roots starting to show. "You should come get something to eat before you dwindle away to nothing."

He followed his mother down to the main level, toward the savory smell of her famous homemade chili, and pulled the newspaper article from his back pocket. "Do you remember this?"

Mom's eyes went bright. "I sure do."

In the kitchen Brooke packed utensils in a small box. Chase's step-father, Doug, placed his empty bowl into the sink, clapped Chase on the shoulder, and squeezed by them to continue working.

"That story was picked up by *People* magazine," Mom said, lifting the lid off the Crock-Pot.

"*People*?"

"They became known as Rebekah's Babies. The gal who wrote the story came here to North Star, hoping to get a picture of the midwife with the four infants, but you know how the Plain folk are about pictures." Mom scooped some chili into a clean bowl. "After the article was published, that birthing center, which of course was also the poor woman's home, turned into a tourist attraction."

He could only imagine how Rebekah and the babies' families would have felt about the attention. The Amish were notoriously private people. Kind, but private. Chase gently nudged Mom aside and finished serving himself.

"I can't believe that was nearly twenty-five years ago." She shook her head. "Somebody needs to tell time to slow down already."

He sat at the table with the article in front of him, his journalistic mind firing on all cylinders. Steam rose from his bowl as he stirred his chili, lost in thought.

Rebekah's Babies.

He couldn't help but wonder where they were now.

*F*inding Rebekah Schlabach's address had been a cinch, as she ran the only Amish birthing center in North Star. Chase just hoped getting answers to his questions would be equally as easy.

He pulled his stocking hat over his unruly dark hair and stepped out of his car. A dusting of white covered the ground and the roof of Rebekah's home. There had been flurries earlier in the morning, but nothing had stuck to the roads.

Chase walked past the horse and buggy parked out front, stepped onto the porch, and knocked lightly on the door. Rubbing his hands together, he shuffled toward the banister, his breath escaping in frozen puffs.

Several seconds later the door swung open, and a man with a scraggly beard stepped out. A young woman came next, fitting a black bonnet over her prayer *Kapp* and talking over her shoulder, her protruding belly obvious even beneath the loose-fitting dress and apron. "*Denki,* Rebekah. *Mach's gut.*"

The screen door whapped shut behind her as she bumped into the man, who had stopped several feet in front of Chase. Judging by their curious expressions, he assumed Englischers didn't typically show up on the midwife's front porch.

"I was hoping to have a word with Ms. Schlabach," Chase said.

The young woman opened the door, its hinges groaning as she called inside, "Rebekah! *Du hosh ptsuh. Sis en hohe mann ahn de deah.*"

Chase was used to hearing bits and pieces of Pennsylvania Dutch spoken by an Amish mother and her children at the grocery store or by men at a work site. But recognizing and understanding were two very different things. The woman could have told Rebekah to stay away or come quickly, and he'd be none the wiser.

But not long after, another woman appeared in the doorway, much older than the first, with dark brown eyes and a few flyaway gray curls escaping her Kapp. Chase took off his stocking cap.

The old woman's eyes twinkled, as if the sight of him standing on her porch amused her. "Are you lost, young man?"

"No, actually I came to speak with you." He stepped closer, pulling the article out of his coat pocket. "About this."

Rebekah eyed the paper, then him.

Chase found himself wishing he'd gotten a haircut before the visit. "I would have called before stopping by unannounced like this, but . . ."

The old woman waited a beat, then let out a welcomed laugh. "But we Amish are hard to get in touch with, ya?"

He smiled. "Yes ma'am."

Rebekah turned to the husband and wife watching the exchange and spoke to them in their dialect. The man tipped his hat at Chase, then took his wife's arm and led her to the buggy.

"I'm sorry to interrupt," Chase said.

"No babies are coming today. At least not by my hand." She waved him inside. "Come in out of the cold. I'll make us some coffee, and we can talk about that article."

Grateful, Chase followed Rebekah through the house into a warm kitchen that smelled like cinnamon and apple pie. His stomach gurgled. He was a sucker for pie.

Rebekah pulled out a chair for him, then got to work making coffee on a gas range. "What's your name?"

"Chase Wellington."

"You are a tourist, Mr. Wellington?"

"I've lived here in North Star all my life, on the opposite side of town."

Metal clinked as Rebekah placed a small steel bowl filled with coffee grounds inside a matching steel pot. There was a distinct tremor in her hands as she worked, perhaps from old age. Chase had a hard time imagining the woman delivering *one* baby, let alone four. But that had been twenty-five years ago.

Rebekah lit the burner, set a timer, pulled the pie from the oven, and joined Chase at the table. "You look much too young to be carrying around an article so old."

"It belongs to my mom. She's subscribed to *The Budget* all my life. I came across the story yesterday while I was helping her and my stepdad move."

"And so you decided to come meet me?" Her question came laced with amusement.

"I was hoping to learn more about where the four babies are now."

"Why?"

Chase expelled a breath. He would tell her the truth and either be met with a polite rejection, because it was none of his business, or the information he hoped for. "I'm a journalist for the *North Star Tribune,* and I would love to do a follow-up story."

Rebekah lifted one of her sparse eyebrows.

The timer ticked softly in the background while he waited, unsure if that quirked eyebrow was good or bad. He ran his hand over his hair, temporarily flattening his cowlicks. "You know how we Englischers are about the Amish."

"Ya, I do." Rebekah twirled her finger in circles around her ear— the universal sign for *crazy.*

Chase laughed.

"I can't say they will want a story written about them."

"I understand, and I promise to respect that." He wasn't now, nor would he ever be, one of those intrusive reporters who cared little about privacy. It was a luxury he could afford since his living didn't depend on newspaper articles. Writing for the *Tribune* was an enjoyable hobby, not a necessity. "I wanted to come here today to see how far I could get, even if only for my own curiosity."

Her eyebrow lifted again.

This time Chase twirled his own finger by his ear. "I know, crazy."

Rebekah scooted away from the table with a smile and removed two plates from a cupboard. "What would you like to know?"

"I was hoping you could tell me the story as you remember it and then where I might find each of the four now."

She set a piece of pie and a fork in front of him. As he ate and then drank fresh coffee, Rebekah told him the story from beginning to end—of the unexpected blizzard, the circumstances that led to four mothers in her birthing center at once, the pipes frozen solid, and no-body to help but one young husband and a teenage boy. Yet somehow, by God's grace, all four babies were born that very night and were healthy and whole.

"It was the most memorable night of my life," she said. "And at my age there have been plenty of opportunities for competition."

"Do all four still live in North Star?"

"Only one. Her name is Savilla Beiler. She lives not too far away and helps me with paperwork." Something like sadness flitted across Rebekah's face. "Savvy has no idea what a blessing she's been to me these past ten years."

"Do you think she would talk with me?"

"I can't say. That's up to her."

"And the others?"

"They might not be so easy to get to. The boy—Andy—lives in

Mississippi. He went down there a while back. Last I heard, he's living in a newer settlement called Kashofa."

Chase jotted down the information in a small notepad he'd pulled from his pocket.

"Little Eden Hochstetler's family moved to Sugarcreek shortly after she was born. Her father took over his father's fudge-and-candy shop. And then there's the fourth."

Chase waited, his pen poised over the paper.

"Baby Anna." Rebekah took a long sip of her coffee, her brown eyes dulling with sadness. "Nobody knows where she is."

"What do you mean?"

"Shortly after Anna was born, she and her mother disappeared. As far as I know, nobody has seen or heard from either of them since."

Chase forced his mouth shut. It wasn't polite to gape. "The family didn't go looking for them?"

"What could they do—drag her back?"

He didn't have a response. He only knew that if Brooke had a baby and disappeared, he wouldn't rest until he'd found her.

"Ruth left as an adult with free will."

"But what about the child's father?"

"He lived several hours away in Chestnut Ridge. By the time he arrived to bring his wife and newborn home, Ruth and the baby were already gone." Rebekah shook her head. "It was a terrible mess. And another day I won't soon forget."

"Do Ruth's parents live here in North Star?"

"Ya, but if you want more information, I wouldn't expect any help from them. Nor would I like you to speak with them at all. What they went through was painful. Best to leave it in the past."

Chase nodded, but as Rebekah told him more about the other three—Savvy, Eden, and Andy—his thoughts spun around the baby who had gone missing. The baby who wasn't spoken about. Her piece of the puzzle turned the story from heartwarmingly sweet to irresistibly intriguing. His mind buzzed with questions.

What would cause a woman to leave everything behind? Why wouldn't the husband go looking for his wife and child? Ruth's parents might not know where their daughter had gone, but that didn't mean she hadn't left a trail.

One thing he'd learned during his years as a journalist—there was always a trail.

*F*or most people Black Friday meant setting the alarm at an ungodly hour to fight the crowds and find the best deals. For Elle McAllister, Black Friday meant coffees to go from Willow Tree Café, pumpkin pie, Christmas music, and tree decorating with her parents. It had been a tradition of theirs for as long as she could remember, and since Mom refused to play Christmas music one second before Thanksgiving ended, and since there was nothing Elle adored listening to more than that particular genre, Black Friday was quite possibly her favorite day of the year. On the rare occasion it snowed, that favorite day elevated itself to heaven-on-earth status.

Today it was snowing. The first real snow of the season.

Cotton-ball snowflakes floated from the clouds, sticking to treetops and roofs and mailboxes. Elle caught several of them on her palm. As a little girl, she couldn't believe that no two were alike. With all the snowflakes in the world, *none* were the same? She'd spent the winter of her third-grade year catching as many as she could, positive she'd find a pair of twins. Most had melted before she could reach any conclusions either way.

A few flakes caught on Elle's eyelashes. She blinked them away, then stomped on the welcome mat outside her childhood home.

Nobody would have guessed that a girl with such wanderlust in her veins would end up settling in the unpretentious town of Peaks, Iowa. Certainly not Elle's parents. They had long been resigned to the possibility that their adventurous daughter would end up in Prague or

Sydney or Cairo, perhaps all three, depending on the year. But here Elle was, still in the place she'd learned to walk, ride a bike, drive a car, kiss a boy. She supposed when it came right down to it, Dorothy knew best.

There was no place like home.

Elle stepped inside to the glorious sound of Bing Crosby crooning about silver bells and shook the snow from her long blond hair. "I feel like I'm stepping out of a giant snow globe."

Mom met her in the foyer, taking the cardboard coffee tray from her hands. "Are the roads bad?"

"Give it an hour and they will be."

Dad walked past them, carrying a box of Christmas decorations into the living room. "Weather forecasters say we could get up to a foot."

"Music to my little ears." Elle unwrapped her scarf and hung it on the coat stand along with her winter coat, slipped off her boots, and followed her mother into the kitchen, where a fresh, homemade pumpkin pie sat uncovered on the counter beside a small stack of plates.

"I'm still full from yesterday," Mom said, pulling one of the coffee cups from the tray.

"But you can't skip pie." Elle unstacked the plates and served one piece for Mom, one for Dad, and one for herself. "It's tradition."

"Says the twenty-four-year-old whose metabolism is still in full swing." Mom took a sip from her cup. "Mine walked out on me years ago."

A brightly colored brochure in the stack of mail on the counter caught Elle's attention. She picked it up, and as she did, a small, handwritten note fell from the fold.

> *To our favorite Iowa couple,*
>   *We hope you can join us! It's a once-in-a-lifetime trip,*

completely on us (no arguing allowed). Last time we saw you,
you both looked like you could use some sun.
 Hugs,
 Diane and Randy

Diane and Randy were Mom and Dad's oldest friends and loaded to the hilt. What was this once-in-a-lifetime trip they were talking about? As soon as Elle opened the brochure, her mouth dropped open. "A Hawaiian cruise?"

"It's nothing." Mom took the note and the brochure from Elle's hands.

"*Nothing*? It's Hawaii!"

"Which I'm sure is beautiful, but we're not going."

Elle's mouth opened wider.

"We'd have to leave in two weeks, and we wouldn't get back until late Christmas night." Mom tucked the brochure beneath the stack of mail, as though putting it out of sight would also put it out of mind, and brought her coffee and piece of pie to the table.

"Mom." Elle's parents had given her the world. Literally. They hadn't just encouraged her to travel in college; they'd supported her financially while she did it. Because of them, she had spent a semester studying in France. Because of them, she'd spent a summer backpacking through Europe. Because of them, she'd gone on a safari in the Serengeti and slept in a tent with the Masai. She wasn't going to let them miss out on a cruise to Hawaii. Not if she could help it. "You have to go."

"No. I *have* to pay taxes. This, my darling daughter, is not a *have to*."

"Dad!"

He popped his head into the kitchen. "Pie ready?"

Elle unburied the brochure from its hiding place and held it up. "Please tell me you're going to take Mom on this cruise."

His attention flitted to the woman under discussion, who sipped her coffee and then shook her head.

Elle put her hand on her hip. "True or false: The only reason you are not going on this trip is because you don't want me to be alone on Christmas?"

"False."

"True."

Mom and Dad spoke at the same time. Mom gave Dad a sharp look, because he, of course, had given the honest answer. Elle narrowed her eyes at her mother.

"Okay, fine. But it's a very valid reason."

"No, it's a very ridiculous reason. I can spend Christmas with Melody and her husband." Melody was Elle's best friend, going all the way back to their elementary-school days. And she was also incredibly pregnant. Overdue, in fact. Elle could spend the holiday cuddling the new baby. "Or better yet, I'll go somewhere. Like Vienna. Or Nuremberg. I've heard both are gorgeous at Christmastime."

Mom looked unconvinced.

"It's one of the perks of my job. I get a built-in winter vacation." Fresh out of college, Elle had snagged the art teacher position at Peaks's only elementary school. The perfect job. Not only because she loved art and kids, but because she could travel all summer long if her heart desired. She lived in a small studio apartment, drove a beater car, and had graduated debt-free (another gift from her parents), which meant she was able to put a sizable portion of each paycheck into her travel fund. "So it's settled. You two will go to Hawaii, and I'll buy a ticket to Germany."

Dad scratched the top of his balding head and eyed his wife. "I think it sounds like a good plan."

The skepticism on her face had receded some but not as much as Dad's hairline.

Before Elle could do any more convincing, her phone chirped from the back pocket of her jeans. She pulled it out and checked the screen. It wasn't Melody's number. It was Melody's husband's number. Which meant . . .

Elle quickly pressed the phone against her ear. "You better be calling for the reason I think you're calling."

There was an exciting heartbeat of a pause and then, "It's a girl!"

❦

"She looks exactly like Josh."

Melody's astonished exclamation a few minutes ago played through Elle's mind as she navigated the slippery roads.

"I'm telling you, Elle. Same eyes. Same ears. Same crazy hair. It's like I'm staring into the face of my husband, only as a pink, wrinkled baby."

The wipers of the Ford Explorer squeaked against the windshield as they pushed aside a fresh accumulation of white. Dad had insisted she drive his car to the hospital since his car had four-wheel drive and hers did not. Elle pressed a little harder on the gas, eager to see this new bundle of joy.

Lila Grace Dowel had come into the world on the best day of the year.

Mariah Carey started singing "All I Want for Christmas Is You" on the radio. Elle turned up the volume and sang along. In high school she and Melody had done a whole bit to this particular song, lip-syncing to each other like nobody's business. But then Melody met Josh and fell in love, and Elle found herself wishing she had somebody else to sing the song to. The problem was Peaks was small and the pickings were slim. Josh said she was too picky. But to Elle it was a matter of not settling.

God simply hadn't crossed her path with the right guy yet.

When she arrived at the hospital, Elle stopped in the gift shop, bought pink balloons and an adorable pair of pink booties, then headed up to the second floor neonatal unit. She buzzed the bell by the security doors and gave her name. Room 237 was at the end of the hall, and as Elle approached, she found herself slowing down, a strange mixture of reverence and *joie de vivre* rising in her spirit.

She stopped when she reached the half-opened door and silently peeked inside, her breath catching at the intimate scene before her. There was her childhood friend sitting in a hospital bed, hair falling over one shoulder as she nursed a swaddled baby in her arms. Standing over them, Josh kissed the crown of Melody's head. She looked up at him, a distinct sheen in her eyes, then stroked her knuckle along the cherub cheek of the suckling baby.

A lump of emotion rose in Elle's throat.

And the niggling questions surfaced.

Had her birth mother nursed her like that when she was born? Did she marvel at how much Elle looked like her father? Did her father even know that she'd been born? Most likely, no. If statistics had any accuracy, Elle had probably been a mistake. Her birth mother had most likely been an unwed teenager unprepared for parenthood. She couldn't know for sure, of course. All she knew was that the woman had given her life. And that would have to be enough.

*T*he water ran green, then red, then gold as Elle rinsed off paintbrushes in her classroom sink—leftover mess from the Christmas tree project her kindergarten class had worked on earlier in the day. She hummed "Silent Night," thinking about the places she could go for Christmas. There were all the European destinations, but perhaps staying closer to home would be a smarter choice. Somewhere simple, like Washington DC or New York City, for a couple of days.

Her phone dinged. Elle glanced at the screen. Friends and family had been checking in throughout the day, leaving messages on her phone or posting birthday wishes on her Facebook wall. "Happy twenty-fifth!" one of her college roommates had written. "You're now a quarter of a century old!" But Elle wasn't sure when she'd reached that particular milestone. It could have been two weeks ago. It could still be a week into the future. It was another of those niggling question marks.

Her "birthday" was December 4 because that was the date her parents had chosen. Her former pediatrician believed it was quite close to her actual birthday, and as an added bonus, December 4 marked the date her parents had officially said yes to adoption. Almost two and a half years later, they received the phone call that made them parents. A phone call Elle's mom had told her about many, many times over the years, never once with dry eyes. One question Elle never had? Whether or not her parents loved her as much as they would have loved a biological child.

She shut off the faucet, tapped the paintbrushes against the sink basin to knock away the excess moisture, and placed them bristle-up in a plastic Hawkeye cup on the counter. She dried her hands, then texted an impromptu message to her mom: "See you in a bit. Love you much."

Elle couldn't imagine anything different from the life she led, nor did she want to. But something about her birth date and the possible inaccuracy of it, combined with watching Melody and Josh turn into such doting, smitten parents, made those niggling questions extra niggly.

When she was a little girl, Mom used to make up all sorts of bedtime stories about her beginning. Some nights she was born on a pirate ship, the beloved daughter of a captain and his wife, who were captured and begged one of the crewmen to take their darling baby girl to safety. Other nights she was a princess like Aurora, flitted away from her kingdom by three fairy godmothers charged with protecting her. Some nights God spun her into existence in the clouds especially for the McAllisters, who had prayed and prayed for a baby. Then he placed her in the care of a stork with specific instructions to take her to Peaks, Iowa. But the stork got turned around in a snowstorm and ended up taking her to the wrong home. Thankfully, God was big enough to right the stork's mistake.

After each story Mom would wrap her arm around Elle's shoulders and tell her that if she wanted to search for the truth, they could search for it together. And every time, Elle shook her head. She liked the stories better.

Her phone chirped again. Mom had responded with a simple "Love you more."

Shaking away the questions, Elle packed her bag and slipped out of her classroom. She didn't need to know. God had given her a good life, a beautiful life. Asking for more than that would simply be greedy.

When she was halfway down the hall, her phone began buzzing. An unfamiliar number with an equally unfamiliar area code flashed on the screen. She considered letting it go to voice mail but changed her mind at the last second and answered with a friendly *hello.*

"Is this Noelle McAllister?" The question came from a man. And since he called her by her full name, he wasn't one she knew.

"This is she." Elle pushed the door open and stepped out into the dark.

"My name is Chase Wellington."

"Hi, Chase Wellington." Snow crunched beneath her boots as she walked across the half-emptied parking lot, waiting for the guy to make his sales pitch so she could politely decline. Dad always hung up when it was a telemarketer, but Elle could never do it. Being hung up on all day had to be disheartening, and listening wasn't so hard. She unlocked her car and slipped inside. "Are you still there?"

"Yes, sorry. This is going to sound pretty strange."

Elle twisted her key in the ignition and turned on the heat, her curiosity officially piqued. It was an odd opening. "Okay."

Another short pause and then, "Were you, by chance, adopted?"

This wasn't a telemarketer.

"If you were, if this is the right Noelle McAllister, I believe I have information regarding your birth mother."

Warmth drained from her cheeks. "Is this a joke?"

"No. I promise it's not. I'm a journalist for—"

Elle hung up and dropped the phone in the passenger seat like a hot potato. She wrapped her fingers around the steering wheel and tried to bat away the web of confusion the man's declaration had left behind. Surely that had been some sort of freaky prank. But then, how had this Chase Wellington gotten her name? How could he have known that she was adopted?

The blog.

Of course, that had to be it. She'd started one her freshman year of college. It began as a class assignment and turned into something so much more—not only a catalog of her travel adventures, but a place to share her testimony from beginning to end. Writing it out had been therapeutic—for her and she hoped for other adoptees too. She no longer updated the blog, but it was still out there in cyberspace. Someone could have easily found it and, from there, tracked down her number.

Normally, Elle would laugh off the call. But today the timing felt much too eerie, much too coincidental. Today that call left her rattled. She eyed the phone suspiciously, waiting to see if the prankster would call back.

When the inside of her car was toasty and warm and her phone had yet to ring, she shifted out of Park and drove to Val's Diner.

Inside, Mom greeted her with a hug and an enthusiastic "Happy birthday!" She'd already snagged the corner booth they loved, and a giant poinsettia sat on the table. Mom bought her one every year, and each year they grew bigger.

"It's so cold," Mom said, sliding into the booth.

Elle nodded, unable to get the shiver out of her jaw. She wasn't sure if it was because of the cold or a side effect of that bizarre phone call. "Aren't you thankful I talked you into Hawaii?"

"I'm still not sure about that."

"Well, get sure. Because if you don't go, you and Dad will be here all by yourselves, because *I* am buying a plane ticket to somewhere fun, and I'm buying it tonight."

A waitress came to their table to take their drink order. Water and decaf coffee for Mom and a Sprite for Elle. As soon as she left, Mom asked Elle about her day. Her students. Melody's baby. Christmas shopping. That handsome new principal at the junior high, who Elle didn't think was really all that handsome. Elle did her best to carry on a conversation, but the phone call kept distracting her.

Halfway through their meal, Mom put down her burger. "Are you sure you want us to go on this cruise, sweetheart? Your father and I don't mind if—"

Elle held up her hand. "Don't even think about it."

"But I can tell something is bothering you."

"Something is, but I promise that something has nothing to do with Hawaii."

"What is it, then?"

Elle ran her fingers through her hair, then proceeded to tell her mother all about the strange phone call. "I have no idea why I'm letting a prank bother me so much."

"What makes you think it was a prank?"

"You think it's serious?"

"We'll never know unless you call him back. If this guy—Chase whoever—turns out to be a jokester or starts asking for personal information, you can hang up and forget all about it. But if he really does know something . . ." Mom slowly shrugged.

Elle rubbed her thumb over one of the poinsettia's red leaves, playing the same scenario in her mind that she always played when she thought about looking for her biological mother—finding the woman who had given her life and knocking on her door, only to have that door slammed in her face. There was a very real possibility this woman didn't want to be found. And then what? Why open a can of worms when her life was perfectly fine?

"Elle?"

"Yes?"

"What's holding you back?" Mom reached across the table and set her hand over Elle's. "Because if the answer is fear, you know what your father and I have to say about that."

Elle sighed. "The good stuff in life waits on the other side of fear."

*C*hase's knee bounced beneath a small table inside Willow Tree Café, his attention pinned on the front door. The coffee and the food smelled delicious, but he was determined to wait for Elle McAllister before he partook in either. He pushed up the sleeve of his navy-blue Henley to check his watch—4:46 p.m. Elle said she finished work at four and could meet him at a quarter past. He was beginning to wonder if he was being stood up. Chase hoped not, especially since he'd come all this way.

It was a crazy move, he knew, but one of his college buddies lived nearby, and Chase was currently between construction jobs, so he'd come under the pretense of visiting an old friend, which didn't sound nearly as insane as meeting with a woman who might or might not prove to be part of an as-yet-unwritten story for a small-town newspaper that paid its writers in nickels and dimes. He couldn't help himself though. The story had gotten under his skin. The more he searched, the deeper it burrowed. Then he'd found Noelle McAllister's blog, read it from beginning to end, and she'd gotten under his skin too.

Chase had inherited his father's addictive personality. It was why he didn't drink or gamble or play video games. It was why he never tried cigarettes in high school. He was all too easily consumed, and this story was consuming him. Whether any of this ended up in the *North Star Tribune* or not, he had this compulsive urge to know whether Noelle McAllister was, in fact, Baby Anna.

He wouldn't blame her if she decided not to come. If Brooke told him she was meeting a strange man who claimed to know something about her past, all kinds of alarms would sound in his head. He'd either go with Brooke to meet the guy or not let her go at all. But he'd spoken with Elle for a while on the phone. He'd sent her his credentials, along with references, and she'd sounded sincere when she told him when and where they could meet.

The front door opened.

Chase sat up straighter as a young woman with long blond hair, fair skin, and rosy cheeks stepped inside. She wore a puffy black North Face coat and a magenta beanie with matching mittens. Everything inside of him perked up. She'd come. He recognized her from the pictures on her blog.

When her attention finally landed on him, she offered up a hesitant wave.

He left his table to meet her up front, becoming increasingly nervous and giddy as he approached—two feelings he didn't commonly have. "Elle?"

"That's me." She let out a breathless laugh and shook his hand. Hers felt dainty in his—not because her grip was weak but because even inside her mitten, her hand was small. "I'm sorry I'm late. I got caught at work."

She had bright blue eyes and a small, slightly wide nose that made her look even younger in person than in her pictures. Her height didn't help. Chase was six feet on a good day, yet next to her he felt like he could play in the NBA.

Elle stuck her hands inside the pockets of her coat. "You found the place okay?"

"Without a hitch." He shuffled to the end of the short line. "You give good directions."

"Where are you staying?"

"Bernie's Bed and Breakfast."

Elle laughed, a sound that chased away some of the unexpected nervousness he had developed since she stepped inside the café. He'd spent the past couple of weeks looking for her, and now suddenly here she was. Looking very pretty, he might add. Combine that with the memory of her blog posts, which had been passionate and funny and welcoming at the same time, and Chase felt a lot like he had in sixth grade when he finally worked up the courage to hold Alyssa Rocker's hand at the roller skating rink.

"Is that a funny place to stay?" he asked.

"No, it's great. Bernie's just"—she smiled up at him—"a little eclectic."

"Do you know she has a female cat named Bill?"

Elle laughed again as they stepped forward in line, and as they did, a little boy launched himself into her arms. He wrapped her waist in a hug and squeezed tight. "Look, Mommy, it's Miss McAllister, my art teacher!"

The woman behind the counter waved to Elle before glancing curiously at Chase. He recognized the look. It was notorious in small towns, especially when one of the town's residents had a stranger in tow and most especially when that stranger was of the opposite sex. The boy's mother handed change to a customer in front of them, and a man stepped out of the back kitchen, holding two plates. He gave Elle a friendly nod as he passed by to deliver the food.

"Hey, C-man," he called, "the kitchen doesn't run right without my sous-chef."

The boy smiled, showing two missing front teeth, said good-bye to Elle, and hurried after the man, leaving every bit as abruptly as he'd come.

"Cute kid," Chase said.

"Caleb's one of my favorites." Elle leaned close, her hair smelling like strawberries. "But you didn't hear that from me."

"So you teach art?" She'd had so many passions when she wrote her blog in college, he'd wondered what she ended up doing. An art teacher seemed like a good fit.

"At the elementary school." She stepped up to the counter and placed her order—a small caramel latte with extra whipped cream and a chocolate croissant. "Robin's croissants are the reason I moved back to Peaks."

The woman behind the register shooed off the compliment.

Elle reached inside her purse, but Chase pulled his wallet from his back pocket before she could find her money. "I've got it."

"Oh, that's not necessary."

"No really, I've got it." He slid his credit card across the counter and peered up at the menu. While he perused his options, the two women talked about Caleb and the funny thing he'd said in art class earlier in the morning, something about his mommy swallowing a baby. Robin laughed and said the baby was due in July. Elle extended her congratulations, and Chase ordered a scone and a large coffee.

When they reached the table, Elle unzipped her coat and unwrapped her scarf. "I can't remember the last time I was this nervous."

"You're nervous?"

"Until a little while ago, I was convinced I was being gullible. That this was some elaborate prank, and you wouldn't be here. But here you are, looking very"—she looked him over, her attention flicking from the bottom of his brown boots to the top of his freshly cut hair—"official."

"Official?"

"Reporterly."

Chase rested his ankle over his knee and bit back a smile, wondering what reporters were supposed to look like.

"I'm not sure how a conversation like this is supposed to go." She took a sip of her latte and quickly wiped the whipped cream off her top lip. "Do we make small talk first, or do we jump right in?"

"Do you want to make small talk first?"

"I feel like it would be the polite thing to do."

"Politeness aside?"

She wrapped her small hands around her mug. "I'm anxious to jump in."

Chase scratched the stubble on his chin, trying to figure out the best place to start the jumping. He knew for sure that this Elle was the same baby who was left on a doorstep at a home in Gary, Indiana, circa 1990. The story had made headlines in Gary's local newspaper. Since she'd been left on a doorstep on Christmas Eve, she'd been dubbed Baby Noel and placed in foster care for several months before being adopted by Mitchell and Vanessa McAllister of Peaks, Iowa. That last bit he'd learned on her blog.

What he didn't know was whether the Elle sitting across from him was also one of Rebekah's Babies. Did Ruth escape her Amish life only to abandon her child to a couple of *Englisch* strangers? It seemed highly unlikely, but Chase couldn't ignore the evidence.

"What do you know about the Amish?" he asked.

Elle blinked at him for several seconds, as if processing the seemingly misplaced question. "The Amish?"

"Yes."

"I don't understand the question."

Chase slid the news article across the table.

Elle unfolded the paper and read. When she finished, she refolded the article and handed it back. "I still don't understand."

"I found that in my mom's attic a few weeks ago. I'd been looking for a special-interest story to write for the holidays, and this felt like a good lead. But when I talked to this midwife—Rebekah Schlabach— she told me that one of the four babies had gone missing. Two days after giving birth, the mother took the child, and the two of them disappeared."

Elle raised her eyebrows and waited for him to continue.

"The mother purchased a train ticket that took her to Gary, Indiana. You were left on a doorstep in Gary, Indiana, three weeks later on Christmas Eve."

She leaned back in her seat, her expression filled with skepticism. And for some odd reason, a tinge of relief.

"That on its own would be a stretch, but I did some more searching and discovered that on December 30 this same woman took another train to Missouri. Only this time there was no record of her taking a baby with her. She left alone."

Chase took a sip of his coffee and watched as a myriad of emotions flickered in Elle's baby blues.

She crossed her arms, her attention dipping to the article. "That can't be me."

"But that's just the thing. It really could be." He folded his arms on the table and leaned forward. "Are you curious to find out if it is?"

*N*ever, not in a million years, would Elle have guessed that when she decided to go somewhere for Christmas, she'd end up flying to Amish country in search of a family that might not be hers with a guy she barely knew. Yet here she was, walking out from the airport into the cold. It was as if she'd stepped into a surrealist painting of her life.

She pressed her hand against her middle as if some pressure might still the hyperactive butterflies. She wasn't typically prone to anxiety, but everything about this situation made her nervous. She'd been jumpy enough while meeting Chase for coffee at Willow Tree, and that had been on her home turf. Now she was in Pennsylvania, preparing to meet him again. The whole thing was certifiable.

Sure, she called the newspaper in North Star to verify that he actually worked there. Her dad—being her dad—followed up on Chase's references. And as an extra precaution, she may have slightly stalked him online as her mom looked over her shoulder, commenting on his cuteness. Even though no signs pointed to his being a psycho, this was still borderline crazy.

A short honk drew her attention to the left.

Chase sat behind the wheel of a silver Dodge Ram parked by the curb a few car lengths away. Elle pulled up the collar of her coat and rolled her suitcase over while he climbed out of his truck, every bit as good-looking as he'd been two weeks ago. He greeted her with a smile-nod-handshake, his palm warm and rough, then took her suitcase and put it in the back while she climbed into the passenger seat, attempting to silence her chattering teeth.

"Hi."

The high-pitched greeting sounded so unexpectedly in Elle's ear she nearly jumped out of her seat. The voice belonged to a girl sitting in the back with the same hazel eyes and dark brown hair as the driver, but she looked too old to be his daughter, unless he'd aged incredibly well. He'd never mentioned a wife or a kid last time they talked. Of course, their conversation hadn't really ever gotten around to him.

"I'm Brooke," the girl said.

"It's, um, nice to meet you, Brooke. I'm Elle."

She grinned an impish grin. "Chase was right."

"About?"

"You're very pretty."

Elle's cheeks turned warm. Chase had said that?

Before the two could get any further, Chase opened his door and slid behind the wheel, rubbing his hands together in front of the vent. "I'm sure my sister's already introduced herself."

Ah, his sister.

"She's one day into Christmas break and already bored." Chase winked at Brooke in his rearview mirror and flashed her a crooked smile. "So I let her tag along."

"You *asked* me to tag along."

"Sorry. I *asked* her to tag along." He pulled his seat belt across his lap. "I thought you might be more comfortable with someone else in the car."

Elle buckled her seat belt as well, thankful for his consideration. She'd worried about the drive from the airport to North Star. She didn't have a problem carrying on conversations with strangers, but an hour and a half was a lot of space to fill, especially when she already had so much on her mind.

Chase merged with the traffic. "We spent the morning wandering around the city."

"I've never been to Philly," Elle said.

"You haven't?" Brooke sounded shocked. "But Chase said you've traveled everywhere."

Elle peeked at the man beside her. How much of her blog had he read? She always imagined travelers or adoptees like herself reading it. Women, mostly, with the same interests and struggles as she had. She'd never imagined ruggedly handsome journalists on the other side of the screen. "I have been to a lot of places, but Philadelphia isn't one of them."

Brooke leaned forward. "Where are all the places you've been?"

Elle started listing them.

Brooke listened raptly. "Chase promised to take me to London when I turn eighteen. I want to meet the queen."

"You want to *be* the queen," Chase teased.

As the two bantered back and forth, Elle looked out the window, the butterflies in her stomach flapping faster. In a little over an hour, they'd be in North Star, Pennsylvania. Population two thousand. An obscure town located in Lancaster County, one Elle never would have known about if not for the gentleman behind the wheel. Was it really possible that after all these years, the answers to her questions were only sixty minutes away?

⌘

Elle was officially charmed. With Brooke's tour-guide enthusiasm. With the easygoing way Chase filled in the gaps around his sister's quips. With North Star's holly-wrapped streetlamps, the twinkling trees in the park, the giant wreath hanging on the covered bridge, the horses and buggies parked outside the shops, and the old-fashioned Country Store and Creamery. She was so charmed, in fact, she could almost forget why she'd come in the first place.

Almost.

Every single time they encountered a man with a long beard or a woman wearing one of those white hats or a tow-headed child on a scooter, Elle caught herself craning her neck and looking closer, as though she might finally see a reflection of herself in another person. It was crazy, this kind of looking. Elle had done it before, when her family drove through Indiana to get to South Carolina one summer break in high school, but the chance of actually running into a relative then had been so infinitesimally small.

But here . . .

Chase opened the door of the Paupers Den, a small coffee shop on the corner, and motioned for Elle to go inside. They'd just dropped Brooke off at a strip mall with some friends in a neighboring town. "The Little Drummer Boy" played softly in the background as Elle walked into the warmth and pulled off her mittens.

"It's no Willow Tree Café," Chase murmured in her ear, "but you can't beat the price."

"Or the atmosphere." Colored, blinking lights framed the large picture window, and a small, eclectically decorated Christmas tree stood in one corner. Add the music and the smell of roasted coffee, and the place was a winner.

Chase stepped in line to order while Elle found them a table. She chose one by the window and watched the people outside until Chase set a caramel latte with extra whipped cream and a cinnamon streusel muffin in front of her.

He took off his coat, revealing a hunter-green sweater that fit him well, and hung the coat on the back of his chair before taking a seat.

"The town is very charming," she said, hoping some conversation would chase away those stubborn butterflies. "Reminds me of Peaks in a way, just Amish-i-fied."

He smiled a slow, amused smile. "Now there's a word."

"You must know a lot about them, having grown up here." Whereas she knew only as much as she'd learned from Google and a couple of Amish romance novels she'd read over the past two weeks. Who knew if any of that was even accurate.

"It's a different way of life, that's for sure."

"Could you do it?" she asked.

"Live like the Amish?"

Elle nodded.

"No way, but I can admire it from afar." He scratched his cheek. Not even dinnertime and already an impressive five o'clock shadow. "You?"

Elle shook her head adamantly.

"What would be the hardest part?"

"Losing the Hallmark Channel."

Chase laughed. It was a rich rumble of a sound that warmed her straight through.

"You think I'm joking, but this time of year the Hallmark Channel is a very real addiction I have. That and Christmas music."

He groaned.

"You don't like Christmas music?"

"I like Christmas music as much as the next guy. But I also have a mother and a sister who listen to it all day long. Nonstop. Starting in October."

Elle let out a mock gasp. "But what about Thanksgiving?"

"It's like the forgotten middle child of holidays."

She shook her head sadly. "Poor Thanksgiving."

"And they sing it too, this Christmas music. Very loudly. My family has been blessed with many things, but singing voices is not among them."

"See now, that just makes me like your sister even more."

"Yeah. Brooke is pretty great."

"Endearing."

"Like you." His eyes twinkled over his coffee cup. They were the kind of eyes a girl could get lost in if she wasn't careful. A ring of light brown melting into earthy green, rimmed with eyelashes so dark Elle wished they could trade. Hers were so blond that the length did her absolutely no good unless she wore mascara.

"I really enjoyed your blog," he said.

The butterflies fluttered awake. Yes, the blog. A reminder that she wasn't here to tour a quaint Amish town or flirt with one of its residents.

A pair of women walked past the window. Both carried baskets and wore plain, long dresses and black capes and those white hats Brooke had called prayer Kapps. Elle's attention lingered even after they passed out of sight.

"This must all be pretty weird for you," Chase said, following her stare.

"Very, very weird." She broke off a piece of her muffin. "My mom and I used to make up stories about where I came from. I've been a long-lost princess, the daughter of sea merchants, an actual pixie, and a child born into the Mafia."

Chase coughed.

"But never once did our stories include the Amish." She played with the bit of muffin in her hand. "Can I ask you a question?"

"Of course."

"Are you, like, taking notes in your head or something? Am I going to read about this whole thing in the newspaper in a few days?"

"That depends."

"On?"

"Whether or not you're comfortable with your story being in the newspaper."

"So if I say no, you won't write it?"

He shook his head.

Elle's eyebrows drew together. "Doesn't sound very reporterly of you."

"I'm more of a storyteller than a reporter." He set his elbows on the table and crossed his arms. "Which means I have this annoying, incessant need to know how things end. Whether or not I report that ending is up to you."

The door to Paupers opened and closed, letting in a gust of cold air and two teenage girls. A young Michael Jackson sang about seeing his mommy kissing Santa Claus, and Elle took a long drink of her latte. "What do you know about this missing baby?"

"Not a whole lot. The mother was named Ruth. The baby was born on November 30 in an Amish birthing center here in North Star. Ruth named the little girl Anna. By the time Ruth's husband came for her and his daughter, they were already gone."

"What do you mean 'by the time Ruth's husband came for her'? Why wasn't he with her in the first place?"

"I guess they lived in Chestnut Ridge, which is a small Amish town several hours away. It's not uncommon for an Amish woman to travel home to be with her mother and sisters for childbirth, especially if it's the first child."

"So Ruth's parents live here, in North Star?"

"Supposedly."

Elle tried to imagine getting married, having a baby, then leaving everything behind. Her parents would be beyond brokenhearted. It was the kind of heartbreak that would never fully mend. Was she really going to intrude upon this couple's life, open up this painful can of worms—on the cusp of Christmas, no less—when there was a real possibility she was nothing more than an unrelated stranger?

"Okay. So let's say they actually are my grandparents. Won't seeing me without their daughter break their hearts all over again?"

Elle's thoughts began to spin. Maybe it was best just to walk away. Leave well enough alone. She and Chase could do a little sightseeing together. He could drive her back to Philadelphia and show her the city. She'd go somewhere pretty for a Christmas Eve candlelight service, and then she'd go home. A simple Christmas trip with a new, unexpected friend.

"I'm not sure this is a good idea," she said.

"But you've gotten so close. Won't you regret not checking?"

Elle frowned into her cup, half-full of latte that was no longer hot. Chase wanted to know how this story would end. But what if the ending wasn't a happy one? What if these grandparents wanted nothing to do with their daughter or their granddaughter? She'd read something about shunning in one of those books. What if these people shunned her?

She dug her fingers through her hair. "What am I going to do though? Show up on their doorstep and ask for a DNA test?"

Chase rubbed his bottom lip. "Actually, there's someone I'd like you to meet."

*E*lle had no idea what an Amish birthing center was supposed to look like, but she certainly wasn't expecting an actual house. She sat on the couch inside the living room, pulling at her sleeves while Chase sat beside her.

"You doing okay?" he asked.

She nodded, a little too fast, trying to distract herself with her surroundings. The room was large with cherry-stained wainscoting and cream walls, a wood stove throwing off heat in one corner, a couch, two chairs, and a beautiful coffee table made from cedar. No family pictures on display. No television or stereo. The only sound was the gentle whooshing from the wood stove, the quiet ticking of a wall clock, and clinking cups in the kitchen.

When Chase and Elle had arrived, Rebekah had been hanging sheets out in the cold to dry. She didn't look surprised by their arrival, which made Elle wonder if Chase had told her they might stop by, but she had stared for a long time at Elle. After a beat, Rebekah had invited them inside, then went to the kitchen to make fresh coffee. With the coffee at the airport, the latte at Paupers, and the nervous energy breeding inside her like field mice, Elle didn't need any more stimulants. She'd much prefer some chamomile tea, but asking felt rude.

Rebekah entered the room with a tray of steaming mugs and a plate of sugar cookies. She set it down on the coffee table and fed some firewood to the stove.

Wanting something to do, Elle took a sugar cookie off the tray. As soon as she bit into it, butter and sugar melted in her mouth, eliciting a groan from her throat. "These are delicious."

"Denki."

Rebekah took one of the mugs while Chase made small talk. Elle tried to chime in, but she had been struck with a sudden bout of attention deficit disorder. She kept looking around, trying to imagine a day twenty-five years ago when this woman delivered four babies at once in this very home. It seemed preposterous to think that Elle might have been one of those babies. And the more she thought about it, the bigger the ache grew in her chest. It felt an awful lot like homesickness. She wanted to talk to her parents, especially her mom, but they were in the middle of the Pacific Ocean, out of reach.

Something Rebekah asked caught Elle's attention. Apparently the conversation had shifted to the reason for their visit. Elle listened as Chase told the story about tracing Ruth's train ticket and finding the news article about Baby Noel.

"You were left on a doorstep?" Rebekah's tone was troubled, as though the idea was appalling.

For some reason an almost irresistible urge to defend the woman who gave birth to her arose in Elle. Instead she gripped her coffee mug over her knees. "Does that sound like something Ruth would have done?"

"I can't imagine any woman giving up her child, but then . . ."

Elle came to the edge of her seat.

Rebekah shook her head, as if she'd thought better of whatever she was going to say. "I didn't know Ruth very well. Not like I know most of the mothers I've helped through the years."

"Why not?"

"I wasn't supposed to help her with the baby. Her mother and her older sister were going to do that. But she was on this side of town when the baby decided to come. An Englischer brought her here, and the blizzard made it impossible for Martha and Alma to join us."

"Martha and Alma?"

"Alma is Ruth's older sister. Martha and John Lantz are her parents. They are very kind people."

Elle swallowed. This was all very bizarre. "Why do you think Ruth left?"

"I don't know with any certainty. Things like this don't happen often in our community, so you can imagine it caused quite a stir." Sadness flooded Rebekah's eyes. "John and Martha didn't deserve what people said. It broke their hearts, what happened. They stayed very quiet about everything. I'm not even sure they know all the details."

"What about the father?" Elle couldn't bring herself to say *her* father. That felt too far-fetched.

"He's still in Chestnut Ridge, last I heard."

"Is he remarried?"

"Oh no. He's still married to Ruth."

"But she left."

Elle wasn't sure Rebekah heard the comment. The old woman nibbled a bite of cookie, her expression glazed over, as though lost somewhere far away. If Elle had to wager, she'd guess that somewhere was the year 1990. "I remember her well. She was a small thing, with big, haunted eyes."

Chase shifted.

Elle leaned over her knees.

"I remember watching tears stream down her cheeks as she held her newborn. I wasn't too concerned. New mothers can be very emotional after a baby arrives." Rebekah set the cookie on a small table beside her chair. "All this time I've assumed Ruth was out in the world with her daughter. I never imagined she'd leave Anna with strangers."

"It sounds unlikely that she would have. I'm probably not this woman's child."

Rebekah looked up from her lap. "You look like her."

The words sent goose bumps marching across Elle's skin. A whole army of them. But Elle told them to stand down. Surely there were plenty of blond-haired, blue-eyed women among the Amish.

"Baby Anna had a small, heart-shaped birthmark." Rebekah touched a spot below her clavicle. "Right here. I remember it clear as day."

The goose bumps spread to Elle's scalp. Every single hair follicle stood on end.

"Ruth kept pressing kisses there."

⚓

Chase watched as Elle's face drained of color. He looked from her to Rebekah, the air in the large room filled with a heated current that had nothing to do with the wood stove. He wasn't sure why he was so shocked. He wouldn't have traveled to Peaks to meet Elle McAllister if he hadn't thought she was Baby Anna. But not until now, this very moment, did the knowledge in his head sink into his heart.

Elle sat there, her eyes so big and blue and vulnerable they did funny things to his emotions. Then she pulled down the collar of her tunic sweater, and there it was—a small, red, heart-shaped blotch.

Rebekah moved her fingers to her lips.

Elle sank back against the couch as though someone had thumped the wind right out of her. "I was born here, on November 30?"

Rebekah's eyes welled with tears.

"John and Martha Lantz are my grandparents?"

The old woman nodded.

Surely Elle had a million more questions to ask, but before she could get one more out, a knock sounded at the door.

Rebekah stood and left the room. The clock ticked into the silence, Elle's shock a palpable thing beside him.

Murmuring voices came from the entryway, a man speaking Pennsylvania Dutch, a woman groaning, followed by a flurry of movement. An Amish gentleman clomped into the room—the same young man Chase had seen when he first visited Rebekah last month. Chase stood alongside Elle and caught a glimpse of Rebekah leading the man's wife into a nearby room.

The young man slipped off his hat and nodded.

Chase nodded back. "We were just heading out." He placed his hand on the small of Elle's back, guiding her to the entryway. As they slipped on their coats, Rebekah came out of the room and pressed a slip of paper into Elle's palm. Chase caught a glimpse of an address.

Rebekah folded Elle's fingers over it. "They would want to meet you."

*C*hase drove them south in his truck, through the festive downtown area, past neighborhoods, past cars and buggies, until houses grew sparse and land plenty. At least once every block, Elle could feel Chase's attention heating up the side of her face.

"They, uh, live on a farm," he said.

Elle nodded numbly. After handing him the slip of paper Rebekah had given her and saying, "Let's go," she'd lost her voice. Whenever she opened her mouth to say something, nothing came out.

"Are you sure you want to go?"

Again she nodded. But Elle wasn't sure she should be nodding. They were headed toward her grandparents' home. In a little bit she would meet people who shared her genes. She'd just left the house where she had been born. Born! On November 30, with three other babies. She finally knew her birthday. And her father was alive, living in a town called Chestnut Ridge a few hours away. After years of mystery, the onslaught of information was too much to process. She needed to call a timeout.

As if sensing this need, Chase pulled over to the shoulder of the road.

Elle sat, unblinking.

He pointed to where the road curved into a bend and disappeared out of sight. "Their farm is up ahead."

She swallowed, but her mouth had gone as dry as the Sahara.

"You don't have to do this."

"But you said . . ." Her voice had returned. It was a little hoarse, but at least it was working. She cleared her throat and shifted her body to face him. "You said earlier that I've come this close. I can't walk away now."

Chase's expression darkened as though he regretted his words.

"You think I'm making a mistake?"

"I'm just a little concerned. You lost your color at Rebekah's. It hasn't come back yet."

She looked down at her fingernails. She'd painted them yesterday—a classic red for the holiday. Did the Amish think nail polish was sinful? She was wearing skinny jeans, too, and jewelry. "What if they want nothing to do with me?"

"I don't think Rebekah would have given you their address if she thought that would happen."

Chase's reassurance might have worked better if he'd ditched the worried expression while offering it. Elle's stomach twisted into the worst kind of knot. They could slam the door in her face. They could tell her to leave and never come back. Elle loved Christmas. Did she really want a hurtful memory to tarnish her favorite holiday?

She shook her head. This was silly. Until a few weeks ago, she'd been fine. Excellent, actually. So she had questions. Big deal. Everyone had questions. God had redeemed her story. She was Psalm 68:6 in action. He set an abandoned baby in a family, one of the best around, if her opinion mattered. Hadn't that always been enough? Did she really need to go looking for more, especially when that more could lead to, at best, an awkward conversation with her grandparents and, at worst, unbearably painful reminders for them and rejection for her? It wasn't worth it.

Elle opened her mouth to tell Chase to turn around when a silent whisper rose up in her heart. *Trust Me.*

The words scared her, because trusting God came with no guarantee of success. It simply meant He'd be with her no matter what came, which should be more than enough. It should. But at the moment Elle wanted the guarantee. She wanted to know without a doubt that what she was about to do wouldn't cause undue pain.

Her hesitancy expanded, reminding her of her mother's advice inside Val's Diner. When Elle was growing up, her parents liked to say that the good stuff in life waited on the other side of fear. Was that true now?

Elle wiped her clammy hands on her jeans and released a shaky breath. "I have to do this. And if I don't do it right now, I'll talk myself out of it later."

"You're sure?"

"Moderately."

With a ghost of a smile, Chase shifted into Drive and pulled onto the road. They drove around the bend and turned down a long driveway that led to a small farm.

There was a barn and a large farmhouse with a smaller home across the drive. They looked like typical farmhouses, except there weren't any electrical wires running to either one. And instead of vehicles parked out front, there were two carriages. Smoke rose from the chimneys. The yard was neat and tidy and snow-covered, with two children playing in it.

As snow crunched beneath Chase's tires, the children stopped playing, and a young man appeared from around the corner of the big house, holding an ax in one hand and a bundle of firewood in the other arm. Chase stopped his vehicle. The young man set the ax against the house and brought his hand up to his forehead like a visor. The sinking sun shone directly behind the truck, no doubt making them difficult to see.

Adrenaline coursed through Elle's veins, making her shiver even though she didn't feel cold at all. Chase had already stepped out of the truck and had come around to her side to open her door. She climbed out into the cold on wobbly legs and approached the young man. It was odd, this moment. She was walking, yet she distinctly felt disconnected from her body.

As they approached, it became clear that the young man was no more than fifteen or sixteen. The two younger children—both boys— closed in fast, their expressions open and friendly and dripping with youthful curiosity.

"Can I help you?" the oldest of the three asked.

"Are John and Martha Lantz home?" Chase said.

The boy nodded. "One of the cows got out earlier this morning, so my *Grossdaadi* is out mending the fence."

Elle's heart tripped over the word. His Grossdaadi? She couldn't be certain, but the word sounded an awful lot like *granddaddy*. Was this boy her cousin? Her *biological* cousin?

"My *Grossmammi* is in the *Dawdi* house, baking."

"My name is Ben," the youngest of the boys said with a smile. His front two permanent teeth were starting to grow where his baby ones had been. "Who are you?"

Elle wasn't sure how to answer that, and movement in the periphery of her vision distracted her. A young woman's face stared out of one of the windows of the big house. As soon as Elle made eye contact, the curtain swayed back into place but not before Elle had a good glimpse. The young woman had been more of a girl, perhaps a little younger than this teenage boy standing in front of her.

He told the two younger ones to go and tend to the chickens like they were supposed to be doing. "*Mamm* and Grossmammi need eggs for baking."

Neither of the boys seemed overly motivated to obey.

"You get your chores done, and I'll take you sledding before sundown."

Their faces lit up like cherubs. They ran off, laughing and kicking up snow as they went. Elle watched them go, feeling very much as if she'd stepped into a time machine, as if somehow she'd time-warped into the past, back when life was slower, more idyllic. Horses and buggies. Gathering eggs from the henhouse. Chopping firewood for the stove. Was this the life her mother had left behind? Why?

The young man motioned for them to follow as he made his way toward the smaller house across the drive. "How do you know my grandparents?"

"I think they're my grandparents too." The words tumbled out before Elle could think. Her tongue had gone and untied itself only to say something that made everyone freeze in their steps.

The young man stared. Elle realized they shared the same eyes, and a rush of curiosity spilled into his. She waited for him to ask questions— many, many questions. Instead, he politely asked them to wait there, set the wood on the porch, and walked inside.

Despite the cold, sweat gathered beneath Elle's arms. The longer they stood there waiting, the more unwieldy the knots in her stomach became. She looked over her shoulder at the big house and saw a different face peeking out at her this time. Another girl, older than the first.

The screen door opened with a groan, its hinges long overdue for some WD-40.

An older woman stepped outside. She looked from Chase to Elle, and as soon as she did, her face went as white as her apron. She took a small step back, her fingers moving to her lips, and for a second Elle thought the woman might faint. As though worried about the same thing, the boy took her elbow.

Elle stood there, unmoving. Unsure what to say. Unsure what to do. Afraid she had broken this poor woman. She shouldn't have come. She should have left well enough alone.

Apologizing, she turned to leave.

"Wait!"

Elle stopped.

With great hesitation Martha crept closer.

Elle stayed very still, afraid if she moved even an inch, she'd scare her off.

When Martha finally stood in front of Elle, her face was soaked in disbelief. And then ever so slowly she reached out and touched Elle's cheek, so lightly it felt like a feather. "Anna?"

It wasn't her name. Not anymore. But Elle nodded anyway.

The woman closed the last morsel of distance between them and wrapped Elle in a tight, trembling hug.

*T*he small home was drowning in bread. Loaves upon loaves covered every square inch of counter space. The fresh-baked scent preceded them into a quaint parlor room while a young girl, who had been kneading dough in the kitchen when Elle and Chase stepped inside, followed close behind. She stood in the entryway, wearing a maroon dress and a gray pinafore smudged with flour, watching as Martha motioned toward a sofa for Elle and Chase to sit.

"Gook as fah deh glenneh breedah," Martha told her before turning her attention to the boy. "Levi, *gey grik deh daudy.*"

The teenager turned to leave as soon as his grandmother finished speaking. The girl dawdled. Levi stopped in front of the door, furrowing his brow disapprovingly. "Kumm, Emma."

Emma looked longingly from Elle to Chase to Martha, then shuffled after him, leaving an all-too-noticeable silence in her wake. Elle clasped her hands between her knees, peeked at Martha, and caught the woman staring.

Martha quickly dropped her gaze and took a step back. "Would you like some coffee?" And then, not waiting for an answer, she rushed from the room.

Elle stared after her, trying to acclimate to the scene she'd stepped into. She had worried that John and Martha Lantz would shut the door in her face. Instead Martha had wrapped her in an impossibly tight hug. When she let go, her apron-white face had turned rosy pink, as though embarrassed by her display of affection.

Chase gave Elle's shoulder a reassuring squeeze. His hand was warm, his presence calming. It felt impossible that earlier today he had still been such a stranger. "You breathing okay?"

"I'm not sure. Everything's feeling very *Twilight Zone*-ish at the moment."

"Someone needs to submit these words to Webster."

"I'll get right on that."

Martha returned with two mugs. She handed one to Elle and one to Chase, then sat in a chair flanking a small sewing table by the window.

Elle searched for something to say, anything to fill the quiet, anything to distract herself from the way Martha kept staring, as though Elle were part ghost, part gift. "This is my friend, Chase. I didn't introduce you before."

"It's nice to meet you," Martha said.

"You too," he replied.

More awkward silence and this time Elle was all out of people to introduce. Her mind was blank, blank, blank. Not a cohesive thought anywhere in sight. All she could think was that this woman—Martha—had the same small nose and the same pointy chin as herself. This was her biological grandmother sitting across from her.

"You're baking a lot of bread," Chase commented.

"Yes, we are." Martha folded her hands in her lap. "My eldest and her husband are hosting the church service tomorrow. There's a lot of bread to bake for church Sundays. My youngest, Amos, is over there now with one of his daughters, helping unload the benches. He should be home any time."

Elle glanced into the bread-laden kitchen. "How many people go to church?"

"There's about a hundred and fifty of us altogether."

"That many?"

The door flung open, letting in a gust of cold air. An older man with a long beard the color of graying wheat strode inside. He stopped abruptly in the entryway, his face registering surprise at the sight of Elle.

Martha stood. Not knowing what else to do, Elle stood too. So did Chase.

Like the other Amish men Elle had seen since arriving in North Star, this man had a beard with no mustache. Unlike the other men, he had Elle's eyes—bright blue and big. He looked every bit as shocked as his wife had, but he showed more restraint.

"This is my husband, John." Martha's voice warbled a little as she spoke. "John, this is Chase and th-this is Anna."

John slid his hat from his head, revealing thinning hair the same color as his beard.

Nobody shook hands. Everyone just stood there, staring.

Finally Martha muttered something about coffee and bustled out of the room again, and John eased into the other armchair, nodding for Elle and Chase to have a seat too. One silent minute later Martha returned with another mug and set it on the end table beside her husband. So far Elle had not taken a drink of hers, but the warmth of the mug was nice between her palms.

"You're Anna?" John finally said. "*Our* Anna?"

"Yes, but . . ." How could she explain that Anna wasn't her name any longer? What would they do if they discovered she hadn't been raised by Ruth? "I go by Elle. It's short for Noelle."

His expression was impossible to read. Yet even in his stoicism, he had an open, friendly face, the kind a grandfather ought to have, only his was marked with sadness. Not a fleeting sadness that came and went, but the kind that carved itself into every contour and wrinkle. The kind that looked much more like an old, old friend than a passing acquaintance.

Beside him, Martha didn't look nearly as stoic. She sat on the edge of her chair, a whole host of emotions puddling in her eyes. "Elle is a pretty name," she said.

"Thank you." Elle waited for them to ask why Ruth had changed it, but neither addressed the elephant in the room. It was obvious by Elle's attire that she wasn't one of them. Maybe they were afraid of what she would say. Or maybe they were simply waiting for her to explain.

"Where do you live?" Martha asked.

"In Peaks, Iowa. It's a small farming town on the Mississippi River."

This seemed to make John perk up. "There's nice land in Iowa."

"Yes, there is." At least that was the word on the street. Elle didn't know much of anything when it came to land. She gripped the coffee mug over her knees, unsure what to say next. Should she tell them that her last name was McAllister? That until Chase came into her life a few weeks ago, she knew nothing at all about the Amish or Ruth or North Star, Pennsylvania?

Martha leaned forward, picking at one of her nails. "Are—are you happy?"

It was such a simple question, and yet the significance of it charged the air.

"Yes. I'm very happy." Elle smiled. "God's given me a good life."

Martha's lip trembled. John took a sudden and concentrated interest in a small fray in his trousers.

The door flung open again.

Elle expected to see Levi or Emma or maybe one of the two younger boys or one of the girls who had peeked out the window of the other house. Instead, a gentleman strode inside, a younger version of John, with a shorter beard. As soon as his attention landed on Elle, his rosy cheeks went chalk white. "Ruth."

And there it was. The elephant in the room had been addressed at last.

The man shook his head, as if rattling clarity into place. She obviously wasn't Ruth, unless Ruth hadn't aged in twenty-five years. "Levi met me halfway down the drive. Said a woman had come asking to meet her grandparents."

A furrow etched itself deep down in the space between John's eyebrows.

"Was he confused?" Martha asked.

Elle looked at the three of them. "Is something the matter?"

"My children weren't aware they had an aunt who left," the man said.

"Oh, I'm so sorry. I didn't think. The words just sort of . . . spilled out."

For some reason this made him smile. A private smile between him and his thoughts, as though Elle's comment had stirred up an affectionate memory. "I'll speak with him later." He stepped forward and stretched out his arm. "My name is Amos. I'm your uncle."

She shook his hand. "My name's Elle."

"Elle?" His forehead scrunched into wrinkles, and for the first time since stepping into the home, he noticed what she was wearing. No dress or apron or black stockings, but skinny jeans and a cowl-necked sweater the same color as her fingernails, a black North Face coat unzipped over the ensemble, and long hair spilling down her back without a covering in sight. "You're Englisch."

"Excuse me?"

"It's a word for non-Amish," Chase said.

Elle pulled at her sleeves, a nervous habit she'd developed as a kid, one that had stretched many a shirt throughout the years. "I was raised by Mitchell and Vanessa McAllister. I only learned about Ruth recently. I had no idea . . ." She trailed off, unsure if she should continue. The more she talked, the chalkier Amos's face became.

He plopped into the last remaining seat—a rocking chair in the corner. "Ruth gave her baby away? How could she do such a thing?"

Elle didn't have an answer, and she was beginning to second-guess her decision to come. In barely any time at all, outrage was already creeping into the room. She looked at Martha and John, wishing she had comfort to offer. Only they didn't look shocked or appalled like Amos. Sad, yes. Shocked and appalled, no.

Amos must have noticed too, because he shifted in his seat. "Mamm?"

Martha looked down at her lap. "Your sister sent a letter."

"And you didn't think us kids would want to read it?" His eyes flashed—with confusion, with hurt and betrayal.

"It wasn't your letter to read," John said, his voice full of authority. Amos might be a grown man, but John was still the father. That was abundantly clear.

Elle waited for this uncle of hers to push, to ask what the letter said. Maybe it explained why Ruth had done it. Why she had left this place with Elle only to leave her baby on a doorstep and disappear.

But Amos did not challenge his father. He grew quiet, and the room crackled with tension.

It was a tension Elle had brought with her. One that fit in no better than she did. "I'm sorry for intruding like this. I shouldn't have come."

"I'm glad you did." Martha's voice radiated such sincerity it was impossible not to believe her. "How long are you staying?" she asked.

"I'm not sure." Elle was scheduled to fly home the day after Christmas, but in the midst of such foreign surroundings, homesickness was getting the better of her. Was she really up for staying a whole week?

Martha gave her a shy smile. "We're having a frolic on Tuesday."

"What's a frolic?"

"A time when the women come together to visit and work. We'll be quilting and baking pies mostly. Your aunts will be there. And some of your cousins. Would you like to join us?"

Elle wasn't particularly good at baking, and she'd never quilted a thing in her life. But Martha's entire being brimmed with so much hope and expectation, how could Elle possibly say no?

*D*éjà vu gripped Elle as she sat inside Chase's car, taking in the childhood home of her biological mother, her breath fogging up the passenger-side window. The only difference between now and Saturday was the knowledge that she wouldn't be turned away. This time she had been invited.

"I can go inside with you if you want," Chase offered.

"Something tells me men don't frolic."

His lips curved into a lazy grin. "The really confident ones don't mind."

She turned back to the window with a smile. On Saturday evening he'd sat with her at a small diner and let her process, in disjointed fits and spurts with plenty of unpressured silence in between, all that had happened. He'd made her smile and then laugh. So hard, in fact, her stomach hurt afterward. On Sunday he invited her to church, then bought her a doughnut afterward. Being with Chase put her at ease and made her forget about everyone and everything else around her. If there was a chart rating people in charm, he had to be somewhere near the top.

"Did you end up going to Lancaster yesterday?" he asked.

Elle nodded. As a service provided by the small inn where she was staying, one of the workers drove her into the heart of the tourist hubbub. Then she escaped to the countryside for a buggy ride with a seventy-eight-year-old Amish-dressed, Englisch-raised tour guide named Art. The air had been cold and clean, the countryside blanketed in snow and lined with frosted trees, the sky so blue it looked more like a painting than real life. "It was very *wunderbaar.*"

Chase laughed.

"I'm familiarizing myself with my linguistic roots."

"I'm sure everyone inside will be impressed."

A fresh round of insecurity assaulted her. "You think?"

Chase's teasing expression melted into something soft, something serious. His hazel eyes held her captive with a confidence she didn't feel. "They'd have to be deaf and blind not to fall in love with you immediately, Elle McAllister."

This did not help settle her nerves that swooped and swirled like snow flurries in a blizzard. His declaration brought heat that rushed up her neck, into her cheeks and ears.

He set his hand on the shifter. "Pick you up in two hours?"

"Are you sure you don't mind being my chauffeur?"

"One hundred percent positive."

Elle narrowed her eyes. Chase wasn't getting paid. He told her on Sunday that he wasn't going to write the story, and he'd solved the mystery, at least the initial one. Sure, he found the new mystery equally intriguing—why did Ruth leave North Star? But was that all that propelled him—this self-proclaimed need to know how things ended? Or was it something more?

"Elle, I've played chauffeur for my kid sister for years. Trust me when I say I'd much rather drive you around. Now get in there and start frolicking already."

With a thank-you and a lingering smile, she stepped out into the cold and crunched through the snow.

Before she reached the front porch of the main house, a woman threw open the door. She had dark hair beneath her prayer Kapp, matching brown eyes, and a warm smile. "You must be Elle!" She opened the door wider, letting out the sound of laughter from inside. "I'm Amos's wife, Arie. Come in, come in."

Arie ushered Elle into the warmth and took her coat. Off to the right, women baked in the kitchen, and to the left, they sat in the living room, quilting. Or at least they *had been* baking and quilting before Elle stepped inside. At the moment they were mostly staring.

She had considered buying a dress or a skirt for the occasion, but Chase assured her that they would want her to be comfortable and that they were accustomed to seeing women in pants. So she'd chosen a pair of boyfriend jeans and a loose-fitting gray knit top. No jewelry, no cute purse or high-heeled boots, and, thanks to nail polish remover, no apple-red nails. Even without the typical accoutrements, Elle felt like a sore thumb.

Thankfully, Martha rescued her. She emerged from the small crowd of women in the kitchen, looking very much like she wanted to give Elle another hug but was too shy to follow through. Instead, she stopped just in front of Elle, her eyes sparkling. "I'm so glad you came."

"I am too," Elle said, despite her nerves that were hopping around like pinballs.

Arie hung up Elle's coat, and Martha began introductions. There was Alma, Ruth's older sister that Rebekah had talked about, who shared Elle's petite frame and pointy chin. A honey-haired lady named Sylvia, who was married to Martha's eldest son, Simeon. A freckle-faced woman named Viola, who was married to Martha's middle son, Daniel. And a few unrelated women, one of whom stared at Elle with the same shocked amazement as Martha had on Saturday when they sat inside the parlor. Her name was Marianna.

Next came the younger women—ranging in age from fifteen to midtwenties—many of whom were Elle's cousins. There were a few babies, some toddlers, and an adorable little girl probably about five named Lydia, who stared up at Elle as if she were some kind of rare, exotic bird. When Elle bent over to say hello, Lydia hid behind her mother's skirt, making the women laugh.

"Where's the young gal who was helping you bake bread on Saturday?" Elle asked. "Emma, I think her name was."

"She's at school."

Right. The one-room schoolhouse on the south end of town. Chase had pointed it out on their way to church.

One of the ladies invited Elle to sit. She did and tried her best to engage in polite small talk. Inside, though, her questions expanded. Surely they were every bit as curious about her as she was about them. But nobody mentioned Ruth or commented on Elle's relationship to Martha at all. Which left Elle with little opportunity to seek answers and plenty of time to take in her surroundings.

Christmas was only three days away, but other than a few sprigs of holly and a candle on the mantel, there were no decorations at all. No Christmas tree in the corner or stockings hanging on the wall. No tinsel or wrapped gifts, no mistletoe or wreaths, not even a nativity scene. And with no electricity or radio, there was also no Christmas music.

But there was plenty of laughter.

After a stretch of time, one of Amos's daughters invited her into the kitchen to peel apples. Now that was something Elle could do. Grateful for a way to contribute, she followed the girl into the kitchen, pushed up her sleeves, washed her hands, and got to work. And while conversation and laughter floated around her, Elle tried picturing her life as it would have been if Ruth had stayed.

This scene and these people wouldn't feel foreign but as familiar as the stamps in her passport. Canning and baking and gardening and sewing and traveling by horse and buggy would have been second nature. She'd probably be married by now with children of her own, and she'd most likely live in Chestnut Ridge, where her biological father lived today.

Her biological father . . .

He prowled on the periphery of her thoughts. What had his life become in the wake of his wife's disappearance? How could Ruth have taken his daughter away from him?

The question stoked her sympathy, but even more it kindled a profound sense of relief. Had Ruth stayed, Elle never would have traveled or graduated from college. She wouldn't have walked the craggy paths of Cinque Terre or toured the Louvre or beheld the breathtaking majesty of the Sistine Chapel. She never would have grown up in Peaks or become an art teacher. Mitchell and Vanessa McAllister would be nothing more than strangers. That last thought was enough to steal her breath.

She was lost in such reverie, such inward speculation at the power of a single decision to alter lives so radically, and the strange and mysterious way in which God worked that she didn't notice Marianna had walked up beside her.

"It was nice of you to come," she said.

Elle smiled at her. "It was nice of Martha to invite me."

Marianna scooped up the large pile of peels, threw them away, and wiped her hands on a dishtowel. "Would you like to go for a walk?"

Across the kitchen Martha's eyes met Marianna's, as though she had heard the question. And so quickly Elle would have missed it had she blinked, Martha gave Marianna a small, approving nod. Curious, Elle agreed.

She put on her coat and gloves, Marianna put on her black cape and matching bonnet, and the two women stepped outside. Their frozen breath escaped into the air as they strolled down the lane.

"Ruth and I were best friends growing up," Marianna said.

Elle looked up from the path in surprise, the questions she'd been withholding making a mad dash to the tip of her tongue. "Really?"

"Yes, really. We raised rabbits together."

"Rabbits?"

"We bred them and sold the bunnies to folks around town. Ruth loved those silly animals. Named every single one. She'd start at A and work all the way through the alphabet and then start over again." Marianna smiled. "The second time through I recommended *Anna* for A, but she said no, she was saving that name for her firstborn daughter."

Elle's skin prickled. It started at her scalp and moved like a wave down the rest of her body. Marianna had handed her a treasured gift, one she could hold close from this day onward, just as Rebekah had in recalling the way Ruth had pressed kisses against Elle's birthmark. *Anna* was a name Ruth had loved since childhood, and she'd bestowed that name on Elle. It was a gesture that spoke of love.

"When we were girls, Ruth had it all planned out. We'd both get baptized at seventeen, married at eighteen. Our husbands would be best friends and handsome, of course. Then we'd have children who would grow up and marry each other, making us true family."

Cattle lowed in the distance. Chickens clucked in the henhouse. Birds chirped up in the frozen tree limbs. Marianna, however, had gone silent. But now that someone had finally opened the door, Elle's curiosity refused to remain standing politely on the other side. She needed to know more. She needed Ruth's disappearance to make sense. Right now it didn't.

"So what changed? If that was the plan, why did she leave?"

Marianna pinned her gaze on something far away as though she were thumbing through fond memories in her mind. "Ruth loved to ask questions. She had this curiosity about things that got her into trouble on more than one occasion and exasperated her poor parents. She was full of passion and wonder. I think that's what drew me to her. I've always been shy and reserved. But Ruth . . ." Marianna shook her head. "She wanted more. And the older she got, the more she wanted it."

"More of what?"

"More than this." Marianna swept her hand toward the Lancaster horizon, where gray sky touched the white-capped tree line. "Ruth felt restricted by our ways. She wanted to continue learning. She wanted to see more of this world God created."

"Sounds familiar."

Marianna gave Elle a sideways smile.

"So is that why she left—to see the world?" But if that were the case, why would she take Elle with her at all? Why not leave her with her father?

"I don't think any of us thought she'd get baptized into the faith. It pained her parents to no end. I can't imagine what I'd do if any of my children walked away. But it's a choice every one of us has to make." A sigh slipped past Marianna's lips, visible in the cold air. "When Elam Hershberger showed up, their relief was profound."

"Who's Elam Hershberger?"

"He's your . . . Well, he's Ruth's husband."

Elle pulled at her sleeves. Elam Hershberger. "Do you think he knows about me being here—in North Star?"

"I'd guess by now he would have heard something."

Elle didn't know what to think about that. Would Elam expect her to come to Chestnut Ridge next? Or might he be on his way to North Star as they spoke? Surely, if he was anything like Martha or John, he'd be eager to see her. "Why were Martha and John relieved?"

"Elam swept Ruth off her feet. And Elam was already baptized into the faith. We first met him at one of the singings. All the girls were smitten, but Elam had eyes only for Ruth. And she fell hard. Before any of us knew it, she was taking classes to be baptized, and the two married that very fall. Martha was sad to see her daughter move away, but it was much better than the alternative. And Ruth, well, she saw it as a grand adventure. Moving somewhere new with the man she loved."

"I don't understand what happened then. Why would she leave if she loved her husband so much?"

Marianna twisted her lips to the side, as if trying to decide how much to tell. She didn't speak again until they reached the edge of a wood and turned back toward the house.

"Ruth and I used to write to each other. The first few months after her move to Chestnut Ridge, I got many letters. But then they slowed. They became fewer and farther between, and the letters she did send were short. I thought my friend was simply too busy to keep up the correspondence. I hoped that meant she was finally with child, since I'd already had two. But then she came to visit, and . . ." Marianna closed her eyes.

"And what?"

"She told me things."

"What kind of things?"

"She said that Elam was mean. She said that sometimes he lost his temper, and when he did, he hit her."

The news came like a blow—the kind that stunned more than hurt.

"Violence goes against everything we believe in. I couldn't imagine Elam hurting an animal, let alone his wife. And he was so friendly, so crazy about Ruth. I just couldn't fathom it. She made me promise not to tell anyone. She wouldn't even tell her parents."

He hit her. Elam Hershberger had abused her mother.

"I encouraged her to tell her new bishop."

"Did she?"

"Yes, and I believe things were better for a time. Elam repented and Ruth forgave him. Her letters resumed, but I could tell she still wasn't happy. When she finally became pregnant and came home to have the baby, she was pale and drawn. She didn't speak of her husband or life in Chestnut Ridge. I tried asking how things were going, but it made her so emotional, so sad." Tears welled in Marianna's eyes. "I didn't know how to counsel her."

Elle reached out and touched Marianna's elbow—a small gesture of comfort.

Marianna wiped her cheek and gave Elle a wobbly smile. "You look so much like her."

"That's what I've been told."

Marianna wrapped her arm around Elle's in the way young girl-friends sometimes did, and as the two walked back to the house, Elle mulled over everything Marianna had told her.

*G*ravel and snow crunched beneath Chase's tires as he pulled to a stop. He was a little early. Ten minutes, to be exact, and more eager to see Elle than he'd ever admit out loud. He could tell himself it was because he was curious to hear what she'd learned about Ruth's mysterious disappearance, but that was hardly the truth.

Over the past few days, he'd developed an addiction: making Elle smile. Every time he managed it—and she rewarded him often—he felt like a little kid in an ice cream parlor. The past two nights he'd gone to bed thinking about her. The past two mornings he'd awakened thinking about her. And the kicker was, none of this concerned him.

As he let the truck idle, he spotted her wandering up one of the footpaths, arm in arm with a woman he didn't recognize.

Chase stepped out of the truck and shut the door.

"Hey." Elle offered him a smile, but something about the gesture fell flat. "Chase, I'd like you to meet my new friend, Marianna. Marianna, this is my not-quite-so-new friend, Chase."

Marianna greeted him kindly, then excused herself and went inside.

Chase stuck his hands in his pockets and waited until the front door closed behind her before asking how everything had gone.

"Good." Elle put her hands in her pockets too and hunched her shoulders. Darkness was closing in, and the temperature was dropping. The cold had turned her cheeks rosy and the tip of her nose red. "And informative."

"You got some answers?"

Her attention wandered to the house. She looked extra tiny some-how, standing there in the waning daylight, wearing a faraway expres-sion on her face. "Marianna and Ruth were best friends growing up. She shared a lot of things."

"Want to share those things with me over a little Christmas shopping?"

Elle's mouth dropped open. Wide. Whether in shock or horror, Chase couldn't tell. Judging by her feelings toward Christmas, it was probably both. "You haven't finished your Christmas shopping yet?"

"Believe it or not, December 22 is progress for me."

She shook her head as if he were hopeless, then headed inside to say good-bye. He leaned against the hood of his truck and waited, eager to hear everything she'd learned. Not because of his need-to-know com-pulsion, but because Elle looked like she needed to talk about it. This had started off as a story he wanted to chase. Now the only thing he cared about chasing was Elle.

He wanted to ask if she'd join him on Christmas Eve, but he was afraid of putting her in an uncomfortable position or himself in an embarrassing one. His mother kept asking to meet this girl who made him so giddy (her words, not his), and then there was Brooke. He could only imagine the level of mortification the two of them together would put him through if Elle actually came.

Invite a girl to a family event? It wasn't something he'd ever done. He'd never felt compelled to. But a few days with Elle McAllister, and he was most definitely compelled. The problem was, his mother would probably start turning jubilant cartwheels or talking about wedding plans. And he and Elle weren't even dating. There was a very real pos-sibility that he'd subject her to Mom and Brooke's shenanigans and she'd go running for the hills.

As his thoughts wrestled with each other—*ask her, don't ask her, ask her, don't ask her*—it started to snow. The quiet, soft kind that fell so slowly it seemed to float in place.

When Elle finally stepped out of the house, she looked up at the floating flakes and held her arms out from her sides. When she walked toward him, she wore a grin so contagious it was impossible not to smile back.

As he drove to the strip mall, Elle told him everything she'd learned from Marianna—Ruth falling hard for Elam, the waning letters, the secret confession, Elam's repentance, Ruth's forgiveness, and her subsequent disappearance. Chase listened raptly, feeling the shock Elle must have felt on her walk with Marianna. Maybe even more so. The Amish were pacifists. They didn't join the military. Violence was abhorrent. And yet Elam Hershberger had inflicted it on his wife. It was very rare, but the Amish were subject to sin every bit as much as everyone else. Adam's and Eve's blood ran through their veins as surely as it ran through his.

"I wrote an article once about abusers," he said. "Unless they get professional help, almost all of them end up as repeat offenders."

Elle frowned. "I don't understand. Couldn't she have lived here in North Star with her parents? Did she have to leave everything behind?"

"The Amish don't allow divorce. If Elam was repentant, the *Ordnung* would require nothing less than forgiveness and reconciliation."

"Even if he slipped into his old patterns again?"

"Even if."

Color rose in Elle's cheeks. "That's ridiculous."

"Nowadays the Amish are more open to counseling and would, I hope, encourage someone like Elam to get help. But twenty-five years ago? I'm not so sure. And if Ruth wasn't convinced it would fix anything . . ." Chase pulled into the parking lot.

"It's weird, knowing where he is."

"Would you ever want to meet him?"

"No. Never." Her answer came too quickly, laced with heat. But it left every bit as fast as it came, a vulnerable uncertainty taking its place. The kind that made him want to step in and protect her. She had no reason to feel guilty about not wanting to meet the man who'd abused her mother.

Chase's grip tightened on the steering wheel. It was a good thing Elam lived several hours away. If he lived in North Star, Chase would be tempted to find him and give him a taste of his own medicine.

He pulled into an open parking place and shut off his truck. "You sure you're up for this?"

"Are you kidding?" Elle dipped her chin. "I am *always* up for Christmas shopping. Even if it's on December 22."

So that was what they did. While Elle helped him pick out gifts for his mom, Brooke, Doug, Gage, and Gage's second wife, he resisted the urge to hold her hand or lean in closer when he stood behind her at the jewelry counter. The feel of her in front of him while she pointed out pretty earrings and lockets had been distracting, to say the least, especially when she swept her strawberry-scented hair over her shoulder, revealing the soft curve of her neck. It took everything in him not to nuzzle his lips against the spot. He'd been so consumed with thoughts of what that might be like he barely remembered what he'd purchased.

Embarrassment be cursed. He was inviting this girl to spend Christmas Eve with him. And he was doing it tonight as soon as he dropped her off at the inn. That was the plan.

But when they arrived at the inn, something distracted them.

A car idled in the mostly empty parking lot, its headlights slicing a yellow path through the night. As soon as Chase and Elle got out of his truck, a man climbed out of the passenger side of the car and approached like a skittish dog. It wasn't just the strange movement that put Chase on high alert, but the man himself.

He was unmistakably Amish, with a long beard, like most Amish men his age. And beneath that beard he had the kind of face that was probably very handsome once upon a time, before life had its way. He stepped out of the shadows into the glow of the parking lot light and stopped suddenly. He lowered his head, peering through the lighted space between them, as if squinting from a different angle might make things clearer.

"Ruth?" The name escaped in a haunted rasp.

The hair on Chase's arms stood on end. This was Elam Hershberger in the flesh.

Chase shifted in front of Elle, wanting to protect her. Not from violence, as that was highly unlikely out in public, but from Elam's presence. She didn't want to meet him—not today, not ever—but he'd come anyway. All the way from Chestnut Ridge. It was too long a trip to travel by horse and buggy, so he had apparently hired a driver.

Elam squinted harder. Shuffled closer. Chase's muscles coiled. Elam pulled his hat off his head. Then he did something Chase had never seen a grown man do, let alone an Amish one. He buried his face in his hat and wept.

Chase stood motionless, Elle equally unmoving beside him. When he looked down at her, her face was pinched and pale. He gently took her elbow and led her past the sobbing man, toward her room. If Elam had demons to battle, let him battle them on his own. Elle didn't need this.

"She was right to leave." The haunted words hovered in the air like snowflakes.

Elle stopped and turned around. So did Chase.

Elam slipped his hat back on his head and wiped his cheeks. "It was like that verse in Romans. I did what I didn't want to do, and what I wanted to do, I didn't." A tear ran down his face. "Do you know what that's like?"

Chase glanced at Elle. Didn't they all?

"Every time I got angry I was sorry. But it didn't matter. I'd get angry and lose my temper all over again. When I came to North Star that day and learned that she'd left, I was relieved. God forgive me, I was relieved." Elam's face began to crumple, but he covered it quickly with his hand, his shoulders chugging up and down like a train engine. "I know I have n-no right to ask f-for it, but can you ever forgive me for the things I did?"

"There's nothing for me to forgive," Elle said. "I'm not the one you hurt."

No, she wasn't. Elam Hershberger had never laid a hand on Elle McAllister. A mother's love had made sure of that.

As though buoyed by that same truth, Elle stepped forward and hesitantly touched Elam's hand. "I'm not the one you need to apologize to."

"But I don't know wh-where to find her."

"I'm not talking about Ruth."

Elam looked up. "You mean John and Martha?"

"They lost their daughter, Elam."

He shook his head.

"If forgiveness is what you're after, you'll never experience it unless you ask."

"I don't deserve it."

"Of course you don't." Elle clasped her father's fingers, comforting the very hands that had hurt her mother. "That's what makes it so extraordinary."

*T*he sound of ringing cut through Elle's sleep. She lifted her head off the pillow and fumbled her hand over the nightstand, knocking over a glass of water in the process. She jerked up and snatched the phone to save it from death by drowning.

A familiar number lit the screen. Smiling, Elle cleared the sleep from her throat and pressed the phone to her ear. "Buddy the Elf. What's your favorite color?"

Melody laughed.

Elle pushed hair from her eyes and leaned against the headboard. According to the inn's bedside clock, it was a quarter past nine. She rarely slept so late.

"Consider this your Christmas Eve morning checkup call," Melody said. Baby Lila cooed in the background. "How are you doing, friend?"

"I'm good."

"Really?"

"Yes, really."

And she was. The last few days had been a lot to take in, especially with Elam showing up in the way he had and Mom out of reach, floating somewhere in the Pacific Ocean. But had Elle not come, she wouldn't have experienced Romans 8:28 in the profound way that she had. The truth of that verse was no longer head knowledge but was lodged deep down in the depths of her heart. God truly did work all things for the good. She just hoped that was a truth Ruth had experienced too.

"Did you leave your room yesterday?" Melody asked.

"I watched the Hallmark Channel and ordered takeout."

"All day?"

"It was heavenly."

"More heavenly if Chase had joined you. You should have invited him."

Elle laughed.

"What?"

"No way was I going to call him and invite him to watch Hallmark movies with me." Especially when she had been convinced *he* would call *her*. But his phone call never came. She'd waited in vain.

Now she found herself worrying. What if after the fiasco with Elam, he'd decided she was too much drama? Or worse, what if his interest really had stemmed from the mystery, and now that the mystery was laid to rest, his interest no longer remained?

Furrowing her brow, Elle climbed out of bed and padded into the bathroom.

"I Googled him," Melody said.

"You did not."

"I did."

Elle shook her head, then put a pad of toothpaste on her brush and began brushing.

"And oh my"—clanking sounded on the other end, as if Melody was putting away pots and pans—"he's very good looking."

Elle spit in the sink. "Tell me about it."

"So what's the plan for today? I forbid you to watch the Hallmark Channel by yourself on Christmas Eve. That's just sad."

"I'll find a church to go to." Chase's church had a Christmas Eve candlelight service at five. She'd read it in the bulletin when she'd attended on Sunday. But she was not about to show up there uninvited.

She'd done her research to make sure Chase wasn't a stalker. She refused to turn into one herself.

"You should call up Mr. Wellington and spend the day together. Go find some mistletoe or something."

"It's Christmas Eve."

"I thought we already established that."

"He's probably spending the day with his family." Elle rinsed out her mouth and dried her lips with a towel. "I'm not going to intrude on his family time, especially when he's already done so much to make me feel welcome in North Star."

"Something tells me he wants to make you feel more than welcome."

Warmth gathered around Elle's collar. "You're funny."

"A regular stand-up comedienne."

"How's Lila doing?"

"Perfect. And also nocturnal."

"Not sleeping?"

"Oh no. She's sleeping. Just not at night."

Elle was leaning closer to the mirror and running her fingers beneath her eyes when a knock sounded at the door. She froze, picturing a weeping, broken Elam Hershberger outside her door. Or Martha Lantz wanting to know why Elle would send a weeping, broken Elam Hershberger to her home when he was the last person on the earth she wanted to see.

"Elle? You still there?"

"Someone's here."

As if on cue, the knock came again.

Elle ran her fingers through her hair, trying to make it less mussed with sleep, then tiptoed to the door and peeked out the peephole.

It wasn't Elam or Martha. It was Chase. Chase was at her door.

Chase was at her door holding one of the miniature prelit Christmas trees she'd tried to convince him to buy on Tuesday at the strip mall after he admitted he hadn't put up a Christmas tree in his apartment this year.

"Who is it?" Melody asked.

"Chase," Elle whispered.

"Fun!"

"I'm in my reindeer pajamas."

"For the love of all that is holy, please change."

"I have to go."

"Okay, but make sure to kiss him!"

Blushing, Elle hung up the phone, ran her hand through her hair one more time, plastered on a smile, and opened the door, her heart fluttering like hummingbird wings. "Hi."

Chase's gaze dipped to her outfit.

She curled her toes and held up her finger. "Don't you dare laugh."

He pulled in his lips, unmistakable laughter in his eyes.

She raised her finger higher. "Rudolph will not be mocked."

"I wouldn't dream of mocking Rudolph."

"As long as we have that established,"—Elle opened the door wider—"you can come in."

"I woke you up."

"No you didn't. My friend Melody did." And she had also told Elle to kiss him, which, looking the way he did—freshly shaved and dressed in his maroon Columbia coat and faded blue jeans—would not be difficult. "You bought me a tree?"

"Everyone should have one for Christmas. You were very adamant about that." He stepped inside and scanned the room for an outlet. "Do you mind?"

She motioned toward the corner. "Be my guest."

As soon as Chase plugged it in, the small tree twinkled. He took a few steps back and stood beside her.

Elle was officially touched. "I can't believe you bought me a tree."

"It's little."

"It's perfect."

Chase slid his hands into his back pockets. "It's an excuse."

"For?"

"To come check on you." He smiled down at her, a self-deprecating gleam in his eye. "I almost called you five different times yesterday, but I thought you might need some space to digest everything, so I told myself to step away from the mobile."

Her heart started fluttering all over again. Chase was still interested.

"Are you going to join John and Martha for Christmas tomorrow?" he asked.

"I don't know." She bit the inside of her cheek, plagued by the same thing as she had been yesterday during the Hallmark Channel commercials. "Do you think I did the right thing, encouraging Elam to go over there?" Maybe she'd meddled in something that was best left alone. "What if they don't even want me to come anymore?"

"Yes, I think it was the right thing."

"Really?"

"They should know their daughter didn't leave for selfish reasons. And trust me, Elle, they want you to come. I've seen the way they look at you."

"They're nice people, aren't they?"

"Like their granddaughter."

Elle blushed. And remembered her pajamas.

Chase rubbed the back of his neck. "So, do you have any plans tonight?"

"I was hoping to find a candlelight service somewhere."

"My church has one. You should come with us."

"Us?"

"My family."

She gave him a sideways look. "Your family, huh?"

His cheeks tinged with pink. It was the first time Elle had ever seen him blush. "Friends do that, right? Meet each other's families?"

Friends. The word left her feeling disappointed, but she scrambled to hide it. "Of course. Friends do that all the time. I'd love to join you and your family."

"How do you feel about ice skating afterward in the park downtown? They play Christmas music and sell hot chocolate. It's a family tradition."

"I love family traditions."

"You don't say."

She slugged him in the arm.

He clutched his bicep. "Is that a yes?"

"I'd love to go."

"Pick you up at four thirty?"

"I'll be waiting."

"Excellent." Chase went to the door and paused briefly in the doorway. "Hey, Elle?"

"Yes?"

"I think your pajamas are pretty adorable."

She picked up a pillow and lobbed it at him.

With a chuckle he stepped outside and closed the door.

Elle knelt in front of her brand-new twinkling tree and touched one of the small branches, giddiness expanding in her chest.

*E*lle held the unlit candle in her hand as the choir sang "O Come, All Ye Faithful." She closed her eyes and soaked up the lyrics.

"Come and behold him, born the King of angels . . ."

Like every Christmas Eve, the miraculous night played like a movie reel in her mind. Angels on the hilltops, heralding the news. Shepherds watching their glory light up the night sky. And the baby in the manger. Immanuel. God with us.

"O come, let us adore him . . ."

When the choir finished, the pastor stepped onto the stage with his candle lit, the sanctuary lights fading to darkness. He said a prayer of thanksgiving to the God who reached down into this fallen world to rescue broken people. Then he shared his light with a person in the front row, who shared his light with the person beside him, who shared her light with the person beside her. Until the sanctuary glowed. One small flame turned into hundreds.

Brooke lit Chase's candle. Light flickered across his jaw line as he smiled and lit Elle's. And then everyone stood and joined the choir to sing "Silent Night." Chase's voice was deep and rich. She closed her eyes and listened, joy licking at her soul.

"Round yon virgin, mother and child . . ."

Her mind fast-forwarded from a night thousands of years ago in a small town called Bethlehem to a night decades ago outside a home in Gary, Indiana. She'd always assumed she had been a discarded baby. But she was wrong. She'd been a beloved child born to a woman who pressed kisses against her chest. A woman who gave her the name Anna. A woman who went to drastic steps to keep her safe.

"With the dawn of redeeming grace . . ."

For so long Elle had been afraid of the truth. She was certain that if she went looking for it, she'd find rejection or apathy. It was better to make up stories with Mom.

But then truth came looking for her. And with it God revealed His love in a way that was unspeakably personal. He'd protected her. He'd placed her in the care of a mother and father who constantly pointed to Him. And now this. He'd led her to grandparents who welcomed her into their home. Aunts and uncles and cousins. Answers she thought would never be hers. It was exceedingly, abundantly more than she could have asked or imagined.

"Glories stream from heaven above . . ."

Elle gazed at the flame in front of her while voices rose in a crescendo that planted a hot ball of emotion in her throat. Hope charged the air like electricity before a lightning strike, so tangible it lifted the hair on her arms.

"Christ, the Savior is born."

"Christ, the Savior is born!"

⁂

"Like my new hat?" Brooke folded her mittened hands beneath her chin and batted her eyelashes.

Elle looked up from lacing her rented ice skates and laughed. Chase's kid sister was wearing a mistletoe headband—red velvet with a protruding candy cane–shaped hook that dangled the tiny sprig of berried evergreen directly over her head.

Chase approached, a pair of hockey skates in hand. "Where'd that come from?"

"Found it in one of the boxes you carted down from the attic during the move. Isn't it great?"

He eyed the skating rink, particularly a group of young teenage boys, one of whom kept catching Brooke's eye and smiling. He had floppy blond hair and baby-smooth skin and wore a scarf, an unzipped coat, and skinny jeans. He looked like the kind of kid who could charm the girls by simply breathing. The kind of kid that made big brothers like Chase frown. "Aren't you too young to be kissed?"

"Maybe." Brooke took off the band and slipped it on Elle's head. "But Elle's not." With a mischievous cackle, she pranced away—as much as a person could prance in ice skates—and joined the group of boys on the ice.

Elle set the headband carefully aside, her cheeks embarrassingly warm.

"I should have warned you," Chase said.

"About?"

"My mom and Brooke." He sat on the bench beside her, close enough that she caught the faintest scent of a woodsy cologne. "You'd think they'd never seen me with a girl before."

"Have they?"

"Very rarely."

"Ah."

Over the loudspeaker "Blue Christmas" faded into "What Are You Doing New Year's Eve?" The trees in the park glittered with lights while kids and teenagers and adults carved the ice with their skates— some more impressively than others. It was like a scene from one of the Hallmark movies she'd watched yesterday.

"Not big on dating?" Elle asked.

"I date." He shot her a devilishly handsome half grin while pulling the laces tight on one of his skates. "I just don't typically bring those dates with me to family events."

"Don't want to scare 'em away?"

"More like I don't want to give them the wrong impression." He got to work on his other skate. "How long was it before my mom started in with the subtle wedding hints?"

Elle laughed. "In the church lobby?"

"Precisely."

But he'd brought her. So that either meant they were so far from dating that he figured she couldn't possibly get the wrong impression. *Or* he didn't mind Elle getting that impression.

As quickly as that second option came, Elle batted it away. It was foolish thinking. Chase had said so himself. They were *friends*. Friends, friends, friends. And as her friend, he didn't want her left alone on Christmas Eve. That was all.

He placed his hands on his knees. "So what'll it be first—the ice or hot chocolate?"

"I have a confession to make." Elle pulled at her sleeves—mock nervousness. "I haven't been completely up-front with you."

Chase leaned a little closer. "Yeah?"

She shook her head sadly. "I'm a horrible, horrible ice skater."

He gave her a lighthearted shove, then told her to sit tight while he walked in his ice skates to a nearby concession stand to get them hot chocolate.

Elle turned her attention to the rink. The Osmonds sang "Home for the Holidays" to the park, but right then, at least, she was glad she wasn't home. There was no other place she'd rather be than here, waiting for Chase and her hot chocolate, watching the rosy-cheeked skaters on the ice. The only thing that could possibly make the night any better was if her parents were here.

Chase set a cup in front of her and took a seat. Was it her imagination, or was he sitting closer than before? "I got you extra whipped cream."

"You know me well." She took off her mitten, stuck the tip of her finger in the mound of whipped cream, and brought a dollop to her mouth. "Life's too short not to get extra."

Chase narrowed his eyes at the rink. Elle followed his gaze. He was staring at his sister, who was holding hands with the blond-haired boy.

She gave Chase a playful swat. "They're fine."

He blew over the surface of his drink, chasing ribbons of steam into the night, looking none too convinced.

"Come on, don't you remember being that age?" she asked. "Young and in love?"

"*We* are young. *They* are babies." Chase flicked his head in the baby lovebirds' direction. "And that kid looks like trouble."

"That kid is cute."

"Code for trouble."

Elle took a sip of her cocoa. His protectiveness was endearing.

They chatted easily, sipping their drinks, and when they finished, Chase tossed the cups toward a nearby garbage can and sank them both. "You ready to get out there?"

She eyed the ice as warily as Chase had eyed Brooke's boyfriend.

"Come on, McAllister, it's now or never."

"I've seen a couple of people fall, you know. And every time they do, they make that loud *oomph* sound."

He held out his hand and wiggled his eyebrows. "I won't let you fall."

He was impossible to resist. Against her better judgment, Elle slid her hand into his and let him lead her to the rink. Laughing, she stepped tentatively onto the ice as a girl swooshed past. She wobbled but quickly stuck out her arms to keep her balance. Chase looked highly entertained.

"The last time I skated I was in pigtails," she protested.

"So, last year?"

"You're funny."

He helped her get going, and they skated very slowly around the outside of the rink, where it wasn't so populated. When Elle felt that she wasn't doomed to slip and hurl herself toward the hard ground, and her arms weren't constantly out at her sides, she decided she could try talking.

"So your brother doesn't come home for Christmas?"

"Not since he got remarried. He and his wife go to upstate New York to be with her family."

"Do they have kids?"

"They say they don't want any."

"Your poor mother."

Chase laughed.

Just as they finished their first full loop and Elle wasn't feeling so off balance, Brooke sneaked up behind them, her *boo* so close and unexpected that Elle nearly jumped out of her skates. Chase grabbed her arm to keep her upright.

"You know," Brooke said, turning around to skate backward, "it works better if you hold hands." She winked, then sped off, leaving Elle's heart racing, her feet too wide apart, and Chase holding one of her arms.

He let go very slowly. "You good?"

"I-I think so."

But she spoke too soon, because somehow her skates slipped out from under her. She flailed, then grabbed for Chase's jacket. He wrapped his arms around her—whether to steady himself or her, she didn't know.

They floundered. She clutched his jacket tighter and squealed. He laughed in her ear. And somehow, miraculously, they remained vertical.

As they steadied, Elle realized that she was in Chase's arms.

When he looked down at her, everything went very still. "I told you I wouldn't let you fall."

The words and the way his eyes smoldered as he said them made her stomach tremble. His attention dipped to her lips. He drew closer. Elle's heart did a quickstep.

But then her phone started playing "Jingle Bells" inside her coat pocket, bursting the moment like a soap bubble.

They came apart, heat rising in Elle's cheeks. She fumbled in her pocket and pulled the singing phone out from its hiding place. "It's my mom!"

Chase set his hand over his stocking cap—the same hand that had pressed against the small of her back—as if to recover from the whiplash, then helped her off the ice while she answered with an enthusiastic and somewhat breathless *hello*. She had been dying to talk to her mother, just maybe not right then.

Chase gave her privacy. She found an empty bench and spilled the entire story to her mother, who had only known that Elle was heading to North Star to learn more about what small-town journalist Chase Wellington had to say. A small-town journalist who had come to mean so much.

By the time she finished explaining everything but that last little bit on the ice before the call came, the loudspeaker had gone through three full songs and Elle felt as if she'd sprinted three full miles.

"I wish you were here, Mom."

"Oh, sweetie, I wish I was there too. Are you going to join them for Christmas tomorrow?"

"Do you think I should?"

"I really do, especially since they extended the invitation. Take the opportunity to get to know them better." Mom paused. "I'd sure love to meet them someday."

"I'd love for you to meet them." And Chase. She wanted Mom and

Dad to meet him. She looked for him on the rink and spotted him skating in goofy circles with Brooke. Those two were naturals on the ice. "And I want to hear about the cruise."

"I'll show you pictures when you get home. We'll celebrate Christmas. Order pizza. Watch *Elf.* Do it up right."

It sounded wonderful. "I miss you."

"I miss you too, sweetheart. Now go enjoy the evening with this Chase fellow. I'll want to know *all* about him when you get home."

Elle laughed, and they said good-bye. When she hung up, she felt fuller and lighter all at the same time. She'd confided in Melody, but that wasn't the same as talking to Mom. She didn't realize how much she'd needed her mother's listening ear until now.

When everyone had had their fill of ice skating and hot cocoa, Elle said good-bye to Chase's family and climbed into his truck. Although the two of them had been alone quite a bit over the past few days, she felt incredibly nervous about it now. Something charged the air as he drove her to the inn, making her hyperaware of her body—and his too. There was a shyness between them that hadn't been there before.

And an unanswered question.

What would it have been like if her phone hadn't rung and Chase had kissed her out on that ice? This filled her with anticipation, because if she knew one thing about the man beside her, it was that he didn't like unanswered questions.

The inn was set up like a motel, with direct access to each room from outside, so Chase walked her to the door. She was sure he'd go searching for an answer to that question, and the expectancy of it was enough to make her body flush from head to toe.

They stopped in front of her room, and she fished inside her purse for her key.

"I had a nice time tonight," Chase said.

"Me too."

"Did you have a good talk with your mom?"

Elle nodded. "It was such a relief to finally talk to her."

"You two are pretty close."

"Very."

Chase rubbed the back of his neck. "I'm sure you have a lot on your mind."

"Mm-hmm." Him mostly. And his lips. She couldn't stop thinking about those. She stood very still, waiting for Chase to finish what had begun on the ice.

Instead he stuck his hands in his pockets and took a step back. "Well, good night."

It left her shocked. And cold. And terribly, terribly disappointed. She forced herself to smile and wave and let herself inside. When the door was closed, she peeked through the curtains. Chase was walking to his truck.

Did he regret not kissing her?

Because she sure regretted not being kissed.

⌘

Coward, coward, coward!

If it were possible to kick himself, Chase would. He'd kick himself right in the backside all the way to Antarctica.

He climbed inside his truck, his regret profound. He'd never wanted to kiss a girl more in his life. Just the memory of Elle in his arms produced enough body heat to melt all the snow in North Star. And there was a lot of snow.

But he'd also never been so afraid to kiss a girl in his life, because kissing Elle McAllister would change everything. He'd finally met a girl who was worth the risk—and then some. But Elle hadn't come to Pennsylvania to start a relationship with him. She'd come to meet her family. She had a lot going on. Did she really need him mucking up the waters?

And besides, what if she wasn't interested? Elle was a friendly person. To him, to Brooke, to his mom and Doug, to her abusive biological father, to strangers on the street. She smiled at everyone. She was generous with her laugh. It would be very, very easy to misread those smiles and put them both in an awkward situation. Sure, for one thrilling second on the ice, he thought she wanted to be kissed, but then her phone rang, and she couldn't answer it fast enough.

But what if he was wrong?

Chase looked out his window toward Elle's room. It was too late. Her door was closed. Opportunity blown.

He started his car, knowing full well he was a chicken. A big, giant chicken. One who would rather imagine kissing Elle than risk being rejected by her. He shook his head and gripped the steering wheel.

Lord, help me. This girl has gotten under my skin.

He peered again at the closed door. Leaned his head back against the seat. Bounced his leg. He liked her. A lot. Way more than he'd ever liked a girl before. A fact that would scare him if liking her didn't make him so ridiculously happy.

Chase squared his jaw and turned off the car. Not giving himself time to second-guess his actions, he flung his door open, jogged across the parking lot, and knocked on her door, his heart thudding as if he'd just done a wind sprint. He waited as one second ticked into two, and two seconds ticked into three, and then the door opened.

Elle stood in front of him, her hand on the doorway. Barefoot. Wide-eyed.

For one electrically charged moment, they stared at each other. Then Chase moved in. Not slow, but fast. He hooked his arm around her waist, pulled her against his chest, and did what he'd wanted to do ever since he met her at Willow Tree Café. He kissed her.

He kissed her, and she tasted like honey. He kissed her, and after a split second, her arms slid around his neck, her fingers into his hair, and she kissed him back. Never mind melting the snow in North Star. The heat this generated could melt all the snow at the North Pole.

By the time they came apart, they were both out of breath. And although they were no longer kissing, Chase wasn't about to let her go. She felt way too good in his arms.

Elle looked up at him, her lips slightly swollen. "What was that for?"

"I figured I got so close before. I'd regret not checking."

Her smile widened. It was the same thing he'd told her in Paupers on Saturday when she was second-guessing her decision to come to North Star. "It sure took you long enough."

"Well, now that I've gotten the hang of it . . ." He dipped his head and kissed her again, a little slower this time. A little softer. The kind of kiss that lingered. "It might be hard to stop."

Elle laughed, but Chase was dead serious. He was quite certain he could spend the rest of his life kissing Elle and never grow bored with it.

"Hey, Chase?"

"Yes?"

"Would you go with me tomorrow—to John and Martha's for Christmas?"

"I'd be honored."

"Your family won't mind if I steal you away for a couple of hours?"

"Didn't you meet my mom? As soon as I tell her I'm spending Christmas with you, she'll probably die of happiness. And then she'll come back to life so she can go buy wedding invitations."

"I like your mom."

"I like you."

"Pick me up tomorrow at eleven?"

"I'll be here." He brushed his lips against her forehead and very reluctantly let her go. This time Chase didn't walk to his car. He floated.

$\mathcal{T}$he large house overflowed with aunts and uncles and cousins, her grandparents, and Chase.

He'd picked her up at eleven on the dot, and just in case she'd imagined last night, he greeted her with a kiss—a wonderful follow-up to the previous night's stellar performance. She'd gone to bed smiling, and she'd woken up smiling, Mariah Carey's "All I Want for Christmas Is You" playing in her head.

He held her hand on the drive over, and he didn't let go as they walked up to the house. Elle was grateful for the comfort. Chase had assured her she had no reason to be nervous, but she hadn't seen Martha or John since she sent Elam their way to seek forgiveness. She had no idea how the encounter had gone. But Chase was right. John and Martha welcomed her warmly.

They ate a feast of turkey and dressing, potatoes, four different casseroles, and cranberry sauce. Elle could hardly breathe she was so stuffed. After the table was cleared, they moved to the living room, where a fire crackled in the fireplace, presents sat waiting to be opened, and Christmas cards hung on the hearth. John sat in one of the armchairs and opened a worn Bible. The young children gathered around his feet while he read Luke, chapter two. The story of Christmas.

When he finished, they sang Christmas carols. Most Elle knew. A few she didn't. And then they exchanged gifts. She wished she had something for them, but she hadn't known the Amish gave gifts, and even if she had, she wouldn't have had any idea what to get. She received two presents—a quilted wall hanging Arie had made and a faceless cornhusk doll from Emma. She was deeply touched by both.

As the gift exchange came to a close, Martha tapped Elle on the shoulder and asked if she would join her in the kitchen. Elle went gladly, eager to be alone with the woman who had not only welcomed her but invited her into the family.

"I thought you might help me set out the desserts," Martha said. "I think we have enough to feed the entire district."

She was right. Every woman, including Elle, had brought some sort of goodie to share. There were pies and brownies and cookies galore. Elle stood shoulder to shoulder with her grandmother and got to work setting the cookies on a platter.

"Elam came to visit us," Martha said.

Elle's stomach tightened. "I might have had something to do with that."

"When Ruth came home to have you, John and I suspected something was wrong. We knew she'd gone to the bishop of Chestnut Ridge, and we knew the bishop had spoken with Elam. People speculated about what had happened." Martha busied her hands with uncovering and cutting the pies. "But I never asked her. I never asked my daughter what was troubling her."

Elle touched Martha's arm.

Her grandmother's hands stilled, and her eyes welled with emotion. "I should have protected Ruth as much as Ruth protected you."

"You didn't know."

"But I should have."

"It wasn't your fault." Elle gave Martha's hand a reassuring squeeze. "What happened wasn't anybody's fault but Elam's. And I suspect he's paid a high price for what he did."

"I miss her so much."

Suddenly Elle knew what she could give Martha. She knew it as surely as she knew God was real and good. "Why don't you tell me about her?"

Martha smiled as though she'd love nothing more and resumed her work on the pies. "She was always so curious, my Ruth. So full of questions. Most I didn't know how to answer."

"I must have inherited that from her. When I was three, my dad called me his little why-fry. He said I asked that question approximately one hundred times each day."

"I'd like to meet your parents someday."

"They'd like to meet you."

Martha's eyes dampened again.

Elle placed a few more delicious-smelling cookies on the tray. "What else was Ruth, besides curious?"

"Imaginative. She loved writing."

"She did?"

"Yes. She wrote poems and stories. I kept some of them." Martha held up her finger, asking Elle to wait, then hurried up the stairs, the steps creaking as she went. It didn't take long for her to return with notebook pages in her hand.

It was bizarre seeing Ruth's handwriting. The script was a little sloppy and small, as though she'd written each piece quickly because the words came faster in her brain than she could pour onto the paper. While Martha continued with the desserts, Elle read two of the poems. They were good—much better than anyone would expect from a girl with nothing more than an eighth-grade education.

"Over the past few years, I'd catch myself wishing we had a picture of her. It had been so long since I'd seen her that the details of her face were starting to blur in my mind. It was an awful feeling. But then . . ." The dampness in Martha's eyes spilled over in a single tear she quickly wiped away. "Then you came. And it was like I could see my Ruth again."

Even if Elle knew what to say, the tightness in her throat would have prevented her from saying it.

"You should have them." Martha nodded toward the pages. "Something to remember your mother by."

"Oh, Martha. Thank you. But I can't keep these." Elle looked down at the papers she held, these pieces of Ruth. Elle didn't need them. She already had a mother. Her name was Vanessa McAllister, and although they didn't look alike, what they shared went so much deeper than hair color and height. She set Ruth's writing in Martha's hands. "These are for you."

Martha sighed. "I wish I knew where she was."

"You can look for her."

She shook her head. "I wouldn't know where to begin. And even if I did, it's not our way. If Ruth wanted to come home, she would."

Maybe. But Elle knew that sometimes decisions were more complicated than what a person wanted. Sometimes fear stood in the way. Perhaps like Elle, Martha needed prompting. And perhaps Ruth needed someone else to take the first step. "I could look for her."

Martha set the notebook pages on an empty space on the counter and got back to work. It was as though the words were too tempting for her to grab, too much hope for her to hold.

"Chase would know where to start," Elle pressed. He'd found her, after all.

Martha's movements slowed as she took in Elle's words. "Even after all these years?"

If there was one thing Elle had learned from this trip, it was that they worshiped a generous God. One who wanted to give His children abundantly more than they could hope or imagine. "Yes, even after all these years."

Martha looked down, then reached inside her apron and removed one more sheet of paper, yellowed with age. She held it out.

Elle recognized the format. "A letter?"

"She sent it two months after she left."

Elle stared at the paper, entranced. She knew Ruth had written a letter, but she never dreamed of asking to read it. And here Martha stood, offering it to her.

"Please take it," Martha said.

"I can't—"

"Not to keep. To borrow. You can return it the next time you visit."

Next time. Elle liked how that sounded, and she knew it was true. She would come back. She'd bring her mom and dad. They could meet these people who shared her eyes and her chin and her hair. They could meet Chase too.

"Maybe something in there will help you and Chase with your search." Martha placed the folded letter in Elle's palm, then clasped her hands. "Merry Christmas, Anna. I'm so thankful you decided to come."

Before Elle could respond, Martha let go of her hands and went into the living room with the platter of cookies.

CHAPTER FIFTEEN

*E*lle sat on the edge of the bed in her room at the inn and unfolded Ruth's letter with trembling hands.

Dear Mudder,

I've tried to start this letter a thousand times, but I don't know where to begin. How does one start a letter such as this? How can I possibly make right what has happened? What can I say to ease the hardship my leaving must have caused?

I don't think I can, so instead I will simply say that I am sorry. It haunts me at night to think of you or Father being ridiculed or questioned because of my decisions. My leaving must have caused a mess at home, and although I cannot stop people from talking, I hope you do not blame yourself. I know all about that. This wasn't your fault. You and Daed are wonderful parents. Nobody could fix the situation I found myself in but me.

I will not burden you with what happened or why I left. That is in the past, where I hope it will stay. I'm not writing to explain my actions. I am writing to ease your heart and let you know that I am okay. So is Anna, though she is not with me. This news must come as an awful shock.

When I left, I thought I could make a life for us out in the world. But the world is a strange place. It is much harder than I anticipated. Finding work has been difficult, especially

*without a high school education. People are not as generous
out here as they are in our community. I found myself unable
to care for Anna, and for reasons you must trust me with, I
could not bring her to you. So I left her with a family. They
are kind, and they have children, and they attend a church
in town. They can give Anna so much more than I could.*

*I hope I can be forgiven. By you and Father. By God. By
Anna.*

*I pray that she will be safe and loved. I pray that she will
have opportunities and a life full of joy. But most of all, I
pray that God will be her Abba Father and that she will
know His goodness. That was my prayer the night I left her.
And that will continue to be my prayer every single day for
the rest of my life.*

Your daughter,
Ruth

Elle wiped a tear from her cheek. God had answered Ruth's prayer a thousand times over. Elle knew it, but did Ruth?

God had given her so much. He could have stopped at His Son, and that would be more than enough. But He hadn't. He'd given her loving parents and all this too. Asking for anything more felt extravagant, but that was just it. God was an extravagant God. He told them to ask. And so . . .

Help me find her, Lord. I want Ruth to know how much You answered her prayers.

Warmth and light gathered inside her—peace. Not certainty that the prayer would be answered in the way she imagined it should be, but a stillness, a knowing that He would give her nothing less than His best, being the loving Father He was.

Elle tucked the letter inside her suitcase, which she'd begun packing for tomorrow. Chase would take her to the airport, and they would say good-bye for now. She'd be back to visit, and Chase was going to help her look for Ruth. Tonight he'd invited her to watch *It's a Wonderful Life* with his family, another Wellington tradition. She couldn't wait to discover all the rest.

A knock sounded on her door.

When she opened it, Chase stood on the other side, wearing Brooke's ridiculous mistletoe headband. He wrapped his arm around her waist and pulled her close. "I figured it'd be a shame for this headband to go to waste. And you do like your traditions."

"Especially this one." She stood on her tiptoes, grabbed the lapels of his coat, and pulled him in for a kiss under the mistletoe. The kind that made her weak in the knees, because Chase Wellington was much too good at kissing.

"Are you having a good Christmas?" he asked.

Elle smiled up at him. "The best."

Mourning Star

AMANDA FLOWER

*E*den Hochstetler peered around the swinging kitchen door to the front of her father's candy shop, Dutch Village Fudge, in Sugarcreek, Ohio. The shop floor was deserted. The round tables and paddle back chairs were in their places, and the glass dome counter that held dozens of trays of fudge and homemade candies sparkled from a fresh cleaning of vinegar and water.

Seeing the coast was clear, Eden pulled her copy of *Jane Eyre* from her apron pocket. She smoothed the weathered cover. She had read this copy so many times that Jane's face was almost worn off and Thornfield Hall was marred with a smudge of dark chocolate—an occupational hazard of reading on her breaks at the fudge shop.

Taking one last peek through the front window, Eden perched on a three-legged stool with her novel. She lovingly opened it to her favorite scene, when Jane decided to leave Mr. Rochester and Thornfield forever. Eden found it so hopelessly romantic, tragic, and beautiful. She wondered if ever there was a better scene to be read, and she needed the comfort of Brontë's words at the moment.

Her callous fingertips ran across the well-loved lines.

"You know I am a scoundrel, Jane?" ere long he inquired
wistfully—wondering, I suppose, at my continued silence and
tameness, the result rather of weakness than of will.
    "Yes, sir."
    "Then tell me so roundly and sharply—don't spare me."

"What are you reading?" a voice asked.

Eden jumped and toppled from her stool, and *Jane Eyre* skittered across the floor. From her spot on the ground, Eden saw her best friend, Gina Gilbert, peering down at her. Gina's body hung halfway over the counter. Through the glass dome, Eden could see her friend's denim-clad legs dangling on the other side.

"Gina Gilbert, what are you doing sneaking up on me like that? And get off the counter. You know my *Daed* hates when you do that. Besides, I just cleaned it. I don't want your fingerprints on it."

Gina hopped down, and her blond ponytail bounced as she hit the hardwood floor. "He's not here, is he? If he were, you wouldn't be reading on the job."

Eden stood up and dusted off her purple dress and black apron. She touched the prayer Kapp on the back of her chestnut-colored hair to make sure it was still in place. Eden avoided her friend's question by asking one of her own. "Why are you here? I thought you had school."

Gina was a nursing student at the University of Akron, Wayne College. Silently Eden envied her friend for going to school and envied her even more for all the lovely books she could borrow from the college library. Eden had visited Gina once on campus and had been completely mesmerized by the size of the library. It was three times as big as the public library in Millersburg, where Eden was a regular visitor. Gina hadn't been as impressed with the library, and Eden decided such a library was wasted on someone who didn't love to read.

"My afternoon class got canceled. The professor is at some type of conference, so I came to check on you. I wanted to make sure you were okay. You took Isaac Yoder's death pretty hard."

Tears sprang to Eden's eyes. This was why she had needed the comfort of *Jane Eyre*. It was hard to believe it had already been two weeks since her Amish district had buried Isaac Yoder. Eden never knew Isaac's exact age, but he had to be well over eighty by the time he'd died.

It was a nice, long life for a person, or so she consoled herself. All the same, Isaac's death had been a shock.

Eden had seen Isaac the very day he died. He'd visited the fudge shop as always and chatted with her as if he didn't have a care in the world. He came in the shop every afternoon for his "chocolate quota," as he called it. Isaac had a serious sweet tooth the likes of which Eden had never seen, and that was saying something since she sold chocolate and candy for a living. Because Isaac knew this about himself, he only indulged his sweet tooth at Dutch Village Fudge six days a week, Monday through Saturday. The fudge shop was closed on Sundays, and Isaac agreed that it was a *gut* thing to forgo indulgences on the Lord's day. On the Lord's day, it was best to go without, to teach a man discipline.

But now Eden could hardly look at the rocky road fudge, a bestseller and Isaac's personal favorite treat. Sometimes he would try another flavor, like maple walnut, chocolate peanut butter, or vanilla, but nine times out of ten, Isaac relied on a thick piece of rocky road to get him through the rest of his day.

Isaac never bought any fudge to take home for later because he claimed then it would not be a treat. Instead he ate his daily ration at one of the little round tables at the front of the shop, usually in the late afternoon after all the Englisch tour buses had departed for the day. While savoring his treat, he would chat with Eden and sometimes Joanna Lapp if she was working in the shop too.

Eden liked it best when she and Isaac were alone. He could enjoy his treat, and she could read. He didn't mind that Eden read novels while no one was watching. In fact, it had been Isaac who had introduced her to *Ivanhoe, Robinson Crusoe,* and so many others, which he loaned to her from his private library. She wondered if she had to return those novels to his family now. She wasn't sure she could bear to part with them.

"That bad?" Gina gave Eden a sad smile. "I know how hard this has been for you."

Eden blinked away the memories of Isaac. She had almost forgotten Gina was standing on the other side of the counter, watching her—feeling sorry for her.

Eden removed a tissue from her apron pocket and wiped at her cheek. "He was such a nice man. I took it for granted he would always be here, ordering fudge. I knew he wouldn't be here forever, but I never expected he would pass away the way he did. It's too horrible. I miss him." Eden tucked the tissue back into her pocket. "Thanks for stopping by to check on me."

"Checking on you isn't the only reason I'm here."

Eden's brow furrowed. "It's not?"

Gina shook her head. "I have something to tell you." She paused. "I heard something about Isaac, but I'm not sure you want to hear it."

Eden picked up her novel from the floor. "Why would you think that? Isaac was my friend. Of course I want to know what you've heard about him."

Gina waved at her over the counter. "Then come out here. There's nobody around, and I think you're going to need to sit down to hear this."

Eden arched an eyebrow. "Are we going to need fudge for this conversation?"

"Doesn't every conversation go better with fudge?" Gina asked. "And we are definitely going to need it for this one. Trust me. I'm going to need a double-wide piece of chocolate peanut butter just to get it out."

Eden slid the glass window open on the back of the counter, exposing the trays of fudge and other chocolate-dipped goodies. She would have thought that after twenty-five years of being around candy every day she would be tired of the smell of chocolate, but nope, that certainly wasn't the case. She found comfort in the rich, soothing scent.

Gina had once told her that chocolate elevated a person's mood because eating it released a chemical in the brain that made a person happy. If that was true, Eden should be happy all the time, because she was always around delectable chocolate sweets. But she wasn't always happy. She especially wasn't happy since Isaac died.

She cut a generous piece of chocolate peanut butter for Gina and a much smaller piece of butterscotch for herself. She set the pieces on a plain white plate and handed it to Gina over the counter. "I'll grab us a couple of glasses of water from the kitchen. You're going to need something to drink if you have any hope of getting that huge hunk of fudge down your throat."

Gina inspected her piece. "It's not even a challenge."

Eden shook her head and went to fetch the water glasses.

When they had settled at the table, Gina took a big bite of her fudge and moaned. Eden broke off a corner of her piece and set it on her tongue. The sweet butterscotch momentarily distracted her from the news Gina was about to share.

Gina gulped her water. "So here's the deal."

Eden sat up straight and watched her friend. Gina had a thick frame, but she wasn't overweight. It was muscle from a lifetime of playing softball. As always, her blond hair was pulled back into a bouncy ponytail. Her overactive hands beat a rhythm on the tabletop between bites of fudge.

Eden resisted the urge to reach across the table and place her hand on her friend's hands to stop them from moving. "The deal?" Eden asked, trying to ignore Gina's jumpiness. Gina was often in motion, but she seemed even more wound up than usual.

Gina wiped her mouth with a napkin. "Yes. I've heard something about Isaac's death."

Eden tensed. "What is it?"

Gina held up a hand to stop Eden from—from what? From

jumping across the table and shaking the information out of her? It was tempting. Gina always took forever to tell a story. It was as if she wanted her audience to beg. Eden was more likely to shake her friend silly than to beg her.

Gina seemed to read this in Eden's expression, because she said, "Isaac wasn't killed in an accident at Yoder Stables. He was murdered."

*E*den stared open mouthed at her best friend. Of all the crazy stuff that Gina could have said—and she had expected something crazy, considering the source—Eden never in a million years expected that. "Wh-what?"

"Isaac," Gina said as if wanting to make sure Eden understood. "Someone murdered him."

That didn't make it any clearer for Eden.

"How do you know this?" she finally managed to ask.

"My dad," Gina muttered around a huge bite of fudge. "He took care of the horse, Bullet." She swallowed. "After, you know, Isaac got trampled by him. The stables called Dad in to check the horse to make sure it was okay. What happened to poor Isaac wasn't the horse's fault."

Gina's father was an equine and livestock veterinarian in the county, and most of his customers were Amish. The Amish had to rely on Englisch doctors for their care and for the care of their animals.

Eden blinked at her friend.

Gina seemed to take her blinking as permission to continue, so she said, "Dad inspected the horse, and there was a puncture wound on his hindquarters. He assumed it was a nail or something sharp the horse backed into while he was stomping around the stall."

Eden winced.

"Anyway, I overheard him talking with one of his vet techs last night, and he said he finally got the lab results back from the horse's blood. I guess he sent it out to check if the horse had an infection or something else that might have made him overreact when Isaac was in his stall."

"What did he learn?" Eden asked.

"There was an amphetamine in the horse's blood."

"What's that?"

"It's a drug that makes animals or people become agitated. Dad thinks the puncture in the horse's hindquarters is from a needle where the drug was injected."

Eden leaned back in her chair. Gina had been right about one thing. Eden was glad she was seated for this conversation. Had she been standing, she would have fallen over. Just sprawled flat on the floor like cooling peanut brittle. "Why would someone do that? It's just cruel."

"Maybe it wasn't the horse the person wanted to hurt. Maybe they did it while Isaac was inside the pen . . ." Gina trailed off.

"Are you insane? You think someone injected the horse with whatever you call it in order to kill Isaac? This might be the craziest thing you've ever said." Eden meant it. She and Gina had been best friends since they were six years old, when Gina befriended Eden on the first day of first grade. As a New Order Amish, Eden went to the public school until eighth grade. Even after Eden left school, the girls remained friends, and Gina continually tried to drag Eden out of her books and into adventures in the real world. She was also prone to saying outrageous things. However, this was the first time murder had come up.

Gina shrugged. "I just think it's suspicious."

Eden shook her head. "It doesn't make sense. Why would anyone do that?"

Gina cut another bit of fudge from her jumbo piece. "I don't know yet, but someone has to find out." Before Eden could ask why, Gina went on. "Dad told his tech that he talked to Isaac's nephew. I can't remember his name. I think it begins with a *j*. Anyway, he told the nephew he thinks the horse was intentionally harmed and that caused

Isaac's death. Dad wanted to go to the police, but the nephew said no. You know how Amish are about cops."

Eden pursed her lips. "Since I'm Amish, I guess I do."

"If the nephew doesn't want to do anything, I think *we* should find out what happened."

Now Gina had really lost it. "If the nephew doesn't want to do anything about it, why should we? It's not our place. Isaac is gone. The community has made peace with his passing."

"It *is* our place—well, yours really, because Isaac was your friend. You were closer to him than anyone. You were much closer to him than some nephew from who knows where. Do you want whoever did this to Isaac to get away with it?"

Eden thought for a long moment.

"Eden?" Gina asked, throwing up her hands.

As usual Eden had taken too long to decide. She sighed. "Of course I don't, but what can we do about it? Do you think we should go to the police?"

Eden bit her lip. Her father would be furious if he found out she had gotten involved. Matt Hochstetler's goal, now that he was nearing seventy, was to have a quiet and peaceful life. Eden was the last of his five children to be born. Her brothers and sister were all married with children of their own. Most of them had married when they were much younger than Eden, and she knew that her elderly father wondered when she would marry. She couldn't help that she compared all suitors to Mr. Rochester.

Eden pushed her butterscotch fudge away and rubbed her temple.

Gina eyed it. "Are you going to eat that?"

Eden mutely shook her head. How could she even think of sweets after the discovery Gina had dropped on her? Gina clearly wasn't as concerned as she alternated between pieces of the chocolate peanut butter and butterscotch fudge.

"Gina," Eden said quietly. She hoped by remaining calm she could make her best friend understand. "You can't go around saying Isaac was murdered."

Gina blinked at her over her fudge. "Why not?"

Eden groaned. "Because. You can't assume Isaac was murdered because of that horse's injury."

Gina frowned. "That's not all of it. Yoder Stables is failing. My dad said he didn't expect to get paid for tending the horse. He did it out of the goodness of his heart. He said now that Isaac is dead, the nephew will have to sell the stables to pay Isaac's debts."

Eden sat up straighter. "That's terrible. Isaac loved those stables." She frowned. "I didn't know he had money troubles." She felt a pinch in her chest for all the fudge and sweets she had sold Isaac over the years. Had he told her he couldn't afford them, she would have gladly given the treats to him for free just for the company. In fact, many times she had refused to take his money, but Isaac was always adamant he should pay like any other customer. Eden wiped her sweaty hands up and down her apron. "That's horrible, but it still doesn't mean he was murdered."

Gina sat back from her plate of fudge. "True, but I think we should go to the stables and check it out."

"Why?" Eden twisted the end of her apron in her hands.

"Because you need closure. I know he was an old guy, but Isaac was your closest friend—other than me, of course. If someone killed me, wouldn't you want to bring my killer to justice?"

"Don't even say that," Eden snapped. "And *closure*? Is that an Englisch word?"

"Yep." Gina seemed undaunted by Eden's reaction. "I just finished my psych rotation in school. Let me tell you, there are some interesting folks out there, but one thing I learned is that everyone needs closure after a tragedy."

So that's where this is coming from, Eden thought. It wouldn't be the first time her friend applied something she had learned in nursing school to Eden. During her orthopedic rotation Gina had been certain Eden was destined to have flat feet from standing all day behind the fudge counter. "I think you should try out your psychology on someone else. Aren't you tired of using me as a guinea pig?"

Gina thought about this for a moment. "Not really. And I'm serious. I really think you need this. You need to go to the stables and see where Isaac died. You've been a mess ever since he passed. I saw you reading *Jane Eyre.* We both know you only break out Brontë when you're really down."

Gina had a point about that. The Brontë sisters were her go-to in times of sadness. However, that wasn't reason enough to drop everything and visit Yoder Stables. "I can't leave the shop. Joanna is off today, and we're in the middle of the Christmas order season. My Mamm and Daed will be back any time now. And when they get back, I need to begin packing mail orders."

"But you still get off work at five."

"Ya," Eden said slowly. "But I can't—"

The front door to the shop opened, interrupting Eden in the middle of her litany of excuses for not joining Gina at Yoder Stables to investigate Isaac's death. She refused even to contemplate the word *murder.* It was too awful and too ridiculous.

Eden jumped out of her seat when her parents walked through the door. At least her father hadn't caught her reading, but talking to Gina was bad enough. He gave her a pointed look as he headed, leaning heavily on his cane, to the back kitchen.

As usual, Gina wasn't the least bit bothered by the arrival of Eden's parents. Gina wasn't fazed by much. Maybe that was why she could talk about a possible murder so calmly.

After Eden's father disappeared into the kitchen, Eden's mother smiled. "Ah, Gina, it is gut to see you. Have you been distracting Eden from her duties again?"

Gina grinned. "Nope. Not me."

"Or perhaps you were planning what to do on Eden's birthday in a couple of weeks?" Mamm asked. "I hope you will come to our home for a small gathering with cake that day, Gina."

"I would not miss it."

Mamm smiled as if she knew better than that, accentuating the wrinkles on her pretty face. She turned to her daughter. "Eden, thank you for watching the shop all day. It was very helpful to your Daed and me."

"Were you able to make all the deliveries?" Eden asked.

Her mother nodded. "Yes, and it's a good thing too. Many of the gift shops needed to be restocked with our candies. Several places doubled their orders for the holidays. We're going to have the busiest Christmas season ever." She smiled again. "It's a gut problem to have, but it is exhausting. I will need to talk to Joanna about increasing her hours at the shop for the next few weeks."

Behind Mamm, Gina made a face when Joanna was mentioned. Gina was not fond of the other Amish girl. Eden looked away before she started laughing.

"I can lend a hand too if you need it," Gina said.

"That's very nice of you, Gina. I will let Matt know," Mamm continued, unaware of the looks passing between the two girls. "Eden, you must be tired from watching the counter all day. Why don't you take the rest of the afternoon off and spend it with Gina? You two don't get to see each other as much as you did when Gina was working here."

After high school Gina had worked at Dutch Village Fudge for a few years to save money for college. She was now in her second year at the Wayne campus. Next year she would be off to the main campus, over an hour away. Eden would hardly see her friend when that happened. She frowned. Terrific. She had something else to feel melancholy about.

"Why don't you girls go to the library you like so much?" Mamm added.

Gina jumped out of her seat, beaming. "That's a great idea, Mrs. Hochstetler. In fact, Eden and I were just talking about books."

Since the Brontë sisters had been a small part of their odd conversation, Eden had to concede that was true.

"It's settled then," Mamm replied. "Now shoo, both of you, before Eden's father comes out of the kitchen with some task for Eden."

"I can't wait to go to the library," Gina announced.

Eden sighed as she walked to the line of pegs on the far wall to collect her coat, bonnet, and the small backpack she always carried, filled with books, including Isaac's. Eden was pretty sure Gina wasn't talking about the library.

*G*ina started up her Jeep as soon as Eden fastened her seat belt. "Closure?" Gina asked.

"Okay, fine." Eden knew there was no point in arguing. Gina wouldn't leave her alone until she got her way.

Eden dug through her backpack and came up with *Ivanhoe* and *Robinson Crusoe*.

"Are you going to read on the way there?" Gina asked as she turned out of the parking lot.

Eden shook her head and was quiet for a moment to make sure her voice remained steady. "These are Isaac's books. I thought if I brought them with us to the stables, we'd have an excuse for being on the property. I need to return them to his nephew anyway. They're rightfully his now."

Gina glanced at her with a smile on her face. "The books are a nice cover. Are you sure you've never done anything like this before?"

"I read a lot of mystery novels," Eden replied defensively.

Gina laughed.

As brave as she pretended to be for both their sakes, Eden couldn't stop the pounding of her heart. What was she doing going to Yoder Stables? What if someone caught them there? Would the books be a good enough excuse?

For once, Gina was quiet. She seemed to sense that Eden wanted some time alone with her own thoughts, or maybe since Gina had already gotten her way, she didn't want to press her luck.

Finally they arrived at the stables, and Gina turned into the long driveway. There was no sign of any activity. Eden had expected a buggy or two. Wouldn't some of the people who boarded their horses be there?

A small whitewashed caretaker's house—Isaac's house—stood at the front of the property. Three enormous oak trees loomed over it and had all lost their leaves for winter. Eden couldn't believe it would be Thanksgiving next week and her birthday a few days later. Christmas not long after that. She thought of Isaac's nephew. Did he have other family? He must have family and friends in Lancaster. As much as she missed Isaac, she knew the grief must be much worse for his nephew, especially this close to the holidays. She wondered what she could do to help other than return Isaac's books.

She held the novels to her chest and was overcome with the feeling that she and Gina were trespassing. If the nephew wanted any help from Isaac's district or neighbors, he would have reached out by now. Isaac had been gone for more than two weeks.

"We shouldn't have come here," she whispered.

Gina glanced over at her as she parked the Jeep. "Don't be such a scaredy-cat. We're just looking around. There's no harm in that. We visited the stables all the time when Isaac was alive."

There could be a lot of harm in it if we get caught, Eden thought.

Gina hopped out of the Jeep. Eden, still holding Isaac's books, followed. Gina, who was nearly six inches taller than petite Eden, was already halfway to the stables by the time Eden caught up with her. Gina grinned at Eden over her shoulder when she heard Eden's boots crunch the frozen grass between them. Eden knew her friend was enjoying every second of their expedition.

She could not feel the same way. This was more personal for her. Gina had known Isaac, but she didn't have the same friendship with the older man that Eden had. Isaac was the closest person she'd had to a Grossdaadi for nearly a decade. Eden was born in North Star,

Pennsylvania, but her father moved the family to Sugarcreek when she was still a baby so he could take over the fudge shop for his ailing parents. The only grandparent she had left was her maternal grandmother, who still lived in North Star with Eden's aunt. Each Christmas her Grossmammi would send Eden a hand-knitted scarf. It wouldn't be long before the package wrapped in brown paper arrived again.

She pulled on Gina's sleeve. "Just so we agree. We go in the barn, look at the stall"—she swallowed—"where Isaac died, and then we leave, right?"

"Right. In and out in no time."

Eden still didn't know what Gina hoped to prove, but she said, "And if we don't find any additional proof that his death was anything but an accident, we drop your ridiculous theory, right?"

"You mean the murder one?"

She winced at Gina's use of the word *murder*. "Yes."

Gina shrugged. "Sure."

Eden frowned, suspicious that Gina was agreeing.

They reached the stable, and Gina pulled on the enormous barn door. It didn't budge. "It's locked."

Relief flooded Eden. "I guess we'll have to call this whole thing off. That's just too bad. Too bad indeed." She tried but failed to keep the happiness out of her voice.

"There has to be another way to get in," Gina muttered, more to herself than to Eden.

"I—" But before Eden could finish her sentence, Gina was already around the side of the stables.

"Bingo!" Gina called triumphantly as Eden followed her around the corner. Gina held a hinged door open like a butler welcoming a dignitary into a great British hall. Eden had never seen such a hall or butler, but she had read about a good many of them in her books. Thornfield Hall had a butler, of course.

"Ready?" Gina asked.

Since Eden hadn't seen anyone on the grounds and since the main door had been locked, she was beginning to feel more relaxed. Although she did wonder where everyone was. When Isaac had run the stables, there had always been one person or another visiting his or her horse. Amish and a few Englisch boarded their horses there, and it seemed like people were always coming and going. Now it was as quiet as a graveyard. Eden grimaced when that image came into her mind.

She stepped inside. The eerie quiet she had felt in the yard extended into the huge stable. Yoder Stables was one of the largest in the county, and the massive building could hold up to fifty horses. Eden had expected to hear horses whinnying and pounding their hoofs on the floor of their stalls. At the very least she expected to see their heads hanging over their stall doors.

But there was none of that. The stable was silent—oddly silent. Nothing moved.

Gina must have felt the same, because she whispered, "Creepy," under her breath.

"Where are all the horses?" Eden asked.

"Don't know. Dad treated that horse, Bullet, here, but that was two weeks ago, right after Isaac died."

Eden dug her hands into the pockets of her black wool coat. It seemed much colder inside than it had outside. She attributed that to the lack of sunshine. She wouldn't allow herself to attribute the chill to anything else. "Let's find the stall and get out of here."

"Good idea," Gina agreed.

There's a first, Eden thought.

The girls moved down the aisle. "I think Dad said Bullet's stall was halfway down on the left. He said there was a big harness on the wall above that particular stall, like it was marked."

Eden knew that stall. It was where Ephraim Lapp always kept

his prize racehorses, like Bullet. She chewed on the inside of her lip. Thoughts of Ephraim were never pleasant. She didn't want anything to do with him, didn't even want to look at the stall that once held his horse.

"There aren't any horses here, so you don't have to worry about running into Ephraim," Gina said.

Eden wondered if her best friend could sometimes read her mind.

As they moved down the stable, Eden heard a scraping sound. A mouse ran out from behind a hay bale. Both girls squealed and grabbed each other.

When the mouse disappeared into one of the empty stalls, Eden dropped her hold on Gina's arm. "This is ridiculous. How many times have we seen a mouse before and never screamed?"

Gina steadied her breathing. "We've never before seen a mouse in a creepy, deserted stable so close to where someone died."

She had a point, Eden thought.

Gina marched ahead, intent on reaching the stall where Isaac died.

Another sound caught Eden's attention, and she froze. The sound came from the door where the girls had entered the barn. There was a scrape of metal and a creak as if the door was opening.

Eden ran toward her friend, grabbed Gina by the collar of her coat, and yanked her into the closest stall. Gina yelped. Eden covered her friend's mouth with her hand and pulled her down into a squat behind the stall door.

"What are you doing?" Gina hissed.

Eden held a finger to her mouth. "Sh."

A man's voice floated down the center aisle, where the girls had just been standing. "I'm telling you, I will make you sorry."

Gina stared at Eden, her eyes the size of goose eggs. Gina cocked her head as if to hear better.

Eden knew it was wrong to eavesdrop, but she couldn't help but hear, so she cocked her head too and wished she had a glass to listen with.

"Are you threatening me?" a second male voice asked.

"Call it what you like," the first man hissed.

The voices came closer, as if they were moving down the center aisle.

Gina and Eden ducked lower behind the stall door. Eden opened it a crack, hoping she could see the two men, but all she saw was the mouse scurrying past the door's opening.

"I need my money. Isaac never paid up, so it's your responsibility now."

"I have let you come here to inspect the property as you asked, but you can't hold me accountable for my uncle's debt."

The other man laughed mirthlessly. "Yes, I can. Unless you want me to get the sheriff involved. I'd be happy to have him do it for me. He's a nice guy, but he enforces the law when he needs to. This is one of those times he would."

"*Nee,*" Isaac's nephew said. "Don't do that."

"I will get my money one way or another. I promise you."

Isaac's nephew said something Eden didn't catch.

"You know I can do much worse to you than calling the police. You and I both know that, don't we?"

"Stay away from my family."

The first man snorted. "Family. You don't have any family. How many Amish men can't claim one relative? You might be the only one."

"Please," Isaac's nephew said. "I have shown you everything there is to see. The horses are gone. I need more time to sell the stables. My uncle has only been gone two weeks."

"Sign it over to me and I will sell it for you."

"Nee," Isaac's nephew's voice was strong.

"Very well," the first man said after a pause. "But my patience is running thin, very thin."

The men's heavy footsteps moved down the aisle and faded away. The side barn door, the same door Eden and Gina entered through, slammed shut.

*E*den peeked over the edge of the stall. Gina did the same. In a half squat the two girls peered out into the stable. Eden imagined that the pair of them looked like groundhogs peeking out of their burrows.

"They're gone," Eden whispered after a beat, still gripping the stall door in her half stance. She forced herself to straighten up. "It's time we get out of here."

"We can't leave now," Gina insisted, standing next to her. "We're almost to the stall where Isaac died. I know where it is. Dad described it perfectly." She pointed. "See, there's the harness he mentioned."

"What's the point of looking when the horse isn't even here?" It was getting close to five o'clock, and the sun was setting. Soon Yoder Stables would be surrounded by darkness. This wasn't a place Eden wanted to be after dark, especially after hearing those two men exchange angry words.

"We still have to check out the stall," Gina protested. "We can't come this far for nothing."

Without waiting for Eden's answer, Gina headed down the center aisle toward the stall with the harness hanging above it. Eden sighed. The sooner Gina was satisfied with seeing the stall, the sooner they could leave.

Gina waited for her in front of the stall. Eden's stomach tightened as she got closer. She couldn't believe she'd allowed Gina to talk her into coming here. How could she be looking at the place where Isaac died?

In her mind's eye she kept seeing him splayed on the floor of the stall, broken and battered. She covered her face with her hands as if by doing so she could escape the image. It didn't help.

Gina reached over and squeezed Eden's elbow, then unlatched the stall door and opened it wide. The stall was empty. Fresh straw lay on the ground, and an old set of reins hung on the wall. Eden was grateful for the fresh straw. She was worried what condition the stall would be in when they arrived. Isaac's death had been violent, so she could only assume that the scene, like the one she saw in her head, would show evidence of the violence. She felt a wave of nausea overtake her.

Gina didn't have the same issues and stepped into the stall. Her dark eyes were bright as she examined everything with the same dedicated attention she gave her schoolwork.

"What are you doing?" Eden asked.

"Looking for a nail or something that might have hurt that horse." Gina circled the stall, sliding her right hand along the wall as she went.

"I thought your dad said it was an injection wound."

"He did, but I want to make sure something else couldn't have caused it."

Eden didn't have the faintest idea how Gina hoped to accomplish that.

A barn cat mewed at Eden's feet, making her jump.

"Where were you when that mouse attacked us?" Eden scratched the cat under the chin. The creature purred, and Eden decided that, like her, the poor little cat must be missing Isaac. Eden bet Isaac gave the cat extra treats. He was that kind of man.

For the first time she wondered about Rocky Road, Isaac's beloved chocolate Lab. What had become of his dog? Many times when Isaac came to the shop for his fudge, he brought Rocky with him.

The cat bumped into the back of Eden's leg as if to comfort her. She was grateful for the cat. It distracted her from whatever Gina was doing.

"I can't find anything," Gina said dejectedly. "Not a rusty nail, loose board, or even a splinter."

"What does that mean?"

"It means the horse wasn't injured by something he backed into inside the stall. It gives more validity to my theory."

"If you say so," Eden replied with far less confidence.

"Hey!" a male voice shouted. "What are you doing in here? No one is supposed to be in here."

The girls turned and found a glaring Amish man standing in the center of the stable. He held a rake in his hand like a weapon. At his feet Rocky sat wagging his tail.

"Rocky!" Eden called.

The dog bolted toward her. His plume of a tail wagged happily as he danced around her. Eden squatted in front of him, her skirt hitting the dusty concrete floor of the barn, but she didn't care. She wrapped her arms around the dog and gave him a hug. Rocky buried his graying muzzle into her neck.

The man lowered his rake. "I take it you two know each other."

Eden stood back up, recognizing the man's voice as one she'd heard in the barn only a few minutes ago. "Rocky and I are gut friends."

Gina had yet to speak. She stared open mouthed at the young Amish man, and Eden knew why. He was very good-looking. Not like a Mr. Rochester from *Jane Eyre*, but more like a Mr. Knightley from *Emma*, she decided. She had never seen him before. Eden knew she would have remembered a Mr. Knightley look-alike in Sugarcreek. His wavy brown hair was barely controlled by his Amish bowl haircut, and he wasn't wearing a hat, which Eden thought was just fine, because hair like that shouldn't be covered by an Amish felt hat. It would be such a shame.

"So you know my uncle's dog. That still doesn't tell me what you're doing here," the man said. He ignored Gina and directed his comment at Eden.

"W-we—" She stopped, collected herself, and reached for her backpack. After digging around for a moment, she thrust the two novels at him. "These are Isaac's. My friend, Gina"—she nodded at Gina, who finally realized her mouth was hanging open and snapped it shut—"drove me out here. Isaac was my friend and let me borrow these books before he died, and I wanted to return them to his family."

He frowned at Eden for less than a second before turning to Gina. "That Jeep outside belongs to you?"

Eden mentally smacked herself in the forehead. Of course Isaac's nephew would come looking to see if anyone was in the barn with Gina's Jeep sitting in the yard as plain as day. The other man, the one who had been arguing with Isaac's nephew earlier, must have seen it too. Did the man in front of her suspect the girls had overheard the argument?

Gina tossed her ponytail over her shoulder and stood a little straighter. The question seemed to shake her out of her stupor. "Yes, that's my car. Who are you?"

"I'm Jesse Yoder, and this is my property. You two"—he pointed at each of them in turn—"are guilty of trespassing."

Eden's cheeks flushed. Jesse was right; she and Gina shouldn't have been there. She stood like a fool, holding out Isaac's novels to Jesse. He made no move to take them.

"We're so sorry for your loss," Gina said. "Isaac was your uncle?"

"Not that it's any of your business, but Isaac was my great-uncle. I just arrived from Lancaster to settle his affairs." He looked back at Eden. "Who are you?"

"I'm Eden Hochstetler." She tried hard to keep her voice steady.

Jesse's face softened. Eden was astonished how the change in his expression made him look even more like the Mr. Knightley in her head.

"Eden," he said. "My uncle spoke of you often. You work at the fudge shop in town he was so fond of?"

She nodded. "My family owns it." She still held the books out in front of her. Her arms were beginning to tire.

Jesse's shoulders relaxed. He took the books from her. "It was very kind of you to bring Isaac's books back. He enjoyed reading so much. I understand that's something the two of you had in common."

Eden frowned. How much had Isaac told his nephew about her? Isaac had barely mentioned his nephew in all the time she had known him.

Jesse smiled slightly. "Was there anything else? Other than you returning the books?"

Eden felt her cheeks flame red. She was staring at him again. "Nee."

Jesse handed the books back to her. "Then you keep them. My uncle would have wanted you to have them."

s the girls strode across the stable yard to Gina's Jeep, Gina asked, "Where did *he* come from?" She fanned herself. "This is one of the few times I've wished I were Amish. Did you see his eyes? I thought I was looking into the deepest depths of the ocean. I have never seen eyes that deep blue before. He should work as a hypnotist with those eyes. They could bring him fame and fortune. It's a shame he's Amish and can't put them to good use."

Outwardly, Eden rolled her own blue eyes. Inwardly, she agreed with Gina that Jesse had lovely eyes.

A tall and painfully thin Amish man holding a black leather harness stomped across the yard toward the barn. He was in a hurry. Eden recognized him right away as Micah King, Isaac's stable hand. Micah had been working for Isaac only a few weeks before the stable owner died. Eden had worried when Isaac hired him because Micah had a reputation for shirking his duties on the job. He had worked for many Amish businesses throughout Tuscarawas and Holmes Counties and hadn't been able to keep a job for more than a few weeks. However, when Eden hinted at her concerns to Isaac one day, the old Amish man told her everyone deserved another chance. Eden had been ashamed that she had questioned her wise friend's judgment, but seeing Micah marching toward the barn, she wondered if she had been right to be wary.

"Micah?" Eden called.

He glared at her, his jaw clenched.

Eden stepped back and bumped into Gina. "Is everything all right?"

Slowly, as if it took an enormous effort, Micah loosened his grip on the harness. "Eden." He nodded at her and Gina. "What are you doing here?"

She held out her small stack of novels. "These are Isaac's. I wanted to return them to his family."

He frowned. "Then why do you still have them?"

"His nephew Jesse told me to keep them."

"And we have to do what Jesse says, don't we? He's the owner of this place now." He scowled in the direction of the horse barn.

"Is something wrong?" Gina asked. "Can we help you in some way? You seem upset."

Upset was an understatement. Micah was furious. He positively shook with anger. "Can you get my job back for me?"

"Your job?" Gina asked.

Micah took a deep breath. "That's right. That no-good waste of a . . ." He trailed off, looking between the two girls.

Eden turned to see Jesse standing behind her and Gina.

Jesse waved at Micah. "Go right ahead. I'm interested in hearing what you have to say. Although it won't do you any gut in getting your job back. There's no job to be had now."

"I'll tell you to your face. You have no right to fire me. Your uncle was a gut man. In the time that I worked for him, he never complained once about my work."

Gina tugged Eden out from between the two men. Eden stumbled after her friend but kept her eyes on the argument happening in front of her. She knew for sure that Micah was not the man Jesse had argued with in the barn. That man's voice had been lower and more gravelly.

"I didn't fire you, Micah," Jesse said, sounding very tired. "I let you go because there's nothing more for you to do here. The horses are all gone. I can take care of the property myself until the stables sell."

"No matter what label you put on it, I'm still out of work," Micah spat.

Jesse came a few steps closer. "I'm sorry you feel that way, but you shouldn't be here. What are you still doing here?"

"I left my harness." He held it up to show Jesse.

"Are you sure that's *your* harness?"

Micah's eyes narrowed.

Jesse clenched his jaw. "You have it now. I think it's time for you to go."

"Fine."

Jesse's shoulders drooped as he watched Micah stomp away. "I'm sorry you had to see that."

"You aren't going to keep the stables?" Eden asked. Rocky trotted to her side and leaned against her leg.

Jesse shook his head. "I can't. My life is in Lancaster." He stopped himself. "Well, you don't want to hear about my troubles."

"We do," Gina insisted.

Jesse laughed, smiling at Eden. "Is she always like this?"

Eden smiled back. "Always. We'd better go."

He nodded. "If Rocky will let you. It might take me some time to sell the stables. If . . . if you want to come back to visit Rocky—I know he's lonely for Isaac—that would be fine with me."

Eden patted the dog's head. "I'd like that. You're taking gut care of him."

"Danki," Jesse said. He turned back toward the barn, whistling over his shoulder for the Labrador. After giving Eden a forlorn look, Rocky trotted after his new master.

"Eden!" Gina squealed, pulling on Eden's arm. "He invited you to come back!"

Eden tugged her sleeve from her friend's grasp. "To visit Rocky."

Gina grinned from ear to ear. "He didn't invite *me* to come back to visit Rocky."

"That doesn't mean anything."

Gina wouldn't stop grinning. "If you say so."

Eden headed to the Jeep.

Reluctantly, Gina followed. "It's too bad that he might have killed his uncle."

"What?"

"Isaac is dead, and that's someone's fault. Jesse Yoder is a suspect."

"That doesn't mean Jesse did it. And keep your voice down. What if he overhears you?"

Gina waved her concern away. "He's way over in the barn. He can't hear us. Besides, why are you defending him? You don't even know him."

"He wasn't here when Isaac died. He said he just arrived."

"Oh, right." Gina's face cleared. "There are other suspects."

"Like who?" Eden asked.

"That mystery guy Jesse was arguing with. The motive there is money all the way. That's a very good motive."

Eden tucked Isaac's novels into her backpack. "What am I going to do with you? I agreed to come here so you would give up this quest, but it's only made it worse."

A half hour later Gina dropped Eden off in front of her farmhouse on the edge of Berlin and Sugarcreek. The two-story home's windows glowed with yellow lantern light, and her father's buggy sat in the drive-way. Her parents were home. Eden hoped they wouldn't ask her about her nonexistent trip to the library that afternoon. She opened the passenger door to Gina's Jeep.

Gina stopped her. "Eden, I know I'm right. There's something strange going on at Yoder Stables."

Eden said good night. There was certainly something strange in the air at the stables, but that didn't mean it was murder. She wished she could make her friend understand that. But how could she when she wanted to know what was going on at Yoder Stables too?

Later that night Isaac and his nephew Jesse were at the forefront of her mind when she laid her head on her pillow—but for very different reasons.

*T*he next morning Eden dried the last of the breakfast dishes while her mother washed. Eden gave her mother a sideways glance as Mamm plunged a casserole dish into the hot, soapy water and scoured the dish until it shined. Mary Hochstetler took dishwashing seriously, as she did all tasks. She had taught her daughter that nothing should be done halfway, not even washing dishes.

After the dish passed Mamm's inspection, Eden accepted it from her mother's hands and cleared her throat. "Mamm, can I make the hotel deliveries this morning? You and Daed did so many deliveries yesterday, and I'm sure you'd like a break to stay out of the cold."

Mamm smiled at her daughter as she began to tackle a frying pan with a scrub brush. "Are you tired of being in the shop all day? I know you tend to become restless when you are there for too many hours. Did you have a nice visit to the library with your afternoon off?"

Eden swallowed. Thankfully, her mother saved her from answering.

"How would you make deliveries? Take the buggy?"

"Gina doesn't have class today, and I'm sure she'd be happy to drive me." She didn't add that Gina would be happy for the chance to snoop into Isaac's death too. "With her Jeep we will be done sooner than Daed and you would be with the horse and buggy."

"Doing work faster does not make it better," her mother said with a soft reprimand in her voice.

"I know that, but I thought it would be better for you, and especially for Daed, if you could stay at the shop today, where it's warm."

Mamm peered out the window above the sink. An inch of light, fluffy snow, which had fallen overnight, covered the backyard. The swing Eden's father had hung from the large red maple tree when Eden was small was dusted with snow. It wasn't December yet, but winter had come early to Amish country, as it always did. In Ohio, winter didn't pay any mind to the calendar. It showed up and left in its own sweet time.

"I do love Christmas," Mamm said with a sigh. "But I can't say I'm looking forward to the cold and snow. The cold bothers your father's legs so much. He would never say so, but he was in a lot of pain yesterday when we were making our rounds. I wish he would take it easy." Her voice dropped an octave. "I wish one of your brothers would take over the business." She sighed. "But neither of them is interested in running the shop, and I'm afraid your father will be working there until he's in his grave. He would never stand for the shop leaving the family in his lifetime."

Eden wanted to take over the shop. It was an argument she'd had with her parents for years, but they wouldn't hear of it. They always argued that she would leave it the moment she married, as her first responsibility would be to her husband and nonexistent children. But that hadn't happened yet and didn't appear to be happening any time soon. Besides, Eden didn't want a husband who would make her give up the business, which had been in the family for four generations. Eden opened her mouth to say all of this but thought better of it. That was a conversation for another day when she had more time and didn't need something else, like permission to be out of the shop to snoop.

Mamm handed her the now sparkling-clean frying pan. "If Gina doesn't mind, then it will be all right. It would be nice to stay in the shop today. I have some new candy recipes I want to try, and today will be my last chance. Next week is Thanksgiving and then your birthday, and after that it will be nonstop until Christmas with all the holiday orders."

Eden thanked her mother, hiding her small smile as she put the remainder of the breakfast dishes in the cupboards and drawers.

As soon as Mamm and Eden reached the shop, Eden stepped into Daed's tiny office and called Gina's cell phone from the work phone. The Hochstetler family didn't have a phone at home.

Gina answered on the first ring. "I'm surprised to hear from you after last night."

"I'm sorry I was cross with you, Gina. I know you were excited."

"It's okay," Gina said, sounding like her cheerful self. "What are you up to today?"

Eden peeked around the office door. She could see her parents working in the kitchen. "I've been thinking about what you said—that something strange must be going on at Yoder Stables. I'm not saying I agree with you that Isaac"—she paused—"was murdered. But something odd is happening."

"Okay," Gina said slowly.

"I think—I think we should find out for Isaac's sake. Isaac was a gut friend to me, and it seems that I owe it to him to find out what happened."

"Oh?" Eden caught the smile in her friend's voice.

"Mamm and Daed said I can make the deliveries today if you can drive me around. It shouldn't take too long, and we should have enough time to pay a visit to the Lapp farm . . ." She trailed off.

"Eden, that's genius. We can talk to Bullet's owner." Gina was quiet for a moment. "Are you sure you want to do that? You and Ephraim didn't part on the best terms."

"That was a long time ago, and I've seen him many times since. He often comes to the shop to pick up his sister Joanna from work."

"I know, but have you really talked to him?"

"It will be fine," Eden said, trying to convince herself as much as Gina.

"Great! The investigation is on!"

"Gina," Eden hissed.

"Oh, can your parents hear you?" Gina whispered back.

Eden shot a glance at her mother, who was concentrating on putting chocolate-covered pretzels into cellophane bags and tying them closed with red and green ribbons.

Mamm glanced up from her work. "Can Gina take you on the deliveries?"

Eden nodded. Her mother didn't need to know about their side trip.

◦⟋⟍⟑⟍⟍◦

Three hours later Gina's Jeep was parked in the circular driveway in front of an Amish restaurant in Walnut Creek.

Eden exited the restaurant after making the last delivery of the day. She opened the Jeep door and hopped in. "They ordered three crates of fudge. That should keep them stocked for a while."

The restaurant was busy. Englischers shivered under the eaves of the wide porch as they waited for a table. Gina nodded to the ones standing in line. "You have to really like pie to stand out in the cold like that."

"You like pie just as much as any of those people do," Eden said, turning up the collar of her winter coat.

"Yeah, but you're my source for all Amish delicacies. It's good to have an Amish connection now and again."

Eden laughed, and as she slammed the back door of the Jeep, Jesse Yoder stormed out of the restaurant.

An Englisch man was a few paces behind him.

"Jesse!"

Jesse didn't slow down or even turn his head. He marched to a horse and buggy tethered to the hitching post a few feet away.

"Jesse," the man in the dark gray business suit called again.

Jesse spun around as soon as he had the horse untied. Gina's Jeep was between the Englisch man and Jesse, and Jesse's eyes widened when he saw Eden through the windshield.

The Englisch man didn't seem to see her, Gina, the Jeep, or the long line of Englisch visitors waiting for a table. He stomped over to Jesse. "This is the last time I'm telling you. If you don't take care of the debt, I will call my lawyer."

Eden's chest tightened. That voice. It was the same gravelly voice she had heard at the stables the afternoon before. This was the man Jesse had been arguing with inside the barn.

"I gave you what I can." Jesse's voice was tight, as if he were talking through a plastic straw. "The rest you will have when I sell the stables."

"You can avoid all that trouble by signing the stables over to me."

"Nee."

The man folded his arms over his suited chest. "What difference does it make if you sell it or I sell it? All the money is coming to me in the end."

"The stables are worth much more than my uncle owed you. I will not let you take advantage of my grief."

A woman came out of the restaurant. "Bryan." Her voice was low, but something in her tone caught the Englisch man's attention, and he spun to face her. "You're disturbing our guests." She gestured at the line of customers staring at Jesse and Bryan.

Jesse took the opportunity to climb into his buggy and drive away. The Englisch woman led Bryan back into the restaurant.

"Whoa," Gina said. "I think that Bryan guy needs some anger-management classes."

Eden silently agreed.

Gina started the Jeep. "Where to next?"

"That was our last delivery, and Mamm won't expect us back for a while yet."

"See, and you said I was driving too fast. It paid off. Let's head to the Lapp farm."

Eden still wasn't sure she was doing the right thing, but she nodded. "Ya, the Lapp farm."

*O*n the way to the Lapp farm, the girls went over their plan. Gina would claim she was there to check the wound on Ephraim's horse as part of her father's veterinary service. Gina worked at her father's clinic often enough that she didn't believe Ephraim would question that explanation.

When Gina turned the Jeep onto the Lapps' property, Ephraim, a squat Amish man with broad shoulders a bit too large for the rest of his body, opened the front door and trudged out to the Jeep in the freshly fallen snow. Ephraim was close to thirty years old, if Eden remembered correctly. He and his sister Joanna lived on the Lapp farm. They had two older sisters who were married with families of their own. Their parents had passed away when they were small, and Ephraim had taken it upon himself to care for his last unmarried sister. At the fudge shop Joanna constantly complained about his overprotectiveness.

"Good afternoon," Ephraim greeted them. "If you're looking for Joanna, your father called her to work at the fudge shop today."

Eden smiled, relieved at the friendly welcome. She hadn't known what Ephraim's reaction would be when she and Gina showed up on his farm. She had known Ephraim and Joanna all her life, but Ephraim's unpredictability had always made her edgy. "My parents appreciate Joanna's willingness to work extra hours during this busy time."

"I'm glad. If you aren't here to see my sister, could you be here to see me?" He watched her face.

Eden's smile faded. At one time she had allowed Ephraim to court her. Her parents pressured her into it, but Eden was never happy when she was with Ephraim. In her mind it never would have worked for them. Ephraim reminded her too much of Mr. Collins from *Pride and Prejudice*. Eden would never marry a Mr. Collins. It wasn't so much his appearance that brought the comparison to mind but his attitude. Ephraim was a little too self-assured for her liking. When she decided to break it off, Eden had done everything she could to discourage him. She thought he had given up any hope. Now she wondered if that was true or wishful thinking on her part.

Gina came to her rescue. "My dad asked me to stop by and check the bandages on your horse."

Ephraim tore his eyes from Eden. "My horse?"

Gina nodded, all business. "Yes. Bullet. He wants to make sure the wound is all healed up."

Ephraim frowned. "Bullet?" His eyes slid to Eden. "He was hurt two weeks ago when"—he swallowed—"when Isaac died. I'm so sorry about that, Eden. I know how much you liked him."

"Thank you," Eden murmured.

"My dad told you about the amphetamine in Bullet's blood work, correct?" Gina asked. Eden decided this must be what her friend sounded like when she was on her clinical rotation at the hospital.

Ephraim folded his arms. "He did. I don't know how that could have happened. I can't agree with your father that someone did that on purpose. Who would want to do something like that to an old horse?"

Gina cleared her throat. "In any case I'm here to check on Bullet." She waved her hand forward. "Can you show us where the horse is?"

Ephraim turned to Eden again, maybe this time for guidance. She gave him a small smile. "I'd like to see Bullet too, to know that he's okay."

Ephraim's face broke into a smile. "I suppose that would be all right." He led the girls to the barn. Gina walked beside him, Eden a few paces behind, her brows furrowed. She hoped encouraging Ephraim in order to earn Gina a look at Bullet was worth it.

"He seems all right to me," Ephraim told Gina. "I've been keeping an eye on him like Dr. Gilbert told me to. Bullet's been calm ever since I moved him to my farm."

"You know my dad." Gina smiled brightly. "He worries about all the animals under his care."

Ephraim smiled. "That's what makes him a gut vet. I was grateful he came to the stables the night of the accident. It gave me real peace of mind. Bullet is my favorite horse. Even though he's retired now, he still means a great deal to me. I boarded him at Isaac's place because of the extra care I knew he would receive there. Isaac was so gut with all animals but especially horses." He swallowed. "I still can't believe what happened. What a terrible accident."

Eden caught up with them as they reached Ephraim's barn. "It's not your fault or Bullet's."

Ephraim beamed at her as if she'd just given him the last piece of pumpkin pie at Thanksgiving.

There I go, encouraging him again. Eden mentally kicked herself.

Leaning into the door, Ephraim used his weight to push it open. The heavy barn door squealed and finally gave way. He clicked his tongue. "I'm going to have to fix that, or it will be a bear to open in January."

The earthy scent of hay and manure tickled the inside of Eden's nose as she entered the barn. The Lapps kept dairy cows. Most of the herd was out in the pasture, huddled under a few tall pine trees, trying to escape the snow. The only cattle in the barn were some late-born calves and their mothers. One of the calves nudged Eden in the hip with her nose as if asking for attention. She patted it on the head.

Ephraim plucked a piece of hay from a feed bag and pointed to the end of the barn with it. "Bullet is in the last stall."

Gina walked up to the horse as if she checked wounds all the time. She had even borrowed a small medical kit from her father's clinic as cover. Eden figured Gina knew enough from watching her father care for so many animals to pull this off.

Gina lifted the bandage. "The wound is healing well. In fact, I think you can remove the bandage."

Eden took a peek at the wound. There was a small indent in the horse's hip, but that was all. Could that tiny mark really be the source of Isaac's death?

"That's gut news," Ephraim said. "If you think it's all right, go ahead and remove it. I'm sure Bullet is happy to have the all clear."

Gina pulled tweezers from her medical kit, removed the bandage, and tucked it into a plastic bag.

Ephraim held out his hand. "I can throw that away for you." Gina handed him the plastic bag, and he walked to the other side of the barn, where a trash bin stood in the corner.

When he was out of earshot, Eden whispered, "Did you learn anything?"

Gina shook her head. "Not really. Other than the horse had a puncture wound that is now healed."

"Danki," Ephraim said as he returned. "I am glad that you came after all. I'm happy to know Bullet is all better."

"We're a full-service vet clinic," Gina said with a smile.

Ephraim nodded. "Ya, that is gut. It's a terrible shame what happened. Bullet is typically such a mild horse. I can't wrap my mind around what got into him. Maybe your father is right, and it was a drug. If so, it does take some of the guilt off my conscience since it was my horse."

"What do you think happened?" Eden asked. "Do you have another theory?"

"Something must have spooked him. That's the only explanation that makes any sense to me. Maybe there was another animal in the barn."

Eden thought about the mouse that had given Gina and her such a fright the day before.

"Is Bullet known for being skittish?" Gina asked. She sounded so much like her father that Eden had to hide her smile.

He shook his head. "But all horses can be jumpy if you catch them at the right time. I've been keeping a close eye on him to see if he develops a limp. That was my biggest worry, but he's been fine." He winced. "I'm not saying that he's worse off than Isaac. I don't want you to think that."

"We don't," Eden said.

He nodded. "Isaac was a gut man." He pressed his lips into a thin line. "I should have been the one there that day, not him. If I had, none of this would have happened. That's what I struggle with the most."

"What do you mean?" Eden asked.

He scratched the white star in the middle of Bullet's forehead. "Even though I boarded Bullet at Yoder Stables, I went to see him every day. The stables are just down the road a mile or so. I would walk over to see Bullet and exercise him. I went every day at three in the afternoon when my work at the farm was over—except the day Isaac died. If I'd been there, Isaac would still be alive. I could have controlled Bullet no matter how upset he became."

"Why weren't you there?" Eden asked. She tried to keep the criticism out of her question, but if Ephraim's face was an indication, she failed.

"Some business suddenly came up in town. I didn't know about it until late in the afternoon, and I knew I wouldn't be back in time to take Bullet out for his daily exercise. On my way to town, I stopped at Yoder Stables to tell Isaac I couldn't make it so he wouldn't wonder what became of me. He offered to ride Bullet to exercise him. I told him that wasn't necessary, that I would take Bullet for an extralong ride the next day, but Isaac must have decided to do it anyway. So you see, had I been there, Isaac would have never gone into the stall with Bullet, and he would still be with us."

Ephraim's dark brown eyebrows knit together. "Eden, I know that you were gut friends with Isaac. Everyone in the county knew he saw you as a granddaughter. To be sure, I was surprised the stables hadn't been left to you. You were the one he talked about the most. No one knew about this nephew from Pennsylvania." He said *Pennsylvania* as if it were on the other side of the planet instead of a few hundred miles away.

"I never expected Isaac would leave the stables to me," Eden said.

"Many did, mind you. Many did."

"I knew Isaac had a nephew. Isaac mentioned him a few times. Gina and I actually met him yesterday." Eden didn't add that Isaac had apparently talked more about her to Jesse than the other way around.

"I have not met Jesse yet." Ephraim's face darkened. "He must have better judgment than his uncle if he fired Micah King. There is not a lazier Amish man that you will meet." He paused. "I should return to work myself." He started toward the barn door.

Before she left Bullet's stall, Eden leaned close to the horse and scratched him behind the ear. "I forgive you," she whispered. She hadn't known what she would feel when she saw the animal that had killed her dear friend Isaac, but it helped her in some way to see Bullet. Maybe she was achieving the closure that Gina was so set on her having.

Bullet's big brown eyes watched her, and Eden wondered if the animal needed a little closure too. She would never breathe a word of these thoughts to anyone, not even Gina. She tucked the look that passed between her and the horse into a little corner of her heart.

CHAPTER EIGHT

*E*den?" Gina called.

Eden scratched Bullet one more time and left the barn. She found Ephraim and Gina standing outside, waiting for her.

"It's a shame Yoder Stables is closing," Ephraim said. "I had heard Isaac was in debt, but I hoped it wasn't true. It's no wonder though."

Eden pulled her gloves out of her coat. "Why do you say that?"

"When he built the stable all those years ago, he thought the Englisch would board their horses there. He was wrong, and most Amish have their own sheds and barns. I kept my horse there, but I am one of a few."

"He built it for Englisch horses? Why?"

"At the time there were plans to put a racetrack in Holmes County to attract more tourists. The Millersburg City Council vetoed the plans, but by that point Isaac was already committed to the stables."

"When was this?" Gina asked.

Ephraim thought for a moment. "Seven or eight years ago, I'd say. I bought Bullet from a racetrack outside of Columbus around the same time."

Eden remembered when Isaac had built the stables. She had thought it was odd that he wanted to take on such a business venture so late in life, as he was probably over seventy then. But she'd never had any thought that something was wrong. It was another aspect of his life, like his nephew, that Isaac kept to himself.

Eden was beginning to wonder if she had really known her friend at all. Had they only talked about books and fudge in all the time they spent together? Had she given him an opportunity to share anything? Or had her nose been too buried in a book to pay much attention?

Ephraim twisted a piece of hay. "Even after the racetrack fell through, other Englisch didn't want to board their horses at Yoder Stables. They wanted the amenities for their horses and themselves that they could find in Englisch stables." He shook his head. "Isaac made a poor investment. It happens to too many of us," he said as if speaking from experience.

A horse and buggy clomped up the Lapps' driveway.

"There's Joanna," Gina said.

"And Micah King." Ephraim tossed the hay onto the frozen ground and stomped over to the buggy just as it came to a stop next to Gina's Jeep. "What are you doing here?" he asked Micah through gritted teeth.

Joanna jumped out of the buggy. *"Bruder."*

Every time Eden saw Ephraim and Joanna Lapp together, she was struck by how dissimilar the siblings were. Where Ephraim was squat, Joanna was lithe. Her features were delicate like the china dolls sold in the antique shops in downtown Millersburg.

But if Joanna and her brother made an odd pair, Joanna and Micah King made an even stranger couple. Joanna's movements were graceful and fluid, and Micah was all arms and legs.

"I asked you a question," Ephraim snapped in Pennsylvania Dutch.

Gina raised her eyebrows at Eden. She knew a few words of Pennsylvania Dutch but couldn't say more than *thank you, yes,* and *no.*

Micah jumped out of the buggy. "I gave Joanna a ride home from the fudge shop as I have always done."

"I asked you not to. I have told you both to stop this."

"Bruder," Joanna said, "it was very nice of Micah to give me a ride."

"Our father wouldn't stand for you riding in a buggy with him. He can't keep a job to support himself. How can he play at courting as if one day the two of you will marry?"

"What if we *are* courting?" Joanna lifted her chin, but Eden noticed her lip quiver.

"You can't be. He is in no position to take care of a wife, and I have not given my blessing."

Joanna's face reddened. "I don't need your blessing."

"You do. I am the only male relative you have."

Joanna opened her mouth as if she wanted to say more, but thought better of it.

"I worked hard for Isaac. I was on the right path," Micah argued.

"You aren't anymore. I heard about Jesse firing you," Ephraim said in an angry voice Eden remembered all too well.

Micah clenched his jaw. "He had no right to."

"Of course he did. Those stables belong to him now." Ephraim's jaw twitched. "I'm asking you to leave. From now on I will pick up my sister from the fudge shop each day. She no longer needs your assistance."

"Ephraim," Joanna protested.

Micah folded his arms. "Joanna is a grown woman. You can't make her decisions for her."

"I'm the head of my family's household," Ephraim said, "and I will make the decisions as I see fit in the best interest of my family. You are not in the best interest of anyone."

Joanna pulled on the sleeve of her brother's coat. "Ephraim, please. Micah really is trying."

"Trying isn't gut enough. If he tried as hard as he claimed, the two of you would have been married by now. It's time you found a more suitable match, Joanna, or at the very least someone with the ability to keep a job."

Joanna dropped her hands. She spun on her heels and ran toward the farmhouse, but not before Eden saw the tears streaming down her pale face.

Micah balled his fists at his side and stomped back to his buggy. Eden watched him drive away before turning to Ephraim. "Why are you so against Joanna and Micah?"

His face hardened again. "He's not worthy of my sister. A man should be able to support a wife before he marries."

Eden opened her mouth to protest, but before she could say a word, Gina touched Eden's arm. "We'd better go. Eden, are you ready?"

She nodded and followed Gina to the Jeep. As they were driving away, they saw Micah King sitting in his buggy at the end of the Lapps' road. He glared at them as they rode past.

Gina nodded at him. "There's another candidate for anger management."

"We seem to be running into a lot of those lately."

Gina turned the corner. "We sure are."

When the girls reached downtown Sugarcreek, Gina stopped a block from the shop. "Are you sure you don't want me to drop you at the door? I don't mind. My homework has waited this long. It can wait a minute or two more."

"It's fine, Gina. I've kept you away from your studies too long as it is. Thanks for driving me around today."

"Thanks for letting me fulfill my dream of being a private eye even if it was a delusional one."

"Have I ever judged you for being delusional?"

"Never." Gina grinned.

Eden climbed out of the Jeep.

"I really do need to study." Gina gripped the steering wheel. "With all this sleuthing, I've gotten way behind in my schoolwork."

Eden waved good-bye as the Jeep disappeared down the road. She stayed on the corner for a few minutes and watched the enormous clock on the opposite corner mark the hour with an almost life-size fiberglass Swiss man and woman dancing to folk music played by a fiberglass four-person band.

"It must have been an Englischer who put that there. An Amish person never would," a voice said behind her.

Eden turned to find Jesse Yoder watching her. A black felt hat covered his lovely hair.

"I'm sure it was," she managed to say.

"Are you on your way to the fudge shop?" he asked.

Eden nodded.

"May I walk with you?"

She couldn't see any reason to tell him no, so she simply nodded a second time.

The sidewalk was cleared after the morning snowfall. As Ephraim had predicted, the snow had begun to melt. Tomorrow it would be just a memory. Eden wished it could stay snow covered until Christmas morning. Rock salt crunched under their feet, and she had to mind her footing to avoid stepping on any slippery spots. She was grateful for the melting ice; it kept her mind on something other than the man walking beside her.

"Can I ask you a question?" Jesse stopped in the middle of the sidewalk. They stood in front of a small bookshop, one Eden frequented almost as often as the library.

Eden stopped and faced him. "I guess so."

Jesse seemed to gather his thoughts. While he did, a minivan drove by, followed by an Old Order buggy. Across the street two middle-aged Englisch women came out of a quilt shop, their arms full of paper shopping bags, and spoke excitedly about the new projects they would create with the fabric and batting they'd bought.

Jesse took a breath. "Why were you at my stables yesterday?"

"To return the novels Isaac lent me. Are you sure you don't want them back? I would happily give them to you."

"Nee. As I said yesterday, Isaac would want you to keep the books. I want you to keep the books."

"Danki," she murmured.

He licked his lips. "I don't believe you."

Eden stood up a little straighter. "Jesse Yoder, I don't know you at all, and you're certainly not in a position to call me a liar."

He held up his hands. "I wouldn't dream of calling you that. I'm only suggesting that Isaac's books weren't the only reason you visited the stables yesterday afternoon."

She lifted her chin. "What other reason could I have?"

"I did this all wrong. Can I start over?"

Eden folded her arms and waited, tucking her hands under her arms to warm them. The temperature was dropping in tandem with the setting sun, and pink and purple streaks danced across the flat clouds in the western sky. Eden wished she was in a better position to enjoy the sunset.

Jesse shoved his large hands into the pockets of his coat. "If you wanted to give me the books directly, why didn't you bring them to the house?"

"How do you know I didn't?"

"Because I was inside the house when you arrived. I saw you and Gina make a beeline for the barn. You didn't even hesitate when you walked by the house."

Eden took a step back and pulverized a huge piece of salt beneath her shoe. It sounded like glass shattering. "Why didn't you come out and meet us, then?"

"I already had a guest," he said vaguely.

Eden knew he must mean the mystery man—most likely Bryan from the Amish restaurant.

Jesse pressed on. "Why, instead of coming to the house, did you head straight for the stables? In particular, to the stall where Isaac died?"

"Gina was curious. She wanted to see the stall. She can be very persuasive."

He shook his head. "It was more than that."

That was the truth. Eden didn't know how to get out of admitting to it without actually lying to him. She wished Gina were here. Her Englisch friend had the ability to tell a convincing story like no one else Eden knew.

"Did you overhear my argument with Bryan Wright in the stables yesterday?"

Eden didn't answer.

"I take that to mean you did."

Eden didn't reply.

"Do you think my uncle was murdered?"

Eden's mouth fell open.

Jesse swallowed and lowered his voice to a whisper. "Because I do, and I want to find out what happened to him."

CHAPTER NINE

*E*den stared at him.

"Judging from your reaction, I made a mistake." Jesse took two steps back, his face coloring. "You clearly don't think the same way I do, and you are now convinced I'm a crazy person who accosted you on the street talking about murder."

"Nee, you didn't." She cleared her throat. "I mean, you're right. I do think something is odd about Isaac's death. Gina and I both do."

His brow cleared. "I thought I had just made a fool of myself in front of you. That's the last thing I want to do." His face turned a deeper shade of red.

"If you think your uncle was murdered, why didn't you go to the police about Bullet's blood work?"

"I see you know about that."

"Gina told me."

He gave her a small smile. "Your sidekick."

"More often I'm her sidekick, not the other way around."

"Not to me," he said quietly.

Eden blinked at him and tried to focus on the conversation about Isaac's death and not worry what he meant by that comment. "Why didn't you agree to go to the police like Dr. Gilbert wanted?"

"Because I was afraid that would be wrong, and I didn't want to drag the Amish community through another scandal like that haircutting incident a few years back."

Eden frowned when she thought about that ugly situation. "Even so, if Isaac was murdered, the police are the best ones to find out what happened."

"Maybe, but I'd rather take care of this myself. Quietly. Isn't that what you've been doing?"

Eden thought for a moment. She didn't know if her and Gina's involvement had been that quiet. She nodded.

"Why?" he asked.

"Gina is helping for the fun of it and because she's my best friend. She'd do anything for me. I'm doing it for Isaac."

Jesse watched her. "You really cared about him."

"Of course I did," she said quietly. "Isaac was my friend."

"The way you talk about him makes me wish I had spent more time with him. When I was a child, I spent a few summers at his farm before the stables were built, and he taught me to ride. He had a way with horses. Most of the time I think he liked horses more than people." He paused. "Except for you."

Eden blushed.

"I'm grateful my uncle had a friend like you in his final years. Your friendship to him was a blessing."

"The blessing was all mine."

Jesse shook his head as if he didn't agree with her. "The guilt of not visiting him more eats away at me. He was the last family I had."

"You never married?" Her face flamed red. She couldn't believe she had asked that.

Jesse gave her a sad smile. "I never saw a reason to. I always saw myself as a confirmed bachelor like my uncle."

"Oh," Eden whispered. She turned away so he couldn't see the disappointment in her eyes.

Jesse touched her arm. "That doesn't mean I can't change my mind."

Eden stared at his hand.

He dropped it and cleared his throat. "I propose we join forces to find out what really happened to my uncle."

Eden chewed on her bottom lip. "I don't know."

"Please. I need your help. I don't know the area well, and I don't know the people in my uncle's district. You do."

"What do you want me to do?"

"Can you meet me at the stables tomorrow morning?"

Eden frowned. Tomorrow was Friday—one of the busiest days of the week for the fudge shop. Her parents would need her, but maybe she could volunteer to pack all the deliveries tonight in order to have the morning off. What could she tell her parents to convince them she needed the free time? She couldn't tell them the truth. "I'll try. I may not be able to get away from the shop. This is our busiest time of year."

He nodded. "I understand. I appreciate you trying. If you aren't there by nine, I will know you weren't able to get away." He paused. "When I told you that Isaac mentioned you to me, it was true."

She looked up into his eyes.

"He wanted me to visit Sugarcreek and meet you. He said he thought we were made for each other. Maybe he was right."

Eden's breath came short, but one thought nagged at the back of her mind. Before he learned about Isaac's debt to Bryan, Jesse had as much to gain from Isaac's death as anyone, maybe more.

Jesse tipped his hat to her and strolled away.

⌒⌒⚜⌒⌒

The next morning at Dutch Village Fudge, Eden covered a yawn with her hand. It was barely seven in the morning, and she was utterly exhausted. She'd worked in the shop packing orders until midnight and then had been back in the shop before six to start new batches of fudge. All so she could visit Yoder Stables that morning.

But she hadn't told her parents that. Instead she offered to do the extra work and asked for the morning off so she and Gina could go to Canton for some shopping. Canton was far enough away that it would give her and Jesse plenty of time to investigate.

Eden cringed to think she was lying to her parents. She had done it only once before, when she was a small child. She had taken a cookie from her mother's cookie jar after being told not to. When her mother discovered the missing cookie, she'd asked Eden if she had eaten it. Eden lied, and her mother said nothing more. Eden had thrown up three times that night, and her mother had never said a word about the missing cookie while she tended to Eden. Eden had never lied again.

But now she couldn't see any way around it. They wouldn't understand her need to find out what had happened to Isaac. She may have doubted Gina in the beginning, but now she, too, believed something was off about Isaac's death. However, she didn't know if whoever injected Bullet with that drug had intended to hurt the horse, Isaac, or both. In any case, there was malicious intent.

Gina had promised to pick her up at eight thirty sharp. Despite Jesse's good looks and ability to say all the right things, Eden wasn't going to visit Yoder Stables without backup. *Backup* was Gina's description, not hers.

The shop hadn't yet opened for the day, and Joanna, who didn't have a key, knocked on the back door. Eden let her inside the kitchen. Joanna's eyes were red rimmed and swollen. It looked to Eden like she had been crying all night.

"Joanna, what's wrong?" Eden asked.

Joanna sniffled. "It's my Bruder. He says that I can't see Micah anymore."

"Joanna, you're a grown woman. If you want to see Micah, you should."

Joanna's mouth fell open. "But Ephraim is my Bruder. I have to listen to him."

Eden pursed her lips. She knew that was the Amish way, but she didn't agree. Maybe she had spent too much time with Gina. She could only guess what Gina would say to Joanna right now. Actually, it was a good thing Gina wasn't there to share her opinion. It would only upset Joanna more.

"I'm sorry, Joanna. I know you're trying to do the right thing. Have you spoken to Ephraim about how you feel?"

She wiped a tear from her chin. "I have, many times, but it makes no difference to him."

Eden ripped a paper towel from the roll behind the counter and wet it in the sink. She handed it to Joanna. "Here."

"Danki." Joanna took the paper towel with her to the small staff rest room next to the office.

Eden frowned. Bullet was Ephraim's horse. How was he tangled up in Isaac's death? She shook the thought from her mind. She was allowing her dislike of Ephraim to cloud her judgment. Bullet was Ephraim's horse, true, but he loved that horse. He would never hurt it.

Eden realized the one question she and Gina hadn't yet asked was where the drug came from. It might be the most important question of all.

*A*s Eden and Gina rode in the Jeep back to Yoder Stables, Gina tapped a beat on the steering wheel. "Okay, tell me everything Cutie Pie Amish Guy said to you outside the fudge shop."

Eden repeated the story about how Jesse thought his uncle's death was suspicious too and wanted their help to find out what had really happened. She left off the part where she asked him if he had ever married. That was too embarrassing to share even with her best friend.

When they reached Yoder Stables, Jesse and Rocky were waiting for them. As soon as she stepped out of the car, Rocky bolted for Eden as if he had been longing to see her all morning.

Jesse smiled. "I told him you were coming."

So maybe the dog *had* been waiting for her, Eden thought. She scratched Rocky behind the ear just the way he liked.

Jesse nodded at Gina. "I see you brought your friend."

"You met Gina the other day," Eden said.

"How could I forget?"

Gina gave him a goofy smile in return, and Eden elbowed her in the ribs.

Gina rubbed her side, shooting Eden a dirty look. "It's good to see you again. Eden told me you want to be part of our investigation."

He arched his left eyebrow, and Eden thought it made him look even more like Mr. Knightley. "*Your* investigation?" He laughed at Gina's insulted expression. "I'm only teasing. Ya, I asked Eden for your help. Why don't we go inside the stable where it is a little warmer?"

"And where we can take another look at the crime scene," Gina added.

When they entered the stable for the second time that week, Eden again felt the rush of emptiness. Now that she knew Isaac had been struggling, she realized the stables weren't as busy or vibrant as they should have been. She never remembered seeing all the stalls filled with horses. She had thought nothing of it because Isaac never mentioned the empty stalls as a problem. She knew now that they had been.

Jesse led them to the stall where his uncle died. The barn cat Eden had met two days before joined them and didn't seem the least bit concerned that Rocky was with them. Rocky pointedly ignored the cat and pressed his warm body against Eden's leg as they walked.

Jesse rested his arm on the stall door. "Why were you looking at the stall the other day?"

"You know about the puncture wound on Bullet's hindquarters?" Gina said.

Jesse nodded.

"And my dad told you about Bullet being injected with some type of amphetamine."

Jesse nodded more slowly this time. "He did. I can't say I know exactly what that is."

Gina stood up a little straighter. "I didn't either, so I asked Dad why anyone would give that to a horse. He said for horse racing." Gina removed a piece of paper from the back pocket of her jeans. "I did a little more digging, and I found out that it's used to increase performance in racehorses. Here's an article I found online about it being illegally used at a horse race in Kentucky." She handed Jesse the paper. "My hypothesis is that whoever injected Bullet with the drug did it for this very reason."

"For horse racing," Eden whispered. The strange suspicion she'd had about Ephraim the day before returned.

Jesse watched her. "What is it, Eden?"

She blinked, momentarily distracted by the sound of her name coming from Jesse's mouth. She cleared her throat. "I know someone who is involved in horse racing."

"Who?" Gina and Jesse asked together.

"Ephraim," she said as if she were betraying a trust. She wasn't fond of Ephraim, but she had known him all her life. She didn't like the direction her thoughts were going.

"He races Bullet?" Gina asked. "Why didn't you say that before?"

Eden shook her head. "Bullet is retired. I don't know if Ephraim races horses anymore. He did maybe five or so years ago. He used to go to races all over the state with the horse he had then. He entered steeplechase competitions. He even took me to one. Ephraim was very good at racing but not as good as he wanted to be."

She shivered at the memory. It had been at the steeplechase that Eden decided she would no longer see Ephraim. He had been furious when his horse finished in third place. He threw his helmet across the field, and it crashed against a horse trailer, leaving a dent in it. He'd frightened her. If that was how he acted in front of her when they were courting, she didn't want to know how he would act if they married.

Jesse's head whipped in her direction. "He *took* you to a steeplechase race? You were courting?"

"Whoa there, cowboy," Gina said, holding up a hand. "Eden and Ephraim went on a couple of dates, or whatever you Amish folks call it, a long time ago. They're not courting."

Eden felt her face grow red. Maybe bringing Gina with her had been a bad idea.

Jesse's shoulders relaxed. Had he been jealous? Eden got a slight thrill at the prospect. She shook the thought away. "But Ephraim loves that horse. Gina and I saw it when we stopped by his farm."

"You stopped by his farm?" Jesse asked.

Gina held up her hand again. "Dude, you need to chill out. It was part of our investigation."

"Oh, right," he said, apparently mollified.

Eden continued as if there had been no interruption. "I don't see why Ephraim would give the drug to his horse if he wasn't racing it. We don't know that he ever gave any of his horses amphetamines in the first place."

Gina perched on a hay bale. "The drug had to come from somewhere. Did Isaac have drugs like that at the stables? I mean, it's illegal to use, but someone has to ask."

"I've wondered the same thing," Jesse said. "I don't know. I asked Micah about it, but he's no help. I have no idea why Isaac even hired him. He has a chip on his shoulder bigger than this stable."

"What did he say?" Eden asked.

Jesse scuffed the toe of his boot on the concrete floor. "That it wasn't his job to question Isaac."

Gina folded her arms. "Doesn't that imply Isaac might have the drug around?"

This time Jesse shrugged. "I can't really take anything Micah says or implies at face value."

"We should look into all the possibilities." Eden chewed on her lip. "Like the money Isaac owed that man Bryan."

Jesse's face clouded over. "Bryan Wright. He owns several Amish restaurants across the county plus one of those big hotels in Berlin. When he saw Isaac's stables were struggling, he made my uncle an offer to help out. My uncle should have never gone into business with him. He got further and further in debt to Bryan until there was no way out."

"Does Bryan have a connection with horse racing?" Gina asked.

"I don't know, but I wouldn't be surprised. He's interested in anything that will make him money. But why kill Isaac? It wouldn't help him get his money."

"His motive might be to force you to sell the stables or even hand the stables over to him," Eden said quietly.

Gina hopped off the hay bale. "I think we need to talk to him."

"But where do we find him?" Eden asked.

Jesse clenched his jaw. "I know where to find him."

*E*den had never been to a golf course before, and in her Plain clothes she felt like everyone was looking at her. Or maybe they were looking at all three of them. Eden had to admit they made an odd trio on the greens: two Amish people in Plain clothes and Englisch Gina trailing after them with her bouncing ponytail.

Jesse led them into the golf course office as if he went golfing all the time. Maybe he did. Eden didn't know what Lancaster Amish did for fun. He asked the woman at the desk where they could find Bryan Wright. Eden was surprised when she answered with no hesitation.

The woman clicked her pen. "You can probably catch him. He and his group just went out, so they should still be on the first hole."

"Not much security," Gina muttered as they left the clubhouse. "What if we were going to hurt Bryan?"

Eden nudged Gina with her shoulder. "Is part of your plan to beat information out of him?"

"No, but still. If I was playing golf, I wouldn't want someone to give me up so easily."

Jesse didn't say anything as he marched to the first hole. The girls had to jog to keep up.

Eden spotted Bryan leaning on a club, talking with two other men. Two golf carts holding golf bags stood nearby.

"Bryan?" Jesse called as they came into earshot.

Bryan turned around, and his face broke into a wide smile. "Jesse, I'm happy you came. I hope you have good news for me." He waved his companions away. "I'll catch you at the next hole. I have some business with this young man."

The other men laughed, climbed into one of the golf carts, and drove away.

Bryan smiled at Jesse. "Are you here to bring me a check?"

Jesse buried his fists in the pockets of his coat. "Nee. The stables haven't sold yet."

"You can sign the stables over to me and save yourself the trouble." Bryan smiled at Gina and Eden. "Who are your friends?"

Gina stepped forward. "Gina Gilbert." She pointed her thumb at Eden. "And that's Eden Hochstetler. We'd like to ask you a few questions."

Bryan shook Gina's hand and laughed. "Oh really? What would those questions be?"

Jesse frowned at Gina. "I—we—want to talk to you about my uncle."

A muscle in Bryan's jaw twitched. "About the money he owed me? I have a contract that shows exactly how much I invested in Yoder Stables."

"I'm not trying to escape from the debt," Jesse said quietly. "I will repay you what my uncle owed you. It's just going to take a bit longer than either of us hoped."

"If you aren't here to give me the money, I don't know what else we have to talk about."

Wind whipped across the golf course, and Eden grabbed her skirts to keep them still. She cleared her throat. "Mr. Wright, do you have any interest in horse racing?"

He studied her. "I do have an interest in horse racing. In fact, I was the one who brought the proposal to the Millersburg City Council to open a racetrack in the county. Those fools on the council were too shortsighted to see the business it would bring to the area."

Eden gripped her skirts. "So Isaac learned about the possibility of a racetrack from you?"

He nodded. "Yes. It's a shame that the racetrack fell through, but Isaac was determined to go forward with the stables. I helped him out where I could. How could either of us know the business was destined to fail with all the horses in this county? Had the racetrack gone through, Isaac would have been a very wealthy man when he died instead of a pauper."

Jesse clenched his jaw but didn't say anything.

Gina flicked her ponytail over her shoulder. "My dad was the vet who treated Ephraim Lapp's horse after Isaac died."

Bryan gave her a blank stare.

"That was the horse that trampled Isaac," she said.

Jesse winced. Bryan didn't say anything.

Gina folded her arms. "Dad found traces of amphetamine in the horse's blood. Amphetamines are used in horse racing, aren't they?"

Bryan laughed. "I can see what you're driving at. You think I injected amphetamine into a horse I've never heard of so it would trample Isaac Yoder. Trust me; there are easier ways to get rid of someone."

Eden shivered, not from the chill in the air, but from the coldness in his voice.

Bryan placed a hand on his chest. "Of course I feel bad about what happened to Isaac, but I had nothing to do with it. And to put your mind further at ease over my ability to kill someone, talk to my secretary. I was in New York on business the week of Isaac's death." He rested his golf club on his shoulder. "I think we're done here." Before he climbed into his golf cart, he pointed at Jesse. "I will forget this insulting conversation, Jesse, as long as you repay your debts." He started the golf cart and drove away.

"Well," Gina said, "that went okay."

"Went okay?" Eden asked. "It was a disaster. We're lucky he didn't threaten to sue us."

"We learned something," Gina said. "The guilty party has to be someone who was actually here to give Bullet the injection."

"Right," Jesse said quietly.

❧

Eden returned to the fudge shop for the afternoon. The conversation with Bryan Wright had shaken her. What were she and Gina doing, running around the county playing detective? She decided to put it out of her head and concentrate on fudge. She was good at fudge.

The shop phone rang.

"Eden," her father called, "it's Gina, and she says she is desperate to talk to you." He gave her a pointed look. "Please don't stay on the telephone too long. It is not for social calls."

Eden nodded and took the phone from her father's hand. She waited for him to hobble away on his cane before speaking. "Hello?"

"Eden!" Gina yelled.

Eden held the phone away from her ear. "Gina, are you all right?"

"Listen to me, Eden. Jesse has been in Ohio for weeks. The day we met him at the stables, he said he'd just arrived. That's not true. He was in the county a week before Isaac died."

Eden's chest tightened. Had Jesse been lying to her all this time? Was everything he had said to her a lie? "How do you know that?"

"I was thinking about our conversation with Bryan, and I thought I could narrow down the suspects to those who had an opportunity to give Bullet the amphetamine. Bryan's out, so I started thinking of other possibilities." She took a deep breath. "I asked my dad who was there the day he took care of Bullet, and he said Ephraim and Jesse. I nearly fell off my chair when he said Jesse, and then he said he had seen Jesse at the stables earlier in the week too, when he was doctoring another horse."

Eden's mouth was dry. "That doesn't mean he gave Bullet the drug."

"I know that, but why would he lie?" Gina was quiet for a moment. "I'm sorry, Eden. I know you like him, but he lied to you."

Eden was in desperate need of a drink of water. "I have to go." She hung up the phone.

As she left her father's office, she found Joanna standing in the doorway, listening. Joanna spun around without a word.

Eden shook off the odd feeling Joanna's interest gave her. After grabbing a drink of water, she returned to cutting the huge blocks of fudge for the mail orders.

She frowned. Maybe Jesse wasn't that different from her. Hadn't she lied to her parents so she could play detective with Gina? She wasn't any better than Jesse, which only made it worse. She forced the knife through a slab of maple walnut fudge. She was a liar too.

A hand cupped Eden's shoulder, and she jumped and dropped the knife. "Eden, are you all right?" Mamm asked.

"Ya, I'm fine. I'm sorry, Mamm."

Her mother studied her face. "You've seemed tense these last few days. You would tell me if something was wrong, wouldn't you?"

Eden couldn't trust herself to speak, so she only nodded.

Her mother tucked a stray hair back into Eden's bun. "All right. Since you came back to work early, I'm going to take your father home. His leg is bothering him something awful from this cold weather. Can you and Joanna close up the shop?"

Eden nodded. "Of course. Go home and take care of Daed. We'll be fine here."

After her parents left, Eden and Joanna worked in silence. Eden wanted to ask her how much of the phone conversation with Gina she had overheard, but she couldn't bring herself to do it.

Sitting at one of the small café tables at the front of the store so Joanna had plenty of space at the counter to slice and wrap a fresh batch of taffy, Eden cut a nine-by-thirteen-inch pan of dark chocolate fudge into two-by-two-inch squares. She kept an eye out for customers so she could jump up at a moment's notice and give them the table. Had she been wrong about Jesse? Could he have been the one who gave Ephraim's horse that drug? What did he have to gain from it? The stables. He inherited everything. He most likely didn't know about his uncle's debt before Isaac died. She kicked herself for becoming attached to him so quickly. She had let his blue eyes cloud her judgment. At least she knew the truth now.

Joanna removed her apron. "Eden, it's closing time."

Eden looked up at the clock in surprise. It was already five minutes after five. She had been so buried in her own thoughts while cutting fudge or helping the flurry of customers who came in throughout the afternoon that the hours had flown by. "I didn't realize—"

The front door to Dutch Village Fudge opened, and Micah King stepped inside.

Joanna gasped. "Micah, what are you doing here?"

"I'm here to take you home."

"Nee, you are not," another man said.

Eden turned and saw Ephraim standing in the doorway to the kitchen with his arms folded across his chest.

CHAPTER TWELVE

"Joanna, let's go," Micah said.

Joanna glanced back at her brother. "Micah, I can't."

Micah's face contorted into a sneer. "Why not?"

Ephraim glared at Micah. "I have told you dozens of times to stay away from my sister. You're no gut for her. I told you that before Isaac died, and it's even truer now that you're out of work. So leave and stay out of our lives."

Joanna grabbed her brother's sleeve. "Ephraim, please. Micah will find another job. You're being ridiculous."

Something tickled in the back of Eden's brain. Bullet was Ephraim's horse. All this time she had been thinking that Ephraim gave the horse the drug, but it never made sense to her. Ephraim would never hurt his horse, and he had nothing to gain from Isaac's death. When she thought about it, no one gained much of anything from Isaac's death. Not Jesse, who was saddled with debt, or Bryan, who would get his money whether Isaac was alive or dead. Eden doubted Bryan would put his own freedom in jeopardy to collect the money sooner. Isaac was nearly eighty, and he wouldn't have lived forever.

Putting that all together, Eden realized that Isaac was never the one who was supposed to be hurt by the horse. It was Ephraim.

Eden's thoughts were coming so fast she could hardly keep up with them. She stood up quickly, toppling her chair.

Hadn't Ephraim said that he went to exercise his horse every day at three? But that day he was away on business. Wouldn't a stable hand know this about Ephraim? And what if that stable hand held a grudge against Ephraim because Ephraim wouldn't let him marry his sister?

Micah was staring at Eden. "Something on your mind, Eden?"

She took a step back, bumped into the overturned chair, and wished she was on the other side of the counter, next to Joanna and Ephraim, not out in the open shop with Micah. "Nee."

"Don't lie to me. You're not very gut at it."

Eden straightened and righted the chair. "The shop is closed. I think you should all sort this out somewhere else."

"Why," Micah asked with a curl to his lip, "when you already have?"

She folded her arms. "I don't know what you are talking about."

"What are you going to do with what you know?" He took a step toward her.

She lifted her chin. "I don't know anything."

"What are you two *talking* about?" Ephraim asked.

Micah's smile was slow, and somehow that made it more menacing. "Why don't you tell him, Eden? Ephraim will be so proud of his clever girl."

"I'm not his girl," she snapped.

Ephraim scowled. "Someone needs to tell me what's going on."

Eden controlled her voice to keep it from shaking. "Micah killed Isaac."

Micah sighed. "The whole plan was wasted in any case," he said to Eden. "A complete waste. The only thing that came of it was that old man's death, not that he was a big loss."

Without thinking, Eden lunged forward. "You take that back! Isaac Yoder was twice the man you will ever be."

"Micah?" Joanna asked with tears in her eyes.

Micah looked from Eden to Joanna.

"Micah? You didn't." Tears rolled down Joanna's face.

"I did it for you. I wanted to take your brother down a peg. Maybe he would fall off the horse and get hurt. I didn't think anything else would come of it. How did I know he wasn't coming to the stables that day? He came to the stables every day like clockwork to ride Bullet."

"But you killed Isaac," Joanna whispered.

"Not on purpose," he yelled. "I didn't do it on purpose. It was your brother I wanted to hurt."

Joanna inched back toward her brother. "Does that make it better?"

Eden's fingers curled around her pan.

"When Joanna and I returned from our buggy ride, Ephraim was there," Micah said to Eden. "He ran out of the barn and shouted to us what had happened, that Isaac was dead. He was so upset he didn't even question where Joanna and I had been, just went to the phone shed and called the police. I was in shock. This was not what I wanted to happen. I didn't even believe him." He closed his eyes for half a second. "I had to see for myself. I went into the barn, and there Isaac was, dead. It was horrible. Ephraim had already removed Bullet from the stall and tied him up a few feet away with a towel over his eyes to calm him. Ephraim had the forethought to do that before he left the barn. When I saw the wound on the horse from the shot, I knew I might be in trouble." He blinked at them. "But days went by, weeks went by, and nothing ever happened." He glared at Eden. "Until recently." He took a step toward her.

"Don't you touch her," Ephraim ordered, coming around the counter. Joanna cowered behind it.

Micah spun around to face him. "I'm tired of you telling me what to do. You order everyone around, especially Joanna. She has a right to decide who she will marry."

"She does," Ephraim said, "as long as it's not you."

Micah lunged at Ephraim, who dodged out of the way and smacked into the glass dome counter. It didn't break, but candies and fudge fell off the trays.

The front door opened again, and Jesse stepped inside. "Eden, there's something I have to tell you. I—" He stopped midsentence. "What's going on?"

"What are you doing here?" Micah asked.

This distraction was all Eden needed. She picked up the heavy pan of fudge from the table and whacked Micah on the back of the head with it. He howled and staggered forward a few steps, bent over and holding his head. She stared at him, and the tray fell from her fingers and crashed to the floor.

Ephraim jumped on Micah's back, forcing him to the ground and pinning him there. "Joanna, call the police!"

Joanna woke up from her daze and ran for the shop's office.

Jesse's mouth fell open. "What is going on?"

Eden ignored his question. "Gina is going to be so upset she wasn't here to see me knock someone out with fudge. She will never forgive me that she missed it."

wo days before Christmas, Eden was in Dutch Village Fudge, packing the last of the Christmas orders in white boxes with red bows. The mail orders had been shipped days ago, and all that was left were boxes of fudge and sweets that would be picked up by local residents that day. In a matter of hours, the holiday rush would be over, and her life would return to a slower pace. Her copy of *Jane Eyre* sat on the counter beside her so she could read a chapter or two as she worked. Even though she now knew the circumstances of Isaac's death, she found herself needing Brontë to get through the first Christmas without her beloved friend. Eden didn't look for Isaac every day as she had the first few weeks after his death, but she still missed the company he gave her.

It was late in the day, and Eden was the only one in the shop. Her parents were at home, and Joanna had quit soon after Micah was arrested. She said she couldn't work there anymore after what had happened in the shop. Eden's parents were not happy when they learned what their daughter had been up to, and she was slowly earning back their trust.

The bell over the shop door rang, and dime-sized snowflakes floated into the shop after Jesse. "I see you're packing fudge *and* reading," he said as he walked toward the counter.

She smiled up at him. "I can multitask, as Gina would say."

"I'm sure you can." He cleared his throat. "I have some gut news."

"What's that?" She taped another box closed.

"The stables are officially sold, and I just gave Bryan Wright the money Isaac owed him. I have no more debt."

"That is gut news. I'm happy for you. It must be a relief to have it all settled before Christmas." She concentrated on her fudge. "You will be able to return home to Lancaster to celebrate with your family and friends."

"I am happy that it is settled." He frowned. "Eden, I'm sorry I didn't tell you I was here in the county the day my uncle died. I should have, but I didn't want you to suspect me more than you already did. I hated the idea of you thinking I was doing something wrong."

"Thank you." She tied a bow around the white fudge box and placed it by the stack of identical boxes. "I probably would have done the same thing in your place. It doesn't make it right, but it is true."

He nodded and smiled at her.

She searched his face and tried not to stare into his dark blue eyes too long. "What will you do now? Will you return to Lancaster?"

He leaned on the counter. "I have a little money left over from the sale. I think I'll see if there is some farmland available and make a fresh start."

"In Lancaster?" she asked, hoping to keep the disappointment out of her voice.

"My life is there."

Eden's heart sank.

"But that was my old life. I can build a new life." His face broke into a slow grin, and she met his eyes. "Here. Like my uncle wanted. My only regret is he's not here to share in it."

"You're here now," Eden said. "I'm sure he knows that and is happy because of it."

"I know he is." He cleared his throat. "To celebrate my new life, I have come to ask if you'd like to go with me to the ice skating pond off Troyer Road. I have heard that many of the young Amish in town are going there tonight. There will be caroling and hot chocolate. I can't carry a tune, but I do enjoy a mug of cocoa."

Eden felt her cheeks heat up, but she forced herself to meet his gaze. "I would like that. I would like that very much."

"Wonderful. I will drop by later after the shop closes for the day." He beamed. "I should let you get back to work." He turned to go, giving her one more smile from the doorway.

After he left, Eden lifted *Jane Eyre* from the countertop and tucked it into her apron pocket until she needed it again. For the moment at least, Brontë was not necessary.

CINDY WOODSMALL

*S*unlight was threatening to chase away the dark as Kore drove toward JK Homebuilders. It was four days shy of being mid-November, and the air had only a mild nip to it. This was his second November to live in Virginia, but it had been much colder last year.

Nature was waking, birds calling loudly as the horse's rhythmic pace added to the sounds. Thoughts of Savilla tried to push past the list of work items he was going over in his mind.

Would he ever completely stop missing her? At least his heart was no longer in shreds. Good progress, he thought. What was it about her anyway? He'd asked himself that question since the first time they met. Her magnetic power over him made no logical sense whatsoever, because outside of Savilla, he was logical. Wasn't he?

He'd been content living *draus in da welt*—out in the world. Then he met her.

For the umpteenth time he wished he hadn't. Maybe one day he wouldn't feel that way. It might help if he simply understood what had happened to cause her to end their relationship.

As he pulled onto the driveway, he saw Jacob and Esther on their screened porch, sitting at a table. The gas fireplace was lit, and Jacob had a mug in hand as he waved.

Kore returned the gesture. He was very grateful for good bosses and friends. Jacob and Esther were both. They had been married thirteen months, and Kore met them about two weeks before they married. Jacob hired him mostly to help Esther with her salvage business. Even though Kore had always heard the first year of marriage was really tough, these two hadn't radiated anything except love and contentment. Oh, and teamwork, joy, and respect. He'd once thought he could have that with Savvy. But it wasn't meant to be. Savilla would find it with someone else. He wouldn't.

He drove the horse-drawn buggy past Jacob's house and came to a stop near the hitching post in front of the office building. He hopped out, removed the rigging from the horse, and put the horse out to pasture. With the shafts of the carriage resting on the ground, the buggy sat at a downward angle, and Kore reached inside, grabbing his overnight bag and his leather binder.

He headed for the office.

"Kore," Esther called.

He turned to see her standing on the top step just outside the screened porch. Kore wasn't sure how far along she was in her pregnancy. His best guess was around six months, and both she and Jacob wanted this business trip to be the last one she needed to go on.

Esther motioned. "Kumm, sit with us before the driver arrives."

He gestured toward the JK Homebuilders office. "I was going to do some last-minute research for—"

"Nah," Jacob said. "You've got a cell. Do that in the truck while Bill is driving. Kumm."

Kore nodded and walked toward the porch. Esther returned to the table, and he could see her and Jacob talking.

After Esther had spent eight months trying to locate a rare buffet for a client of hers, she had found one that would be on an auction block a couple of hours away. Unfortunately, neither she nor Jacob could attend that auction, so they had sent Kore with more than enough money to win the bid.

His failure to win that bid caused this current trip to be necessary, and he wanted to do all he could to make it successful. The problem with tracking down odd pieces was that most were at auctions or antique stores. Finding them at either place took time.

Esther's usual business didn't include finding rare pieces. She typically reclaimed items from houses being torn down or renovated, and she repurposed them. Before she met Jacob, she sold those—old wood floors, window frames, molding, doors, even antique doorknobs and hardware. After she met Jacob, they began using the items to give character to the homes he built or remodeled. They were quite a team. But a few months ago a wealthy woman made Esther an offer she couldn't refuse—to decorate her entire home in French circa eighteen hundreds pieces.

"Nice morning for November." He opened the screen door and set his overnight bag to the side, but he kept his leather binder with him.

"It's the start of a nice day." Jacob picked up the percolator from the center of the table and poured coffee into a mug. "I doubt we'll get to eat breakfast outside many more days before next spring, even with the gas fireplace."

"True." Kore took a seat.

Jacob set the cup of coffee in front of him. "So how many towns and antique stores do you plan to hit before nightfall?" He then tried to refill his cup, but the percolator ran out of coffee, and he put it back on the table.

Kore opened his binder and took out the list of towns and stores he hoped to get to today. "If Bill makes good time driving and Esther is up to it, I'm thinking twelve to fifteen."

Jacob looked over the paper. "Sounds good."

Esther passed Kore a plate with a bacon biscuit and a blueberry muffin before grabbing the percolator. "I'll get more coffee on to perk."

When she went inside, Jacob leaned in closer to Kore. "I wish I could go with you guys, but with work what it is, I can't get away today. I may be able to meet you late tomorrow or early the next day. Don't let Bill get stubborn about making good time. He gets a destination in mind, and he doesn't like to make stops."

"Got it. I have no problem asserting myself in a situation like this." Kore once again wished he'd gotten that piece at the auction two weeks ago.

He'd arrived at the auction house early, and he was fully focused on his task when he noticed from the corner of his eye an unattended toddler. The toddler nearly suffered a dangerous accident, but Kore grabbed him in time—in time to save the boy but miss the final bidding on the buffet.

Jacob passed the itinerary back to Kore. "It looks great. I appreciate the time and effort you've put into planning this."

"It was the least I could do."

Esther returned to the porch without the percolator, but she did have a newspaper. "Mandy will arrive on foot and Bill in his truck, and both should be here in about fifteen minutes, probably at the same time as that second pot of coffee is ready." Mandy was one of Esther's younger sisters, and she would go with them.

Esther passed the newspaper to Kore. "I'd like to make a visit here."

Kore opened the paper, and his heart jolted. It was the *North Star Tribune*. "You want to go to North Star?" Disbelief filled him.

"There's a little antique store on the town square that's having a great sale. At those prices we're sure to come away with something. Since your plans have us within thirty minutes of the place by tonight, I was hoping we could mosey into North Star. Problem?" Esther asked.

"Well . . . no. I guess not." He noted the red circle around a shop she wanted to go to. Closing the newspaper, he shrugged. "It's a beautiful little town, especially around Christmas. They've probably started hanging the decorations by now, but they'll all be up by Thanksgiving, so in about two weeks. You and Jacob should wait until then and make a visit."

"Ya, sounds nice." Esther sat across from him. "But the sale is happening now. It sort of sounds as if you're avoiding that place."

He drew a deep breath. "My girl . . . my former girl lives in North Star. And my family. Anyway, Savilla is a seamstress, and she works in Tang's Tailor Shop, which is next to the antique store."

Esther angled her head. "Don't stop now, Mr. Silence." She folded her hands, sitting up straight and looking very interested. "The floor is yours, Kore."

Jacob chuckled. "She's teasing . . . sort of. You don't have to tell anything."

In his thirteen months of living in Virginia, Kore had shared some personal stuff but not much. "My life in a nutshell—by Kore Detweiler." He chuckled, but his laughter sounded hollow.

"That's what I want to hear"—Esther stacked Jacob's plate on hers—"only it doesn't need to fit inside a nutshell."

"Well . . ." It did seem as if it was time to tell his friends about Savilla. Maybe a little sharing would prove helpful. "My parents are pretty great. They work hard, have a strong faith. And I have one remaining grandparent, *Mammi* D, who is truly a woman of God. Despite my upbringing I questioned God about everything. I left home at seventeen, seeking answers to a million angry questions. Unlike a lot of Amish parents, mine understood, and they kept an open-door policy. So a couple of times each year I would return home for a few days. I couldn't tolerate the idea of living in one place, but I loved my family. During one visit I met an Amish girl from a nearby district—Savilla Beiler. I suppose *met* is the wrong word. She lives only a few miles from my home, so I guess I'd known her for years, but we hadn't attended the same school, and we weren't in the same church district. To my way of thinking, we were invisible to each other until . . . we weren't. She's the kind of girl who outshines everyone else." At the mention of her, Kore could feel the smile lifting his lips even as his heart ached. "She was different, you know?"

Jacob's eyes locked with Esther's, and he winked. "I completely understand."

Kore had thought she was perfect for him. The only thing that required any patience was her back issues. At times she would be confined to her bed with the pain, but within a couple of days, she would be herself again.

He realized Jacob and Esther were waiting on him to talk. "Oh, sorry. I got lost in my thoughts for a minute. Even though I thought she was the best, I wasn't about to let go of my freedom for a girl, so I told her I only wanted to be friends. She seemed to want the same thing, which was a relief. We talked on the phone every Friday night, but mostly we communicated through letters. And inexplicably I began to change. She didn't talk about answering to an angry God—you know the usual 'God demands this and that.' We talked about things so much deeper, about how real life works, and I began to understand how the Amish ways had the power to unlock the best in a person. My anger over the restraints of religion was slowly molded into respect. Of course, I never told her any of that. I was too cool to admit I'd dissented from faith for all the wrong reasons. Over the next few years, I found excuses to return home more and more often. Savilla was there to welcome me each time. When I was there, we dated, but she never asked for a commitment. Three years ago, when I was twenty-five, I realized I was too in love with her to pretend otherwise. I moved back home and started going through instructions to join the faith so I could marry her."

"She knew why you were joining the faith?"

"Ya, she was really excited at first, seemed every bit as much in love as I was. We talked of marriage and our future, but we didn't set any definite plans for when we would marry. Around the time I joined the faith, she began to change, and she no longer wanted to talk about getting married. I thought it was because my furniture-making business was floundering, so I poured more and more time into trying to make a go of it. But there were too many Amish furniture makers and too few people interested in buying it. I recently read that oak furniture has been going out of style for a while now, and maybe that's true. Anyway, one day she finally said, 'It's not going to work out between us.'" Talking about it had familiar dark clouds churning inside him. "She said she wanted to go back to being friends. So we parted ways. I threw in the towel on my business, spent a week selling what I could, and gave the rest away. After paying to break the rental agreement on the shop, I closed the doors. A week later I heard about Jacob's homebuilding business, so I left and came to Virginia."

"That was more than a year ago, and you haven't been back since?"

"Nee. Just not ready to chance bumping into her. I'm afraid of what I might say."

"I'm feeling that same way about now." Esther reached across the table and took the newspaper back. "Let's skip going to North Star."

The idea of Esther unloading her thoughts on anyone was amusing. Kore knew her as someone with great restraint and gentleness.

Jacob set his coffee cup on the table, his brows furrowed. "It's strange that she let you go through all the steps to marry her before breaking up with you."

Before Kore answered, Mandy called out. *"Hallo?"*

"On the porch," Esther responded.

Bill drove his truck onto the driveway.

Jacob stood and picked up plates. "All I ask is that you make sure

Esther gets out of the vehicle to stretch her legs at least every ninety minutes. That's what her doctor said—no longer than ninety minutes of riding at a time."

Kore rose. "I have the three days planned in every possible way—hotels, restaurants, and shops. Nothing will go wrong."

CHAPTER TWO

*E*arly afternoon light spilled into the birthing room as Savilla eased the swaddled newborn from his Mamm. "Welcome, little one."

His Mamm, Miriam Yoder, smiled up at the wee thing before she relaxed against the bed, exhausted after giving birth less than an hour ago. She radiated enough love to last this baby a lifetime. Miriam's husband sat next to her, holding her hand as they whispered things only meant for the two of them.

Savilla swallowed hard, resisting the heartache that wanted to taunt her. She would never know this kind of intimate friendship or unbreakable bond with a man.

Her lot in life wasn't one she would've chosen, but she trusted that God knew what He was doing. Maybe, for reasons that escaped her understanding, she didn't deserve a better lot. Whatever was the cause of her destiny, she was at peace with it.

But peace didn't stop heartache.

The baby boy in her arms opened his eyes, squinting against the sunlight. She smiled. "Everything is so very new to you, ya?" She cooed while tucking the thin, downy swaddling blanket around his chin, getting it out of her way so she could take in all of his beautiful face. Pulling him close, she breathed in the aroma of the newborn. Nothing had this same delicious smell. To her the scent meant the start of new life—the dreams and hopes yet to be fulfilled—and Savilla prayed for this little one.

Miriam lifted the clipboard Savilla had placed beside her. "Do we need to fill this out now?"

"It would be helpful. It won't take more than a couple of minutes, and I need the info to prepare the birth certificate." She studied the baby, fascinated by the power this helpless little being had over the adults who surrounded him. "Be especially careful with the spelling of your son's name, because that's how I'll list it on the birth certificate. Once I have the birth certificate in order, I'll bring it to you to sign, give you a copy, and log the original at the courthouse."

Rebekah delivered the babies, and Savilla did the bookkeeping. She had been doing the paperwork on every infant born at this clinic for the last ten years. It only took her about an hour, sometimes two, each day, which was good, because her seamstress work often required twelve-hour workdays.

She and Rebekah made a great team, although Rebekah had been delivering babies long before Savilla was born. She'd even delivered Savilla on a snowy night almost twenty-five years earlier.

Miriam studied the bundle in Savilla's arms, and she squeezed her husband's hand. "Today's date—November 13—will stand out as enormously important to us for the rest of our days."

Miriam's husband smiled, his eyes glistening with moisture. "Ya, it will."

Savilla had seen this same beautiful, inexplicable look in hundreds of parents—the power of love unleashed.

Regardless of how many times she'd witnessed this afterglow, when she held each new bundle, her eyes moistened at the enormity of what a newborn meant—to the parents, the family, the community, and God.

Rebekah opened the bedroom door and motioned for Savilla. "Could I see you in the kitchen for a minute?"

"Sure." It wasn't unusual for Rebekah to call her from a room. Few business-type conversations were allowed to take place where babies were born.

Birthing rooms were hallowed ground.

Savilla traced the little one's cheek. "I gotta go, cutie pie." She gently placed the newborn in his Daed's arms. It was the couple's first child, and the man looked as terrified as he did thrilled. She kept her hand under the baby's head. "He's not as delicate as he appears as long as you remember to support his head at all times. When picking him up or passing him to someone else—just splay one hand, keeping it behind his shoulders and head simultaneously, while holding his bottom with the other hand." She demonstrated. "Always. No exceptions for two to three months, and you'll be just fine."

"Ya." The Daed's nervous whisper made her smile.

Savilla left the room, closing the door behind her. She entered the kitchen, heading for the cabinet to get a glass. "What's going on? I'm supposed to meet Sarah Glick in just a bit to discuss seamstress work." She turned on the faucet and filled the glass with water. "Did you know the youth are planning an extra-special Christmas caroling this year?" She took a drink of water before turning back to face Rebekah. "The plans are heartwarming and . . ."

Something in Rebekah's demeanor made her pause. Maybe Rebekah was simply worn-out. She couldn't continue doing this job much longer. It was exhausting work, and it required a sharp mind and steady hands twenty-four hours a day. At seventy years old Rebekah had a sharper mind than most young people, but her hands and arms were growing weak, even trembling of late. Savilla knew that her knees ached with arthritis too.

Savilla closed the gap between them. "Is something wrong?"

Rebekah's eyes watered. "Elizabeth Detweiler fell last night. Her daughter-in-law found her this morning, unconscious."

"What?" Savilla nearly dropped the glass. "But I . . . I was at her place all day yesterday, helping her organize her storage spaces."

At seventy-three years old Elizabeth had remarkable coordination and energy. Her stamina constantly amazed Savilla. Still, before Savilla left her place last night, she'd hurriedly gone through each room, moving boxes and trying to make sure nothing was in the way for Elizabeth to trip over.

Had Savilla missed something? The thought terrified her. She set the glass on the table. "Is she going to be okay?"

"No one knows yet. When the EMTs arrived, they checked her vitals, and they were weak. That's all anyone knows right now."

Savilla trembled as she sat in the closest chair. "While I cleaned out her closet yesterday, she sat on her bed, and we laughed and talked for hours. She is too full of life, too amazing to lose her . . ."

"I know, honey. Everyone will feel that way."

"What if I left a box or some discarded items in her path?"

Rebekah took a seat next to her. "Regardless of why she fell, it was an accident. You know Elizabeth. If this incident moves her from this world to the next, she's ready."

Savilla pondered Rebekah's words. By Elizabeth's own confession just yesterday, she had lived a full and wonderful life, and as a widow for the last decade, one who missed her husband something fierce, she wouldn't mind leaving this world.

Elizabeth had spent her life in obedience to the Lord, marrying and blessing this earth with the fruit of her body. She had eleven children, sixty-one grandchildren, and fifteen great-grandchildren. What would Savilla leave behind when she passed? A dried-up heart, disfigured insides, and a shoe rack full of fancy lace-up boots she was forbidden to wear.

Rebekah reached across the table and touched the back of Savilla's hand. "I hate to add to your shock and concern, but I don't want you caught off guard when family starts arriving later today and tomorrow."

Savilla's heart jolted as she realized what Rebekah was trying to get at. "Kore will come home."

"Ya, that's right. There's no way he won't come home as soon as possible."

If Savilla had taken a moment to think, she would've realized that. Kore had a special bond with his Mammi D, and to Savilla's knowledge he hadn't been home for a visit since leaving here soon after they broke up.

Rebekah squeezed her shoulder. "Maybe it's time you told him the truth."

"No." Savilla stood and grabbed her sweater off the back of the chair. "I need to go. Tell Miriam I'll come by her home tomorrow or the next day so she can sign the birth certificate."

"Savilla, you loved him and he you. A secret of this magnitude should never have been kept from him. He deserves the truth."

"He deserves better than any truth I could share. What I gave him was freedom to find someone else, someone worthy."

"Even if that is the case, you should be painfully honest and let him decide."

Savilla placed both her hands on the table and leaned in, staring into her friend's eyes. "I won't." She narrowed her eyes. "You said I could trust you, and I did. Promise me you'll stay out of this."

Rebekah pursed her lips, tears filling her eyes. "He won't hear it from me."

With the vow made, Savilla hurried out of the house, gulping in air. She wasn't ready to see Kore. Not yet.

Embarrassment heated the back of her neck. How self-centered could she be? Elizabeth was in the hospital, and that should be the only concern on her mind.

But it wasn't.

*K*ore put away his paperwork as the driver pulled the truck into a parking space. They were in a small historic town about an hour west of North Star. The proximity to home had made it impossible to stop thinking of Savvy. They'd once come to this old town just for the fun of it and spent an entire day going through the old stores, paying special attention to the many flavors of ice cream offered at the local creamery.

Bittersweet memories had niggled since before dawn, and he was weary of it. He pushed those thoughts aside, trying to stay focused on today. This was the third day that the four of them—Bill, Esther, Mandy, and Kore—had been working their way north, stopping at two estate sales and thirteen antique stores. They'd found some good items but nothing resembling the French buffet at the auction. Their next destination was directly in front of them, Endless Memories Antique Store.

Mandy studied it. "Looks small." Unlike Esther, Mandy easily became restless. On the upside she could scour a store quickly and not seem to miss anything that might be of value to her sister.

Kore unfastened his seat belt. "It's two long and narrow stories with an attic. You won't get bored."

They got out of the crew cab, and Kore held open the door of the antique store. Bill headed for the creamery. The driver got them to their destinations as needed. That was the limit of his contracted work. But he never failed to be back at the truck before Esther was finished shopping.

When Kore's cell phone rang, he stayed outside the store and pulled it from his pocket. The word *Home* flashed on the screen, and he ran his finger across it. "Hallo?"

"Hi, sweetie." His Mamm's voice sounded different—hoarse and sad.

"You okay?"

"It's about your Mammi D."

As she explained the situation, his chest felt as if someone were pouring buckets of scalding water into it. What had he been thinking to stay away for as long as he had?

⸎

Black carriages were parked in the field and along the front of the barn at Kore's parents' home. Savilla's Daed brought their rig to a stop, parking it between two other horse-drawn rigs.

A lot of Mammi D's family had already arrived, as well as many people she'd known over the years. No doubt many folks were also at the hospital, but this was the original homestead where Mammi D had raised her children, and her loved ones had gathered here for comfort and to do what loving families did—support and nurture one another. Savilla steadied her breathing. Was he here?

Surely not. The news of Elizabeth's accident couldn't have reached him more than a few hours ago. He lived six hours away. If he'd dropped everything to get here, he would've still had to hire and wait for a driver to arrive. If he went to the hospital first, that would delay his arrival too.

Her desire to avoid seeing him was why she and her Mamm had rushed to get this food cooked. Like all Amish women in this area,

Savilla was expected to help provide food, and once she delivered her dishes, she wouldn't return.

She hoped, by God's mercy, that she would be spared having to face him. But she knew there would be no avoiding the other Detweiler brothers, and their goal during each encounter was to make her pay for hurting Kore.

Mamm turned around from her place in the front seat. *"Du gut?"*

"Ya." Savilla had gone by Mammi D's place after leaving the birthing center, and she saw nothing Mammi D might have tripped over. Then again, her daughter-in-law might have moved the item.

Mamm frowned. "You don't look as if you're okay."

"I may need chocolate before bedtime, lots of it."

A hint of a smile crossed her Mamm's lips. "I like that kind of talk. My favorite or yours?"

"Both." Savilla wasn't at all sure she could have survived the last year if her mother hadn't changed from an uptight rule keeper to a woman who could embrace Savilla's lot in life and learn to chuckle instead of cry in the midst of complete heartache.

Daed set the brake, and he and Mamm got out. He held open the door on the driver's side of the carriage, waiting for Savilla to squeeze between the front seat and doorframe. As she worked to climb out, he offered his hand. He never did that. Why today? Did her Daed feel sorry for her because Kore, the dragon slayer who now had a good position with JK Homebuilders, was on his way home, and his pitiful ex-girlfriend needed a hand getting out of a buggy?

"Nee, Daed." She shook her head. *"Denki, Ich bin ganz gut."*

At her assurance that she was quite good, Daed nodded and withdrew his hand, but compassion reflected in his eyes. Maybe his offer had more to do with her past health issues than pity, but she doubted it. He'd yet to show much concern about that, and she'd been on her feet for six months now.

She stumbled out of the carriage, and Daed grabbed her arm, steadying her. He looked at her lace-up boots with their heel. He sighed, pursing his lips and shaking his head. "Seems as if you could've made a better choice on your footwear while coming here of all places."

"Maybe so." She'd been stripped of more than she could admit to herself, but during the journey she'd discovered a few new loves. Stylish boots were one of them. The ones she currently had on were solid black, and technically they fit the Amish dress code—except for the three-inch heel.

Old oak trees stood guard around the homestead. The once lush green leaves of summer had reached the peak of showing their true colors weeks ago. Various shades of red, yellow, purple, orange, and magenta were long gone. Now brown leaves fell like rain as the mid-November winds pushed gray clouds across the sky.

A sea of people dressed in Amish attire filled the yard, some talking in small groups and others waiting in line to enter the home. The Amish wasted no time gathering at one main home when someone was seriously injured, ill, or had passed away. Savilla prayed Mammi D would recuperate and this gathering would become a celebration, and if that happened, even more people were likely to arrive.

Mammi D's cabin, built after her children were grown, was small with a tiny kitchen. Her cabin might hold thirty people if most of them remained standing and didn't mind close quarters. If Kore's homestead wasn't large enough to hold all the visitors, Mammi D's place wouldn't have held even the food that was being brought in. But it would take a lot of food to provide for the eighty-something people who made up her immediate family.

Her Daed opened the hatch and pulled out two large baskets containing the food she and Mamm had cooked. He passed them the baskets before leading the way toward Kore's house and joining the back of the line of visitors.

Sweat ran down Savilla's back despite the cool temperature. Her heart pounded, as did her head. All she wanted to do was fulfill her duty and get out of here before Kore arrived.

Trying to shift her uptight focus, she thought about Mammi D's cabin. Since Savilla sewed all the time, she tended to think in terms of yards, and Elizabeth Detweiler's small cabin was about a hundred and sixty yards away or, based on what Kore had once told her, about one and a half football fields from here. The place was surrounded by trees and couldn't be seen from this spot. No one really knew why she insisted on living so hidden. When she gave up the old homestead and her children built her a cabin, she could've requested that it be built next to or adjoining the main house, but she was too independent for that.

Savilla understood that sentiment. She rented a dilapidated room above Old Man Miller's carriage house. It was bitter cold in the winter and steamy hot in the summer, but it didn't cost much, and it was hers. All freedom came with a price, didn't it? She had to be very organized to both live and work in the same space, but when she was at her parents' home, her family was always under her feet . . . or maybe she was under theirs. Either way, one outdated room above an Amish garage solved that problem.

Daed began talking to friends who were in line ahead of them. Savilla's heels kept digging into the soft dirt. She hadn't realized pointy heels did that. The only place she'd worn them was inside or on sidewalks. Until she was in the house, she would need to keep her weight on the balls of her feet.

Mamm gasped.

"What?" Savilla whispered.

Mamm clutched her basket closer to her body. "Nothing."

Savilla searched for what had made her Mamm gasp.

As if there was no one else on the lawn, Kore looked right at her, their eyes locking. He smiled, a faint but sincere smile as he nodded his head. Unwelcome tears singed her eyes. With a basket in hand, she lifted her fingers slightly and waved. A man near him moved, and it became clear that there was an attractive young woman beside him.

You can do this. You can.

But she wasn't at all sure she could. Her legs felt like the wobbly limbs of a newborn calf.

"Did you know he was seeing someone?" Mamm asked.

She shook her head. "Nee, but be happy for him, Mamm. It's what I want." From the moment she knew they couldn't survive as a couple, she'd spent a lot of time praying he would find the *one,* marry, and have a huge, loving family. But fresh tears welled, and she dug into her pocket for a tissue.

"Struggling a bit, Savvy, as Kore finds happiness?" The voice of Kore's brother David, filled with biting sarcasm, came from behind her.

"He doesn't know," Mamm mumbled. "Show mercy."

She wiped her face, took a deep breath, and turned. "Hello, David. I'm sorry for what your family is going through. Any news?"

"Ya, here's some news for you." David lifted one eyebrow. "I was sort of hoping *you* wouldn't come."

Mamm turned, reaching for him quickly as if she was going to slap him upside the head. Instead she straightened his bent collar. "Of course our family would come." She dusted off his jacket and smiled. "We love Elizabeth. We're praying for her recovery."

With that said, Mamm grabbed Savilla by the arm and turned around quickly. Savilla's heels stuck, and she tripped, going forward several steps before getting her balance. People snickered. When she looked up, Kore was right in front of her.

"Sorry." She straightened, pulling the basket closer. "New boots." Her cheeks burned, and she was sure they were flushed. "I . . . I'm so sorry about Mammi D."

"Ya." He kept his eyes on the basket in her hands. "It's rough."

Since Kore understated every emotion, those two words carried a lot of weight. She wanted to know how he was doing and encourage him, but she'd lost that privilege. "You . . . must've been close by when you got the news."

"Ya."

If she had held on to the illusion that they had managed to remain friends, she was facing the truth right now. They had nothing left between them but tension and awkwardness.

He held out his hand for the basket, and she released it without argument. "Lydia." He nodded a polite hello before lifting her Mamm's basket too. "David will take these inside for you." He looked past them, a calm, steely anger in his eyes. Had he known his younger brother was being unkind?

David took the baskets.

Kore went to her Daed and shook his hand.

Daed clasped Kore's arm. "Any news?"

"A little. I spent a few hours at the hospital before coming here. Mammi D has a severe concussion and a broken collarbone, arm, and wrist. So far there's been no change for the better concerning her vitals."

Would Kore have told her that much if she'd managed to get the question out? It didn't seem like it.

Kore thanked her Daed for coming, and then he disappeared into the crowd.

Stars twinkled against the black sky, and the outdoor glider beneath Kore creaked and whined as he swayed back and forth in a rhythmic motion. It was nearly midnight, and the old homestead was finally quiet. After ten hours of reminiscing and updating family, friends, and near strangers about Mammi D's condition, Kore longed for a bit of time alone.

He stared into the woods, looking down the well-worn path that began at the edge of his parents' yard and continued deep into the woods until it stopped at Mammi D's front door. Regardless of how busy she was or even if she was under the weather, she had always welcomed him with open arms and a squishy hug.

Surely she would recuperate. He would be at the hospital right now except he felt he needed to stay near Esther so he was within hearing range if she needed anything. Jacob would want that. Mammi D had an entire hospital staff watching out for her, not to mention numerous grown children.

Had Kore just seen movement on the path? Hoping to spot a deer, he rose and went to the edge of the wood, staring into darkness.

How many times as a child had he run down that path to show her something or talk? There weren't many women like his grandmother—Amish or Englisch. Her spirit for adventure kept her young, and whether she was playing softball with the grandchildren or comforting Kore during life's many heartaches, she exuded a love that knew no bounds. She was a ball of energy that gave sacrificially to anyone of any faith, color, or background, and she managed to do so without ever getting crosswise with the Old Ways.

Something scampered through the woods, and muffled childlike voices rose from nowhere, seeming to shush one another. Was it his imagination, perhaps the stress of today mixing with the memories of yesterday?

Remaining in place, he kept a watchful eye. A twig snapped, and a faint yelp seemed to ride on the wind. "Hallo?"

Suddenly the woods seemed eerily quiet, as if even the nocturnal creatures had paused their movements. Was that whimpering?

"Kore?" Mamm called, and he turned. "Do you mind having a little company?"

He motioned for her. His Daed wasn't coming home tonight . . . unless Mammi D passed away. The doctors said her status was that serious.

Kore's Mamm came outside, sliding her arms into a thick coat as she descended the wooden stairs. A moment later his brother David came outside, following her.

Kore studied the woods for a long moment. Clearly his imagination was getting the better of him. He returned to the metal patio glider in the middle of the side yard. When Mamm sat next to him, he put his arm around her shoulders. "How are you holding up?"

"Okay." She wrapped the coat tighter around her. "I know she's seventy-three, but she seems too young to die."

"She's a fighter, Mamm. Don't give up on her yet."

David took a seat in one of the Adirondack chairs Kore had built nearly four years ago—back when he thought it was a feasible business to make and sell his own furniture.

His Mamm leaned into his embrace. "When I married your Daed, it didn't take long to realize I had the best mother-in-law a girl could ask for."

"She's pretty remarkable." Kore squeezed her shoulder. "And I'm praying you get a chance to remind her just what she means to you as you wait on her hand and foot while her bones and concussion heal."

David tapped the palms of his hands against the cedar armrests. "Let's not forget she's also ridiculously strong willed."

"Ya." Mamm looked skyward. "She's accepting of people, resolute in her decisions, and a closet nonconformist."

Kore shifted, putting his forearms on his legs, thinking about another person he cared for who had those traits. It'd been awkward seeing Savilla today, talking as if they barely knew each other. What had happened between them? When she'd said they weren't going to work out, he pushed back, angry and asking questions, but she never gave a reason, only a sincere apology. He'd walked out, slamming the door behind him. Isn't that how breakups worked?

He needed to think about a different subject. "I appreciate your warm welcome of Esther and Mandy." Kore pulled a lighter out of his pocket, fidgeting with it. When he arrived here, he sent Bill back to Virginia. "Jacob will join them here tomorrow. Esther is in a time crunch to find certain pieces, and I was interrupted from that, so he is going to try to make up for it."

"It's not a bit of trouble." Mamm raised a finger. "Change of subject though. You know what I've been thinking?"

Kore ran his thumb across the spark wheel of the lighter, and a long flame, usually meant to light candles and kerosene lanterns, danced in the cool night air. "That it's late, and we should get some sleep?"

"No. I think we need to empty Mammi D's attic, you know, since your aunt found her at the bottom of the steps."

Kore released the button on the lighter, and the flame disappeared. "I'm not following you."

"Savilla was helping Mammi D clean and organize her storage spaces yesterday. After Savilla left, Mammi D went into the attic by herself, so today I asked Savilla to go through everything in the attic, get out all Mammi D's personal items, and mark everything else to be removed."

Savilla felt too involved with his family, but it couldn't be avoided. Mammi D loved her.

"The best remedy for keeping Mammi D out of the attic is to empty it." Mamm folded her arms. "I've asked Savilla to get as much done tomorrow toward that goal as possible."

"Not sure I care for that plan. Maybe emptying the attic isn't really a fair thing to do to Mammi D while she is in the hospital."

"You might be right. Perhaps I should wait and let Elizabeth decide." Kore's Mamm looked tired.

David lifted his foot and nudged Kore's leg. "So how old is that Mandy girl?"

"Nineteen, I think."

"Any chance you and her have a little something going on?"

Even if there weren't almost a decade between him and Mandy, Kore couldn't make himself see her or any woman in that light—as if she could be a person to date. He shook his head. "Nee. Nada. Nil."

Mamm patted Kore's knee. "It's late, and the morning will start early." She rose.

"I need a minute with David."

"Don't be long, okay?" Mamm asked.

"Sure thing." When his Mamm was out of earshot, Kore turned to his brother. "What'd you say to Savvy today?"

"Nothing."

"I saw the look on her mother's face."

"I . . . I didn't mean for Lydia to hear me."

"Which tells me that whatever you said today, you've said much worse things when others weren't around. Right?"

David shrugged, and Kore knew the answer.

"Come on, David, grow up. You're twenty years old. You think you have a right to be rude to Savilla because she broke up with me?"

"It's not about a breakup. I hate her for cheating on you."

David's words knocked the air out of Kore, and it was more than a minute before he could take a breath. "She what?" Disbelief tried to immobilize him. "Why would you say something like that?"

"Because it's true. She left here right after you. I didn't know where she went, but I was suspicious she had someone else, especially after she returned home months later skinny, detached, and unhappy."

"Maybe she left to help expand her business and had a rough go of it with the back issues she suffers with."

"Come on, Kore. Stop being gullible. She'd had a fling and returned brokenhearted. Served her right. Our cousin Amon called from Ohio to let us know he saw her walking arm in arm with some man. After she returned looking a lot worse for the wear, rumors ran wild. Rather than moving back home with her parents, she rented that dump of a place above Old Man Miller's carriage house." David shifted against his seat. "So in my book she deserves far worse than anything I've dished out."

Anger thudded hard in Kore's chest. "Even if all you're saying is true, the only person with the right to call her to task is me."

"Would you, even if you were around?"

"Insult her? I hope not. My goal is to avoid her." But knowing all this, if Kore couldn't avoid her, he knew the question would begin to eat at him.

"Exactly my point. You're mellow and kind, and we help give her what she's owed."

"You and who else?"

David slumped, apparently realizing what he'd said. "Noah and Joe."

Kore's head pounded. What had his seventeen- and nineteen-year-old brothers dished out? "That's just wrong, regardless of what she's done. Every one of you will make it up to her. Clear?"

"Someone needed to set her straight."

"And that someone was either me or no one. You can't get offended at her on my behalf and dole out your version of justice. Across the board in all scenarios, that's wrong."

David slunk in his chair, looking sullen. "Just how are we supposed to make it up to her?"

"Figure it out." Kore tapped his temple. "And whatever kindness you come up with, I want proof of it."

"I don't get why you're so angry with us."

Kore counted to ten. "What you've been doing is sneaky and underhanded. I know you were raised better than that. Do us both a favor and just go inside, okay?"

David left.

Kore stood at the head of the path, looking into the darkness. An owl hooted in the distance and the wind kicked up. Something about the woods niggled at Kore. He walked down the path a bit. A faint noise rode on the wind. Was that a dog whining? He whistled.

Again the wooded area grew quiet. He waited. The aroma of an autumn night in the woods filled his nostrils, and dozens of memories filled his mind—of him and his Mammi D and of him and Savilla.

Tired of thinking of Savilla, he turned to go inside. Maybe sleep would bring him some much-needed relief.

*T*he attic boards beneath Savilla creaked as she pulled out another box. She rubbed her hands together, warming them. Maybe she should've started a fire in the hearth when she arrived six hours ago. But there was no sense in starting one now. It would be dark in about three hours, and she would begin her walk home a good forty-five minutes before then. By the time the fire was giving off enough heat to make a difference in the attic, it would be time for her to leave.

She knelt. What treasures would she find this time? More items picked up at a yard sale? Dresses from Mammi D's younger days? Cookbooks?

Mammi D was a bit of a collector. Savilla agreed to do this task of organizing and labeling, but she disagreed with Kore's Mamm about removing everything from the attic. Thankfully that wasn't the task she'd given Savilla. If Mammi D got better, Savilla would look for an opportunity to gently share her thoughts about emptying the attic.

She opened a box and saw numerous antique kitchen items.

A loud thump made her jolt. She moved to the top of the stairs. Something creaked, as if a cabinet were being opened . . . and then the fridge.

She had locked the door behind her so that none of Mammi D's family could enter and accidentally surprise her. She hated being startled.

"Hallo?" She sent out a distant warning of her presence. Glass shattered and footfalls hit in quick syncopation. Clearly her plan to speak from afar hadn't kept her from frightening someone. But why didn't the person call back? She went down the steps and into the small kitchen.

No one. A casserole dish and its contents were spattered on the floor. "Hallo?" Through a window she saw bushes rustling as if someone had run through them. Savilla moved closer, staring through the glass. She saw no one, but her heart raced. Was someone out there?

How had anyone gotten in? And why? Savilla searched through the home and found an open window in Mammi D's bedroom. When she closed it, she discovered a broken pane. Had that person broken the glass while Savilla was in the attic? Wouldn't she have heard that?

Savilla grabbed her coat. She would go by the Detweiler home and let them know what had happened.

Such an odd thing. Why would someone break into the home today and never before, as if the person knew Mammi D wasn't here? Why would anyone take leftovers from the fridge?

Feeling a little eerie and isolated, she didn't take the time to clean up the broken dish before she left the cabin. She wanted to be gone long before dusk settled. It would be disconcerting enough to walk through the woods alone while knowing someone had been watching the cabin.

While taking the key from its peg, she saw movement near the shed. She eased the sheer back and saw two scrawny, jean-covered legs disappear into a hole on the side of the building.

A child?

Savilla shuddered, fearing who else might be with her. She grabbed a hoe from the mud room and tiptoed toward the shed. Once on the path, she heard whispers.

"I want to go home."

"Sh."

Savilla couldn't believe her ears. Surely not. "Hello?" With her temples pounding, Savilla eased open the door. "Jade?" she whispered.

Savilla hadn't seen her in more than a year, and if it was Jade, she was a lot taller and skinnier. Wishing she'd brought a lantern, Savilla tiptoed forward, peering around barrels and crates.

The girl jumped out, spreading her arms as if she were a barricade. "Go home!" She shooed Savilla back.

"Jade?"

The girl struck a match, and her threatening posture melted. "Savilla?"

"Ya."

"It's you!" She blew out the match and ran to Savilla and put her arms around her. Jade's arms tightened and she broke into tears. Savilla saw the two younger ones—Chad and Demi—huddled in a corner. Four suitcases of various sizes were scattered about, some open with clothes hanging half out.

"It's okay." Savilla held her. "How long have you been here?"

"Since school let out yesterday. Where's Miss Elizabeth?"

Savilla had plenty of questions of her own, like why were Chad and Demi remaining huddled in the corner? And why hadn't Jade gone elsewhere, at least to Kore's home? "Jade, honey, where are your parents?"

"Out of the country. They left yesterday morning after dropping us off at school, and then the school bus let us out a few blocks from here, just like it was planned. We were supposed to stay with Miss Elizabeth."

These children, ages eleven to five, had been on their own since yesterday afternoon? Savilla's knees felt a little shaky, but this wasn't the time to sit. "When you got here, the house was locked?" And they'd spent the night on their own, a fierce warrior protecting her two younger siblings, but in reality they were three young, confused children.

"Yeah, we were going to sleep inside, but an older man came by, looking over the place, locking up everything. I was afraid he'd come back, so after he left, I broke in and got the suitcases we brought to Miss Elizabeth a couple of nights ago, and we slept out here. I didn't know it was you inside the house today."

"It's okay, Jade. Just take a breath and relax."

"But I don't understand. Mom, Dad, and us kids were here night before last. Mom brought in dinner, and we ate with Miss Elizabeth. Everything was arranged, and then we got here Friday afternoon, and Miss Elizabeth was nowhere."

"Ya, we'll talk about Miss Elizabeth in a minute. Why are Chad and Demi staying in the corner?"

"I think my sister's got a fever. I told Chad to stay with her. Demi has hardly quit whining since we got here last night, 'cept when she's asleep."

Savilla couldn't see the girl well, but since she was quiet, she could only assume she was asleep. "How about if we take Demi inside and let me get a look at her."

"You can't turn us in. It would cause all sorts of trouble for us, and then Mom and Dad will have to return, and they'll never be able to bring our brother home."

"Where exactly did your parents go?"

"To Uganda to get our little brother. Maybe we can get through to them later, but I've been trying, and the phone goes straight to voice mail without even ringing. They're going to be there for weeks, maybe even past Christmas."

Savilla's head swam with dizziness. Why would parents need to fly to a third-world country to pick up a younger sibling?

"You must have aunts, uncles, friends of your parents—someone you can stay with."

"Maybe. We can't try until I reach Mom or Dad. If anyone causes a stink, they will be forced to return, and that'll cause them to lose all rights to adopt Aidan. You've gotta trust that I know what I'm talking about. My parents have been trying to bring him home for two years!"

"Okay, Jade. I hear you. Just take a breath. We'll figure this out."

Chad moved to a spot behind a barrel and peered over it, only his tousled black hair and blue eyes showing. "I'm hungry."

"Sh." Jade motioned for him to return to the corner. "So where's Miss Elizabeth?"

"She's . . . unable to . . ." What could Savilla tell her without adding grief on top of her fears? "See, she fell and broke a couple of bones in her arm. But right now we need to have Demi seen."

"She can't go to a doctor unless you have permission to be her guardian. My parents have traveled out of the country a lot, and I know how this works. Like I said, you gotta trust me."

Were Jade's fears well founded? Savilla had no experience in such matters. Amish people had no shortage of blood relatives to care for them when a parent wasn't able to. "I know your parents moved here from Germany a decade ago, but haven't any other relatives moved to the States?"

She shook her head. "No. Please promise you'll do your best to help us."

Savilla's eyes moistened as she held up her pinkie. Jade clutched it with her pinkie, trembling. This bright, demanding girl had the heart of a child.

*C*onversations buzzed around the kitchen table as many of the Detweiler men—brothers, uncles, and cousins—talked while finishing a piece of shoofly pie and drinking coffee. But Kore had to fight to keep his focus on what was being said.

Savvy had cheated on him?

That question had hounded him even while he'd spent most of the day at the hospital. His parents were there now. Mammi D's vitals were improving, and the doctor said she would be moved from ICU sometime today, but she'd yet to regain consciousness. The doctor was much more optimistic today, and Kore's family was optimistic, and their sense of fellowship was strong. He continued to listen to the many stories involving Mammi D. Memories were so powerful, able to make a person feel loved for a lifetime, able to motivate a person to pass on that love.

Children's voices upstairs rose with laughter. The boys were playing a game of marbles. He didn't know what the girls were doing, but the youth, including Esther's sister Mandy, were outside sitting around the firepit, talking. Every room was filled with men, women, and children. Jacob and Esther were still here. A hired driver had taken them to various antique stores for a good bit of today. Esther purchased several sale items at the North Star Antique Store, but rather than heading back to Virginia, they'd chosen to stay another day in hopes of going to more antique stores tomorrow. Mandy was having a great time with Erma, one of Kore's many girl cousins. The two hit it off, and Mandy was in no rush to go home.

One of Kore's cousins rose from his chair next to Kore and went to the coffeepot. David moved from a seat at the far end of the long table to the now empty chair.

"I had an idea I wanted to run past you." David leaned in, talking softly. "You know how the youth go Christmas caroling each year. Some of the youth are getting Savilla to make their clothes. We're dressing in specific, coordinating colors this year so we'll look sharp while caroling. Families like that sort of thing. Since Savvy is a seamstress, I thought I'd ask her to sew the clothes for me, Noah, and Joe."

"Asking her to do you a favor is the best you can come up with?"

"I'll do it nice like, so she'll know it's an apology, and she'll make money from it. Worst case scenario, she leaves pins in the outfits, and we get stuck and bleed as the evening goes on. If she doesn't want to help, she can say no. Clearly, declining people isn't an issue for her."

"Seems a little opportunistic to my way of thinking. You need the clothes made, and she's skilled at it."

He shrugged. "I'm trying, Kore. I don't know her like I used to. She's changed."

"Ya, so you've said, as if that excuses you. Maybe some of that change is because you and two other men have been getting your digs in for the past year. Buy her an upgrade for her carriage. Maybe new wheels."

"She doesn't own it anymore."

Fresh confusion stirred up dozens of questions. "She sold the carriage she spent all those years saving to buy?"

"Ya."

She used to joke that she'd give up her beloved sewing machine before she'd let go of that custom-made carriage.

David opened his mouth to say something else, but Kore barely lifted his hand, stopping him. He wavered between wanting to know more and leaving well enough alone. She lived in a dump and had sold her carriage? Kore needed a few answers, but there were too many ears around this table, although thus far everyone else was involved in different conversations.

He stood and nodded for David to go with him. He grabbed his coat off a peg and kept going until he was twenty feet from anyone else. Sunlight cast a golden glow, but dusk would take over soon. The temperature had dropped a lot since yesterday, and he hoped the crisp fall air would help clear his head.

David followed him out the door, shoving his arms into his coat.

Kore put his hands into his coat pockets. "Does she still have Zena?"

She'd gotten that horse on her tenth birthday, had loved it, and slept in the barn with it during storms to comfort it. Savilla was still doing that during really bad storms until a couple of years ago.

"Ya, Zena's still hers. From what I hear, the horse and her sewing machine are about all she's held on to this past year."

This insight into how she was living didn't line up with the young woman Kore once knew. Ready for time alone, he decided to go for a walk, but he should at least tell Jacob where he was going. Last he saw of Jacob, Noah was challenging him to a game of chess. Kore went inside and to the family room. Esther was on the couch, talking to one of Kore's aunts. Jacob was sitting across a chess table, smiling as Noah shook his head. Clearly his younger brother had lost . . . again.

"Jacob." Kore stepped closer. "I'll be back in a bit. I'm going for a walk."

Jacob stood. "I could use a walk to stretch my legs. Do you mind?"

"Not at all."

Jacob turned to Esther. "Care to go?"

She was on her feet before he finished the question. "I need to run to the rest room. Jacob, would you get our coats from the bedroom?"

"Sure."

"I'll meet you outside." Kore left the house, and once he was in the yard, he realized David was waiting for him.

"I thought of an idea you might like." David buttoned his winter coat. "When the youth go caroling, for the most part we only go to the grandparents' homes. The roster of where to sing is already too full, but maybe I could get the group or at least a part of the group to go to Savilla's carriage apartment, and we'd sing for her."

"Your plan is sounding better." He could see Savvy really enjoying that. She loved Christmas music, and the Amish had no way of listening to it like the Englisch did. In years past they would eat out at an Englisch diner on the square of North Star that played Christmas music starting the day after Thanksgiving. "Actually the caroling idea isn't bad at all. And if she agrees to do the sewing, pay her really well."

Jacob and Esther came out the back door.

"You ready?" Kore asked.

"Ya."

"Have a preference on which direction?"

Esther gestured toward the path that led to Mammi D's. "Since arriving I've heard so much about years of your family going to her place that I'd like to see it."

It was late, and Savilla would be gone by now. "Works for me."

They went across the yard and onto the path. Jacob and Esther bantered back and forth, and even though Kore didn't feel like adding to the conversation, he enjoyed their company. His quietness didn't seem to bother them. After Esther saw Mammi D's cabin, if she felt up to it, they could stroll down her driveway that led to the main road.

When they rounded a curve, he saw Savilla coming their way. His heart jolted. Was there any truth in the rumors about her? What the gossip described didn't sound like anything she would do. Then again, neither did living alone above an old carriage house or selling the carriage she'd worked so hard to purchase.

"We have company," Esther said.

"Ya, Savilla." Maybe she was on her way to his house to ask about Mammi D.

"Oh." Esther paused for a moment. "Maybe walking this way wasn't a good idea."

"It's fine, but I thought she'd have gone home by now."

His heart thudded harder as they continued walking toward her. Wisps of curly honey-brown hair hung about her face, probably from the hard work of cleaning out the attic. Once within a few feet of one another, everyone stopped cold.

She gestured down the path toward his home. "I . . . uh . . . need to see your Mamm . . . or Daed, I suppose."

She seemed nervous again, like yesterday with David. He could understand that incident for numerous reasons—Mammi D had been seriously injured, David had said something inappropriate, and Kore hadn't seen her since the breakup. But why was she nervous now? "I'd like you to meet the people I work for, Jacob and Esther King." They were also friends, but the first description explained enough.

Her lips formed into a smile, but no other part of her face showed any hint of friendliness. "It's nice to meet you." When she tucked stray hair behind her ears, her hands were trembling. She returned her attention to Kore. "I apologize, but if your goal is to visit inside Mammi D's place, it's not a good time for that."

He'd had no plans to go inside, but her statement had him curious. "Why not?"

She shook her head. "I just need a little time. Late tomorrow afternoon . . . please."

"Again, why?"

Jacob touched the back of his hand against Kore's arm. "We'll just go on back to your place."

"No, that's not necessary. Just give us a second."

"Sure." Jacob and Esther walked in the direction of the cabin, going about a hundred feet before stopping to wait for him.

Kore jammed his hands into his pockets, trying to harness his frustrations. "Is it just routine for you to be secretive about everything these days? What were you going to tell my parents that you can't tell me?"

"It's their property, and I was going to ask if I could stay the night."

"Ya, 'cause that explains so much. Why would you tell me I can't go in my grandmother's home? I can't imagine what the issue is. No one here cares if the place is a little messy."

She rubbed her forehead with the back of her thumb, not a move he had seen before. "I need you to go home. I apologize if what I said made you uncomfortable because you were going to take your boss through the house, but—"

"I'm not worried about what anyone thinks. You should know that." As he mulled over her behavior—her disheveled look, her nervousness, her refusal to let them inside, he knew. "Something's wrong."

Savilla wrapped her sweater tightly around her waist. "Please, just go home, Kore."

He shifted. "Have my brothers done something again?"

Surprise flickered through her eyes, perhaps that he knew they'd been out of line. "No."

He waited, but she offered nothing else. During the breakup he'd had to accept what she wanted without getting a satisfactory answer, but not in this. "Am I invisible, Savvy? Or do you see me standing here waiting for an answer? I'm not budging until I get one."

She licked her lips, staring at the patch of ground between them.

"Okay," she whispered. "The truth is I . . . I could use some help but not yours."

Not his? Offense ran heat through him, and for several long seconds he wrestled with the desire to walk off. Then he did something he hadn't done in a very long time. He stopped reacting to her words and stresses, and he simply studied her, taking in the many emotions reflected in her face and her stance. She was more than just nervous. She was desperate for him to leave. "You're afraid that letting me in on whatever is going on is the same as inviting me into your life again."

She grimaced, guilt written on her face.

Anger pounded. "Don't worry, Savvy, we're as done as if I were getting married tomorrow."

*K*ore's words hit hard, and Savilla tried to keep the pain from showing on her face. *This is what you wanted. Kore moving on was the plan.* The realization brought some needed relief, and she drew a ragged breath.

He had pegged the reason she hadn't asked for his advice concerning the children. His parents owned the land and Mammi D's home, so they needed to know what was going on. That's why she was headed for their place. But Kore knew the children, so his insight could be helpful. "I . . . do need your advice."

"What's going on?"

"Remember Jade, Chad, and Demi?" Of course he did. Kore and Savilla used to help Mammi D take care of them from time to time, although their main task was entertaining them. She and Kore had some very special nights out with the three in tow. Their Englischness caused Savilla and Kore to branch out beyond their normal dates—like going to a carnival, the roller-skating rink, and bowling.

His slow blink indicated he was already putting the situation together. "Don't tell me Mammi D agreed to keep them, and they showed up today needing overnight care?"

"That would be the easy version of what's happening. They arrived yesterday afternoon, and I found them hiding in the shed about two hours ago—cold, hungry, and scared."

"Hiding?" Kore pressed his hand against his mouth, staring skyward. She'd seen this look before, and she figured the clamped hand was to prevent him from speaking his frustrations. He lowered his arms. "I should've followed my instincts last night."

"What do you mean?"

"Never mind." He shook his head, looking as dismayed as he did frustrated. "Parents have to put their children first, so Patti and Hank need to come home from wherever they are."

"It won't be that easy this time. They're out of the country, and Jade and I haven't been able to figure out how to reach them yet."

"What?"

Savilla hurried through an explanation. The situation with the children would be difficult to make clear under any circumstance, but it was especially tough as Kore studied her, seeming as if he was searching her face and body movements to help him understand.

Kore sighed. "What a mess."

"Ya." Savilla had fixed sandwiches for them, although Demi wasn't hungry. Right now Jade was sponging Demi's face and arms with room-temperature water while Chad read aloud to both the girls. "Speaking of difficult situations, how's Mammi D today?"

"Better. Still unconscious but being moved out of ICU."

The relief hit harder than Savilla expected, and she moved to a tree stump and sat. "Thank God." She closed her eyes, taking in the good news. It might be a good holiday season after all. Dusk settled fast, and darkness threatened to close in around them.

"So." Kore snapped her out of her moment. "You said you can't get through to their parents?"

"Jade's phone died."

"Okay, that's an easy fix." He pulled a cell from his pocket. "If she knows the number, I can call it. My younger brothers have a solar-powered battery charger in the barn loft and a converter for recharging their phones. We can get her phone working again."

"Jade said getting a cell tower connection in Uganda requires time and patience. I'm not sure whether that means a few hours or a few days. But whether we connect or not, Jade says one wrong move could force her parents to return, and if that happens, they'll lose their right to adopt Aidan from Uganda. Is that possible?"

"I don't know. She's a smart kid."

Jade had explained to Savilla, as best she could, all there was to be afraid of if they made a wrong move. "She made one trip to Africa with her mom, and she loves Aidan. All three children hurt for how he's spent his life in an orphanage."

"I get all that, Savvy, but you have to be practical. Does Jade know anyone who can keep them for a week, let alone maybe five to seven weeks? My guess is no, or the parents wouldn't have asked a seventy-three-year-old woman to keep three children for that long." His tanned face deepened in color as emotions welled. Did he think the couple was taking advantage of his grandmother's nurturing nature?

"You're being unfair, Kore. Mammi D took a liking to Patti and Hank when the couple first moved to the area. Both are transplants from Germany, so they have no family here. I doubt any friends can take on three children with the craziest, busiest month of the year coming up. Most people are so frazzled they're barely keeping their sanity while dealing with their own children, let alone someone else's. Mammi D has chosen to be the local grandma those kids don't have."

"This kind of commitment was asking too much."

"Only Mammi D could decide that. Clearly, she thought sacrificing to keep three children for an extended period of time was worth it so Aidan could be adopted." She stood. "You know what? I'll figure this out on my own. Just let your parents know that, for tonight, I'll be at Mammi D's with the children." She started to walk off.

"And then what, Savvy?"

She turned. Apparently where she had once stirred love and humor in Kore, where she'd once been a friend and a support, she now easily stirred anger and frustration.

"I don't know, and I get that you're tired, under stress, and you don't like me very much these days, but evidently all you have to offer is your negative opinion. That's not the kind of advice I was looking for."

An almost inaudible laugh escaped Kore. "Nice to see you haven't lost your ability to stand up for yourself . . . at least with me."

She held her palms up, silently asking what he meant.

He walked to her. "Why didn't you put my brothers in their place the first time they made some snide remark?"

"Because I take ownership of what I've done, and from their point of view, I deserve far more than a few hurtful remarks. I understand that."

He barely shook his head. "That's ridiculous, Savvy. You don't allow anyone to pick on or bully you for any reason. It's not healthy or helpful for you or them."

She was weary of his tone, his anger boiling over. One day, in just another year or two, he would be grateful she'd released him. Until then, Savilla needed to avoid him when she could and find the internal fortitude to cope when she couldn't. "I'm glad Mammi D is doing better, and I hope the news about her continues to be only good."

With that said, she returned to the cabin.

*T*rying to shake off what she did to him, Kore began walking toward Jacob and Esther, and they met him halfway. "Sorry."

"No problem," Jacob said. "Everything okay?"

"Not exactly." Kore motioned toward the cabin, and the three of them walked in that direction. He wasn't ready to retreat. He needed time to think, and right now he wanted to sit in the outdoor furniture in Mammi D's front yard. "She doesn't want me drawn into it, and I don't want to be."

"It?" Jacob asked.

As Kore explained the situation with the three Adler children, they arrived at the furniture and sat. "It's a ridiculous predicament. If Savvy wanted my help finding somewhere for the kids to go, I would be on board. But she wants to take on keeping them so the parents can stay in Uganda, and I'm out." Kore leaned back, tapping the ends of his fingers together.

Jacob's brows knit. "It seems like way too much responsibility for too long. Most good neighbors would barely keep three children for an afternoon."

"Question." Esther raised her hand. "I hate to burst the bubble of good men, but your logic is faulty. It's cold and dark. Savilla is inside with three young children and no fire." She pointed at the chimney.

Why wasn't smoke coming out of it? Kore didn't know. "She doesn't need me taking care of her. Whether the need is fire, food, or what have you, her name fits the situation—Savvy." He gazed at the sky, looking past the barren treetops to see a few twinkling stars. That sounded good, but everyone needed help at times, and for Savvy, *now* was one of those times. Maybe she didn't have a fire because her back pain kept her from toting the needed wood.

When she returned to North Star, she may have been as skinny as David said, but she was a picture of health now, and that could mean she had surgery while she was gone, couldn't it? He shook free of those thoughts. They were too personal.

He had a practical matter poking at him. Two years ago he and Savvy had agreed to be Mammi D's backup for the Adler children, just in case she was under the weather after agreeing to keep the children. What would Mammi D expect of him in this situation?

"Great." He slumped in his chair. "Just what I need, some ridicu- lous reason that makes me agree to knock on that door and spend hours helping my ex." He stood. "A couple of years ago I gave Mammi D my word concerning the Adler children. I can't leave just yet, but you guys go back to my house. Get warm, eat, and rest."

Esther angled her head, eyeing her husband. Jacob stood and helped her up. "We volunteer to help. If nothing else, we make great referees . . . maybe."

"The youngest is under the weather."

Esther shrugged. "I won't snuggle close, but we've traveled all over the place and have been waited on by servers who clearly had a cold, or worse, and we didn't let any of that stop us."

Gratefulness mixed with a spot of relief. "Denki."

"You're welcome, but you will need to make it up to us. About the time the baby is born, we'll need all-night sitters."

Kore chuckled. "Dream on."

They followed him as he went to the door and knocked.

Savvy opened it. Kore stared at her and she at him. Was she as unsure as he was?

He managed a smile. "I needed a few minutes to bury my pessimism, and now I'm here to help."

Wariness melted from her beautiful face, and she returned his smile. "Denki." Peering behind him at Esther and Jacob, Savilla smiled while opening the door wide for them.

"No." Jade tugged on Savilla's sweater. "No strangers." Jade's wide eyes held fear. Didn't Jade recognize him? Kore wanted to ask, but he held his tongue.

Savilla knelt, looking up at Jade. "Sweetie." Savilla fidgeted with a large gold button on Jade's coat. "You were three children on your own earlier today, and now there are four adults who want to help. You can't live in the shed or the cabin on your own. You need food and heat. You have to get to school and do your homework at night. Demi may need a doctor if she doesn't start feeling better in the next day or two, and without signed papers of guardianship, I don't know that I can take her. I need advice and help."

Jade glanced at Jacob and Esther before frowning at Savilla. "You better know what you're doing."

"Jade, honey, I know what's not going to work, and sometimes that's all the information we have." Savvy stood.

Kore rubbed his hands, warming them. "This place could use some heat."

Little feet thundered against the wooden floor, and Chad slid to a stop, looking up at Kore. "Hey, I know you." He turned to Jade. "We know him. It's Kore, remember?"

Jade seemed to look at him for the first time. Recognition flashed in her eyes, and a sweet smile lifted her whole face. "Kore."

He poked her shoulder. "I was beginning to think you'd forgotten me." Kore put his hand on Chad's head. "Any helpers to get wood and build a fire?"

"Me." Chad raised his hand. "My dad let me use a hatchet a few times to make kindling from sticks that had fallen from trees."

"Ah, a good worker." Kore put his hands on the boy's shoulders. "We won't use a hatchet, but I'll need your kind of help."

The next four hours were a blur of activity as the adults worked on different tasks. They built a roaring fire, went for groceries, cooked a meal, and administered the newly purchased acetaminophen to reduce Demi's fever. They told Kore's parents what was going on, recharged Jade's cell phone, and found the original papers from the children's parents where Patti and Hank had granted Mammi D temporary guardianship.

The sink was filled with dirty dishes, and the children were finally asleep, stretched out on homemade pallets on the living room floor near the fireplace.

Savilla and Esther had made dinner, and the seven of them had eaten together. Despite the awkwardness between Kore and Savilla, they'd managed to speak nicely to each other. The banter and laughter passed easily between the adults and the children, providing a nice distraction.

Now Kore sat at the kitchen table with Jacob, Esther, and Savvy. He had a pen in hand, making notes on a legal pad concerning every aspect of this endeavor. Well, he had been making notes, but he was currently doodling circles. Black ink, going round and round and round. The movement sort of harmonized with his inner turmoil. Had Savilla broken up with him to be with someone else? If so, who? If not, what had happened that she chose to destroy a strong, loving relationship? He'd never imagined having the kind of friendship with anyone like he'd had with Savvy. So what happened?

He couldn't put the questions to rest, especially as they'd spent the last four hours working to help a family they were once acquainted with to be able to stay together. She could rearrange her life to fight for the Adler family but not for her and Kore?

The grandfather clock ticked loudly in the silence as the adults tried to work out a reasonable schedule.

"So . . ." Jacob broke the silence. "Your seamstress work is done solely out of your apartment. Is that right?"

"Ya, but Monday I can move what I need to do my sewing here."

What had happened to working out of Mr. Tang's place on the square? She had really liked working there, and Mr. Tang appreciated her skill. Since the man was Englisch, his shop ran an air conditioner and ceiling fans during the hot months, and heat was adjusted by the touch of a button in cool weather. She could walk to get a sandwich, and she'd loved watching people pass by, especially after the Christmas lights went up. Why would she give that up to work in the closed-off space of a carriage apartment? "You don't do any sewing for Tang's Tailor anymore?"

"Nee."

Short answers seemed her specialty tonight. She was different—still kind and gentle, but she was walled off somehow. David had said she was detached, but that wasn't really the right word. She was hiding behind a barricade. It was subtle, but he saw it as clearly as if there were a No Trespassing sign around her neck. The Savilla he once knew had been open and relaxed about her life—or at least he'd thought she was. Had he only seen what he wanted to?

The chimes on the grandfather clock began tolling eleven.

Esther peered into the living room. "I hope the clock doesn't wake them."

"I can stop the pendulum. That'll stop the chimes." Savilla rose. "I need to check on Demi anyway to see if her fever has broken." She took the candlestick holder by its handle. "While I'm up, I want to get a few more blankets out of the attic."

"Need some help?" Esther asked.

"I know that attic like the back of my hand. You have done too much work already. Just sit tight."

Kore watched Savvy disappear, his eyes lingering.

Esther turned the knob on the kerosene lantern, raising the wick a tiny bit. "After working side by side for a few hours, I can easily see why you were willing to give up your Englisch travels to return home for her."

"Ya." Kore set down his pen. "That's the easy part—seeing her personality and the quality person she is. Understanding some of her decisions is a totally different topic."

Jacob removed the legal pad from in front of Kore, turning it so he could read the list. "According to Savilla's schedule, if you could keep the children on Saturdays, that would be a lot of help."

He didn't like the idea, but he could do it. Mammi D would want that of him. "I'll leave after work on Fridays, stay at Mamm and Daed's, and walk here Saturday morning to get the children out of her hair."

"That's one way of doing it," Jacob said. "But I see no reason why you couldn't take off early on Thursdays, even be here in time to share that evening meal with them, and be available to help Savilla all day on Fridays."

Kore looked up, pinning Jacob with a stare. "I know what you're thinking—reconciliation between Savvy and me. That's not going to happen."

"Okay." Jacob held up his hands in surrender. "I was just checking. Besides, I guess she could be seeing someone."

Esther yawned. "Amid all the strategy we've discussed, brainstorming how she could keep up with her paying jobs while taking care of the children, she's not once mentioned needing to talk to a guy about her plans or needing a weekend night off so she can go on a date."

Kore had noted the same thing. Maybe David was right. Whoever she had been seeing was gone from her life.

Jacob stood and moved behind his wife. He rubbed her shoulders. "Kumm. You're sleeping for two." He kissed the top of her head. "You need rest."

She nodded, and they headed to the bedroom. Savilla had put clean sheets on the bed a few hours ago. The four of them would stay the night, hoping to receive a call from the children's parents.

Savilla walked back into the kitchen. "I made up the couch for you."

He supposed he should move to it and try to get some sleep. She would sleep in Mammi D's tiny guest room.

"Thanks." He tapped the end of the pen on the table. "It's a huge undertaking to provide a place, meals, and help with homework for those children for that length of time."

"It will be worth it to the family, maybe especially to Jade and Aidan."

"I'm sure we'll hear from the Adler parents soon, and I'll talk to Daed tomorrow about you and the children staying here for a while— for several weeks."

She gestured toward the legal pad. "I think you've listed everything I will need to do and how to do it."

"I hope so."

Her smile carried gratefulness. "I really appreciate the help, Kore. There aren't many men who would set aside their personal feelings to lend a hand like this."

"It's not as if I had much choice, but you're welcome." He read over the list one last time. He imagined Mammi D's cabin wasn't set up for sewing like Savvy's apartment was. But it was clear that the children couldn't stay at Savvy's. He knew the place. It was tiny, and it would be quite cold in winter. "Why live above the carriage house, Savvy?"

She blinked, seemingly caught off guard by his question. "Oh. That came out of the blue."

"I didn't want to ask in front of the others."

"Unlike my parents' home, it's quiet. Since it's on the edge of town, it makes a good place for people to pick up what I've sewn for them, and I can get to Rebekah's really easily from there. But more than anything, I needed space."

He put the pen on the table, fidgeting with it. "I . . . I don't get it. From what? I was gone."

"From dreams that were broken. I needed a new place to start fresh."

From broken dreams? Theirs or hers with someone else? He flicked one end of the pen, making it spin on the table. "You could ask the church ministers if you can keep the Adler children at their home until the parents return."

She pulled her cup of cocoa closer. "No. Jade could be grown with children of her own before the ministers hand down a decision. Besides, Mammi D's is better situated for my needs. I can get to my apartment and the birthing center much quicker and easier from here than from the Adler place."

He nodded, and they fell into silence, each watching the light from the kerosene lamp dance on the tabletop. She was staying up, hoping to hear from the Adler parents. He remained there because he couldn't make himself leave the room. Questions hounded him about the breakup, and he had to ask. It wasn't wise or guarded, but he had to at least question her.

"I need to know something . . . if that's okay."

She ran her fingers around the rim of her mug, but she didn't respond.

"Savvy, I heard that you left North Star not long after I did. Rumors say you had someone . . . somewhere."

She stared at the table, her eyes filling with tears. "Would . . . accepting that help?"

Accepting it would only cause a multitude of other questions, starting with, when had they met? How did she get to know someone so well while dating Kore that she would break up with him? What did the other guy offer her that Kore couldn't? Did his failing business make that much difference to her? What had happened that she and *whoever* didn't end up together? But while pondering those things, he realized she hadn't actually given him an answer. She'd simply asked a question.

He kept his eye on the pen, making it spin on the table again. "Truth would help. I just thought we were so good together . . . until—"

"We were. There was no one else."

His heart seemed to stop for a moment. It helped to know that, but at the same time, the news simply confused him. If there had been someone else, the breakup would have made sense. Or if he and Savvy had been prone to arguing or grated on each other's nerves. But none of that was a part of their relationship—not that he knew of.

Using her thumbnail, she scraped a dried spot of hot chocolate off the table. "What happened wasn't about you or even us. We were great friends, but marriage . . . I . . . I thought I could do it, but . . . it wasn't the right thing . . . for us."

Did that mean she didn't want to marry at all or just not him? He'd known she was unusual concerning her views on marriage. Most Amish women longed for marriage. She'd been very relaxed about it. That was part of what had made their relationship work so well when he was living Englisch and their only contact was his occasional visit home and his phone calls. Whether he was coming to North Star or simply calling, she was there for him, content to be his friend. He was the one who started pushing for more, and it began with him moving back home to go through instructions so they could marry.

Still, she had been excited about those changes at first, hadn't she? Maybe he'd pushed too hard too soon, and she just wasn't ready.

Reaching across the table, Savilla stopped the pen from spinning. When he looked up, their eyes locked. "I promise that if you haven't found the right girl yet, you will, and when you do, you'll have children. Your house will overflow with love and happiness, and you'll have it all. I can't give you that."

Her countenance radiated that she believed her words with all that was in her. He had a lot less faith concerning it. She had been the one. The only one.

Jade's phone shimmied across the table, buzzing as the word *Mom* showed on the screen. Kore gestured toward it. "She'll want to talk to you."

*S*avilla put more of her sewing items in a large basket. She paused, looking around her carriage-house apartment, trying to plan for all the personal and work items she would need while staying in the cabin with the children.

She glanced at the clock. Ten. She'd promised Chad and Demi that she would be at the stop, waiting for them when they stepped off the bus. She was learning quite a lot about being the sole caregiver of children. When she was attending school as a child, the day seemed quite long. Now that she had a full workday to accomplish before the children returned home, the school day seemed quite short. She had made breakfasts, packed lunches, and walked them to the bus stop. The elementary school bus ran last, so once Demi and Chad were on it, Savilla had hurried to the birthing clinic and gotten her paperwork done for the day. She didn't know why Demi had run a fever Saturday and some of Sunday, but she seemed fine now.

The elementary school let out at a quarter past three. This schedule cut Savilla's typical workday from fourteen hours to about six, unless she could squeeze in a few hours of sewing after the children arrived home from school or after they were in bed.

The rhythmic thudding on the steps leading to her carriage apartment announced that someone was arriving. Had she forgotten that a client was coming by? Since most of her work came through decorators, businesses that needed uniforms, and wedding planners, Savilla didn't see clients often, and when she did, the visits were scheduled in advance. Still, she needed to put a sign in the window, one that gave people Mammi D's address. A moment later there was a tap at her door.

"It's open."

The hinge creaked as it slowly opened. "Hi." David Detweiler remained outside, looking unsure of himself. "May I come in?"

"Depends. What's your purpose?" She was in no hurry for him to come inside and close the door. She had on her coat, and it was just as cold inside as out because she hadn't started a fire in the potbelly stove. It would take longer to build heat than she intended to be here.

David seemed to be searching for words. Kore had been right. She shouldn't let anyone give her a hard time over her decisions. Maybe she'd allowed it because she felt she deserved whatever verbal lashings came her way. But no more. She was without Kore, and that was a high enough price.

"An apology and a helping hand . . . if you'll accept it."

She left him standing in the doorway. "Ah. I see your big brother's handprints all over this visit."

His eyes fixated on the rough-hewed flooring. "Ya. He's angry with us."

"And you're angry with me."

David shifted, looking uneasy. "Pretty much, ya."

She walked closer, knowing he needed to look in her eyes as she spoke. "I didn't cheat on Kore. I don't date, not that it's anyone's business."

David's blank stare indicated shock and embarrassment, and she knew he needed a minute to absorb her words.

When Kore had shared that rumor with her the day before yesterday, she'd been dumbfounded. Of all the possible rumors about her strange behavior, she'd expected ones about her being a little nutty or taking up drinking and leaving to get clean, but cheating? on Kore?

That one hadn't entered her mind, and when he brought up the topic, she had to be honest. Her goal in the breakup was for him to find someone else. If he thought she'd cheated on him, he might be leery of trusting the next woman in his life. She hated the thought of him with another woman, but love wanted the best for the other person. She no longer fit that description.

David's eyes finally reflected acceptance of what she'd said. He believed her. "Then I really am sorry." He looked mortified. "I just . . . I still don't understand why you ended it with him."

"You don't have to, do you?"

"I guess that's true. It sounds as if my younger brothers and I have a lot to make up for."

"*Gut.*" She smiled. "It seems I'll need a good bit of help until the Adler family returns home."

"And I would appreciate getting to be helpful during this time."

"He's that angry, huh?"

There weren't many men like Kore, and she would always grieve losing him.

David removed his black felt hat, nodding. "He is, but I really am sorry. Oh, and one other thing I need to clarify. I also have a request for you to sew some clothes for me and some of the other youth for a Christmas caroling event—for pay of course."

She motioned for him to come in. "Apology accepted. A helping hand is welcome. And sewing is what I do best." She moved to the window and peered out. "You drove a wagon."

"*Ya,* I thought that might be more useful than a buggy, especially that rickety little thing you own."

"Good thinking." She went to her bolts of fabric. "I need the first ten of these boxed up."

"Got it."

The task of planning and sorting was much more difficult since

her supplies were limited and she would work from here one day each
week . . . maybe.

Kore needed a home base for keeping the children on Saturdays,
and she couldn't imagine being able to spread out her work in that small
cabin with three children underfoot. His parents had enough on their
plate, so Kore taking the children to his house wasn't a good plan.

Maybe he should take the children to the Adler home on Saturdays. The church ministers wouldn't object to Kore staying in an Englisch home all day once a week. But they would balk at Savilla staying
night and day, seven days a week for a month or more, especially since
there were rumors flying around about her. Mean ones.

She went to a cubby and pulled out a box of hanging files. This
held all the information concerning her various projects and the dead-
lines. She needed to take this with her.

Thoughts of Kore remained close as she worked. He was gone
when she woke Sunday morning, and she hadn't seen him since. Esther
and Jacob hung around about half of the day, helping her with the children before returning to Kore's parents' home. Today they were going
through some antique stores in Lancaster before meeting Kore at the
hospital so the three of them could grab a bite of lunch together.

Once she'd understood what Esther was searching for, Savilla realized she might be of some help. Because of Rebekah's position as a
midwife, she was well connected in these parts. The husbands of the
women in labor spent hours talking to her about their businesses and
family matters. Rebekah was a wealth of information. When it came
to finding antique French furniture, Savilla imagined Rebekah knew
someone who knew someone who could lead them to a boatload of that
kind of furniture. Well, okay, maybe not a boatload but at least a few
good pieces. Savilla had asked Rebekah about it while at the clinic earlier today, and Rebekah said she'd make some calls. Savilla gave her
Esther's cell number in case she got a lead.

"Hey, David, any word on Mammi D?"

"She's breathing on her own, and her vitals are excellent, but that's all the improvement thus far. We were told her latest scan indicated good brain activity, and the bruise inside her skull is healing quicker than expected. She could wake at any moment, so Kore hasn't left the hospital since before daylight yesterday morning. Any updates on the Adler family?"

"Not since before midnight on Saturday. Kore probably filled you in on that conversation, right?"

"Ya."

After the Adler parents finally got a cell tower connection and heard the panicky messages from Jade, they were beside themselves when they got through to Savilla. She and Kore both had to talk to Patti and Hank to make the situation clearer and to assure them their children were fine.

Patti cried a lot, upset to be caught in such a difficult situation, sickened by all her children had gone through. Of course she was saddened by the news of Mammi D's accident, but if she rushed home to her children, she would be leaving Aidan behind forever.

Savilla had to share her honest opinion—the Adler family was in a battle to bring that boy home, and they needed to stay and fight. She assured Patti and Hank that she would be diligent to provide a safe environment for the children.

While Savilla gave additional reassurances, Kore woke Jade so she could talk to her mother. That seemed to help both mom and daughter. Before the conversation was over, the two younger children also spoke to their parents. Savilla imagined that was going to be one very expensive phone bill, but they got everything as straight as they possibly could. In the end the only way the parents could feel comfortable staying in Uganda was if Savilla promised that either she or Kore would be with the children the entire time they weren't in school. It helped that when Savilla and Kore were a couple, Patti and Hank had come by Mammi D's one evening to visit while Savilla and Kore were there. The four became acquainted pretty well that evening.

Before the phone call ended Saturday night, Patti and Hank expressed sincere gratitude to Savilla and Kore. Oddly, it was Savilla who felt blessed by this predicament. It was eye-opening how deeply it touched Savilla's mind and heart to be a part of helping these children. She'd never experienced assisting a family increase their young brood outside of the birthing center. The joy and sense of awe it stirred in her was surprising. She was honored that God had involved her.

The children, especially Jade, were in a much better emotional state all day yesterday. But it was clear to Savilla that they were scathed by the trauma of staying by themselves Friday night and most of Saturday. She and Kore had some work cut out to generate a sense of security for them until their mom and dad returned home. It was hard to imagine that the children might be without their parents over Christmas, but the Adlers had known that was likely to happen the moment they received the call to go to Uganda.

She pointed out a box of goods. "Would you take this down for me?"

David grabbed the box and hurried out the door.

His showing up was a lifesaver actually. Otherwise she would have had to haul these things to Mammi D's and unload them by herself. She could have asked her parents or one of her siblings for help, but life was busy for everyone. Besides, it was important to stand on her own two feet. Or not. Stand or fall, she would not be a needy single gal for her already-overworked friends and family. But since David volunteered, it would make this transition day much easier.

They moved bolts of fabric to the wagon and a dozen almost-finished uniforms for a local machinist shop. When it was time to move the half-made bridesmaids dresses for an Englisch wedding, she lined the wagon with sheets and took those down herself, not wanting David to snag the chiffon or smudge the burgundy fabric.

When she reentered the room, David was kneeling with her personal mail scattered all around him. He was grabbing up papers, and she saw her invoices from the hospital on the floor. Her heart skipped a beat. She'd told him to grab the file box in the cubby, but she had set the file of client info on the counter earlier.

Stupid, stupid mistake, Savilla.

But why had the items spilled? Her heart raced, but if she didn't remain cool about it, it would be a dead giveaway. She ambled his way. "Have a mishap?"

David jolted. "Ya." He set the box upright. "But I'm not sure this is the file you meant for me to grab."

She knelt, scooping up pages of unpaid bills. "This is personal mail, mostly bills. Just shove everything back in the box. I'll organize it later." Trying to sound calm and move without looking harried, she made short work of picking up the papers. They crammed the stuff back in the box.

While he returned the box to its cubby, she saw a few hospital bills on the floor near the client box. The dates and amount still owed were highlighted in yellow. She went to them, snatched them up, and tucked them inside the client box before David saw. "You know, your wagon is full, and I should probably take this box with me. We wouldn't want a box of papers falling out of the wagon and littering the roadway."

Her heart pounded, and she hoped he'd seen nothing that was telling. If she asked him what he had seen, it would only draw attention to the very thing she was trying to hide. All she could do was hope that either he hadn't noticed where the bills were from or he would keep his mouth shut.

*K*ore wasn't sure what had possessed him to tell the driver to stop at Savilla's apartment. The best way to handle their arrangement with the Adler children was minimal contact between Savvy and him. He needed to be kind and friendly for the children's sake, reliable and helpful for her sake, and distant for his sake.

So why was he here? He had to be. He was as drawn to stop as old friends were now committed to holding a family together. It was inconvenient and unwelcome, but nonetheless, people huddled together around the kitchen table at midnight and agreed to temporarily dismantle their lives for this. To do any less was unbearable. And so it was with Savilla and him. He was here because it would be unbearable not to be.

He turned from the front passenger seat of the truck to catch a glimpse of Jacob and Esther. "How about I release the driver, and we'll use Savilla's rig?" If she wouldn't agree to that, they could use David's or walk.

Jacob nodded. "Fine by us." He held up Esther's phone. "We are free until the private showing of the pieces in Lancaster tomorrow afternoon at one."

Once the driver stopped his car, Kore paid the man. Cold air slapped him in the face when he got out of the heated vehicle. David was at the wagon, strapping down his load. Savvy was at the top of the stairs, coat on and a box in hand as she locked the door.

"David." Kore spoke softly. He motioned for David, and then he moved to the foot of the stairs to wait for Savvy.

Even though she was coming down the steps, she didn't see any of them until she was on the third to the last step. She gasped. "Kore."

"In your own world much?"

She chuckled. "I prefer to call it the power of focus."

"Ya, well, you and David focus on this—Mammi D is awake. Has her full memory, as far as we can tell."

"Ach, wie wunderbaar!" Her smile, the way her eyes soaked in the news with such joy—that's why he was here. His news was amazing, but it wouldn't have been completely satisfying without this moment. Only now he wanted more.

David grinned, slapping him on the back. "Ya, what she said—oh, how wonderful!" Kore sensed David had apologized. Savvy was hard to figure out in some areas, but one thing he did know about her was that she didn't hold grudges.

"I agree. It's great," Kore said. "She won't be released for a week or more, and then she may be moved to a rehabilitation hospital before coming to Mamm's place, but it's wonderful news."

"Hey, Kore," Jacob said. "Tell her Mammi D's first words."

"She started waking a few hours ago, and every time her first words were 'the children . . . the Adler children.'" Kore took the box from Savvy. "That's all she could manage before she dozed off again . . . or whatever they call that when someone is in and out of that type of consciousness. Anyway, I was able to assure her each time that they were being well cared for. When she was finally alert, she drilled me on the topic." He laughed. "I glossed over the rough start the children had. We can talk about that when she's stronger. I told her about our plans and how we're juggling the responsibility, and she sends her love and gratefulness to you."

"And you," Savilla said.

"What I got was a wag of her finger, assuring me it's a good thing I stepped up to the plate." He laughed. "Family expectations are written in stone. You know that."

"Without a doubt."

Had a trace of something sad flickered in her eyes?

"We have more good news," Esther said. "You were right to ask for Rebekah's help. She called me about ninety minutes ago with the name and number of a collector who could help us. Five or six calls later, we made contact with a woman who texted images of two pieces that meet the criteria of what my client is looking for. Can you believe that? Two pieces, and we'll look at them tomorrow to decide which one is better."

"I think it's a little-known secret how very connected an older midwife is in a community that's knit together by generations of parentage."

Kore shifted the box. "Speaking of being connected and knit together and such, let's celebrate the great news about Mammi D."

"I'm really excited about the news, but"—Savilla glanced at the wagon stuffed with her seamstress items—"I have work to do, a lot of it, and it's only three hours before the two youngest children are out of school."

Kore hadn't felt this good in a really long time, and he wasn't easily dropping the idea of a luncheon celebration. "David will take all the stuff to Mammi D's and unload it while the four of us grab a bite at Paupers Den."

"Ya, I can do that," David said. "Because there were two of us loading the wagon, you're way ahead of where you thought you'd be by this point of the day. Go, drink some coffee and eat a sandwich."

"Ya, what he said." Kore smiled.

Savilla narrowed her eyes at Kore. "Why do I want to say 'get thee behind me'?"

"Because Esther is standing in front of you?"

Esther's mouth opened wide at the insinuation that she was the one tempting Savilla. Then she broke into laughter. "Thanks, Kore."

"Sorry. I'm wired right now, and I couldn't resist." He pointed at the rig. "Paupers Den? Best coffee in town. Charming setting. Probably already playing Christmas music." He didn't need to sell Savilla on what the place was like. His description was a coded message, a way of saying "let's rewind to when we were just friends hanging out." The encrypted meaning wouldn't escape her. The first time they did anything together, they'd agreed to keep the relationship as just friendship, and then they'd walked into North Star in mid-November and had coffee and sandwiches at Paupers.

"You're sure?" She lifted one brow, obviously aware of his meaning. "I'm sure."

Her eyes closed as if relief was pouring into her as it had into him when Mammi D woke. "I would like that, Kore."

The four of them went to her rig and climbed in, the girls in the back and the men up front. Why had she sold her really nice carriage for this piece of junk? He tucked the file box on the seat between him and Jacob before he took the reins in hand.

Savvy turned to Esther. "I'm looking for a way to help the children get over the trauma of arriving at Mammi D's and finding that no one was there for them. All they could voice last night and this morning were fears that I might not be there for them after they arrived home from school."

"They need something positive that fills the same spaces—like rather than thinking about if you're going to be there, they could be focusing on an after-school treat or something."

"Like chores." Kore teased. "That would do it." He looked in the rearview mirror, and Savilla's eyes met his. "Oh, I've got it—a puppy." He teased.

Savilla's eyes widened. "That would do it!"

He laughed. "You can't give them a puppy without parental consent."

"Ya, I can, because—" They entered a covered wooden bridge. Had her facial expression changed, or were the shadows inside the wooden tunnel playing tricks? Maybe she was being pulled into the same powerful memories as he was. Two years ago late one night as he drove her home from a date, he'd stopped the carriage in the middle of this bridge, and they'd kissed for the first time.

Trying to break free of the memory, he focused on the creaking of the rig and the clomping of the horse's hoofs as they crossed the bridge. The noise of it was too loud for her to be heard anyway, so the pause in conversation didn't raise any questions. When they came out from the bridge, she seemed lost in thought. Did the loss of who they once were haunt her as it did him? She didn't resume her comments.

"You were going to tell us why the puppy idea would work," Esther said.

"Oh, uh, I have a birthday coming up in two weeks, so they can be told the puppy is for me. They'll love it just the same and be just as excited to have it around. If their parents are on board with having a dog, I'll give it to them."

"I'm not sure about this plan, Sav." Kore tapped the reins against Zena's back and clicked his tongue. "If the Adlers don't want a dog, you'll have a pet for ten to fifteen years, and you live in an apartment up a long flight of steps."

She shoved his shoulder. "Bury the pessimism, buddy. I'm sticking to my idea. You're in charge of telling the children tonight about the birthday present and finding a good dog as soon as possible."

"Me?" Kore chuckled. "How come I'm getting stuck with doing chores?"

"Oh, zip it, Detweiler. You'll spend a week or two finding a puppy that's well suited for the family, and you'll be a hero in the children's eyes for bringing it into their lives. I, on the other hand, will be stuck housebreaking it, and I'm likely to spend the next decade and a half taking care of it."

"And your point?"

"You know"—Savilla leaned in toward Esther, speaking conspiratorially—"I hope the puppy doesn't whine as much as Kore."

"Hey!" Kore glanced at her in the mirror. "I heard that."

"Even over all your whining?" Savilla grinned, looking at him in the mirror. Then she seemed to realize something outside the carriage. She extended her arm between him and Jacob, pointing out the front window. "Look, they're already putting up Christmas decorations."

North Star at Christmastime had always been a favorite of theirs. Kore knew that, even with a friendship rebuilt between Savvy and him, it'd be the last they observed together. He noted the holly already on the streetlamps. "Let's break some Amish rules and make this Christmas season really special for the children. Christmas tree in Mammi D's home, wreath on the door, stockings on the mantel—the works."

"That's perfect, Kore."

The next six weeks would be gone before he knew it, and there was nothing he could do to hold on to this Christmas or have another one similar to it. All he could do was enjoy it until it became a hundred old memories and heartache.

CHAPTER ELEVEN

S avilla felt a little hand tapping on her shoulder.

"Savvy." Demi's sweet voice matched her gentle pats.

Savilla opened her eyes to see only the black metal of her machine. She was slumped in her chair, her forehead pressed against the frame of the sewing head. She took in an achy breath as she straightened her spine. "Morning, sweetie." Savilla rubbed her eyes, willing her body to wake.

"Mornin'." The little girl smiled, holding a faceless cloth Amish doll that Savilla had found in the attic.

The Christmas tree in the corner of the room caught her eye—cut, set up, and decorated yesterday, the Friday after Thanksgiving. Kore had returned from Virginia on Thursday morning, and he spent Thanksgiving Day with his family while the children and Savilla had Thanksgiving with her family.

Mammi D had been released from the hospital the day before Thanksgiving, so Kore had time with her on Thanksgiving Day, and Savilla got a chance to visit her yesterday at the Detweiler home while he stayed with the children at the cabin. Seeing Mammi D and getting to talk to her had been the best Christmas present ever, a really early one because it wouldn't be the first of December for a few more days yet.

Kore came to the cabin Friday midmorning. Savilla once again set aside all her sewing projects, and they began giving the children a Christmas season that was as close to what they were used to as possible. Kore hitched a horse to a flatbed board on wheels. A flatbed board usually had runners, and it was used for hauling wood during a snowy winter. But since they didn't have a covering of snow just yet, they used one with wheels, and the children rode on it while he and Savilla took turns leading the horse as they searched for the right Christmas tree.

What a perfect day yesterday had been. It only confirmed what she already knew—whether working or playing, she and Kore were a matchless team.

Once they found the ideal tree, they dragged it back to the cabin. After several failed attempts, Kore figured out how to get the huge tree to stand up inside. It was now stable . . . they hoped. How did the Englisch get their Christmas trees to stand properly?

Savilla had popped popcorn, and all of them helped sew it onto a string to lace around the tree. They made homemade ornaments using every imaginable thing—scraps of material, pine cones, spray paint, and cookie cutters to cut out some kind of dough made of flour and salt.

After dinner Kore helped her clean up the kitchen before leaving. Once Savilla tucked the children in bed, she tried to sleep, but her seamstress work kept calling to her, so she got up, lit two gas pole lights, and started working.

Still trying to get moving, Savilla brought the little girl's hand to her lips and kissed it. "You hungry?" Her voice reminded her of a bullfrog. Why was it so cold in here? She rubbed her eyes, feeling the tiredness in her achy muscles. "Coffee." Savilla breathed. "I need coffee." She stretched, and her breath caught in her throat.

Demi was beside her, but three faces were less than ten feet away, near the front door, staring back at her—Jade, Chad, and Kore.

A half-dozen thoughts hit—the day had begun, she was in her nightgown, her hair was down, the children were up, the room was way too cold, and Kore had already arrived. Desperate to cover her shimmering white gown she'd made from leftover wedding-dress material, she shot out of the chair and grabbed her housecoat, which she had peeled out of last night because sewing on a nonelectric treadle machine was a workout. At least she'd designed this nightgown to be very modest—long sleeves, no plunging neckline—but the satiny material was thin with ruching at the waist, making it fit snug. Trying to shove her arms into the fleecy robe, she dropped it. Twice! Finally with it on, she pulled it tight, wrapping her arms about her waist. Who needed coffee? She was now wide awake, and her heart was pounding in her ears. Nightgowns for her were much like her beloved boots—with so much womanhood scrubbed from her life, they helped her feel feminine and attractive.

Demi wiggled her hand, as if saying hello all over again. "Me and Bell are hungry."

Savilla's eyes moved to Kore's. What was he doing here this early? They'd agreed he wouldn't arrive before eight today. She glanced at the clock. It was 8:03.

She turned her attention to Demi. "And what would you and your doll like for breakfast?"

"Candy."

The answer caught Savilla off guard, and she laughed. Children had a way of zapping all tension from a room. They were also skilled at adding it. "I'm afraid that Bell needs more nutrition than candy, and you need to set a good example for her."

"I did set a good example." The little girl frowned, while bobbing her head. "I had eggs, fruit, and yogurt for breakfast all week. Daddy says that Saturdays are a minivacation from the workweek and that we should have fun."

"Ya, Amish daddies say that Saturdays are for making up for work missed during the school week." She placed her hand on the little girl's head. "I think we should blend the two ideas. What do you think?"

"If you say that's a good thing to do, I agree."

Savilla took the girl by the hand. "Then let's get that started."

"Wait." Chad caused them to stop short. "In our house the men cook on Saturdays. I want me and Kore to fix breakfast . . . after we get the fire going again."

"Ah, the fire being out explains why it's so cold in here." Smiling, she mimicked shuddering while smoothing the boy's hair.

Chad looked up at Kore. "Can you cook?"

"Of course he can. My mom and I taught him how to make several things—homemade doughnuts, funnel cake, and hot chocolate." They would prepare the goods to sell at the Amish-made ice rink during the winter, and they'd use the proceeds to help pay bills or buy Christmas gifts for poor families with sick children—Amish or Englisch.

"That true?" Chad put his little hand in Kore's, looking proud to be like him.

Kore's attention didn't move from Savilla, but he nodded in response.

Savilla, go to the kitchen! But she couldn't make herself move. Her eyes stayed glued on their hands. Kore's large palm gently swallowed Chad's hand.

Kore needed to find the right woman and have sons of his own. And daughters. Her eyes stung with tears, and her breathing was labored. *Dear God, it hurts.*

Somewhere inside she found a glimmer of strength to pull herself together. She pointed at Chad's feet. "If you're going outside to get wood, you'll need something on those bare feet . . . and your coat."

Jade held out her hand for Demi's, and the little girl took it. "Come on, Chad," Jade said. "I think your boots are under Miss Elizabeth's bed."

The children left, and suddenly she and Kore were in a room that seemed to be shrinking by the second. She should be happy. Live in the moment. Extract every ounce of joy from this magical time God had given her. In the words of the poet Horace, she needed to *carpe diem*— seize the day. Her life seemed to fit with what the poet was saying. It was not hers to see the end that God had for her. She had today, and today was beautiful.

She started toward the kitchen. "I'll make coffee."

Kore grabbed her arm, stopping her. "What happened to us, Savvy?"

He was shaking with intensity, and she opened her mouth to finally tell him the truth. Oh, how she longed to break her silence. But the words wouldn't come. She stood there like a voiceless waif, tears in her eyes, wishing for the millionth time that she could bear him children. Men like Kore were loyal to the death. If he knew her secrets, he'd stay by her side for all the wrong reasons.

Hell would freeze over before she would do that to him. If she had known before they fell in love that she would be unable to bear children, she would've told him, giving him the choice to move forward with the relationship or say good-bye. But she hadn't known until after he left the Englisch world and moved back home. Her specialist had been dealing with women with this condition for twenty-nine years, and he said he'd never seen a case as bad as hers.

Her heart would break when he fell in love with someone else. It would break again when her dreams of having his children came true for his wife. But she couldn't make herself say anything that would prevent that from happening.

Kore released her arm. "Okay." His sultry whisper was haunting. He pressed his palms against his eyes and took a deep breath. "We leave it as it is." He lowered his hands, taking a step back. His breathing was labored as he held out his right hand. "Teammates until the parents return home."

"Ya." She was sick of tears filling her eyes. It had to stop. She demanded it stop. Sniffling, she held out her hand. "Teammates until then."

K ore ignored the heaviness inside his chest as he pulled a pan of cookies from the oven. The cabin looked, felt, and even smelled of Christmas.

The fresh sugar cookies actually had little to do with Christmas. Monday would be Savilla's twenty-fifth birthday, but Kore couldn't be here then, so the children were celebrating it tonight. Saturday was a good day to have a birthday party. Besides, Savilla and the children would go to her family's home after school on Monday to have a meal and cake on her birthday. Since birthday cake was on the menu for Monday, Jade, Chad, and Demi wanted to make Christmas cookies for Savilla.

No wonder Savilla had been slumped over her sewing machine when he arrived this morning. She couldn't catch a break to get work done. But Savilla was at her sewing machine now, her right foot going to and fro on the treadle as fast as possible. The girls, Jade and Demi, were at the kitchen table icing and decorating already-cooled cookies. Chad was filling up the woodbin again, preparing for another cold winter's night. The boy could bring in only a few pieces at a time, but he loved being given that job.

Kore glanced outside, checking on Chad. He was gathering two pieces of split wood from the pile. A wintry sunlight spread across an orange and purple sky as the sun began to set. All three of the children seemed to be doing well. One thing that seemed to help them was corresponding with their parents. Phone calls from Uganda were nearly impossible, but e-mails were another matter. So either Savilla or Kore took them to the library regularly to use the Internet and computers.

After a bit of research about dogs, Kore felt a Labrador would have the right temperament in the long run for either the children or Savilla. It'd taken him two weeks to find an excellent breeder—one who didn't do puppy-mill breeding and didn't allow familial interbreeding. If Savilla intended never to marry—if that was really the issue—he hoped she would keep this dog. The Lab pup sounded as if it would be a really good dog.

In order to get the puppy here in time for her birthday, Kore had to enlist Jacob and Esther's help. The owner of the puppy was in southern New Hampshire, and since Jacob and Esther had gone to Maine to spend Thanksgiving with his older brother's family, they were going to get the puppy on their way home.

Were the holidays always this nonstop busy if one was responsible for children?

Chad walked in the front door with an armful of wood and dumped it into the bin. Kore received a text message. He pulled his phone out and read it. Jacob and Esther were pulling into the driveway. Time for Savvy and Kore to sneak out to the shed as planned. He'd wanted her to get a few minutes with the puppy without the children underfoot. After all, it was likely to be her dog for a lifetime, and if she needed to back out, now was the time!

He left the kitchen. Savilla was at her machine, but he caught her eye and nodded toward the back door. She acknowledged his gesture and began gathering the yards of material that flowed from the machine and surrounded her.

God, what is her issue? It was an old prayer, one he'd begun asking the day she broke up with him.

Chad stood over the woodbin, knocking dirt off his coat.

Kore walked to him. "That's a good job, buddy." He helped brush debris from Chad's coat. "Hang up your jacket and join your sisters at the table. You'll want to decorate cookies for Savvy's birthday party tonight. We'll have supper in a bit."

Chad hurried out of the room, yanking off his coat as he went.

Kore took his jacket off a peg, and while Savilla slid into her coat, he moved to the table. He rapped his knuckles against the wood. "We are going to step outside for a few minutes. If you need us, open the back door and call us. Do not argue. Do not leave the house. Are we clear?"

Chad mumbled around a mouthful of cookies. "Got it."

Demi pointed to a specific cookie. "I made that one for you, Kore."

"Thank you. I'll save it until after we have some dinner." He gestured to the two younger ones. "Jade, you got this?"

She put a dollop of blue icing on a cookie. "With my eyes closed."

"Chad." Savilla placed a glass of milk in front of him. "That's the last cookie you can have until after supper."

"Okay." He gulped down the milk.

Kore opened the back door, and Savilla went out.

He closed the door behind him, whispering, "Jacob and Esther are in the shed with the puppy."

"Okay." She crossed the porch and started down the steps. "I'm not sure I understand the secretiveness. You think I would change my mind about the puppy at this point?"

That seemed like a bad question coming from her, but he held tight to his thoughts. "Indulge me."

His words came out sharp and sarcastic, and she stopped short and turned toward him. "Are you up for this? If not, I can make an excuse to Esther and Jacob for—"

"I'm fine, but thanks." He sighed. "Today just feels as if it's been a week long." But it was his fault more than hers. She'd made her wishes known a year ago, and he pushed against them this morning, hoping to get an answer. He got one. The same one he'd gotten during the breakup—they weren't going to work out. Apparently to her that was sufficient.

"I'm sorry, Kore. This is really difficult for both of us."

"Is it?"

The back door opened, and Kore hushed.

"Hey." Chad licked icing off his thumb. "Jade said I need a blank piece of paper to make a birthday card."

"Go on to the shed, Savvy. I'll get it."

"Okay. I have some blank paper in my file box with client info. It's on the top of the bookshelf."

"I'll find it." Kore went toward Chad. "Right?"

Chad nodded. "I know where the box is, but I can't reach it."

They went inside. Kore grabbed the file box from the shelf and set it on a table. He pulled out a stack of blank paper and passed it to Chad. "Good?"

Chad flipped through it. "Thanks!" Then he frowned. "Wait." He pulled one paper from the stack. "You better put this back." He held it out. "It's not blank."

Kore glanced. "You're right. Thanks."

Chad ran to the kitchen, and Kore glanced over the paper, hoping to figure out which folder it needed to be placed in. But this wasn't one of Savvy's work orders for logging info. This one was addressed to her. Did she have a folder in this box for bills due? He looked at it closer. What was this?

He studied the various blocks of information, the date, the money owed—and his world tilted. It was from a hospital in Ohio, and the date on it was a few weeks after their breakup. He glanced at the money owed. Good grief. Had she replaced an organ with a gold nugget? He read the procedure. He didn't recognize all the words, but he knew the main one—*hysterectomy*.

His thoughts sounded like an auctioneer rattling off bids—loud, quick phrases that made perfect sense if one was paying attention. And suddenly Savvy's every move made sense.

His chest hurt as if his heart were imploding.

Savilla held the wiggly black pup as it nuzzled her neck. A kerosene lantern hung on a peg, casting a warm glow. Esther was sitting on a makeshift chair beside a wooden crate that had hay, a blanket, and a huge red ribbon.

Jacob added fresh hay to the puppy's crate. "You can rename her, but we call her Korvy."

"That has a perfect ring to it." Savilla held the puppy in front of her as it wriggled, trying to lick her face. "Korvy it is." She pulled the pup close again.

Esther rested her hand on her protruding belly. "We thought the children might like that it's a part of each of your names—Kore and Savvy."

"I like that. Very sweet, and you two have been amazing throughout this whole thing with the Adlers. I can't thank you enough."

Jacob winked at his wife, and Savilla couldn't help but take note of the couple. They had it all—each other and a baby on the way, their first. The way Jacob looked at his wife with such pride and joy tugged at Savilla's heart. Their marriage didn't have any empty, aching holes in it. In a few months, they would hold their newborn while radiating enough love to last a lifetime.

The puppy's sharp teeth dug into Savilla's chin, and she moved it away, letting it nibble on her fingers.

Savilla loved Kore so much, and doubts concerning her hard-line stance about her condition were pelting her like a hailstorm. Was it possible to have that kind of relationship with Kore even if she couldn't bear him children? They'd kept Jade, Chad, and Demi for only two weeks, and they'd bonded. She and Kore loved them, not as if they were their forever family or even as much as they would if they were together for months or years, but enough that Savilla had begun to wonder, had she been completely wrong all this time? Could Kore have the life he'd dreamed of with her at his side, or would asking him that make his sense of loyalty overrule his real desire?

She had been so sure that this earth needed more people like Kore to have their own offspring, and her heart had broken, knowing she would never have a child.

But maybe . . .

The shed door flew open, and Kore filled the room like an ominous cloud. "What have you done, Savilla?" He held up a paper.

Her heart moved to her throat. *Dear God, no.* A few days after moving her stuff here, she'd gone through the client file box and removed the few hospital bills she'd stuffed inside, hadn't she?

The hope she'd begun to nurture moments ago became as barren as her body.

"Concerning our relationship?" Her voice wavered, but she set her will to staying calm. "I did what I thought had to be done." She put the dog into the crate and stood straight to look him in the eyes. "I hope one day you'll forgive me." She moved toward the wall, intending to skirt past Kore.

He took a few quick strides and put his hand on the wall, blocking her. "How is it possible I didn't know of any symptoms or that you had this kind"—he shook the paper at her—"of issue going on?"

"I was too embarrassed to speak of the real problem."

A knowing look entered his eyes. "Back issues." He scoffed.

She lifted her gaze to his, staring into his disbelief.

He fisted his hands and put one on each side of her, trapping her in place. She could feel the desire in him, a longing to be close to her even as he teetered on the edge of resenting her. "Was I no more to you than a man who could father your children, and when you learned you couldn't conceive, you didn't need me?"

"What? No! Tell me you know better!" Her distress echoed off the walls, and she hated that Jacob and Esther had become innocent bystanders in this dreadful fight.

It seemed that his anger steadied rather than escalated, as if her words brought some balance to the chaos inside him. "Then why?" His warm hand brushed wisps of hair from her face. "Tell me why you would do this to us—send me packing rather than lean on my love for you?"

"*I* am barren, Kore. But I will not make *us* barren!"

He withdrew his hand, a dark cloud filling his handsome face. "*We* are not barren! Maybe some couples are, but not the two of us. *We* have the power to produce abundantly—whether it's earning money to give to needy families or helping the Adlers or doing whatever else God puts in our path."

"The highest calling of a woman is to—"

"No! Don't you dare finish that archaic lie!" He cupped her face, keeping her full attention. "The highest calling is *not* motherhood. The highest calling is whatever God asks of us."

His fingers trembled as he held her face in his hands. "I only wanted you and the life we would carve out. That's all." He mumbled as he lowered his lips to hers, kissing her like never before. Savilla melted in the moment, too weak to resist. She wanted to have his forgiveness and to start fresh.

He was right—they weren't barren. Why couldn't she have seen that before now? As her arms tightened around him, he pulled away, releasing her.

As he caught his breath, he studied her, and Savilla saw a dawning

in his eyes. "Who does this, Savvy? Tell me what kind of person de-
ceives and destroys what we had because one dream needed to be trans-
formed into another?" He stepped away, staring at her as seemingly
more of the puzzle pieces came together for him. "I deserved to know
the truth. You should've asked me what I wanted to do—marry you or
find someone else."

"You're too loyal, Kore. You would've stayed."

Defiance flickered in his eyes, and it seemed to fill him within a few
seconds. "You think so?" He straightened. "Maybe not."

He walked out, leaving her there with Jacob and Esther.

Savilla slumped against the wall sobbing.

Esther put her arm around her shoulders while passing her tissues.
"Sh." Esther's breathing was labored. "It's going to be okay."

Would it ever be okay? She doubted it. "What have I done?"

Esther took a deep breath, and Savilla realized she was crying too.
Esther directed Savilla to a place to sit. "We wanted to leave and give
you and Kore space, but . . ."

Savilla sat, shaking from deep within. "You feared Kore might lose
control and hurt me. He wouldn't. Not ever."

"Do you need me to get you some water or something?" Jacob asked.

"Ya," Esther said. "Why don't you do that and give us a minute?"

"Sure." Jacob left.

"That was a lot of pent-up pain unleashed." Esther lifted Savilla's
chin. "I'm so sorry."

"Ya, me too. Endometriosis. My specialist said it was the worst case
he'd ever seen, and he did all he could with laparoscopic surgeries and
medicines to keep me from having a hysterectomy, but the pain became
unbearable. You know the Amish. We don't discuss our monthly cycles
at all, especially with any man, so I was too embarrassed to tell Kore
how rough my cycles were. I just said it was back pain, and he thought
that's what put me in bed several days each month."

The door swung open. "Hey." Chad motioned. "David's here to wish you a happy birthday. I'm supposed to tell you that Mammi D sent a card." His eyes grew large, and he ran inside. "A puppy! Can I hold him?"

If she and Kore needed anything right now, it was three distracted children. "Ya." Savilla stood. "It's a she. Why don't you take her inside for Jade and Demi to see?"

Chad beamed. "David is staying for dinner. It's a good thing we made all those cookies, huh?"

"It is." Savilla put her arm around his shoulders. "Let's take the puppy to your sisters." She couldn't hide out in this shed for the rest of the night. Had Kore stayed for the children's sake, or had he left?

She opened the back door.

The children were all smiles as they welcomed the new puppy. Kore was at the sink with a glass of water in hand, staring blankly out the window. Jacob ushered the children into the living room, which was barely a whisper from them. Esther followed suit, talking with David.

Savilla eased closer to him. "I'm sorry, Kore. I really, really—"

"I'll continue to come on Saturdays until the Adlers return. I'll pick them up and take them elsewhere while you work. I can manage that for, what, four more weekends at the most? But after that, I'm done with being *friends*."

"Can you feel our pain right now? That's what I felt when I learned I couldn't have children, and I came up with a plan that would keep you from being trapped inside that prison like I was."

"Ya." He took a long sip of his water. "That plan didn't work." He swished the water around in the glass, studying it. "Clearly you're the kind of woman who can devise another one." His steely blue eyes met hers before he walked off.

*E*sther's letter burned a hole in Savilla's apron pocket. It had been brief and filled with love and encouragement. Savilla shivered, pulling her black cape around her tighter as she sat inside her rickety carriage, staring at a drab brick building in Lancaster.

It'd been a very long ride to get here, or at least it seemed so. Could she make herself go inside? Esther's handwritten words assured Savilla that an afternoon volunteering at an Englisch group gathering would be good for her. The purpose, according to Esther, wasn't to change Savilla but to open her mind and heart to the God of possibilities so that healing would begin.

Whatever Savilla found inside that building wouldn't alter the situation between her and Kore. That wasn't Esther's purpose, but Savilla knew that Esther hoped today's experience would make a difference. What would Savilla see inside? A room of infertile women, she imagined. They would talk of their pain and drink coffee.

Savilla sighed, but she was desperate to find an ounce of peace through some venue—even this one.

The bank sign across the street flashed the words *Merry Christmas* in an array of small yellow bulbs. The next item on the screen flashed the date, followed by the time and the temperature: December 16; 12:35 p.m.; 34°. People with their own problems had posted a sign wishing her a Merry Christmas.

Why had Savilla so fully believed Kore couldn't be happy in life unless he had biological children? She knew one reason was because her infertility made her feel unworthy of him, but he wasn't the one dumping that on her. Based on what he'd told her when he learned the truth, that kind of thinking angered him.

A good number of Amish, maybe most of them, would believe she was cursed to be barren, but what did it matter what any of them thought? The only opinions and desires that mattered were Kore's and hers. Given time, God would provide a few good friends who loved them for who they were.

If she'd been honest with Kore from the start, he could have helped her get past her ignorance, her fears that he would never be happy if he stayed with her. And she now knew that he would've stayed, not only out of loyalty, but out of the love he had for her, out of faith in what God would create through their union—something as strong or stronger than the bonds of biological children.

But Kore was gone now. He continued to remain true to his word and arrived at the cabin on Saturdays to pick up the children.

Savilla pulled out Esther's letter and skimmed a few of the many lines Esther had copied from somewhere.

> *To all women . . . if you're walking the hard path of*
> *infertility—we walk with you. Forgive us when we believe*
> *or say foolish things. We don't mean to make this harder*
> *than it is.*

Those simple sentences conveyed such understanding, a kind of grace she hadn't expected from anyone, and she soaked it in.

She closed the letter and got out of her rig. She looped the reins around a wall anchor in the side of the brick building. Her heart pounded as she went inside and climbed the stairs to the second floor. Would the other women ask her to tell her story? Could she simply serve coffee and cookies while listening? Nothing inside her wanted to be here. As she went down the hallway searching for the door with the correct room number, she heard laughter and music from somewhere. Apparently there was a group somewhere celebrating Christmas a little early. She would much rather be a part of that group, but she trusted Esther's opinion.

Savilla opened the door. Christmas music surrounded her. Children were dashing about, blowing on party favors—silent ones that rolled out and in with each blow. Adult men and women were in a circle playing a game with a large group of children between four to ten years old—their laughter reminding her of what paradise must be like. How many hard days had passed, how many tears were shed to work toward a moment like this? At the far end of the room, teens tossed a basketball into a hoop, careful not to knock over roaming little ones.

Was she in the wrong room?

A middle-aged woman with straight salt-and-pepper hair that fell just above her shoulders approached her. She smiled. "Savilla?"

"Ya . . . yes. I'm sorry I'm late." Although she'd arrived in plenty of time, she'd had trouble making herself get out of the rig and come in.

"You're fine. I'm Kelley Riley, the regional director. We're having a party of sorts today, so we can use the extra set of hands. Welcome to Forever Care Family Services. We're a private organization dedicated to providing safety, security, nurturing, and love to all children—because every child deserves those things, not just those with good biological parents."

The magnitude of Savilla's closed-mindedness hit her. How could she have been so blind? She'd been acting like a child playing house—doing all within her power to set up her life exactly as she imagined it should be, or she didn't want to play. Rather than taking her dolls and going home, she'd sent Kore away.

No wonder she and Kore hadn't worked out. She didn't know how to love beyond the borders of her narrow dreams. She hadn't known how to let life . . . God . . . do the leading. And she'd assumed what Kore needed. Hadn't asked. Hadn't been vulnerable enough to tell him the truth. Just assumed.

Another line came to her from Esther's letter: "To all women . . . if you're foster moms or adoptive moms—know that we need you."

Who did the word *we* refer to in the lines Esther had written: *we* walk with you . . . *we* need you?

The Trinity? Christians? Society? Children? Or was the *we* faith, hope, and love?

Maybe it was all of the above, and the thought stirred her heart.

The life in front of her wasn't a secondhand one. It was a privilege. It was life, perhaps not born by her body, but nonetheless from God's own hand.

God, forgive me.

The office door to JK Homebuilders opened. Kore didn't look up from studying the discrepancies between what he'd ordered in roofing materials and what had arrived.

"Hi," Esther said.

He glanced up. "Hi."

She had a basket in hand. "Jacob will be here soon. You hungry?"

Kore wasn't, but he needed to eat. "You got enough?"

"I do." She set the basket on his desk. "May I sit?"

"I won't be good company."

"Ya, well, it won't be the first time." Esther sat in the chair opposite his desk.

"I'm sure." He pushed back from the desk. "I've never apologized to you or Jacob. I'm sorry you had to witness that fight."

"I'm not. I mean, you deserved privacy, but seeing what I did gave me an understanding of some things I needed to tell you. But you needed time to cool off. I think nearly three weeks is long enough."

Had it only been three weeks? It felt more like a lifetime. He looked at the calendar sitting on his desk and realized that the children's last day of school until after New Year's was tomorrow. What was he going to do, still only show up on Saturdays when Savilla was so behind and construction work came to a standstill during the holidays? He leaned back. "What's on your mind?"

"Every couple has a love story. Jacob and I have one that I treasure, but I've never witnessed any love like Savilla has for you. She freed you, Kore. Psalm fifteen asks who can dwell with God in His holy mountain, and then it lists characteristics of those who qualify. One trait is people who are willing to do right even if they have to swear to their own hurt. Savilla swore to her own hurt, and she freed you."

"She cut my heart out."

"Just yours?"

He stared at the scattered papers on his desk. "I thought it would help to know the truth. I had no idea it could make unbearable pain more intense."

"It's a hard thing to face—infertility. Complete anguish at times, I imagine. Anyone who brushes it off or quips platitudes to couples in similar situations is just wrong. Maybe they are too weak to cope with feeling that kind of pain, so they have to find ways to dismiss it. Some are so black and white with their understanding they can't separate their narrow-minded judgments from love's gracious faithfulness."

"I hurt for Savvy. Even so, I don't know that we could be good for each other, not after what she's done."

"And maybe not after knowing what life has done to her body?"

"It's a lot to take in. She had my path planned out. I was to get over her and marry someone else." He scoffed. "Ya, what happened to *that* plan?"

Esther put her hands inside her coat pockets. "Your Mammi D was seriously injured, and when you showed up for that, Savvy was strapped with three children and needed your help. It's enough to make me wonder if God is at work, drawing you two together again."

"That sounds nice, but this isn't God." He looked through the window, watching the empty treetops sway in the wind. "Her plan was never going to work. I wasn't going to find a wife and have a family. I've always liked the idea of women and have talked to plenty, hoping to uncover a connection, but Savvy was the only one I ever connected with."

"I feel it's important you know a few things, but I'm not interested in trying to influence your decision or hers. It's just information to use or toss aside."

"About?"

"Well, you know that years before I met Jacob, I ran a home for unwed expectant Amish girls."

"Ya, you're still pretty involved volunteering your time."

"That's right. The goal of everyone involved is to keep moms and babies together, to reunite the pregnant girls with their disappointed parents. That's what is best for everyone, and with some patience and intervention, that plan works almost every time. But on a rare occasion, maybe once every four or five years, a situation arises when the girls need an adoptive parent, and when that happens, the girls almost always choose to locate an Amish family."

"Why are you telling me this?"

"Because it may matter. Adopting, fostering, delivering—it's all a way for love to flow in a healthy, needed manner. A way of welcoming a baby into your hearts."

He nodded. "Denki. I appreciate you sharing that, but Savvy and I are broken."

"Maybe so, but look at how much healing you brought to the Adler children. They were traumatized by what happened, and they're doing great. The children told me they look on that night they spent by themselves as if it were a great adventure, their personal sacrifice to make sure Aidan could cross the Atlantic to become one of them."

Did Kore really want to let things end with Savvy? Or was he trying to punish her?

$\mathcal{S}$avilla put another sweater in an overnight bag. The grounds were covered in snow, and Kore would be here in a few minutes to pick up the children. Once they left, Kore wouldn't return for anything until it was time for the children to get ready for bed. She'd packed enough clothes that if their first round got wet from the snow, they could change into warm, dry ones.

Demi jumped onto the bed. "I need help." She sat up, bouncing her feet at Savilla. The little girl's boots were on the wrong feet and the shoestrings were in knots.

"Yes, you do." Savilla knelt in front of her, untying the laces. "How did this happen?"

"Chad was rushing me."

"Was not!" Chad yelled as he barreled through the door, dressed in coat, hat, and boots. "You were being a slowpoke."

"That's enough." Savilla glanced at the clock. She had three minutes to get the kids ready to walk out the door. Kore always arrived at eight sharp and was gone by one minute after . . . if not sooner. Savilla switched Demi's insulated boots to the correct feet and retied them.

She closed the overnight bag and zipped it. "Chad, set this beside the front door."

"Yes ma'am." He saluted and ran with the rolling bag trailing behind him. Jade walked in the back door, holding Korvy. "He's eaten, played, and been walked. He should sleep all morning while you work."

"Denki."

Three knocks in quick succession vibrated through the room. Her heart thudded with anxiety, but as soon as he was gone, she would focus on her work. "Okay, guys." She shooed them toward the door. "Let's go."

Jade passed her Korvy.

Chad jerked open the door. "Morning! Can we go sledding today?"

"I was thinking the same thing, but it'll be later." Kore reached inside, lowered the handle on the suitcase, and picked it up. "Breakfast is first, followed by some Christmas shopping. When the library opens, we'll go there to read the latest e-mails from your folks and write back to them. Lunch will be at my Mamm's house, where you will regale Miss Elizabeth with stories from your lives. Then we go sledding."

Jade looked to Savilla. "He probably has a list with that same schedule somewhere."

Kore pointed at her, a smile in place. "As a matter of fact, it's on the Notepad app on my phone."

Chad grabbed his hand. "Come on. Let's get started."

Kore set the bag on the porch before he looked at Savilla. "I could use a minute to talk."

Her heart pounded. "Sure. Whenever you need."

He walked inside, not stopping until he was close enough to pet the dog she held. "Now?"

"That's fine." If she didn't pass out from her heart racing.

He gestured toward the door. "Why don't all three of you gather kindling just like I've shown you? Pile it on the porch, and I'll be out in a minute."

"No thanks," Demi said.

Jade put her hands on the young girl's shoulders and guided her toward the door. "It wasn't really a question." Jade turned back and waved at them. "Hey, Demi, let's team up against Chad to see who can get the most sticks."

"Okay." Demi ran off the porch.

Chad frowned, eyeing Kore and Savilla. "You guys too?" He buttoned his coat in quick, choppy movements. "My parents are always doing that. Taking breaks to talk, just the two of them. Mom giggles, and Dad whispers stuff while smiling. Sometimes they smooch and hold hands. I'll tell you what I tell them—you people are sick." He marched outside and slammed the door.

They both laughed as Kore stroked the pup. Tears fell from Savilla's eyes, and she quickly wiped them away, hoping he hadn't seen.

He lifted the puppy from her. "Hank Adler was able to patch a call through last night—around three in the morning our time. All the preliminary stuff has been approved, and they are supposed to have a final court date on Monday. Might be home next week, right before or right after Christmas."

"That's wonderful!" Savilla was so excited for the Adlers, and the blessing of being a small part of this adventure stood out clearly in her soul. She and Kore had been instrumental in holding everything together stateside. Whatever else she'd destroyed, she'd been a part of keeping the Adler children together and safe, and that warmed her soul like the fire in the hearth warmed this cabin.

But Savilla's life was similar to the blazing logs in the fireplace—both would be stone cold within a day of the Adler parents taking their children home.

She dreaded what was ahead for her and Kore—the emptiness. Savilla swallowed hard, wishing the room had more oxygen in it. "If you need a place to crash with the children this afternoon, you can come here. I'm meeting clients at my apartment for fittings."

"Okay." He put the pup in her crate. "I don't want to be angry anymore, Savvy."

She tried to gain control of her breathing, but pain and hope were flooding her. "You've been justified to feel as you have."

"I know." He closed the crate so the puppy couldn't climb out. "But you weren't the only one who handled the breakup wrong. I should've fought harder for answers. I should've returned to North Star so we could talk. I should've asked my family how you were doing, and I would've known something was wrong. There's a list of things I should've done differently."

"On the app on your phone?" She hoped a little levity helped.

He chuckled. "Not this time. It's more of a list in my mind that refuses to fade."

"Of the two of us, I was the most wrong, by a lot."

"Ya." He released a long sigh. "I'll give you that. Although . . . if I was the one who couldn't give you children, I don't know that my initial reaction would've been wiser. I hope so, but . . ." He shrugged. "Anyway, I'm unsure where this leaves us. Not because of the infertility, but because you controlled and manipulated me, withholding information I had a right to know. I never saw that side of you, and it's disturbing—both you having it and my not seeing it."

"You didn't see it because it didn't exist, not until I learned I had no other option than a hysterectomy."

"Maybe so." He drew a deep breath. "I need to go."

As the door closed behind him, warring emotions rolled through her—the desire to cry and to dance—depending on whether Kore was easing his way into a forever good-bye or just needed time to finish letting go of his anger.

*K*ore's toboggan whooshed Demi and him down the snowy hill. She squealed with delight while keeping her arms, clad in a puffy yellow coat, locked around his knees. The temperature was dropping fast, and the winds had kicked up. He needed to draw this outing to a close before the children were too cold, tired, and hungry to be their usual selves. Before partnering to help take care of these children, he hadn't realized the amount of effort involved in keeping moods on an even keel.

A dozen families were on this hill sledding. Excited chatter and laughter echoed through the cold air. Kore recognized Wayne Umble and his sister Nellie speeding past them, the siblings racing on saucers. He was glad to see Nellie back in North Star.

The moment caused him to catch a glimpse of what Savilla must have been thinking—that family life was inexplicably valuable. He could see that as he watched people sled. Her mistake was to overvalue the importance of the biological factor. It held value, no doubt. Everyone alive was biologically connected to someone. But the real significance of family was found inside the bond of love, not DNA.

The speed of his and Demi's sled lessened until it came to a halt. He helped her stand before he got off the toboggan. She looked tiny inside the mounds of layered clothes. The only skin peeking out was the oval part around her eyes, nose, and mouth.

Demi put her gloved hand into his and pointed. "Look, they're heading straight for us."

Kore crouched, keeping the wind from chafing her face. "They are. Think they'll make it this far before the sled stops?" They stayed in place, watching as Chad and Jade laughed while swooshing down the hill, the toboggan spraying snow along the way.

"Nope. We went the farthest, and I wish Savilla was here to see it."

Kore sighed. "Me too." But he wasn't sure how he felt about that feeling. He and Savilla. It's all he'd wanted for way too long. And now he didn't know what he wanted other than to find a place to file all his thoughts and emotions concerning her. "You can tell her all about it tonight."

"Did you see that?" Chad yelled, grinning. "I think we went faster than you guys. Come on. Let's race!"

"I think we need to call it a day on sledding. The wind is picking up, and the temperature is dropping."

"No, please, please, please!" Chad grabbed Kore's hand, tugging him toward the top of the hill.

Demi's eyes pleaded with him to continue sledding, and Kore wondered if the children were on the verge of another crying spell. The longer the Adler parents were gone, the harder the emotional toll on the children. Their feelings were on a roller coaster, especially as Christmas grew closer and the children's parents were so far away.

Snow began to fall, and a gust of wind swooshed. Kore stuck to his guns. "No more for today."

Before the tears in Demi's eyes could fall, Kore had an idea. He picked her up. "Is there anyone here who would like to see Savvy's place?"

Demi nodded, wiping her gloved hand across her eyes.

"Would we!" Chad grabbed the rope to his toboggan and took off running toward the horse and carriage.

It was past time Kore got a peek inside her apartment. He needed—

or rather wanted—to get to know all the parts of her life she'd kept hidden.

Jade picked up the rope to the other toboggan. "Maybe she can get done early, and we can do something, all five of us."

"Doubtful. It's her last Saturday to work before Christmas, and a lot of people need their items before Christmas Eve."

"But you'll ask?"

"Doubtful." They trudged up the hill toward the carriage.

Demi patted him on the face. "Hey, mister. I'm hungry."

Kore laughed. After Demi called him that one time because she couldn't remember his name, the phrase became an inside joke that all five of them used at times, especially Demi. "Hungry again?" Kore bounced her one time on his hip. "How is it you're no bigger than a minute but you have the appetite of a day?"

Jade grinned. "How come you're as big as a day and have no more appetite than a minute?"

Using two fingers, Kore barely pushed her, making her giggle. "That was clever. Not true, but clever."

She feigned a curtsy. "Denki."

"Amish don't curtsy."

Jade's eyes grew big in that mocking and joking way of hers. "Imagine that . . . something the Amish *don't* do."

"Point taken. They also don't get out of school a week before Christmas."

He approached his rig and set Demi in the buggy before helping the other two climb inside. He closed the buggy door and went to the horse. "How you holding up, old boy?" The horse nuzzled him, and Kore stroked him before removing one of the blankets he'd placed over him a few hours ago. "How about some oats and a warm barn soon?"

The horse nodded as if he understood Kore's question. Kore got in the buggy and spread the blanket over the children's laps. "The Amish way to warm a blanket—horse-body heat."

"You stole it from the horse to give to us?" Chad asked.

"The horse needed it while standing still in the elements." Kore released the brake and tapped the reins against the horse's back. "He's still got one much thinner blanket on, but if he had on both, he'd get sweaty, and that would make him very cold once we stopped."

"I'd like a horse of my own." Chad buried his hands under the warmed blanket.

"I doubt that will be under the tree Christmas morning," Jade said.

"But there will be something?" Chad studied Kore.

Their parents had never imagined they'd get the call concerning Aidan before they went Christmas shopping. The process had dragged on for so long, how could they have known?

"Ya, a little something." He'd picked up a few items for Chad, and Savvy had purchased some stuff for the girls. He and Savvy went shopping at separate times, of course.

Kore tugged on the left rein, intending to stop at a nearby diner to feed the children. The snow was falling harder now, large flakes that swirled peacefully. The streets of North Star were decked out in electric Christmas decorations, making all of life feel as if it were wrapped in hope.

After picking up to-go food at the diner, they piled back in the buggy, carrying the bags of hot food. When Kore pulled into the Millers' driveway, there were several horses attached to buggies in the carriage house. One of them belonged to his brother David.

Kore drove his horse under the shelter too. He got out and covered the horse again before giving him some oats. Then he helped the children navigate the steep stairs to Savvy's place.

Jade knocked.

"It's open," Savvy called.

Jade turned the handle, letting them inside. Kore closed the door behind him. In the long, narrow room were eight to ten Amish men, three of whom were his younger brothers. About half of them had on their coats while the other half were putting them on. Where was her bed or kitchen? All Kore saw was a Coleman camping stove, a cooler, a cabinet where her sewing machine sat when it wasn't at Mammi D's, and shelves of fabric in a narrow, desolate room.

Savilla stood at a wooden island counter, writing a receipt while talking to David. "I've pinned the correct name on each shirt and pair of pants. If you want them to fit well, don't get them mixed up." When she glanced toward the doorway, her eyes held inquisitiveness as they met Kore's. "Hey, guys."

He held up the plastic bags. "We brought food."

"Oh." She seemed caught off guard. "Make yourself at home?"

"Here's a tip, Savilla," David said. "When you say that, it's not supposed to be a question."

Savilla tore off the receipt and slapped it against David's chest. "My tip for you guys—don't wear the new clothes before Christmas caroling this Wednesday. If you do, they'll have stains on them, and the girls, who picked up their dresses earlier, will be unhappy."

David took the receipt, looking serious. "Denki, Savvy."

The room began to echo as each man uttered "Thank you."

"You're very welcome. I love what you're doing, so bless the families by singing your hearts out on the eve of Christmas Eve."

All the young men made their way out the door, and the room grew quiet. Kore held up the bags. "Hungry?"

She glanced at a clock. "I am, and I have about thirty minutes before the last customer comes by."

Kore looked around. "Where do you eat . . . and sleep?"

She knelt, helping Demi out of her snowsuit. "It's all here. You just have to find it." Her eyes lit up. "That reminds me." She shook her finger at Kore. "I have something for you."

"Coal for my stocking?" Kore set the bags on the counter where Savvy had been writing out the receipt. There was no reason they couldn't work through some of the awkwardness between them from the fallout. Doing so wasn't the same as a commitment. So far in his life, he'd been too quick to walk away when something didn't suit him. He'd left the Amish. He'd left Savilla.

He was ready to learn to be a different type of man.

Chad tossed his coat, boots, and snowsuit into a corner.

"Some ideas about a distinctive kind of furniture to design."

Kore put his coat and hat on a peg. "I gave up that business." He'd walked away from that too, left the world of craftsmanship as if he had no skill or desire for it.

"So no fashioning gifts for family or friends?" Savvy asked.

Kore hadn't planned on it, but like a lot of other stuff recently, he probably needed to reconsider it. "I'll think about it. So tell me, do you sleep on the floor?"

She went to a cubbyhole and pilfered through a square basket. "No. I sort of sleep on the wooden bench that doubles as a seat at the kitchen table." She pulled a manila envelope from the basket and then shoved it back into its spot and passed the envelope to him.

He used the envelope to point. "That area is less than two feet wide and three feet long. Also, there isn't a kitchen table."

"Isn't there?" Savvy stood, hands on hips. "Hm." She picked up a three-foot tall two-by-four piece of wood that had been leaning against a wall. "I was sure I had one somewhere . . ." She winked at Jade. "Follow me."

Straining, she pulled a shelf away from the wall and lowered a hidden leg, making the shelf become a table directly in front of a wooden bench that was attached to a wall. "Every piece of furniture does double or triple duty." She pushed the shelf back into its spot and then un-latched hooks on the wall and slowly pulled down a bed. Its frame had been a bench seat for her table moments earlier. "None of it works eas-ily." She stood, rubbing her back and taking a deep breath. "But with enough effort I can make it all work, and I need the space." She pointed at the envelope. "Open it."

He did so and found himself looking at drawings she'd made of double-duty furniture. "This is interesting."

"Ya, I thought so."

"Did you draw these yourself?"

"Uh-huh. I wanted to send you the information eight months ago, but it didn't seem like a good idea. Then I forgot until you started ask-ing questions about my furniture."

"I've heard of pieces like this, but I've never seen any." He inspected it. "Did you design this yourself?"

"Ya. Daed did the carpentry work. Since he's a dairy farmer, his carpentry work is crude at best. But what he has made gets the job done, and that's all that matters."

Surely Kore could use her designs but make the pieces so every part moved smoothly and effortlessly. He was excited about the idea, and he had one week to accomplish his goal in order to make it a Christmas gift. That's not what she had in mind. Her goal was to give him a dif-ferent way to build furniture, possibly a successful way.

Kore moved to the window and peered out. A streetlamp show-cased huge white flakes falling.

Savilla glanced his way. "Is it snowing again?"

"Ya. Began about an hour ago."

Jade pulled to-go containers from the bag. "You should see down-town North Star tonight—the snow falling against all the Christmas lights. It reminds me of Bedford Falls, only much prettier."

"Bedford Falls?" Savilla asked.

Jade set a large plastic bowl of soup on the counter. "From the movie *It's a Wonderful Life.*"

"Ah." Savilla got out several bowls from a cabinet. "I've heard of that movie." She dished out food, and the children began eating.

Now that Kore understood how Savvy was living and the extent of her medical bills, he had ideas that could improve her life. "Savvy?"

She passed Demi a napkin before walking to Kore. "Ya?"

"Your finances," he spoke softly. "There's no reason you should be this"—he gestured at her surroundings—"strapped for money." He'd seen what she owed. "There are ways to work with the hospital to have your monthly payment lowered. They aren't going to offer you that, but you can push for it."

She gazed up at him, looking genuinely interested. "Are there?"

"Absolutely. Let's eat. Afterward we could take the children for a ride, look at Christmas lights through the falling snow."

"What does that have to do with helping me work through some of my bills?"

"Nothing."

Her pursed lips slowly formed into a smile. But before she could respond, someone knocked on the door. "That's my last client for the day. Let me take care of this, and I'll be finished with work for the night."

It sounded as if she could be game for a long night without much sleep. After a sightseeing trip in the horse-drawn carriage, they could get the children tucked into bed and talk.

They needed to talk—until dawn, probably. He was unsure about her . . . about them. Was their love strong enough? Would he know the answer by morning?

CHAPTER SIXTEEN

*T*he smell of honey ham and shoofly pies wafted through the air. Savilla walked to Mammi D's fridge and read the list Kore had written yesterday. Neatly printed across the top were the words *Christmas Eve.*

Today's schedule was full, brimming with love, light, and three wriggly children. Savilla could almost float away she felt so good.

Forgiven.

Understood.

Accepted.

That was her, and she felt it to her toes. Seemed odd. It was downright preposterous actually. She had more optimism today—as a twenty-five-year-old woman who couldn't have children and who would tell the love of her life good-bye soon—than she'd ever had before. The strength found in trusting God, in yielding to His wisdom, had a power all its own.

The newborn babe in the manger didn't know what would face Him, not as an infant. He learned about it as He grew, as He became able to comprehend. She wanted to follow that pattern, even though it would be in a much more flawed way, of course. Following Christ's example, Savilla wanted to stay connected to God and to do as He directed. Accept that heartache was part of life. It had been for Jesus, His mother, and His disciples. He couldn't stop all the hurt, or at least He hadn't. But what He did do was love, forgive, and encourage people through the pain.

She would do the same—for herself and everyone in her life. She'd learned the truth about pain the hard way, but now that understanding was hers, she wouldn't let go of it.

Laughter belted out, vibrating the room. She went to the doorway of the kitchen. Mammi D looked up from her spot on the couch, her arm still in a cast and a sling. The children were on the floor near her, all of them playing a board game that was spread out on the coffee table. Six dice were spattered on the board, and multicolored cards sat in stacks. What was this game?

She smiled at Savilla. "I won." Her eyes sparkled. "And I have no clue what the game was about."

Savilla laughed.

Mammi D narrowed her eyes as she once again looked at the decorated Christmas tree in her house. "I never would've imagined having one of those, but it is pretty, isn't it?"

"Ya," Chad mimicked. "Gut and wunderbaar."

Jade tickled him. "You're not Amish."

Savilla glanced at the clock. Kore should be back any minute. Since his work with Jacob and Esther was similar to the public schools—shut down until after the first of the year—he'd stayed in town all week, but she had no idea what he'd been doing. It didn't matter. They were on good terms, and she had peace about her future. That was enough to know.

On her way out the front door to bring in a few sticks of firewood, she paused and kissed Mammi D on the top of her head. When Savilla stepped outside, she saw Kore coming down the path, only twenty feet from the cabin. He waved before pointing behind her. She turned.

Was it possible?

A car pulled onto the driveway and came to a halt. The Adlers! Kore approached the car. A man got out, grinning. "Kore."

"Welcome."

The man engulfed him. "Thank you."

A woman hopped out of the vehicle. "How can we ever thank—"

"Mom!" Jade ran outside and plowed into her mom's arms.

Chad hurried out too, clomping around in his untied boots. Demi had on her princess house shoes as she scurried through the snow. The driveway was in utter disorder with tears and grins and introductions to the newest member of the family—Aidan Adler, a beautiful child with skin as dark as night and eyes full of hope.

Chills covered Savilla. Love was love, whether the child came from the mom's belly or from the other side of the world. What a beautiful lesson to learn.

"Come in." Savilla led the way. "We were hoping you'd arrive in time for Christmas Eve dinner, and here you are."

The chaos during the next few hours warmed Savilla's heart. Kore's too. She could tell by his smile as he interacted with everyone. But before dark she and Kore were giving the children good-bye hugs as their parents packed all their belongings in the car, taking their unopened Christmas presents and Korvy the Lab with them.

Patti wrapped her arms around Savilla. "Hank and I have been praying for you nonstop since we talked six weeks ago. Kore too. Asking God to bless you above all that you could ask or think." She squeezed tight. "Thank you."

The house felt empty and way too quiet as she and Kore went back inside. Tonight would be Mammi D's first night to sleep in her own home. Every item on Kore's list on the fridge had been checked off. He and his brothers had taken her sewing machine and all her sewing items back to her apartment yesterday. Mammi D's house was in order, except for the Christmas tree that would remain for another night or two. Savilla had put gifts to Kore under it. New shirts, pants, and dress jackets. Finding the hours and energy to sew the items hadn't been easy, but her determination had won out.

Savilla plunked into a chair. "It's time for this Mary Poppins to go home."

"You're welcome to stay," Mammi D said.

"I know, but it's time to go home."

Still, no one budged, including Savilla. They watched the fire and breathed. Finally Kore stood. "I'll drive you. How about a spin through North Star first? See the Christmas lights one more time before Christmas?"

"Sure."

He was returning to Virginia the day after Christmas. She wasn't sure what that meant for them, but she knew that nothing was final. Every ending was the start of a new beginning. It was just a matter of finding the new beginning.

She hugged Mammi D gently. "Love you. Glad you're home."

"Same to you. Stay safe and warm, child."

If Savilla thought this house was quiet with the children and puppy gone, she couldn't imagine how quiet her apartment would be.

Kore drove them through the town. The *clippety-clop* of the horse's hoofs was relaxing, and it mingled well with the twinkling lights and holly-trimmed lampposts. Neither of them was very talkative. Tired maybe. Adjusting to the transition. There were still people bustling about.

Savilla relaxed against the bench seat, trying to enjoy these waning moments. "I don't think I've been in North Star on Christmas Eve before. It's a happening place, as Jade would say."

"Yep, as Demi would say."

They laughed. She drew a deep breath. "Thank you."

He nodded, a warm smile on his face. "Let's get you home."

When they pulled into her driveway, she saw light coming through her frosted windows. "Someone must've left a kerosene lantern burning after delivering my stuff."

"Looks like it." Kore followed her up the steps, probably to make sure she didn't slip on the steps.

She unlocked the door, and the air was instantly filled with "Joy to the world, the Lord is come! Let earth receive her King."

She glanced at Kore. He shrugged, but he knew what was going on. She could see it written on his face. The scheduled evening of caroling was last night, and yet the young people were here at her place on Christmas Eve. What a treat. Easing into the room, she saw two dozen Amish youth dressed in coordinating colors and each with a candlestick holder and a lit candle.

The place was warm. She spotted the gas-burning logs heating the room instead of the wood-burning stove. Someone must have installed it since she had last been home. That meant heat without hauling wood up here. She looked behind her, peering up at Kore. The look on his face was priceless. He had been working here, ready to surprise her with a wonderful Christmas present. He removed his coat and hat and held out his hand for her coat.

She passed it to him, her attention moving about the room. The makeshift double-duty furniture had all been replaced. She didn't know whether to enthusiastically inspect it or remain in place, listening to the carolers.

"Kore . . ." Should she just say "thank you" when she wanted to take his hand into hers and never let go?

David had one hand behind his back when he stepped forward. Without missing a word in the song he was singing, he passed her a puppy.

Kore petted it. "Korvy's sister. I hope I didn't misread you about having to let go of Korvy."

"You didn't. Thank you." The puppy snuggled in the crook of her arm, ready to sleep. "I can't wait to play with all the double-duty furniture."

"It's made of reclaimed wood, which is what Esther acquires in her business. Your idea will sell. I already have orders through Esther simply showing pictures of this stuff to her clients." From behind her, Kore put his arms around her waist. "I love you, Savvy." He kissed her cheek. "If I could choose any life I wanted, I would choose the one with you. It's as if God wrote it in the stars that we were meant to be together."

With the singers in perfect a cappella harmony, the puppy asleep in her arms, and Savilla surrounded by the furniture Kore had built for her, she turned and kissed him full on the lips. "It's always been you, always." She kissed him again.

"Merry Christmas," Kore mumbled while kissing her.

Star of Grace

MINDY STARNS CLARK AND
EMILY CLARK

*A*ndy Danner sat on the roof of a Craftsman-style home, looking out over the neighborhood, a glimpse of the brownish-blue gulf in the distance. Though he and his fellow crew members were based farther inland, about an hour north of here, he always enjoyed it when a job brought them down this way. The Mississippi coast was a beautiful place to visit, though about as different as could be from where he'd grown up in Lancaster County, Pennsylvania.

He'd come to Mississippi last May, intending to stay for a week. Instead, he'd stuck around for six months now. He hadn't minded the weather so much—not the intense spring storms, nor the astonishing summer heat, not even the crazy fall winds. But today was especially beautiful—sunny and warm with a slight breeze coming off the water—and he couldn't have been more irritated. This was mid-*November,* for goodness' sake. They should all be wearing coats and gloves by now. The trees should be bare of their leaves, the beautiful show of autumn colors past, the grass around them mostly brown. Instead, the people here were still in their shirt sleeves.

It was ridiculous.

Even as he had the thought, Andy grimaced, knowing that wasn't what was really bothering him. Besides, just because Lancaster County was gearing up to look like a Christmas postcard right about now, that didn't mean the weather was correct there and wrong here. They were just different, much like the foods there were different from the foods here. The accents too. He would adapt to all of it, even the climate if necessary, even the parts of his life here that made him feel like a Canada goose in a Carolina henhouse.

Telling himself to get back to work, Andy held a roofing nail in place and drove it flush with a single whack of his hammer. Some of the crew used diesel-powered nail guns, but he preferred the feel and precision of hand driving.

Andy had learned how to build when he was a child. His father was a dairy farmer, but he was also known for his carpentry skills, and he'd passed those skills down to his sons. Andy had taken to the craft more than any of his brothers, and he had decided at a young age that he might like making carpentry his life's work—though he'd never expected that work to take him out of North Star, away from home. Away from Nellie.

Then again, he'd never expected Nellie to break his heart the way she had. The fact that he left town soon after to go on a short-term mission trip to rebuild the homes of storm victims along the gulf had been at least somewhat understandable to his family, friends, and community members. The fact that he'd stayed here once that trip was done, accepting a construction job with an Amish crew based out of a small, relatively new community south of Hattiesburg, had not. He often called home on Sunday afternoons, and every time he did, at least one family member got on the line and tried to talk some sense into him, especially after Nellie had a change of heart, moved back home, and decided she wanted to reconcile. *"What's keeping you away, Son?"* had been his mother's latest plea. But even though he tried to explain, she didn't understand. None of them did.

What kept him away, Andy thought as he drove another nail into place, was the knowledge that all his plans and dreams could be crushed in an instant, as if by a single whack from a hammer, shattering into a million pieces.

❦

Sam Danner was running out of time. He loved autumn in Lancaster County, loved working beside his older sisters to harvest the pumpkins in the patch so they could make fresh pumpkin pie, loved raking the leaves into a giant pile with his older brothers and sometimes jumping into that pile together afterward, scattering the leaves again.

But now that they'd reached the middle of November, it was starting to feel less like autumn and more like winter. Through the window nearest his desk, he could see that most of the trees lining the playground had already lost their leaves. The sun was rising later—and setting earlier—with each passing day. And the air was definitely colder. It was time to stop thinking and start doing, time to get to work.

Time to tackle the Great Christmas Challenge.

Sam worried that he might already be too late. How many days did he have exactly? He needed to take a closer look. Raising his hand to get the teacher's attention, he pointed from his pencil to the sharpener mounted on the wall near the front of the room. She gave him a nod, so he made his way there.

As he stood at the sharpener, slowly turning its handle, his eyes were on the calendar posted on the bulletin board directly above it. Though the page currently showing was November, it also included tiny versions of October and December. Today was November 13, and the deadline for the challenge was December 23. Sam quickly calculated the time between now and then in his head. He had five weeks plus five days to reach his goal. Would it be enough?

Sam finished sharpening the pencil, pulled it out to check the tip, and gave it a quick blow before returning to his seat. There he flipped open his notebook to the inside back cover and drew yet another circle around the figure he'd scribbled at the center of the page just last week: $318.

He had five weeks and five days to earn $318.

Sam looked up from the paper, absently tapping the pencil's eraser against his chin. Between school and chores and helping out at his family's produce stand, he didn't have a lot of free time. But he could probably squeeze in an hour or two each day after school and maybe three or four hours on Saturdays—*if* he could talk someone into hiring him.

That was a very big *if.* The problem was that, at just twelve years old, he was too young for a real job—though he knew he could handle a lot more than some folks might give him credit for. Thanks to all the chores he did around the farm, not to mention the hours spent toting heavy pumpkins and big baskets of fruits and vegetables and canned goods at the stand, he was very strong for his age. He was also good with customers and knew how to use a cash register and make correct change. Surely someone somewhere needed a guy like him, if only temporarily.

Sam turned to a fresh page in his notebook and began listing possible jobs he could do. It was too late in the season for mowing or weeding, but maybe he could offer to rake or to wash windows or just do general yard and garden cleanup. What else? He added to the list, going faster as he went. House painting, baby-sitting, animal care, and more.

The list kept growing, and he'd managed to fill nearly half a page when he heard his name called. He looked up and to the left, where the girl beside him was giggling. He had missed something.

"Sam," said Beth, his teacher. She was standing to the right of his desk, fidgeting with the strings of her Kapp, which was something she did when she was irritated. "How many spools of thread does Sally have?"

He blinked, utterly lost. "Thread?"

Beth grunted. "Have you been listening to a word I've said?"

"Sorry." His face grew hot as he discreetly closed his notebook. Normally he was an attentive student, but it wasn't every day he tried to pull off something of this magnitude.

"Let's go through it again." Beth moved toward the front of the class. "Sally has twelve spools of blue thread, and she has two fewer spools of green thread than blue thread. She also has five more spools of red thread than blue thread. So how many spools of thread does Sally have total?"

"Um . . ." Sam did the calculations in his head. "Thirty-nine?"

Beth gave him a curt nod as she took her seat at the desk. "Correct. All right, Wayne. Can you come up to the board and show us how Sam arrived at that answer?"

Sam turned and shot a glance at his best buddy, Wayne Umble, who sat directly behind him in class. Wayne was a great guy, but math wasn't exactly his strong suit.

"Uh . . ." Wayne faltered, not rising from his desk. "He ran over to Sally's and asked her?"

The class chuckled, but Beth didn't even crack a smile. She simply gave a sigh and then moved on to the next seventh grader in the room, the girl across the aisle who had giggled at Sam before. "How about you?"

Beth held out a piece of chalk, and soon the girl was up at the board, writing out the number of spools, color by color. Almost immediately Sam's mind began to wander again, back to the Great Christmas Challenge.

It had started two weeks ago, when the first snow flurries of the season appeared. His big brother Andy loved snow, and even though those flurries had lasted for only an afternoon and barely left a dusting on the ground, the sight of the flakes swirling around in the sky made Sam miss him even more than usual.

He had four other siblings, but Andy was the one he'd always been closest to, despite the twelve-year difference in their ages. Andy was the one who'd taught Sam to fish, to swim, to hit a volleyball just right. The one who called him *Boova* for "little brother." The one who left town last spring after his girlfriend broke up with him and hadn't come back since.

The one Sam missed something terrible.

For the first few months after Andy went away, most of their phone conversations revolved around Sam trying to talk Andy into coming home. Finally they had agreed to disagree, and after that Sam tried not to bring it up quite so often. But the day after the snow flurries two weeks ago, his sister started taking orders at the family produce stand for her Christmas fudge, and he realized that the holidays weren't that far off. Andy usually called home on Sunday afternoons just to chat with whoever was around, so the following Sunday, Sam was the one waiting in the barn when the phone rang, and he launched into his pitch straightaway. *"Even if you're not willing to move back home for good,"* he'd pleaded, *"at least you should visit. You could come for Christmas. We could even keep it a secret from Mamm, maybe make it like a special Christmas Day surprise for her or something."*

Sam hated to beg, but he just knew in his heart that if he could get Andy home and face to face with Nellie, who was really sorry for what she'd done and wanted to reconcile, the two of them would make up and get married, and Andy would never leave North Star again.

To Sam's great disappointment, however, Andy wasn't having any of it. He threw out a few objections, mostly about not being able to miss work, and finally closed the subject by saying, *"Even if I could take off, I can't afford a driver or a bus or a train to get there. It's just too expensive, and I'm barely getting by as it is."*

The conversation had ended there, but Sam wasn't giving up that easily. The very next day he paid a visit to the travel agency downtown after school and had a long chat with a very friendly—and patient— agent. The following Sunday when Andy called again, Sam was ready for round two. Knowing his brother as well as he did, he figured the best way to approach the matter was by issuing a challenge.

"What if someone else paid for your train ticket?" Sam had said. *"Then would you come home for Christmas?"*

"Someone like who?" Andy replied. *"Mamm or Daed? No thanks, Boova. I don't want them spending their hard-earned money on me like that."*

"I'm talking about me," Sam explained. *"What if I paid for it? Would you come then?"*

"No sir. You're not dipping into your savings on my account."

"Ya, right," Sam retorted, explaining that the only savings he had at the moment amounted to less than five dollars, tip money he'd earned a few quarters at a time at the produce stand by carrying big pumpkins out to people's cars. *"It takes twenty-seven hours, one change of trains, and $318 round trip to get from Hattiesburg to Lancaster on Amtrak. So that's my challenge. If I pay for it, will you do it?"*

The question gave Andy pause, but finally, grudgingly, he accepted his little brother's offer with a laugh.

"Sure, kid," he said. *"If you can earn that much between now and Christmas without letting it interfere with school or the stand or your regular chores, then yes. I'll come."*

Sam's heart filled with joy, knowing if he could just get Andy home, he'd end up staying for good.

Andy even agreed to a set of dates so Sam could reserve him a spot on the train—those dates being subject to his boss's approval, of course. By the time their call was over, Sam was nearly walking on air. All he had to do to get Andy here on December 25 was reserve a seat for him on the train that left December 24 and be sure to pay for it by December 23.

Sam wasn't dumb. He was fully aware that the only reason Andy had said yes was because he didn't think his little brother could pull this off. How could a twelve-year-old earn that kind of money that fast?

Sam had no idea, but he knew he had to try. With God's help, somehow, he was determined to make it happen.

*N*ellie Umble scooped up a generous portion of vanilla ice cream and packed it into the waffle cone. Since her promotion last month from floor worker to bookkeeper, she'd spent less time manning the counter at the North Star Country Store and Creamery and more time in her small office in the back, balancing the books, tracking profits, and performing numerous other money-related tasks. But with the new ice cream flavors in—cinnamon cider and, her favorite, pumpkin spice—the store was having a busy week, and she needed to pitch in now and again.

She walked the cone to the counter and handed it over to a young man, one of the Detweiler boys. He smiled, said, "Denki," and joined some cousins enjoying their own similarly delectable choices. Nellie watched him go, pleased that such an ordinary thing as this creamery could make people so happy.

She turned to the next person in line and immediately smiled, recognizing a family friend, a local Amish midwife.

"*Guder Nummidaag*, Rebekah," she said. Good afternoon. "What can I get for you?"

The wiry, gray-haired woman's eyes sparkled as she greeted Nellie in return and then requested a single scoop of mint chocolate chip in a bowl, not a cone, with sprinkles and a dab of whipped cream on top. To go.

"You got it," Nellie said, punching in the buttons on the cash register and announcing the total.

Soon Rebekah had paid, been served, and exited the store, but even after Nellie moved on to other customers, the sprightly midwife stayed on her mind. Rebekah was a minor celebrity of sorts, at least around here, thanks to her actions one fateful night almost twenty-five years ago when she single-handedly delivered four babies during a terrible late-November snowstorm. The story of her courage and endurance that night had made the local paper, which wasn't too unusual, but then the tale was picked up as a human-interest piece by a larger syndicate and in the end became a bit of a national sensation.

Nellie hadn't even been alive back then, but she had a connection to the woman just the same. Andy Danner, the love of Nellie's life, had been one of those born that night, one of the four infants who'd come to be known in the press as Rebekah's Babies.

Thinking of Andy now, Nellie's heart grew heavy. She tried to busy it away, going on to the next customer and then the next, but it was no use. Finally, when she felt the threat of tears, she quietly excused herself, went to her office, and pulled the door tightly closed behind her.

She needed to think, to breathe, to hold the sobs at bay.

Hers were tears of sadness, yes, but also of shame, and her mind began pounding with the knowledge of what she'd done, of the tremendous mistake she'd made.

She and Andy had been so good together. First neighbors, then friends, then finally much more than friends. They had made a perfect pair. Everyone said so. God willing, they would have gone through life hand in hand, as happy as any couple had ever been.

But six months ago she'd ruined it all in a single, impulsive, regrettable, irrevocable moment, one that she wanted to take back more than anything on earth.

As soon as school was over, Sam and Wayne headed for downtown North Star, as they always did on Friday afternoons. Wayne's sister Nellie worked at the creamery, and she liked to treat them to what she called "Free Fridays." Ordinarily that was more than enough to justify the walk, which was about half a mile from their Amish school and in the opposite direction of home. Today, however, Sam's motives were a bit more complicated.

He needed to speak to Nellie about more than just ice cream.

Downtown North Star was a neat place, with shops, restaurants, and lots of friendly people, most of whom Sam had known his whole life. In the summer it often swarmed with tourists, but this time of year there was always a lull—at least until Thanksgiving. That was when the town would go all out with holiday decorations, including twinkle lights in the trees and big red bows on every streetlamp. Then the tourists would come back in droves to shop in the stores, take tons of pictures, and gape with curiosity at any Amish person who happened to stroll past.

The North Star Country Store and Creamery sat on one of the four corners of the main intersection and was a major hub of activity. Though the store sold all sorts of things, from peanuts to paintbrushes, by far its most popular area was the ice cream parlor in back. Even after the weather turned cold, people still came in for ice cream, especially on the weekends.

When the two boys got to the store, they both groaned at the line, which stretched halfway past the jam-and-jelly aisle. At least it seemed to be moving quickly, so they stepped in place behind a pair of Englisch tourists, a couple who seemed to be bickering about whether to go to the outlet malls in Ronks or stick with the smaller shops around here.

"I want to get your mother a quillow for Christmas," the woman said in a whiny voice, referring to the quilt pillows that were so popular with visitors to the area. "I need a smaller, local shop for that, not a chain store."

Sam tuned the people out, forcing himself to focus on what he was going to say to Nellie. The Umbles—Wayne, Nellie, six other siblings, and their parents—had lived next-door to the Danners for years, so talking to Nellie wasn't like talking to a stranger. Yet Sam still felt odd about it. Things had been kind of weird between the two families ever since last May, when the whole mess happened. First Nellie broke up with Andy and ran off to Kutztown, then Andy got all weird and went to Mississippi, and then Nellie finally came back in September, but Andy stayed gone. Regardless, the two families were still next-door neighbors and lifelong friends, so Sam would just have to act as if everything was normal.

In the meantime there was one other reason he was here—to get a glimpse at the community bulletin board, just in case there might be some sort of job listing. Mounted on the wall to the right of the counter, the bulletin board was popular with lots of folks in town. Sam wasn't quite close enough to read the signs and fliers and ads posted there, but he could make out several photos of furniture—no doubt castoffs people were hoping to unload—and a big sketch of a fire truck, probably for a mud sale or a spaghetti dinner or some other sort of fund-raiser.

As the customers ahead of him got their orders and left, he and Wayne drew closer to the board until finally he could make out the words. There was a lot to take in.

For Sale: Master bedroom set. Call for details.

Lost Cat: Answers to the name of Mittens.

Help Wanted: Part time, temporary. No experience necessary. Good pay, flexible hours. Heavy lifting required. Contact Vincent Cook.

Sam's heart skipped a beat. At the bottom of the sign were strips of paper with a phone number written on each one. He noticed none of them had been torn off yet, which probably meant the paper had been put there recently. If Sam was the first one to call, maybe he'd get the job, even if he was only twelve years old. Excited and hopeful, he waited until Wayne was looking in the other direction, and then he pulled loose one of the strips and stuffed it into his pocket.

When it was at last their turn, Sam and Wayne stepped forward excitedly. Wayne's eyes were on the ice cream choices down in the case, but Sam was looking around for his brother's ex-girlfriend, who was nowhere to be seen.

"Where's Nellie?" he asked the young woman behind the counter, an Englischer from the north side of town who always seemed either bored to death or harried beyond belief. Today was one of her harried days.

"I don't know. In the back, I guess," she said, glancing impatiently at the long line behind them. "What can I get you?"

"I'll have a waffle cone with one scoop of peanut butter crunch and one of chocolate," Wayne said. As she grabbed the cone, flipped open the freezer case, and began digging, he turned to Sam and added, "Nellie doesn't serve at the counter much anymore. She got a promotion."

Sam's eyes widened, and Wayne nodded.

"Something to do with money or books. She tried to explain it to me, but it was complicated. Whatever it is, she's a part of the office staff now, full-time."

Full-time. Office staff. In other words, permanent, Sam thought excitedly as he let those words sink in. A big smile spread across his face despite himself. *Wait until Andy hears about this.*

"Well?" the girl asked. She'd handed Wayne his order and was tapping her fingernails against the counter as she waited for Sam to place his. Then a young woman appeared behind her.

"Are these two giving you trouble?" she asked the girl, shooting Wayne and Sam a wink. It was Nellie, looking beautiful as usual. Today she was dressed in maroon, her blond hair tucked back under her Kapp, her green eyes soft and playful yet a little bit sad as well. Ever since she'd come back to Lancaster County in September, she had carried that sadness around with her, and Sam felt sure it had to do with how much she missed Andy and how sorry she was that her actions had hurt him so deeply.

"I'll take care of these guys," she said to the girl, who was visibly relieved. Then Nellie motioned the two boys to the far end of the counter, away from the busy throng. "I see Wayne got his already," she added as she playfully reached over and gave him a poke on the shoulder. He jerked away with a groan, but Sam knew Wayne liked his sister's attention. Turning to Sam, she asked what he would like.

"Just a small cup of vanilla," he replied. He was thankful for Nellie's "Free Fridays," but he knew they weren't really free. He'd seen her slip her own money into the cash register a few weeks ago when she thought he and Wayne weren't looking. He later told Andy, who confirmed that she'd been paying for their cones for years, all the while pretending they were on the house.

Nellie eyed Sam knowingly. Then she went to the freezer case and got to work. When she returned, she held a waffle cone topped with three big scoops of rocky road, Sam's favorite, with chocolate sprinkles on top. She smiled at his surprise as she handed him the cone, cautioning him not to tip it over.

"Nellie, you didn't have to do that," Sam said shyly.

"I know," she replied. "But I also know you'd prefer that to a small cup of vanilla."

Sam knew he was blushing. He could feel the heat in his cheeks. Of the many girls in Andy's old youth group, Nellie had always been Sam's favorite by far. It wasn't just that he'd known the Umbles so long they were like family or that she was a good sister to Wayne or that she'd always treated Sam like an actual person who mattered and not just some dumb kid. It was that she was the best one for Andy.

If only Sam could make his brother forget what she'd done. If only he could talk Andy into giving her another chance. Sam took a deep breath, ready to say what he'd come here to tell her, but at the last second he held it in. With all these people around, it wasn't the right time to share with her about the Great Christmas Challenge. He was pretty sure he wanted her to know, but for some reason he felt hesitant talking about it in front of Wayne.

"Thanks, Nellie," he managed instead, and she responded with a nod.

"You're welcome, Sam," she replied. "Give my love to your family," she added, and their eyes met for a brief moment.

He knew, and he knew she knew he knew that what she really meant was, *Give my love to Andy.*

*T*he only thing Andy enjoyed more than the solid feel of a hammer in his hand was the pleasure of having used that hammer to work his way down an entire row of shingles. He had just reached the far edge of the roof and was about to start on the next row when he heard the sound of a ladder creaking and looked over to see his boss's head pop above the roofline.

"Hey! Andy!" the man called, gesturing him over with a wave.

Though a good twenty years older than Andy, Ivan had become a close friend and mentor to him over the past six months. As Andy stood and moved in his boss's direction, bending low for stability as he went, he thought about how much he admired Ivan's work ethic and character, not to mention the way he treated the men in his charge.

"There's a call for you, my boy," Ivan said when Andy drew close and knelt in front of him. Clutching the ladder with one hand, Ivan dug into his pants pocket with the other, finally producing a cell phone, which he handed to Andy. Though Ivan was Amish and his community was fairly conservative, he was allowed to have a cell phone on the work site in case of emergencies.

Andy had a regular wall phone at his disposal in the shanty near the garage apartment he rented from an Amish family in the town of Kashofa. That was the number his family was supposed to use when they wanted to talk or to leave him a message, though he had given them Ivan's cell number as well, just in case they had a more urgent need to reach him.

Taking the phone now, Andy's pulse surged, and he braced himself for whatever had prompted this call.

"Hello," he said, sounding tight and tentative even to his own ears.

"Three scoops," said the excited voice at the other end of the line.

"Excuse me?"

"Nellie. At the creamery. She gave me three scoops of rocky road with sprinkles on a *waffle* cone, even though all I asked for was a small scoop of vanilla in a plain old cup."

Andy let out a long breath, not sure whether to fuss at his little brother or laugh. Before doing either, he gave Ivan an *okay* sign with his thumb and forefinger, letting him know things were fine, that it wasn't a true emergency. Ivan responded with a nod, then pointed toward the ground and began descending the ladder.

Andy held the phone away from his mouth and called after him. "I'll bring it down to you in a bit."

"No rush," Ivan replied from below.

Returning his attention to the phone in his hand, Andy took another deep breath and formed his words carefully. "And you're interrupting me at work to tell me this . . . why?" Before Sam could answer, he added, "Where are you calling from anyway? Why am I hearing traffic?"

"I'm downtown, at the pay phone by the post office. Right across from the community center. Wayne had to buy stamps for his mom, so I decided to call you while I was waiting for him." He went on to say he'd be making one other call after this one, to inquire about a job that he'd spotted on the bulletin board in the creamery.

"Is that why you called? To tell me you may have found a job?"

"No," Sam replied, sounding frustrated. "I was just mentioning that 'cause I thought you'd want to know."

Andy adjusted his position on the roof from kneeling to sitting and let out a sigh. "Okay. So what's up?"

As irritated as Andy felt, a part of him couldn't help but smile. He missed his kid brother so much sometimes it was crazy. The two of them had always been close, from the first time his mother placed the fussy, squirming infant in his twelve-year-old arms. He had looked down at that baby, and that baby had looked up at him, and suddenly the squirming and fussing stopped. They just stared at each other for a long moment, and then even though Mamm said it wasn't possible at such a young age, Andy was certain the baby had smiled.

That infant had grown into a fine young man, one who was the same age now that Andy had been when he'd first met his baby brother. There was much to admire about Sam, Andy thought, including his drive to get things done. His energy. His enthusiasm for his various pursuits. But sometimes that enthusiasm led him to do things he shouldn't, like using his big brother's emergency number just to talk about ice cream.

"She's staying this time, Andy," Sam said. "I'm sure of it."

Andy squeezed his eyes shut, trying to muster some patience for dealing with the endless refrain. "Sam, we've been over this. You know how I feel."

He rubbed his eyes with the palm of his hand. Nellie couldn't be trusted, no matter what she said or did or how strongly she'd managed to convince Sam otherwise. *She left once,* Andy reminded himself every time he thought of her. *She planned and schemed behind my back, and then she made her move. Even if she's sorry about it now, there's always a chance she might do it again. How could I ever believe otherwise?*

"I know," Sam replied, frustration creeping into his voice. "It's just that she's got a full-time job now, as a money manager or something. She's different from how she was before. She seems more sure of things, more sure of herself. Like she finally knows where she belongs. I'm not explaining it right, but I can feel it."

"I don't want to have this conversation."

"But she's sad too, you know?" Sam pressed onward. "She smiles and stuff, but you can see it in her eyes. She misses you."

"I have to get back to work," Andy said, his jaw clenched. "Don't call this number again unless it's an emergency. Okay?"

"All right, all right," Sam replied. "Just remember your promise. If I earn the money, you're coming home for Christmas."

"How could I forget?" Andy could feel his exasperation fading into something more like pity. Poor Sam was convinced he could pull this off, but Andy knew the truth, that it would be nearly impossible for him to earn that much money in so short a time. Try as he might, this was one mountain Sam was not going to be able to move.

They said their good-byes, and once Andy had hung up, he headed down the ladder to return the phone to Ivan. He found him standing out back, watching two workmen smooth the last of a large, wet square of fresh cement.

"Everything okay?" Ivan asked, tucking the phone in his pocket.

Andy nodded. "Sorry about that. My little brother needs a better definition of what constitutes an emergency."

Ivan chuckled. "The two of you are close," he said more as a statement than a question. Andy had talked about the kid often enough that it had to be obvious.

"Yeah."

"Hey, listen," Ivan added when Andy turned to leave. "Just so you know, the offer's still open, if you're interested. I can arrange a meetup. You only have to say the word."

Andy shook his head, trying not to groan. Ivan was an aspiring matchmaker, at least on behalf of the eligible young women in his community. He was always trying to pair Andy off with one girl or another, and according to him, almost all of them were interested. Andy knew

Ivan's intentions were good, and he was sure the women were nice enough. But he always said no, because they just weren't right for him.

They just weren't Nellie.

Back up on the roof for the final hour of the workday, Andy tried to concentrate on the task at hand, but it was pointless. His mind was far away, on thoughts of home, of his family, of his former life. He loved being a carpenter, but he wasn't all that crazy about using those skills for house repair and construction. He would have much preferred a quiet workshop of his own somewhere, a square of sandpaper in his hand, a sturdy curve of mahogany just aching to be made smooth. Instead he was surrounded day after day by noise and commotion, by the buzz of electric drills and the slams of nail guns.

It was enough to make a man miss the quiet of a barn, the smell of hay in the loft, the crispness of a winter morning. Though he'd never wanted his father's dairy farming life, thinking about his family, about Sam, about being back in North Star made Andy's insides ache.

Before he could stop himself, Andy's mind once again returned to Nellie, the one person he most wanted not to think about. He just couldn't help remembering what it had been like to be with her. The way a dimple formed in one cheek when she smiled. The way her hair smelled. The tendrils that sometimes came loose from her Kapp to curl delicately at her neck. He thought of their walks through the patch of trees that separated their families' farms, walks where they discussed marriage and life and all their dreams and plans. With Nellie at his side, Andy could've had everything he wanted. The best wife in the world. A wonderful mother to all the kids the Lord chose to bless them with. And an intelligent helpmate who shared his goal of operating their own cabinet-making business. He would have been the creator, the crafts-man, and she the administrator and money person. Together they would have made the perfect team.

Andy shook his head, trying to chase the memories away. All of that was gone now, and he didn't want it back. He could never be with someone he couldn't trust.

And despite whatever Sam had to say about it, Andy knew he could never trust Nellie again.

The next morning Sam pulled on yesterday's clothes to do his chores of tending the horses, mucking out their stalls, and feeding the chickens—messy endeavors all. Then he went back into the house and cleaned himself up, changing into a fresh pair of trousers and a nice white shirt, before joining the family at the breakfast table.

Sam had thought long and hard last night about how he would approach the matter of the Great Christmas Challenge with his parents. In the end he decided not to tell either one of them—not because he made a habit of keeping things from them, but because he realized that Andy's appearance in North Star on Christmas Day would make the perfect surprise for them both, the most excellent gift he could ever give.

Once breakfast and devotions were done and he'd helped his sister open and stock the produce stand for the day, he went back into the house and told his Mamm he was going out for a while, a statement that almost always meant he was heading over to Wayne's. Sam wouldn't lie to his Mamm if she asked, but neither would he correct any mistaken assumptions she might make.

Fortunately for him, she was busy at her sewing machine and too distracted to pay all that much attention.

"Okay," she replied over the drone of the generator outside the window. "Just make sure to get back by one so your sister can take a break and get some lunch."

"I will."

His steps light, Sam pulled on his jacket and hat and headed to-

ward town, covering the distance between his house and the neighborhood he was looking for in about ten minutes. Once he'd turned off
Danner Drive and into the neighborhood, he still had to go several
more blocks to reach the house he was looking for.

As he walked, Sam went back over yesterday's phone conversation
in his mind. He'd made the call from the pay phone in town as soon
as he'd hung up with Andy. The man, who had identified himself as
Vincent Cook, had sounded kind of old and not all that friendly. He
answered Sam's questions with short, clipped sentences. Then he responded with a few questions of his own, like what hours was Sam free
and if he had ever done this kind of work before. The man seemed
satisfied with Sam's answers, so when it sounded like the call was about
over, Sam asked if he could have the job. Vincent laughed, a strained
cackle that ended in a coughing fit.

"You have to come for an interview first," he rasped. "How's tomorrow, say midmorning?"

Wayne had emerged from the post office not long after Sam's call
was done. As he watched his buddy approach, Sam decided to tell him
the whole plan after all, just as a security measure. He wasn't supposed
to go into the homes of strangers, but he figured as long as at least one
person knew exactly where he was and when he should be back, he'd
be safe. Wayne had listened with great interest and even offered to come
along if Sam wanted, but he'd said, "No thanks, just swing by the produce stand later to make sure I'm not dead or something."

Now the time for that interview had come, and Sam was finally
on Holly Lane, the tan ranch-style house the man had described just
ahead. Moving up the walk toward the door, Sam noticed that the
garage was half-open, and as he went past it, he heard a cough from
inside, the same kind of cough he'd heard over the phone yesterday.

Pausing at the threshold of the garage, Sam dipped his head under
the door and looked around. "Hello? Is somebody there?"

"Back here," croaked a man from deep within. Then he coughed some more.

Sam ducked inside, removing his hat as he stood up straight amid a massive amount of clutter. The space was nearly full from end to end with towers of boxes, tons and tons of them stacked one on the other. There were old bicycle parts on the ground and broken pieces of furniture and Christmas decorations strewn across the piles. No wonder Vincent wanted to hire help. This was way more than one man could manage on his own.

Sam followed the sound of coughing to the left side of the garage, where he spotted a short, elderly fellow struggling beneath the weight of a box.

"I'll get that," Sam cried as he dropped his hat and ran up to take the box into his arms. The guy released it and then bent forward, pulling out a handkerchief and coughing loudly into it. "Are you all right?" Sam asked once the ruckus ended.

"I'm fine, I'm fine," Vincent grunted as he stood up straight. He wiped at his mouth with the handkerchief, carefully folded it, and tucked it away in his pocket. "Don't worry. I'm not sick. I'm allergic to dust. Every time I come out here and try to get things organized, it sets me to wheezing."

"That's not good," Sam told him.

"No, it's not." He cleared his throat and squinted at Sam. "I assume you're the young fellow who called about the job?"

Sam nodded. "And you're Vincent Cook?"

"Last time I checked," he quipped.

Sam smiled but didn't offer his hand for a shake because he was still holding the box. "Nice to meet you, Vincent. I'm Sam."

The man's brow furrowed. "How old did you say you are?"

"Uh, twelve."

"That's what I thought. None of this 'Vincent' stuff, then. It's 'Mr. Cook' to you, boy."

Sam's smile faded. Of course. How dumb of him. Englischers always started out more formally with each other than the Amish did.

"Sorry, Mr. Cook. No offense intended."

"All right, then." The man gave a nod, and his attention seemed to shift to their surroundings. Eyes still squinting, he peered around as if in search of something. "We can get started as soon as I find my glasses," he explained finally. "I can't see a thing without 'em, but they've fallen somewhere over there."

"I'll get them," Sam replied. "But I'll need to put this box down first. Where would you like it?"

"Just set it on top of the others." He pointed toward the right side of the garage.

"Mr. Cook," Sam said, "there are a lot of others."

The man hobbled over to the pile he had meant to indicate and told Sam to place it there. "You see how heavy it is, so be careful now," he warned.

This surprised Sam. The box was barely heavier than a fifteen-pound pumpkin. He raised it up and set it on top of the pile.

Mr. Cook grunted. "You're strong for your age."

"I help out a lot on my parents' farm."

Mr. Cook nodded. "Someone with a good work ethic. That's the type of fellow I'm looking for."

"*Looking* for?" Sam said lightly, attempting a quip of his own. "I thought you said you couldn't see a thing without your glasses."

Mr. Cook chuckled, though it came out more like a clearing of his throat. "And a comedian besides," he said, shaking his head, though he didn't seem displeased. "Come on. Let's find them."

Together they moved back toward the area in question, and then

Mr. Cook wiggled a stack of boxes just far enough out of the way for Sam to squeeze through. Behind there he noticed an old rocking horse, some engine parts, and a set of golf clubs. Peering around, he finally spotted the glasses, which were peeking out from underneath a long wooden toy box.

"Got 'em!" Sam called, scooping them off the floor and brushing away a big glob of dust with his fingers.

"I have a lot of stuff, I know," Mr. Cook apologized as Sam squeezed back out through the boxes and handed over the glasses. Taking them carefully, the man held them up to the light and studied them for a moment before wiping the lenses with the tail of his shirt. "You can see why I need help. I'd like to get all these things sorted out. You know, box up what's important, give the rest away. There's even more inside the house. But we'll start out here. Interested?"

"Yes sir," Sam replied. "I need this job. More than anything. I can only offer you a few hours a day right after school and maybe a little more on Saturdays. But I promise you I'll work hard and do it right."

Mr. Cook studied his glasses again, breathed on the lenses, and then wiped them in slow circles this time, seemingly lost in thought. "All right," he finally said. "You're strong. You seem polite. And apparently you're punctual. I guess you're hired."

Sam shook Mr. Cook's hand with vigor, his vision of the perfect Christmas coming together at last: The call to Andy to tell him he'd earned the money. The secret arrangements and ruses he'd have to use to get his parents to the train station on Christmas Day. His mother's tears and the joy on her face when she realized they weren't there to pick up some package but her own son Andy, home after all these months. Sam could practically feel his heart swell with the joy of it all.

He let go of Mr. Cook's hand, realizing he might've been a little too enthusiastic. Taking a step back, he was about to ask when he could start when the man finally put on his glasses.

Immediately something changed in his features.

He stared at Sam for a long moment, looking him up and down, and then he opened his mouth to speak—and began coughing instead. He tried to pull out his handkerchief but dropped it in the process. Sam bent forward to retrieve it, but Mr. Cook pushed him away.

"Amish," he finally managed to gasp between coughs. "You're *Amish*."

The way Mr. Cook said the word sent a shudder through Sam's body. There was so much anger in it, almost fury or rage.

Sam looked down at his white shirt tucked into his broadfall trousers, his navy suspenders. He'd left his hat near the door, but otherwise he knew he looked like every other Amish boy in this community. He brushed some dust from his sleeve and pushed his hands into his pockets.

"You didn't mention that on the phone, that you were Amish," Mr. Cook said accusingly, as if it were something bad, as if it fell into some category that made him unfit for the job. "I can't believe I didn't notice the accent. Of *course* you're Amish."

Sam could not think of a reply. In his entire life no one had ever said anything like this to him. The Amish and the Englisch coexisted peacefully in this town, just as they did throughout Lancaster County.

Mr. Cook looked pale. He moved toward a rocking chair, the only available piece of furniture in the place, and lowered himself into it. "I can't work with someone who's Amish," he said, his voice quiet but firm. "The deal is off."

Sam was about to protest, but Mr. Cook began coughing again. Sam waited until he was done and asked if he'd be okay, if he'd like some water or something.

"Just go," the man wheezed. "And don't come back."

Stunned, all Sam could do was look around for his hat, pick it up, and head out the way he came in. He walked down the driveway to the street and just kept going, his mind spinning like a wooden top as he retraced his steps through the neighborhood.

The tears didn't come until he was nearing Danner Drive. Not wanting to be seen in such a state, Sam stopped walking and tried to bear it, just as he'd seen his brothers do when they'd accidentally smacked their thumb with a hammer or gotten their foot stomped on by a feisty cow. But this pain wasn't on the outside. Sam's whole heart hurt, and he couldn't understand why. He couldn't help but cry.

A few minutes later, once he'd finally regained some control, Sam began walking again. When he came to Danner Drive, he paused and thought for a long moment.

Then he turned in the opposite direction and began striding purposefully toward town, wiping the tears from his cheeks as he went.

*W*hy don't you tell me why you're really here," Nellie said, keeping her voice soft as she looked at the young man sitting on the other side of her desk.

"I told you," Sam replied, his cheeks growing pink. "I wanted to know if you need any more pumpkins for the ice cream. The crop's almost done, so you better order them now."

"Thanks for asking, Sam, but we're fine," Nellie replied. Then she stood, quietly pushed the door all the way closed, and returned to her seat. She leaned forward on her elbows, fixing Sam in her gaze. "Now tell me the truth."

He looked panicked for a moment. She'd noticed when he first arrived that his face was red and blotchy, as if he'd been crying. She thought about pointing this out, to encourage him to tell her what was wrong, but instead she waited in silence until he finally blurted the words he'd obviously been burning to say.

"You still love Andy, don't you?" he demanded. "You still want to marry him."

Nellie took in a breath, startled by his forthrightness, his perception, and his intensity. Considering the state he was in, she decided to level with him, even if it was none of his business.

"Yes," she whispered, "I do."

Sam's wide brown eyes filled with fresh tears, and the sight nearly broke her heart.

314

MINDY STARNS CLARK AND EMILY CLARK

"Why, Sam? What's wrong? Why are you so upset?"

He swiped angrily at his cheeks. "If you love him so much, then why don't you tell him? Why don't you ask him to come home?"

Nellie could see a myriad of emotions on the boy's face—anger, sadness, frustration, hurt. She didn't know what had brought this on, but once again she felt like she needed to be honest with him.

"I did," she said.

His eyes widened.

With a nod she continued. "When I first came back from Kutztown, I wrote Andy a long letter, pouring my heart out to him. I told him what a mistake I'd made and how sorry I was and how very much I wanted to undo all the pain I had caused him." Now it was her turn for tears, though she managed to blink them away and keep going. "I asked if he could forgive me and move past what I'd done to him. To us. I asked him if he would come home so we could try again and do it right this time."

"And?" Sam asked, looking quite surprised.

"And he wrote me back, a brief note scribbled on a scrap of paper and shoved into an envelope. I don't remember how he worded it, but basically the sentiment was 'too little, too late.'"

Sam swallowed hard. "And so you gave up? You stopped trying?"

Nellie shook her head. "No, Sam. I started praying. Every day I have prayed for God to soften Andy's heart. To show both of us His will. To guide us in making decisions. I keep telling myself that maybe I should move on, that I should give up hope. But then something stops me—this feeling I get, like the Lord is telling me to be patient because He does have a plan for us."

"Me too. I think that too, all the time. I even tell it to Andy."

Nellie nodded, resisting the temptation to ask how Andy responded.

"Whatever God has in mind here," she said instead, "I know one thing. He has been using the situation to help me grow. I've gotten so much closer to Him in my pain."

"Yeah?"

"Yeah. I'm ready to join the church now. I've already told the bishop I'll be taking the membership classes in the spring."

Sam looked away, and something about his expression twisted Nellie's stomach into a knot.

"What?" she asked.

He shrugged. "It's just that . . . well . . . you've done the classes before, remember?"

There was accusation in his tone, but she tried not to let it hurt her feelings. Yes, she remembered. She remembered very well, especially her last day, when she was supposed to stand up and reaffirm her decision and her commitment—and instead turned and ran out the door.

"What do you want from me, Sam? Reassurance that I know what I'm doing this time? That I've changed? That I can be trusted now, even knowing what happened before? Because frankly, there's no way for me to convince you otherwise, just like I can't convince your brother. Sometimes it's more about faith and letting a person's actions speak for themselves."

Nellie pursed her lips, not sure if she'd said too much or not enough. Either way, she let her words sit between them, watching the sweet little brother of the man she loved as he grappled with issues he was too young to fully comprehend.

"Why did you come here, Sam?" she asked yet again. "Do you need something from me?"

This time he rose, still clutching his hat in his hands, rubbing his fingers back and forth along the brim.

"I need you to write Andy another letter," Sam said. "Remind him of what he already knows. That you love him. That you're sorry. That you want him home."

Nellie sighed. "You think that'll make any difference?"

Sam shrugged. "I don't know. But maybe this time he'll remember he still loves you too."

~~~⚜~~~

The whole next week Sam searched every day after school for work. He asked neighbors, checked more bulletin boards, even read the want ads in the newspaper. But he was always too young for the jobs, or they required more hours than he could give, or they turned out to be volunteer rather than paying positions.

By the end of the week, Sam felt more hopeless than ever, so when Wayne was ready to head into town after school for ice cream, Sam declined.

"What?" Wayne gasped. "But it's Free Friday."

"I don't have much of an appetite," Sam replied. Then he turned and headed for home, knowing he had hurt Wayne's feelings but needing very much at that moment to be alone.

The day was cold, the bitter kind of cold that crept under clothes and chilled all the way to the bone. The closer Sam got to home, the colder he grew. But as he got to the driveway, he headed not for the warmth of the house but for the dairy barn.

He knew what he needed to do.

Sam found his Daed tending to their newest cow, Gerty, who'd been having a little trouble settling in with the rest of the herd. They'd had to segregate her in her own stall for now, and Daed was standing at the door, talking gently to the animal as he attempted to pull out some briars stuck in her hide. Sam joined him, watching Gerty's breath turn to steam in the air as her nostrils flared and snorted.

"She still giving you trouble?" Sam asked, pretty sure he could detect a rebellious glint in the cow's eyes.

"Ya," Daed replied, "she made a run for the Umbles' yard at grazing time today and got stuck in some thorny bushes in the trees. She's making it as difficult as she can to get them out now, but we'll get there."

Ever since they'd brought Gerty home a few weeks ago and realized how agitated she was, Daed had insisted on being the one to handle her, including cleaning out her stall. She had a bad temper, and he didn't want anyone getting kicked.

As Daed pulled an especially large thorn from her side, Sam spoke softly to her so she'd remain calm.

"Something on your mind?" Daed asked once the thorn was out, shooting Sam a quick glance.

"I've been keeping a secret from you and Mamm," Sam blurted.

Daed's face remained calm. "Oh?"

Before he could stop himself, Sam was telling his Daed everything: his challenge to Andy, his attempts to get a job, his encounter with Mr. Cook. The only parts he left out were the conversation with Nellie, which wasn't his right to share, and his crying like a baby all the way to town.

Daed pulled out another thorn, seemingly lost in thought. The cow sidestepped a few times and snorted, but Daed's touch seemed to calm her. After a while he spoke.

"You were right to tell me all this, Son. I'm glad you did. I only wish you'd said something sooner."

The disappointment in Daed's voice almost made Sam want to cry again.

"But I think you should keep your secret a little longer."

Surprised, Sam looked at his father, whose face wore a mischievous grin as if, despite the disappointment, he was also a little pleased.

"You mean don't tell Mamm?"

Daed shrugged. "Tell her you've gotten yourself a job after school, yes. Maybe even tell her you're earning money to buy her a Christmas present. But don't tell her what that present is."

Sam felt a smile creep across his face. "Really?"

"Ya. I think your heart was in the right place when you made these plans. And I think if you can pull it off, it'll be the best gift she's ever gotten." He rubbed Gerty's neck before starting on the next briar. "I can even help you pay for it."

"Actually, Daed, you can't. The only way I could get Andy to agree to come was if I earned all the money myself. He was definite about that."

Daed gave a nod. "Very well, then I can help in other ways. I'd be happy to handle the whole get-Mamm-to-the-train-station-under-false-pretenses thing."

Sam smiled. "Really?"

"Sure, why not? I think it's high time we had a visit from dear old Almena."

"Almena?"

"From Indiana. Almena Schrock, your fifth cousin once removed. I don't know why I never thought to invite her out here before."

Sam laughed. "Maybe because she insists on bringing her pigs with her?"

"And her pet skunk," Daed added, and then they both laughed.

They returned to the thorn removal and worked together in comfortable silence. Then finally Sam spoke, his voice somber. "I should have come to you from the very beginning," he said, shaking his head. "Or at least after the whole thing with Mr. Cook. I can't forget the way he looked at me. So much anger, Daed. Such hurtful words. It's probably best that it didn't work out." Even as Sam said it, he knew it wasn't true. He had wanted that job with Mr. Cook. He needed it. Until the moment the man put on his glasses and everything changed, Sam had actually even liked the old guy.

Daed was quiet for a while. He sifted through the pouch of tools around his waist until he found a large pair of tweezers, and Sam knew by the absent look in his eyes that he was thinking. When he spoke, Sam was surprised by his words.

"Sometimes people use anger to cover other feelings. Like grief."

"Grief?"

Daed shrugged. "I'm familiar with Vincent Cook. He's not a bad sort. He just hasn't had an easy time of things these past few years."

Sam waited for his father to elaborate, but it seemed that no other details were forthcoming.

"What are you trying to say?" Sam finally asked.

"Just that people don't start out bitter. Sometimes they let circumstances make them that way."

Sam blinked, considering, as his father continued.

"When Vincent said those terrible things, he was probably just taking his pain out on you. But that doesn't make it right." Daed took the tweezers and pulled an especially deep thorn from Gerty's side. She snorted loudly and knocked her head back and forth, but after a few soothing strokes on her hip, she calmed again. Then he locked eyes with Sam and added, "It's never our place to judge, Son. Only to love."

"To love?" Sam echoed.

Daed nodded. "People like Vincent need someone in their life who will show them love—God's love. Who will show them the meaning of grace."

CHAPTER SIX

*T*he next day, after all of Sam's Saturday chores were done, he stood at Mr. Cook's front door, his fist suspended in the air. He wanted to knock, had intended to knock, but now couldn't bring himself to do it. He put his hands back into his pockets and stepped off the front porch. He wasn't sure what to do.

He was about to forget it and just go home when he noticed for the first time the condition of Mr. Cook's front yard. It was covered in dead, rotting leaves. Sam remembered seeing a couple of tools leaning against the side of the house near the garage, so he walked over there and was pleased to find, between a shovel and a pair of long-handled clippers, a rake.

Sam got right to work, starting at the far corner of the front yard and making his way slowly down and across. He was just past the halfway point when he heard someone call out to him. He spun around to see Mr. Cook looming in the open doorway, a scowl on his face.

"What are you doing, boy? Get out of here."

Sam hesitated for a moment. Then he steeled his resolve, turned his back to the man, and continued raking.

After a bit more hollering, the noise finally stopped, followed by the slam of the front door.

Sam relaxed a bit, blowing out a breath and tackling the next section of lawn. It took him another half hour or so, but he didn't hear anything else from inside until he finished raking together the final pile of leaves.

It was Mr. Cook, again from the porch, but this time he cleared his throat instead of yelling.

"Bags are in the garage," he growled. "Right-hand side, near the front."

Then he went back into his house and closed the door, albeit more softly this time.

Stifling a victorious smile, Sam walked to the garage, yanked up the rolling door, and found the bags right where Mr. Cook had said they would be. He carried a stack out front and managed to fill nearly ten before he was done.

"I'm not paying you for today," a voice said from behind him. "Raking leaves was never part of the job description."

Sam took a deep breath and turned to face the older man. "Yes sir, I understand. I just noticed they needed doing is all."

"Doesn't matter how good it looks now, I'm not paying."

"And I'm not charging," Sam replied. "But I am still interested in the job if it's available."

Mr. Cook made a grumbling sound. He crossed his arms over his chest. "Haven't filled it yet, if that's what you mean. Heard from a few others, but they weren't even worth considering. The last applicant actually fell asleep during the interview."

"Fell asleep? Were you that boring?" Sam teased.

Mr. Cook grunted. "Nope. He was that lazy."

"I see."

They both chuckled, and only then did Sam realize how dark it was getting. That always seemed to happen in the fall; as the sun set earlier each day, dusk would catch him by surprise.

"All right, fine, you can have the job," Mr. Cook said. Then he added quickly as if to salvage his pride, "But only if you show up on time, you do exactly what I say, and you don't mess around."

Sam grinned.

"You'll start Monday, four o'clock. Don't be late."

"Oh, I won't."

Sam was about to turn and go when Mr. Cook held up an index finger and added, "One more thing. I'll be right back." He disappeared into the house, emerging about a minute later with what looked like a battered old flashlight. He fiddled with it for a minute, whacked it against the palm of his hand, then finally got it to come on.

"There you go," he said, holding it out toward Sam.

Wow, that's awful nice of—"

"See you next week," he added gruffly, waving off Sam's thanks as he went back inside and closed the door.

Sam grinned most of the way home.

On Monday, Sam could barely concentrate for the second half of the school day. He was too excited about his new job—excited and nervous and maybe a little bit scared. What if he made some big mistake, like dropping and breaking something valuable? What if he put things away wrong and got all mixed up and ended up labeling the important boxes as giveaways? What if Mr. Cook yelled at him again just for being Amish?

Those were the kinds of questions that swirled around in Sam's mind, distracting him from his schoolwork and getting him in trouble with the teacher not once but three different times.

Wayne wasn't too happy with him either, which he made clear as they walked part of the way home together after school. "Today I shot a whole bunch of spitballs at you while the teacher was writing on the board," Wayne grumbled, "and you didn't even notice."

Sam's eyes widened. "*You* shot spitballs at *me,* and you're the one who's mad?"

Wayne shrugged. "I'm not mad. I'm just saying it's time to stop daydreaming and pay some attention to what's around you."

Sam was about to reply when he saw Holly Lane up ahead. He checked his watch and realized he needed to speed things up a bit if he wanted to be on time.

"Sorry, Wayne, gotta run," he said.

Then he crossed to the other side of the road and jogged toward the home of his new employer, making it to his destination a few minutes before four.

The work time went quickly, though it was nothing like Sam had expected. For two solid hours Mr. Cook mostly ordered him around like a servant. He had Sam pulling boxes down from up high and then taking those same boxes and piling them on other shelves. He had Sam carry at least twenty garbage bags to the curb out front, only to make him bring half of them back in again so he could go through them one more time. Sam tried not to complain, but it was all so inefficient and frustrating. He wanted badly to say something like "Make up your mind!" But he held his tongue. Maybe Mr. Cook was testing him, making the job as irritating as possible to see how much he could take.

But finally, after a while, Sam realized that maybe Mr. Cook wasn't intentionally giving him pointless tasks. It was more like he was trapped by indecision.

Once when Sam was carrying an especially large box from the curb back to the garage, the bottom collapsed, and all the contents fell out. Fortunately, it was only clothing and nothing breakable.

But Mr. Cook ran over and began frantically scooping the clothes off the driveway and into a bag, like he was about to cry or something, and Sam was more confused than ever. What was the big deal? They were just clothes and not even fancy ones at that. A few dresses. Some blouses with flowers on them. A flannel nightgown or two.

It wasn't until he saw the nightgowns that it struck him these were women's clothes.

"Whose are those?" Sam blurted. Then he winced, wishing he could take it back as he waited for the man's reaction.

All he got was a glare. Mr. Cook continued stuffing the clothes into the bag. Unfortunately, that bag had a hole in it from earlier when Sam had caught it on a nail in the wall of the garage, and the clothes started coming out the other side. Sam stooped to help, but Mr. Cook waved him off.

Sam responded by running to the garage and retrieving a fresh bag from the box. Then he brought it out to his employer and gingerly handed it over. It took a minute, but when Mr. Cook realized what it was, he seemed to calm down a little. With a sigh he started over, this time transferring the clothes from the old, busted bag to the new one.

"They were my wife's," he said finally. Then he sighed again, adding, "I can't bring myself to get rid of them."

His wife's. Of course. Mr. Cook had been married, but she must have died. The thought made Sam's heart ache.

Slowly he squatted down and began to help, and this time Mr. Cook did not stop him.

"She passed on three years ago," he said after a while. "Sometimes I forget that she's gone. I'll wake up and roll over to tell her something. Or I'll read something funny in the paper and open my mouth to share it with her before I remember she's not there to hear it."

Sam wasn't sure how to reply, so finally he just said, "I can see why it's hard to make up your mind about this stuff."

And he really meant it. Sam hadn't experienced much death, at least not at such a personal level. But he did remember how it felt when Andy called near the end of his Mississippi mission trip to say that he'd decided to stay down South. The next day Sam was helping Mamm deep clean Andy's abandoned room when he spotted one of his brother's work boots under the bed. Later, after his mother went down to the kitchen, Sam had grabbed the old boot, snuck it into his own room, and tucked it away.

For the longest time Sam kept that stupid boot. The thought of getting rid of it brought tears to his eyes. He didn't know why, but with Andy so far away, knowing his boot was still here somehow made him feel closer. Even though it was just a boot.

"Here's a thought," Sam said, trying to keep his voice light. "Why don't we work on everything else first and save the clothes for last? Maybe it'll be easier by then."

Mr. Cook was quiet for a while. Finally he nodded. "Yes, good idea. Let's leave her stuff for last."

They both grew silent again until the older man added gruffly, "And I suppose you can start calling me 'Vincent' if you still want to. That is how you Amish do it, isn't it? First names for everyone?"

"Usually," Sam said, deeply touched by the offer. "Thanks. I guess 'Vincent' it is."

*T*he next afternoon went a bit more smoothly as Sam and Vincent began to develop a rhythm. The older man was coughing pretty bad at first, so finally Sam grabbed the rocking chair and set it up just outside the open garage, suggesting that Vincent direct everything from there without being right in the middle of it, breathing it all in. He was skeptical but gave it a try and soon found that it really did help. On the downside, once he was no longer coughing so much, he was able to boss Sam around even more, barking out orders like a military man.

On Wednesday, Vincent seemed even crankier than before, almost surly, a mood Sam chalked up to the weather. It had been a cool week, but today was positively frigid, so much so that after about ten minutes, they decided to save the rest of the garage for another time and moved to the inside of the house instead.

They started in what Vincent said was a guest room, though it was stuffed so full of boxes and things that no guest could possibly use it. They followed the same routine, with Vincent sitting just outside the door in the hallway ordering Sam to open this box or that, see what was inside, and sort it from there.

Things progressed fairly well with the piles, though Vincent's mood seemed to be getting worse. Finally, at the end of their first hour of work, he announced that was enough for today and Sam could go home.

"But I can stay till seven tonight if you want," Sam objected. "I'd rather keep working if you don't mind."

"I do mind."

Sam hesitated, adding, "Well, see, the reason I was hoping to put in some extra hours today is because I won't be getting any at all tomorrow."

"Tomorrow?"

"Ya. Thanksgiving. You weren't planning for us to work on Thanksgiving, were you? Because I know my parents wouldn't allow that."

Vincent seemed surprised, and Sam realized he hadn't even known the holiday was coming. Sam wondered if he had any plans at all, or if now that his wife was gone, he'd just eat a can of soup or something, all alone in his big, empty house. More than anything Sam would've loved to invite him to share the day with his family, but he knew that was out of the question. If Vincent had trouble accepting just one Amish boy, there was no way he would be open to socializing with an entire extended Amish family.

Just then there was a knock at the door.

"I'll be right back," the older man growled as he rose and headed up the hall.

The visitor sounded like a woman, though their exchange wasn't quite loud enough for Sam to hear what they were saying. All he could tell was that she sounded friendly enough, but Vincent was gruff and curt in return. Their conversation lasted for only a minute or so, and then the door closed and the woman was gone.

After that, Vincent shuffled past the guest room with what looked like a white Styrofoam box in his hand. Curious, Sam waited until the man returned to his chair before he spoke.

"What was that?" he asked.

"What?"

"The woman at the door. The white box you were carrying."

Vincent grunted. "Not that it's any of your business, but that was what's known as 'Christian charity.'" His words were tinged with sarcasm. Sam gave him a questioning look, so he added, "Food. From the church. Gloria brings me a hot meal three times a week. Guess that officially makes me a shut-in. Or just an old man."

From the way he said it, Sam couldn't tell if it was meant to be a joke or not, so he turned back to the box at hand and kept going.

"Didn't I tell you we were done for the day?"

Sam hesitated. "Yes sir, and I asked you if I could keep going since we won't work tomorrow."

Vincent was silent for a long moment, just watching him, and then he spoke. "What's got you working so hard anyway?" Eyes narrowing, he added, "Are all you Amish kids forced into earning money for your families? Is that it?"

Sam took a deep breath, trying to ignore the taunting tone in his voice. "No way. No one's forcing me to work. I'm doing this on my own."

"Why? You trying to get enough money to run off or something? Do your parents even know you come here?"

"My Daed knows, yes. But Mamm doesn't. We're keeping it a surprise."

"A surprise."

"Ya, I'm trying to earn the money to buy a train ticket for my brother to come home for Christmas. He lives in Mississippi."

"Why can't he buy his own ticket?"

"Because he doesn't even want to come."

Vincent's eyebrows raised.

Sam hesitated, wondering how to explain. "The problem isn't Pennsylvania or our family or anything. It's . . . There's this girl, and she broke off their engagement, and after that he didn't want anything to do with her . . ." His voice trailed off, uncomfortable with sharing such personal information.

"There's always a girl," Vincent huffed.

"Well, anyway, we miss him really bad—especially our Mamm,

who would just give *anything* to see him—so I came up with a challenge. I said, 'I know you're not willing to buy a ticket home, but if *I* bought one for you, would you come then?'"

"And he said yes?"

"Not at first. I had to keep bugging him awhile, and he made me agree to certain conditions. But finally he said yes. He promised if I paid, he would come." With a soft chuckle Sam added, "I'm sure the only reason he made the deal is because he thinks I won't pull it off. But I will. I just know I will."

By the time Sam was done with his explanation, he realized Vincent was gaping at him, incredulous.

"So you mean to tell me you're doing all this lugging and lifting and sweating . . . for someone else? For your brother? For your mother?"

"Yes sir," Sam said. "But for me too, I guess. I mean, I really miss him."

Vincent grunted, rose, and hobbled off toward the kitchen. Sam returned to his work, hoping that was the end of it and he would be allowed to stay till seven after all.

But then Vincent appeared in the doorway and held out a small wad of money. "Here," he said. "Your wages for the day. Now go on."

Vincent stood there, arm outstretched, and Sam knew not to argue the point further. Instead he mumbled a quick "thanks," took the money, and stuffed it into his pocket. Then he followed Vincent down the hall to the door, where he retrieved his hat and coat and headed out.

Sam was disappointed, of course, though as he walked home in the gathering dusk, he tried to console himself with the thought that at least he'd been able to put in a full hour, which meant he now had five dollars more than he had before, and that was better than nothing.

Except it wasn't five dollars. It was fifteen. Sam realized it later that night when he was getting ready for bed and emptied out his pockets onto the dresser. His arrangement with Vincent was five dollars an hour, paid in cash at the end of each workday. On Monday he'd worked two hours and had been given ten dollars. On Tuesday he'd worked three hours and had been given fifteen dollars. But today he'd only worked one hour, yet the man had given him fifteen dollars.

Vincent had made a mistake, Sam realized, one he needed to know about sooner rather than later. It was too late to return the money that night, but the next morning, after chores and breakfast were done and everyone was bustling around, getting ready for their Thanksgiving trip to his oldest sister's house, Sam checked with his Mamm about when they would be leaving. He had just enough time to return the extra cash.

The day was chilly but sunny and bright with a blue sky and tiny wisps of clouds. Rather than walk, Sam grabbed his scooter and rode there instead, making fast work of the trip.

Once there, he knocked and waited, listening until he finally heard heavy footsteps inside coming closer. The door swung open to reveal Vincent looking tired and scruffy in a dingy bathrobe over a T-shirt and some old flannel pajama pants.

"What?" he barked.

"Sorry to bother you," Sam said, "but I'm afraid you made a mistake yesterday. You were only supposed to give me five dollars, but you accidentally gave me fifteen."

He held out the extra bills toward his employer, who simply stared at him in return, then shook his head like Sam was an idiot. "It wasn't a mistake," he said gruffly. Then he closed the door in Sam's face.

Confused by the entire encounter, Sam pulled his Daed aside once he got home and told him what had happened. In response, his father just laughed, reaching out to tousle his son's hair.

"Makes sense to me," he said. "You were expecting to work for three hours, but he made you go home after one. Seems only fair that he pay you for all three."

It didn't quite make sense to Sam, but if Daed said it was okay to keep the money, he would keep it.

Grinning, he headed up to his bedroom, dug out the jar he was using as a piggybank, and dropped the bills inside. He didn't have anything close to $318 yet, but every little bit helped.

With Sam's duties at home and school and work, he stayed so busy that the next three weeks flew by. Thanks to several unseasonably warm days in a row, he and Vincent managed to clear out the entire garage. Once they were done, all that was left was the rocking chair the man had sat on as they worked.

"That chair's so old," Vincent said, "I won't even bother trying to give it away. Why don't you just drag it to the street for trash."

Sam blinked, regarding the heavy wooden piece in the drive. "Are you kidding?" He stepped forward to give it a closer look. The handiwork was outstanding, the seat hand caned, and when he checked under the left arm, he saw the emblem he was looking for. "This was locally crafted, Amish made, from mahogany. You don't throw a piece like this away. It's worth a lot of money."

Vincent grunted, skeptical.

"A *lot* of money," Sam repeated, "like at least a couple hundred dollars. Why don't I put a flier for you on the bulletin board in the creamery? I bet it'll sell fast."

"All right," Vincent relented. "Do that. In the meantime slide it over there."

With the garage empty, the work inside the house became a lot easier, because now Sam could cart stuff out there and put it into organized sections. Though Mrs. Cook's clothes still remained untouched in the corner, the piles they'd designated as "Keep" and "Give Away" both slowly grew.

Vincent was still bossy, which Sam had gotten used to and didn't really notice anymore. But he remained at times indecisive, which Sam still found frustrating. Finally he came up with a solution. In the garage Sam added a new category, a pile he called "Not Sure—Decide Later."

That made Mr. Cook feel better. It also allowed them to move at a faster clip, and soon they had finished with the guest room too. From there, they went on to the rooms Vincent used most regularly—the kitchen, living room, and bedroom—which meant leaving plenty of items in place while still packing up everything that wasn't necessary.

At the end of each workday, Vincent paid Sam in cash, and slowly the bills inside his secret jar grew. He wanted to tell Andy all about it, but he wouldn't be calling home for a while. According to the most recent message he'd left on their machine, his work crew was heading to a job in Florida, which would last for a couple of weeks, and he probably wouldn't be in touch until they returned.

At least Daed seemed proud that Sam was working so hard, and though his Mamm voiced concern that he'd been awfully busy lately, she didn't seem suspicious of the reason behind all the time he spent away from the house. As long as he got his chores and homework done and didn't look too exhausted at the end of the day during devotions and family time by the wood stove, Mamm didn't try to stop him.

It helped that harvest officially came to an end after Thanksgiving, which meant no more restocking produce or carting pumpkins around or helping customers with their heavier purchases. His sister would keep the stand open through Christmas, as usual, but only for baked goods, homemade canned items, and of course her famous fudge, which flew off the shelves as fast as she could make it. The December shoppers were mostly tourists, and though business remained brisk, there wasn't much need for Sam's help beyond the occasional carting of boxes or manning of the cash register.

That meant he was able to put even more time in at Vincent's. By mid-December they'd made it through almost the entire house, including the attic, which they had worked through as quickly as possible, because it was so cold up there.

Eventually all that remained were a few dwindling piles in the basement, a big linen closet in the main hallway, and one last bedroom they hadn't touched at all yet. Vincent continued to gripe and snarl, but he never yelled—at least not until one Saturday when Sam apparently did the unthinkable.

The two of them had been heading for the basement to work when they were interrupted by a knock on the door. The food-delivery lady. Knowing it wouldn't do any good to continue down on his own, Sam simply waited nearby as Vincent and Gloria exchanged pleasantries. Sam had noticed lately that their little doorway chats were growing friendlier and longer each time she came, so finally he stopped hovering and decided to occupy himself by checking out the linen closet and that last room, just to see how much work still lay ahead.

The linen closet wasn't too bad, he decided, though it wasn't going to be very good for Vincent's allergies. The stack of sheets and blankets on the top shelf looked as if they hadn't been touched in years. There were some containers in there as well, and as the two lovebirds wrapped up their conversation, Sam pried up each lid in turn and looked inside.

Photo albums, which would no doubt go into the "Keep" section. As Vincent closed the front door and headed to the kitchen with his food, Sam snapped down the last lid and stepped out of the closet, sliding the doors shut again. Then he moved to the bedroom at the end of the hallway just to take a quick look at what else awaited.

He turned the knob and was pushing the door open when he heard from behind him a bloodcurdling yell, a tremendous *"Stop!"* that burst from Vincent's lungs like a cannonball.

Startled, Sam dropped his hand and spun around to see the man hobbling quickly up the hall toward him, his eyes wild.

"Don't you *dare* go anywhere in this house I haven't said you could go!" he cried furiously.

Speechless, Sam raised his hands as if in surrender and backed away from the door. Pushing past him, Vincent grabbed the knob and gave it a strong tug, pulling it closed again.

"I'm so sorry," Sam said, trying to understand what was going on. "I didn't mean to pry. I just wanted to see how much stuff you have in there."

Releasing the knob, Vincent slumped against the wall. He pulled his handkerchief out of his pocket and blotted his forehead.

"I didn't know," Sam insisted quietly.

"No, you didn't know," Vincent replied in a calmer tone. Then he surprised Sam by adding, "I shouldn't have yelled like that."

Swallowing hard, Sam simply gave the man a nod and waited for whatever was next.

The two of them stayed right where they were, the only sound the distant ticking of a clock. Finally, with a deep weariness, Vincent drew himself up, took a breath, and held it for a long moment before slowly blowing it out.

As he did, it struck Sam how much this man had changed over the past few weeks. Like a flower blooming in the spring, Vincent Cook seemed to have opened up somehow, not just with Sam but with the food lady too. Though he could still be bossy, he'd begun speaking in a lighter, less menacing tone. He'd stopped acting like a bear that just wanted to find somewhere dark and go into hibernation. He'd started to move differently too, almost as if with every pound of stuff that got carted out of this house, he lost a pound of some unseen burden. Now that this had happened, however, Sam feared the blossoming flower was about to close itself tight again, never to open.

Sam braced himself for what he knew would come next, for Vincent to say they were done for the day and he needed to go home.

Instead, the man tucked his handkerchief into his pocket, gestured toward the basement stairs, and said simply, "After you, son. We've got more work to do."

⸙

Andy's crew finished their job in Florida right on schedule, making it back to Kashofa on the afternoon of December 19. Ivan had hired a van and a driver for the long, boring ride that terminated at his house. From there, it was up to each of the men to get themselves home.

As the van turned into Ivan's driveway, Andy saw the line of buggies parked there. Before the driver even pulled to a stop, the front door of the house swung open, and folks began pouring out. Seeing all the smiling wives and waving children, Andy felt a sudden pang of sadness, a loneliness that he tried to push aside but could not. There was a flurry of activity as each man gathered his stuff and headed to his respective family, leaving only Andy to fend for himself.

"Andy," Ivan said from the doorway of his home, "won't you come in and join us for supper?"

"That's all right," Andy replied, though the thought of a home-cooked meal made his stomach growl. All he had at the apartment was a loaf of frozen bread and a couple of frozen dinners. But he was road weary and just wanted to be alone.

He did, however, accept a ride to his place, not because it was far—the farm where he rented a garage apartment was less than a mile away—but because his toolbox was extra heavy, plus he had the duffel bag that had served as his suitcase for the trip.

Fortunately, Andy's Amish landlady offered laundry services for an additional fee, so once he was home and showered and had the wood stove all fired up, he gathered his dirty clothes and carted them over to the main house. The woman there took them with a smile and then told him to wait because she had a few things for him.

She disappeared into the house and a minute later reappeared with a big stack of mail. She handed him the entire pile, followed by a covered plate of hot chicken pot pie, saying she'd made extra because she knew he would be home today.

"And a quart of milk," she added, giving him the glass bottle. "What good is chicken pot pie without some milk to wash it all down?"

Andy thanked her for the mail, the food, and the milk, saying a silent prayer of gratitude as he walked back to the apartment. What a wonderful reminder that at least he wasn't completely alone.

He began going through the mail as he ate, looking at the envelopes one by one but not yet opening them. He knew what most were—cards for his birthday, which had come and gone while he was in Florida. There were a few without return addresses, but all the rest seemed to be from friends and relatives back in Lancaster County.

Only after he had finished his supper and washed the dishes did he settle into the easy chair next to the wood stove and allow himself to open his mail. He started with the one from his parents, glad to see that tucked inside the card was a long note from his Mamm, written out by hand on her familiar white stationery. She started the letter by saying she didn't have much news, but then her writing went on for three whole pages. Mostly she talked about the day-to-day happenings around the farm. She mentioned Sam being "so busy these days" with "a nice little after-school job helping out an elderly gentleman, an Englischer." As he read her words, Andy couldn't help but feel a pang of guilt. It sounded like Sam was working hard—too hard, maybe—for the money to bring him home. Andy sighed. When would Sam realize that the task was too large for him, that he'd never earn enough for a ticket by then?

The poor kid just needed to accept the truth: ticket or not, Andy never wanted to return home again. Ever.

After finishing Mamm's letter, he went through the pile and dug out the three cards that always served to remind him he was one of Rebekah's Babies. He started with the card from Rebekah Schlabach herself, the midwife who had delivered him twenty-five years ago during a late-November snowstorm. The other two were from fellow "babies"—an annual tradition begun by Savilla's and Eden's mothers when they were young and continued by the ladies themselves once they were older.

When he'd read the three cards, he turned his attention to the rest and went through them slowly, savoring each one in turn. He ended with the three that had no return addresses. Of those, one was from his brother Duane, a silly card with a picture of a chimpanzee dressed as a farmer on the front and inside the words "You just get better looking every year."

He moved on to the next-to-last one, but just as he was about to open it, he realized with a start that it was from Nellie. Return address or not, he would know that delicate script anywhere. Hands shaking, he set it aside and opened the other, a simple card from the bishop of his church back home, wishing him a happy birthday and assuring him that he was in their prayers.

Andy needed those prayers now, he thought as he reached for the final, unopened envelope. He considered leaving it for later or maybe tossing it into the fire without reading it at all, but then suddenly, somehow, the envelope was open and the letter was in his hands, and he was devouring every word.

> *Dear Andy,*
>
> *Happy 25th birthday! I don't know how you're feeling as you read this, if you are glad to hear from me—or pained. If*

it's the latter, I'm sorry. I won't write to you again. But I have to write now, as there are a few things I need to say.

I had a visit from Sam recently, one that has left me aching with loss and missing you even more than I already did. He came by the creamery one afternoon, all worked up about our relationship—yours and mine, I mean—and why we haven't been able to find our way back to each other by now. I managed to calm and reassure him, I think, but I have to admit that my heart has been pounding with the very same question.

I don't know if your feelings have softened toward me at all since you last wrote, but if it makes any difference, my love for you has remained as strong and steadfast as ever. I still want you back. I still love you. I still see the future you once painted for us.

If you don't yet feel the same, I understand. Just as I needed time to grasp the truth about my real motivations, you need time to decide where you belong. My only plea is that you don't confuse time spent seeking God's will with time spent running from pain. He binds our wounds, including broken hearts, but only if we invite Him in to do so.

I guess that's all I wanted to say for now. Please know that you are constantly in my prayers and on my mind and in my heart.

All my love forever,
Nellie

*A*ndy reread the letter three times before tucking it back into its envelope. Then he cradled it in his hand, almost unable to bear holding it and yet not willing to let it go. As he sat beside the fire, it all came rushing at him—the love he'd once felt for Nellie, her shocking betrayal, the hole it had left in his heart ever since.

It had happened last spring, on a Sunday that started out much as any other. By that point they had been together for quite a while, were deeply in love, and had already made plans to marry in the fall.

First, however, Nellie would need to become, as Andy already had, a member of the Amish church. Membership was a process that required a series of eight classes followed by baptism. Every year at least one or two of the people who started the classes dropped out partway through, usually because they weren't quite ready to give up their worldly ways.

Andy had never once considered that Nellie might be among those who didn't make it. Of course, she'd had a time of *rumschpringe* like everyone else, during which she'd gotten the world out of her system—or so he had assumed. In the months leading up to the start of the classes, she had thrown away her Englisch clothes, stopped driving the little Kia she kept behind the barn, and—hardest of all—had given up her plans to go to college. Nellie was smart, especially with numbers, and a part of him understood why she'd worked to get her GED, why she wanted to further her education. But he also knew there was no reason to do any of that if she planned to marry an Amish man and live an Amish life. He'd told her as much, many times, saying she'd already been taught everything she needed to know, thanks to her upbringing and her previous schooling.

At the beginning of each membership class, which took place in a separate room during part of the Sunday morning service, the candidates showed their intent to commit by declaring one by one, "I am a seeker desiring to be part of this church of God." By Nellie's fourth membership class, one of the other members had already dropped out.

The service that week was being held in the home of Andy's brother Duane, who lived on several back acres of their parents' farm. It was a beautiful morning, and Andy could remember having trouble concentrating on the hymns they were singing. He had plans to take Sam fishing later that day, and even as he sang along with the congregation, his mind kept going to thoughts of bait and fishing holes and a new lure he was eager to try.

It was between songs, in that brief moment of quiet broken by the shuffling of pages in the *Ausbund,* when a sob came from the second floor, followed by the sound of footsteps running down the stairs. Though every person gathered for worship should have kept their eyes where they belonged, more than a few heads turned and necks craned to see what was going on.

Andy tried not to look, though he couldn't help but catch the flash of a blue dress in his peripheral vision as whoever it was dashed out the door. He thought about Nellie's various classmates, trying to decide which one had likely ditched and run. As the congregation launched into the next song, Andy glanced toward the window and was shocked to see that the young woman who'd gone flying from the house was none other than Nellie.

He was on his feet in an instant, a reaction that would later bring a reprimand from the bishop, but he hadn't been able to help himself. He had simply jumped up and hurried out the door. Then he took off running after her, not catching up until she was halfway home, in the hollow between the two farms.

At first she was so hysterical that all he could do was hold her as she cried. There in the hollow, they were out of sight and alone except for a few curious horses lingering along the nearby fence. When Nellie finally gained some control over herself, Andy led her to a tree stump and sat her down. Then he knelt in front of her, took her hands in his, and looked into her eyes.

"What happened?" he asked, giving her hands a squeeze.

"I can't," she replied in barely a whisper.

"Can't what?"

"I can't," she repeated, a little louder this time. "I can't do it. I love you, and I love the church, but I can't give up my dream. Not even for that."

Andy was stunned. "What dream?"

She blinked, sending fresh tears down her cheeks. "Education. Learning. I just keep thinking about what you said, that I already know everything I need to know for the life we plan to lead. You meant it as reassurance, but every time I think of those words, they sound more like a prison sentence to me."

Andy let go of her hands and rocked back on his heels. "A prison sentence? Is that how you see our marriage?"

Nellie's eyes grew wide and pleading. "No, Andy. No! Of course not. But as much as I want to be your wife, I know I can't join the church with this . . . thing . . . burning inside me."

"Going to school isn't the only way to learn." Andy ran a hand through his hair. Just a short while ago he'd been thinking about fishing with Sam. Now his world had been turned upside down, and Nellie was acting crazy. "There's reading, for starters. You can pick up a lot that way."

She shook her head miserably. "I'm not talking about general knowledge, Andy. I want to learn mathematics. Accounting."

"So take a vocational class or a correspondence course. In light of our plans, the bishop would probably give his approval."

She sighed, fixing her gaze on Andy. "But I want more. Do you even know what the world of numbers is like for me? It's part of who I am—and always has been."

"You don't have to tell me. I learned that with the cabbages."

"Cabbages?"

He nodded. "When we were kids. You remember. I wanted a scooter, so Mamm gave me a space for my very own garden plot and told me I could keep the profits from whatever I grew myself and sold at the stand. By the time fall came around, I was so excited because I had eight good cabbages."

Nellie smiled. "That's right. But then I explained it would take eleven for you just to break even—and at least fifteen if you wanted to make a decent profit."

"You were always saying things like that."

"Because that's who I am. I take in numerical data and understand where things balance and where they don't and what needs to be done to make them right." She looked around as if the trees and sky might give her a better way to explain. "Do you have any idea how frustrating it is to scoop ice cream all day, knowing full well that I should be the one in the back room doing the books? That I should be handling things like billing and procurement and bank reconciliations? Mrs. Potter wants to retire. They've been looking for her replacement. But they won't even consider me."

Before Andy could ask why it mattered, given that her job there was only temporary, she continued.

"I told them how I handle my Daed's payroll and tax filings, how my analysis of his ROI on the corn versus the hogs helped him make changes that brought the farm into the black. Daed says I was born knowing more about numbers than most people learn in a lifetime."

"I agree. So why bother going to school if you already know so much?"

Her hands clenched into fists. "Because there's so much more *to* know," she cried. "Not to mention how tired I am of being treated like I'm incapable of doing anything that requires more than half a brain."

She exhaled slowly, calming down a bit before she continued. "Twice a year," she said evenly, "I sit down with Daed's accountant and go through the figures with her. I watch what she does, how she has the same affinity for numbers that I do. But because of her education, she's able to take it to a higher level."

"You covet her life? Over your own?"

Nellie's cheeks flushed a vivid red even as her chin set stubbornly. "She says I should be an accountant, that I could even become a CPA like her if I work hard."

"But why would you want to? What would that prove?"

Suddenly he caught a glimpse of something like guilt in her eyes. He realized this had nothing to do with learning and everything to do with credentials. A degree would make people respect her. A degree would prove her worth to the world.

"It's not about proving anything," she said, unable to meet his gaze. "It's about using my talents to the best of my abilities."

"No it's not. You're lying, Nellie—to yourself and to me."

Her face coloring even deeper, she rose from her perch on the stump and moved toward the fence. A beautiful mare stood on the other side, grazing on the early spring grass, and as Nellie approached, the horse raised its head and swung it toward her. Nellie stroked the animal's broad neck, silent for a long moment.

"I'm leaving, Andy," she said finally, turning to look at him. "I'm going to stay with a friend I met when I was taking my GED classes. She just moved to Kutztown, near the university, and she's starting summer school in a few weeks. I already got accepted. I'm going to enroll and start when she does."

Andy could hardly believe Nellie's words. Throughout this entire conversation, he had assumed this was a spur-of-the-moment thing, a temporary panic, an act of impulse.

Now he realized it was nothing like that at all. It was planned. Thought out. Premeditated. She was breaking up with him so she could go to college—for all the wrong reasons.

"What about us?" he managed to mutter.

"You could come with me," she whispered desperately, though Andy could tell by her expression that she knew what his answer would be.

He gave a single shake of his head.

"Then once I start down this path," she added, "I guess there is no us."

There is no us.

Even now, sitting in his stupid little apartment in Kashofa, Mississippi, Andy could feel the pain those words had wrought. He had often reminded himself of them—every time he missed her, every time he forgot he didn't want to love her anymore, every time some memory crept in and filled his mind with images of her and made him want to take her back.

There is no us.

Looking down at the letter he still clutched in his hands, he wondered if he was being too harsh. Yes, she had broken things off with him that day. Yes, she had packed up and driven away from her Amish life the very next morning. Yes, she had gone to summer school at Kutztown and reportedly had done really well, earning good grades across the board.

But apparently, by the end of just that one semester, she had come to understand what Andy had suspected all along, that it wasn't knowledge she had craved so much as validation. Certification. Some tangible proof of her abilities.

Once she realized that her driving force had been pride and not a true desire for more schooling, as she'd originally claimed, she also knew without a doubt that what the world offered—even the educated world—was not the life God had in mind for her. That life was waiting back in North Star, back among the Amish. Back with Andy.

She moved home, confessed and repented to the whole congregation. Gave up her car and her textbooks and her college classes. Placing herself in God's hands, she embraced the Amish lifestyle in full. As a sign of her newfound humility, she even went back to scooping ice cream at the creamery. If they eventually offered her the promotion after all, she said she would probably accept it. Not because she still needed or craved the validation but simply because she knew the higher wage would bring her and Andy that much closer to their dream of opening their own business.

She told him all this in a letter once she was back home and settled in, explaining what had happened and why and how much she had come to regret her actions. She loved him, she said, and she would wait for him as long as it took.

"I understand if you might have trouble trusting me at first," she'd written. "But I'm a different person now, a new creature in Christ, a woman with a repentant heart who is content and eager to live the life we were planning before I threw it all away."

That letter had come in September, and it had made Andy furious. He just kept going back to that one line: "I understand if you might have trouble trusting me at first."

At *first*? He would never, ever trust her again!

Now she was reaching out to him once more, and his reaction was not so much anger this time as sadness. He wanted to believe what she said was true. He wanted to believe she would not betray him again. But how could he? It wasn't just the pride that had led to her actions that concerned him. It was the deceit. The omissions. The steps she'd taken behind his back to create a new life for herself. Trust her again? No way. As his grandfather used to say, only a fool stands behind a mule twice.

With a groan Andy rose and moved to the window, the letter still in his hand. Should he write back with a better response this time? A longer one, explaining that she could stop waiting because they were never going to reconcile?

Or should he not react at all? She needed to move on just as he needed to move on. He should focus on his new life here, start putting down some roots, maybe even let Ivan set him up with someone after all. Perhaps the only way to convince Nellie of that would be to ignore this latest letter of hers completely.

But that still left the matter of Sam. Andy hated the thought of how deeply his little brother had been affected by the breakup between him and Nellie. Worse, he realized now it had been a mistake to accept Sam's challenge over this stupid Christmas train ticket thing. He'd given the kid false hope in a situation where no hope existed at all. What had he been thinking? No way was Andy going to make that trip, even if it meant having to break his word to his Boova.

Tomorrow was Sunday, but he wasn't sure if he would call home or not. Though he wanted to see where things stood with Sam's quest, a bigger part of him wasn't ready to face the fallout. If he was lucky, Sam had failed. If he wasn't so lucky, Sam had succeeded, and Andy would have to break his promise. Either way, he was not going home. Which meant all of Sam's work had been in vain.

And Sam would be the one hurt most of all.

On Sunday afternoon Sam went up to his room, closed the door, and pulled out his secret jar. Though it was nearly full now, he had not yet counted its contents, not even once. But today was December 20. He needed to know whether or not he had made his goal—or at least if he was close enough to make it by the purchasing deadline of December 23.

Amtrak could hold reservations without payment for only seven days, and then they would expire. So for the past month Sam had stopped by the travel agency in town once a week, checked to see if seats were still available on the train he wanted, and then made a new reservation, which held for another seven days. That was the only way he had been able to keep a spot for Andy despite not yet having the money to pay for it.

But that train would leave the station in just four days, which meant he had to have all the money in three. No matter how nervous counting the total made him, he couldn't put it off any longer.

His hands practically shaking, Sam unscrewed the lid and began pulling out the bills and straightening them into stacks. As he did, he calculated just how much he needed to have if he wanted to make the full amount by Wednesday. There were still three potential workdays between now and then, and after a quick calculation Sam realized that meant there needed to be at least $285 in the jar. He would have time to earn the remainder, if need be. Then, if everything went as planned, he would buy the ticket Wednesday evening, Andy would get on the train Thursday morning, and he would arrive in Lancaster Friday afternoon. A true Christmas Day surprise.

Sam began to panic. What if he didn't have enough? What if, even with three more workdays, he still couldn't make the total? What if when Andy finally called, he'd have to tell him he'd failed?

Sam couldn't imagine such a thing.

Heart pounding, he finished laying out all the bills in neat piles by denomination. Then he climbed down off the bed and got on his knees.

Lord, thank You for the money You've already given me, he prayed. *Now help me have enough, or at least help me get the rest in time, whichever You think is best.*

He stayed like that awhile longer, listening to the quiet of his room, feeling the wood floor beneath his knees. God had gotten him this far. Surely He would bless this effort.

Climbing back on the bed, Sam began to count, first the tens, then the fives, then the ones. By the time he was done, he simply couldn't believe it. The total came to three hundred dollars. All he needed was another eighteen bucks. Another four hours of work over the next three days. He had done it. This was actually going to happen.

Talk about cutting it close!

He put the money away again, grinning all the while. Sometimes God was just so good to him he thought his heart might burst.

CHAPTER TEN

*O*n Monday, Sam told Vincent the good news, that he'd nearly reached his goal.

He thought the man would be happy for him, but instead he got sort of quiet and weird for a while. Then he started barking out commands, and Sam went back to work.

They put in three good hours, which was long enough to finish the rest of the basement. That brought in another fifteen dollars. He was as good as done.

Halfway home, with a gasp he amended that thought. Financially speaking at least, if he added in his tip money from the stand, he was *completely* done.

As soon as he reached the house, he ran up to his room, jerked open the dresser drawer, and dug out the little leather pouch where he stashed his other cash. Sure enough, there was nearly $5 in coins inside, enough to bring the total to more than the $318 he needed.

He had done it! He had earned the money to bring his brother home.

Sam knew he wouldn't be able to wait until after dinner to tell his father the news, so as soon as he'd tucked all the money away again, he ran outside to look for him. He finally found his Daed in the workshop, fiddling on some piece of machinery that had to do with the milking machines. Once they were alone, Sam told him the good news. As disappointing as Vincent's reaction had been earlier that day, Daed's was the opposite. He looked so happy it made Sam's heart soar. He even thought he spotted tears in his father's eyes, though he turned away before Sam could tell for sure.

With Sam settled on the workbench and his Daed still tinkering with the machine, they slowly plotted out the details of their plan. Tomorrow afternoon, Daed said, if Sam could come home right after school and handle his father's afternoon chores, he would slip away and make arrangements for a driver to take them to the station on Christmas Day in time to meet Andy's four o'clock train. So they wouldn't have to perpetuate their fib for too long, however, he would wait until Thursday night to inform his wife that they were getting a visit from a distant relative on Friday afternoon.

She wouldn't be happy about it—not that she minded hosting folks in their home. But it would be awfully short notice. Besides, she had never even heard of this person, and hiring a driver and going all the way into Lancaster to the train station was going to completely disrupt the peace and togetherness of their Christmas Day. In the end, however, they both knew she wouldn't put up too much of a fuss. She was a good wife, and if this was something her husband wanted, she would go along with it.

Once their plan was in place, all that remained, Sam said, was to buy the ticket and tell Andy the good news.

"Maybe you should do that in reverse order," Daed replied, busying himself with a wrench and a loose bolt. "Tell Andy first, and then buy the ticket."

Sam wasn't sure what his father was trying to say, but by the odd turn in his demeanor, he was obviously trying to prepare Sam for some sort of disappointment.

"I don't understand," Sam said finally. "You know Andy *promised,* right?"

Daed nodded, twisting the wrench till it stopped. "Still, it never hurts to be prudent."

"Prudent?"

Daed shrugged. "Things happen, Son. Andy hasn't called yet to say he got back from Florida. He could be stuck down there for work. Or he could be sick, too sick to travel."

"Or he could change his mind and say he isn't coming home after all," Sam said flatly, knowing that was what his Daed really meant. Trying to keep his lip from trembling, he added, "Andy wouldn't do that."

Daed was silent as he set aside his tools and then tested the valve he'd been working on. "Nellie hurt him awful bad," he said finally. "Sometimes it can take longer than you'd think for a man to get over something like that."

Sam did not want to have this conversation. He trusted Andy. He knew he would keep his word.

But he also respected his father. So even though he was certain Daed was wrong about this, he would do as he said and talk to Andy first and then buy the ticket.

"I've got until six o'clock Wednesday evening to take the money to the travel agent," he said.

Daed nodded, relief flashing in his eyes. "Well then, we'll just have to make a point of talking to Andy before then."

❧

The next day after school, instead of heading straight to Vincent's, Sam made a beeline for his own house. He hated to be late for work, but it couldn't be helped. He had promised to cover several of his father's chores today so Daed could run into town and make arrangements for a driver on Christmas Day.

Once he got home, Sam worked as quickly as he could, going through the tasks Daed had told him needed doing. He raked away the old hay and sprinkled down the new. Then he weaved among the machines to check on the hookups for each cow. He realized his speed was making the cows antsy, but what else could he do? Vincent was probably getting worried about him. And the sky was growing darker by the minute. Snow had been predicted, and it would start falling soon.

Last, Sam got to Gerty, who had apparently graduated just this morning from a single stall to a larger exterior pen. She was still touchy, and he was careful not to get too close as he stepped through the gate and tended to the food and water there. But at least she was in with a few other cows now. She would slowly adapt to this place, and then they could finally set her to work alongside the other cows at the milking machines.

Once Sam was finished in the pen, he was free to go. After a stop at the mud sink to wash his hands, he was out of there, making quick work of the trip to Vincent's by going on his scooter. As he soared along Danner Drive, it struck Sam how much he enjoyed this job as well as the time he spent with Vincent. They still had more to do, but once their task was complete and the work came to an end, Sam realized he was actually going to miss it.

Just as he reached Vincent's house and slowed his scooter to a stop, a car turned into the driveway and pulled up next to him. Glancing inside, he saw that the driver was a woman about Vincent's age, with silver hair and kind eyes. When she noticed Sam, she smiled through the window and turned off the engine.

"You must be Sam," she said, getting out of the car.

From her voice he realized this was the food lady, which made sense, as this was about the time of day she usually showed up.

He nodded. "You're Gloria?"

She smiled. "Why yes, I am."

This was the first time he'd actually seen the woman face to face, and he understood why Vincent liked chatting with her at the door. She was old, but she was pretty. And there was something appealing about the way she held herself, about the warmth in her eyes.

"Can I carry the food in for you?" he asked, propping his scooter against the fence and gesturing toward the white box on her passenger seat.

"That's okay. I've got it," she replied, but she made no move to retrieve it. Instead she stood by the car a moment longer, looking as if there was something she wanted to say. "I've heard a lot of good things about you. You've accomplished so much here—and not just with the house. With Vincent too."

Sam knew what she meant, though he took no credit for it. Vincent had changed because God was working on him.

"It's been fun," he said with a shrug, realizing that he actually meant it. Despite the crankiness and the commands and the never-ending possessions, his time with Vincent had been fun. "It sure is nice of you to bring food here all the time," he added, trying to deflect the attention away from himself.

"Oh, the church provides it. I just deliver it."

"I know he appreciates it though."

She looked toward the house, her brows furrowing the slightest bit. "That's good to hear. I worry about him. He's been through so much, you know? It's hard enough losing a spouse, but then . . . with his son and everything, and all in the same year. I can't imagine."

Sam's heart gave a thud. Vincent had lost a son? Sam could barely breathe at the thought.

"Anyway," Gloria said, turning her gaze toward him again, "I'm happy to do it. Hopefully, one of these days I might even talk him into coming back to church."

"Back?" Sam echoed.

"Well, you know, with everything that happened and the reporters hounding him all the time, and people being so nosy . . . I suppose it was easier for him just to close his door and hide from the world. Though he's been hiding now for three years." Her somber face slowly spread into a smile. "And then you came along."

Sam could not form a coherent reply. He could barely speak at all, especially when she added, "And the fact that you're Amish, well, it makes it even more special. Isn't that just how the Lord works?"

Sam was about to respond when he heard his name being called. He turned to see Vincent in the doorway, waving him toward the house. At that moment he wanted nothing more than to run in the opposite direction, to go somewhere that he could think.

Instead, with tremendous effort he managed to mumble a quick "Excuse me" to Gloria and then trotted up the drive to Vincent. His head was spinning, his heart was pounding, but somehow he managed to act normal enough that the man didn't seem to notice anything was wrong.

"Are you okay? I was worried," Vincent said. "What took you so long?"

"I'm sorry," Sam replied. "It's a long story. I can tell you later."

"See if you can get them all in the trunk," Gloria said from behind him. Sam turned to see her coming up the walk toward them, the container of food in her hands.

After a beat Sam realized she was talking to him. "Ma'am?"

"The bags. I'm hoping you'll be able to squeeze everything in the trunk. I left it open. If not, the rest can go in the backseat."

Confused, he looked to Vincent for an explanation.

"Go out to the garage and get all those bags of clothes from the corner and load them in Gloria's car."

Sam blinked. "The bags. Of your wife's . . . of women's clothes?"

Vincent nodded. "Those are the ones."

*I*t took a lot of trips to get everything to the car, and Sam was glad. Vincent was inside the house with Gloria the whole time, which left Sam alone with his thoughts.

And he had a whole lot of thoughts to work through.

For one thing, now that he knew Vincent had a son and the son was dead, a bunch of things suddenly made sense. The pain in the man's eyes. The room at the end of the hall.

It must've been his son's room. No wonder he hadn't wanted Sam just wandering in there, poking around. No wonder he had yelled that way. Just thinking about someone else going in at all must've hurt something terrible.

What Gloria had meant by the Amish comment though, Sam didn't have a clue.

When he finally finished in the garage, he closed the trunk of the car and headed for the house. As he stepped inside, he heard Vincent laughing, a hearty laugh, the same kind of laugh he'd given one day last week when the two of them were working in the basement and Sam had accidentally spilled a box full of Styrofoam peanuts on Vincent's head. Sam had been lifting a box onto a high shelf when he tilted it back too far. Vincent was standing directly behind him to steady the ladder, right in the line of fire, and the white peanuts had poured down on him like rain. Sam had cringed, waiting for one of the man's usual explosions, but instead he'd begun to laugh. In his disbelief Sam had laughed too. Then they had laughed together for a couple of minutes before finally drying their eyes and cleaning up the peanuts. Vincent had a nice laugh. Sam was happy to hear it again now.

He continued into the kitchen, where he saw Vincent and Gloria sitting across from each other at the table. They were both drinking coffee and kind of looking at each other in a special way.

Could people fall in love when they were that old? Sam wondered. He supposed they could. The way Vincent and Gloria were looking at each other now reminded Sam of the way Mamm and Daed looked at each other sometimes. Of the way Andy used to look at Nellie.

He cleared his throat before walking into the room.

"All finished?" Gloria asked. "Thank you so much for doing that."

After chatting a few more minutes with Sam and Vincent, Gloria said she had to go. Vincent walked her to the front door, and though he wasn't trying to look, Sam couldn't help but see Gloria turn and impulsively give Vincent a big hug.

"You're doing a brave thing," she said as they pulled apart. Then she turned and headed for her car.

She was talking about the clothes, Sam realized, and she was right. Considering how attached Vincent had been to them, it must've taken a tremendous effort to finally let them go.

Rather than closing the door behind her as usual, Vincent stood in the hallway, seemingly oblivious to the cold air rushing in at him, and watched her leave. After a long moment Sam joined him, and they stood side by side.

When her car was finally out of sight, Sam turned to Vincent, unable to stop the question from escaping his mouth. "So why did you give the clothes to her? Is she going to start wearing them or something?"

Vincent shook his head, a faraway look in his eyes. "She's affiliated with an organization that clothes the needy. She's going to pass them along."

Sam nodded, swallowing hard, deeply proud of his friend.

Much to Sam's surprise, the next task Vincent had in mind was an even bigger deal than giving away his late wife's clothes.

"So what do you think?" Vincent said, turning toward him in the hallway. "Are we ready to tackle the last room in the house?"

Stunned, Sam blurted the first thought that came into his mind. "I am. But are you?"

Vincent thought for a moment and then spoke in a more somber voice. "Not really. But it has to be done."

With that, he turned and headed down the hall, going right to the very door he had screamed at Sam about. This time he twisted the knob, pushed it open, and flipped on the light.

Pulse surging, Sam followed, pausing in the doorway and looking inside.

It was a sewing room, he realized, with a big electric sewing machine in the corner and stacks of folded fabric all around. But as he stepped inside and took a closer look, it wasn't hard to see that at one point it had been a young man's bedroom, with its heavy oak furniture and Eagles and Phillies posters still gracing the walls.

The room wasn't near as messy as the others had been, and Sam was deeply relieved. This was not going to be easy for Vincent, not at all, so the faster they could get it done, the better.

On the other hand, Sam realized that once this room was finished, they both would have reached their goals, and his job here would come to a natural end—a thought that made him rather sad. It would be nice not to be so busy anymore, but he would miss spending time with his friend Vincent.

As Sam took a step inside, he noticed a heavy coat of dust covering almost every surface. "You better be careful with your allergies," he said, gazing around. "Looks like nobody's been in here for years."

Vincent didn't reply, and when Sam looked at him, he realized that the man had lowered himself onto the bed and was now just sitting there, his face riddled with conflicting emotions.

"Three years, actually," he said. "I couldn't bring myself to come into this room, not even once."

Sam nodded, leaning against the nearby desk. "Too painful?" he asked, hoping Vincent might share some details of how his son died.

"Too ashamed," Vincent replied. Then he put his hand to his eyes and began to cry.

Sam didn't know what to do, whether he should leave the poor man alone for a while or put a hand on his shoulder to comfort him. Finally a thought struck him, and Sam turned and went up the hall to the master bedroom, to the dresser where Vincent kept his handkerchiefs. Thanks to all the packing and sorting they'd done, Sam knew where almost everything was in this house now, including these.

When he got back to the room, the man was still crying, though not as loudly now. It was more like soft sniffling. He already had a handkerchief, but he took the fresh one Sam offered with a soft, mumbled, "Thanks, son."

Finally Sam stepped over to the desk, rolled out the chair, and had a seat. Maybe what Vincent needed most right now was for someone to be here with him. Maybe what he needed was not to have to do this alone.

"How old was he when he died?" Sam asked cautiously, sensing that Vincent might want to talk about it. He thought that was a less intrusive question than the one he really wanted to ask, which was *how* he died—not to mention all those strange things Gloria had said earlier at the car.

But from the look on Vincent's face, he shouldn't have asked the question at all.

"Excuse me?" Vincent said.

Sam was embarrassed. "I said, how old was he when he died? I mean, if it happened three years ago, he must have been—"

"My son isn't dead," Vincent interrupted.

Sam's eyes grew wide. "He's not?"

The man shook his head, dabbing at his cheeks one last time and then tucking the handkerchief into his pocket. "No. He's not dead. He's in prison."

✦

The story unfolded slowly as the two of them sat in the dusty bedroom, the snow gently falling outside. The facts of the matter were simple but shocking. Because of his struggles with alcoholism, Vince Junior had lived a troubled life. He had been in and out of minor scrapes and scuffles and tangles with the law since he was young. As Vincent put it, "He vacillated between rehab, sobriety, and drunken binges."

Vince Junior had been sober for a while when, three years ago, his mother—Vincent's wife—passed away after a lingering illness. Vince Junior had never dealt well with sadness or pain, and not surprisingly, he starting drinking again within days of her funeral.

One night just a month or two later, he was driving down Summit Hill Road, inebriated, when he rounded the corner at North Star Lane and came upon a horse and buggy ahead of him. The crash had been fast and horrific, and the Amish woman driving the buggy had been instantly killed.

Vince Junior was barely injured at all—at least not on the outside. His wounds were on the inside. Once he sobered up and realized what he'd done, he could barely live with himself. In the end the state charged him with involuntary manslaughter, and he was convicted and sentenced to five years at Rockview.

"It sounds strange, I know," Vincent said, "but he actually seemed relieved when his sentence was handed down. He felt so horribly guilty, I think he wanted more than anything to be punished, to pay for his crime."

Sam thought about that, about all the people in the world who struggled with guilt and shame, believing it was up to them to wipe away their own sin. They didn't know that only God could do that—had already done that when He sent His son.

"You were, what, nine years old when it happened?" Vincent said. "I'm surprised you don't remember it."

"I do, sort of," Sam replied. He recalled the incident, though he was fuzzy on the details. He hadn't really known the woman who died, nor had he learned the names of the others involved.

"Well, anyway," Vincent continued, "the whole story became a huge deal for a while—though not so much the part about a drunk driver killing an Amish woman. What the press kept focusing on was the way the Amish community surrounded Vince—and me, for that matter—almost immediately after it happened, offering us love and care and absolute forgiveness."

Sam nodded. Of course they had. The Bible said it straight out: if they didn't forgive others, then God would not forgive them.

"Even the woman's husband was a part of that crowd. He visited Vince Junior in jail and cried with him and hugged him and told him that once he repented of his sin, what he'd done was as far as the east was from the west." Vincent blinked, and twin tears traveled down his wrinkled cheeks. "He tried to meet with me too—they all did—but I wasn't having any of it. Forgiveness? A clean slate? The very thought boggled my mind."

He pulled out his handkerchief, dabbed at his cheeks, blew his nose. "I grew to hate the Amish after that. What right did they have to forgive my son? Who were they to come here and tell me it was all okay? How could they show up in court the day of his sentencing and plead not for the maximum punishment but the minimum?"

"I don't understand," Sam said, trying to put himself into the mind-set of someone who had not grown up with these ways, who had not been taught to think like this.

"They had no business forgiving him," Vincent cried, his eyes wide, his expression intense.

"But why?" Sam asked.

"Because *I* hadn't forgiven him!" The man closed his eyes, lowered his head. "I, his own father, had not forgiven him. I kept envisioning that woman's family, how his selfishness destroyed their lives. I still haven't—or at least I hadn't, not until these last few weeks. I can't explain it, but for the first time since they took my son away and locked him up, I've found myself wanting to go see him. To apologize to him. I've found my heart somehow . . . softening toward him. I've decided that maybe you Amish weren't so wrong about that forgiveness stuff after all."

Sam's eyes widened. "You've never gone to see him?"

Vincent shook his head. "Rockview Prison is in Bellefonte, which isn't that far away. Maybe a two- or three-hour drive. But I've never made that trip, not even once. Haven't written, haven't accepted any of his calls."

"That's so sad," Sam said, trying to imagine it.

Vincent looked at him. "It is sad," he replied. "For him and for me."

*B*y the time Sam got home, the snow was still falling, and the ground was completely covered in white. Sam headed straight to the barn in search of his father, so eager to tell him about what had happened today. Sam and Vincent had talked for so long that they hadn't done any actual work. But there would be time tomorrow for that. Today had been about healing and forgiveness and friendship.

Daed wasn't in the barn, so Sam headed to the area out back, where the animal pens were. As he did, he began to sense something in the air, a feeling that all was not right. He told himself there was nothing going on, that it was just the snow, but somehow he knew that wasn't true. It was something else. Something bad.

The moment he emerged from the far side of the barn, he saw that the gate to the largest pen was hanging wide open. Cows were wandering freely on the grounds, pushing their noses through the snow to the frozen grass below and swinging their tails lazily.

Sam's first, panicked impulse was to run around and gather them up. But he stopped himself, afraid he might spook them, and walked to the nearest cow instead. Gripping her firmly by the rope around her neck, he pulled her toward the barn, and after a few tugs she gave in, carrying in her mouth the last of the grass she'd been chewing.

Sam locked her away and then went back for another, realizing as he gathered the cows one by one that this was his fault. He was the person who changed the food and water in the pen earlier this afternoon. That meant he was the person who had left the gate unlatched.

It made sense. He'd been in such a rush to finish and get over to Vincent's that he'd probably flown right past that step without even realizing it.

As Sam led what he hoped was the final cow into the barn, he scanned the yard and then the stalls, counting heads. They were all there. All except one.

Gerty.

A chill ran through Sam's body. He didn't know why, but suddenly he was overcome with nausea. He ran into the barn and grabbed the high-powered flashlight, flicked it on, and scanned the landscape with the beam. Finally he spotted her in the distance, near the silos, just standing and chewing as if she was exactly where she belonged.

Sam approached Gerty slowly, carefully, but it wasn't until he got closer that he saw it. What he'd somehow known he'd see but was too afraid to admit.

Daed. Sprawled on the ground. Red blood pooling on the white snow around his head.

⸎

Sam and his mother spent the next five hours in the hospital's third-floor waiting room, talking and pacing and waiting for news, which came only intermittently. Most of all they prayed. Over the course of that time, they were joined by a veritable parade of loved ones, each of whom showed up simply to support and love and reassure and pray.

The diagnosis finally came around midnight, once all the scans and tests and x-rays had been done. It ended up being "a good news, bad news thing," as the doctor put it. The good news was that Mr. Danner did not have a brain injury. The bad news was that he did have a broken jaw, which would need surgery in the morning.

Sam was a mess, but Mamm was solid as a rock. She was upset, of course, especially when news was slow in coming. But even in the worst of it, she never lost the peaceful expression in her eyes. She never cried tears of fear or self-pity, only tears of compassion for the man she loved.

Once Daed was finally settled into a room for the night, the two of them were able to join him and stay for as long as they wanted, even though visiting hours were over. Daed couldn't talk at all, and his face was swollen and bruised, especially where Gerty's hoof had connected with his jaw. But he didn't seem to be in too much pain, thanks to the medications. Mostly he just drifted in and out of sleep.

At some point Sam must've fallen asleep as well, because he was in the middle of a dream when he felt a hand on his shoulder, gently shaking him awake. It was Mamm, who said they might be more comfortable out in the waiting room, which had lounge chairs long enough to stretch out on. Not that either of them got much sleep that night anyway. Sam dozed off and on, sometimes waking to find his mother snoozing on the adjacent chair, other times opening his eyes to see her sitting up or pacing or speaking in soft whispers to one of his sisters or brothers or uncles.

It was nearly dawn when he woke to the sound of one of those conversations. His eyes still closed, he tried to go back to sleep, but he couldn't help overhearing what they were saying.

". . . could be thousands of dollars. We just won't know till it's all over," Mamm whispered softly. "At least they've agreed to send him home as soon as they can."

The voice that spoke softly in reply was that of Sam's older brother Duane, who assured his mother that they'd come up with the money somehow. "We'll all pitch in. Hopefully, that'll cover most of it. One way or another, God will provide."

Those words stayed on Sam's mind for hours, even after the sun came up, and they all prayed together in Daed's room and then watched him be taken to surgery. They were on his mind when the surgery was over and he watched them roll Daed back in again. He thought about how this whole thing had been his fault, that if not for his negligence with the gate, there wouldn't be any expenses. They were on his mind when Mamm was off handling the paperwork for Daed's release, and Sam seized the opportunity to borrow a cell phone from one of his teenage cousins who was on rumschpringe. Settling on a bench down a quiet hall, Sam dialed the number he'd memorized months ago, the one where he could always reach Andy in an emergency.

⌒⌒✠⌒⌒

Mamm had called Andy last night to tell him what had happened to Daed. But as Sam listened to the rings and then waited for Andy's boss to take him the phone, he tried to figure out how to break this additional news, that although he had managed to reach his goal and earn the $318 in time, he had decided to hand that money over to their parents instead to help cover Daed's medical bills.

As it turned out, though Andy sounded sad for Sam's sake that his plan hadn't worked out, he was also clearly relieved. He tried to hide that part from his voice, but Sam knew his brother too well. And he knew Andy really hadn't wanted to come at all, a thought that pained Sam's heart.

His next phone call hadn't been any easier. He had to tell Vincent that he wouldn't be able to come to his house for a while, that he couldn't help him finish his son's room or get the last few things out of the garage, at least not until Daed was better and Sam wasn't needed so much around home.

"Well I guess I shouldn't be surprised," Vincent snapped. "After all, you did reach your goal. You got what *you* needed out of this."

Sam blinked, startled. Did the man really think he didn't want to come back? That he was just using this as some sort of excuse not to finish the job?

"I really do want to come," Sam protested. "But I can't, not now that this has happened."

"Yeah, sure, kid, whatever you say."

Sam's heart surged with anger. "You know what, Vincent? My goal doesn't even matter anymore. I'm not buying Andy's ticket. I'm giving the money to my parents to help pay the medical bills."

Vincent hesitated. "I thought your community took care of things like this."

"Yeah," Sam replied, "they'll help when it's necessary. But I wouldn't feel right taking money from them that I could have contributed myself."

"I see what you mean," Vincent said, the edge now gone from his voice.

"Anyway," Sam continued, calming back down, "I really am sorry about this. I promise I'll be in touch with you as soon as I have some free time and can work."

"Don't apologize, son. I know family has to come first."

The words were the ones Sam had wanted to hear, and he was glad Vincent was no longer mad, but in a way his disappointment was even harder to take. Sam had wanted to be there for his friend to the end, and instead all he had done was let him down.

At least he was too busy for the rest of the afternoon to give it much more thought. Getting Daed home and up the stairs and into bed had taken the efforts of Sam and Duane. After that, Mamm got Daed settled. Then she went to the kitchen to sort out all the food that had been delivered by members of the community, and the two brothers headed out to the barn to work alongside several parishioners who were there already, tending to the dairy and the milk and the cows.

Daed slept straight through the night and then on and off for much of the following day. As he did, Sam worked even more, feeding and washing and mucking and cleaning and whatever else he could to assuage his conscience. In the end, however, nothing he did would take the guilt away.

By the time the sun began to set on Christmas Eve, Daed was quietly snoozing in the bedroom, Mamm was busy cooking some soup for him in the kitchen, and Sam was out in the barn, tending the cows. He'd been joined by two of the older Umble brothers from next door, both of whom had dairies themselves and knew way more about what needed to be done than he did. To Sam's relief, they told him that they had removed Gerty not long after the ambulance had sped off toward the hospital. Once Daed was feeling better, they said, he could decide what to do with the difficult bovine, but in the meantime they would keep her safely segregated, out of harm's way.

After all the commotion of the past two days, Sam was glad when everyone else left and things finally settled down. As he and his sisters shared a quiet supper of cornbread and vegetable soup at the table, Mamm ate upstairs with Daed, though his bowl held only the liquid and none of the vegetables or the meat.

Sam waited until the meal was over and his sisters were tending to the dishes, then he summoned his nerve, went to his room, and retrieved the jar. Taking a deep breath, he walked to the doorway of his parents' bedroom and gave a soft knock.

"I have something for you both," he said when they looked his way.

Mamm waved him in, so he walked over to the foot of the bed and continued.

"I know that $319.75 is nowhere near enough to cover the medical bills, but at least it should help." With a lump in his throat, he unscrewed the lid, lifted out the wad of money, and handed it to his mother. "Guess this means you won't be getting a present from me after all," he added, "but I hope this kind of makes up for it."

He looked at Daed, whose expression went from surprise to sadness to something like acceptance. Finally he gave Sam a nod, and then he reached out and took Mamm's hand. She turned toward him, and the gaze they shared was one of deep parental satisfaction.

"Aw, Sam," Mamm said, the words catching in her throat as she turned back again, "seeing you grow into such a fine and Christlike young man is more than enough for me."

Sam had planned to apologize too, to admit the accident was his fault. But in that moment, seeing the proud look in his parents' eyes, he just couldn't bring himself to do it. The words lodged deep in his throat and refused to come out.

Giving them a nod, he simply turned and went back to his room, empty jar in hand, knowing he was about as *un*-Christlike as anyone ever could be.

*T*he next morning Sam awoke early, got dressed in the predawn darkness by lamplight, and made his way out to the barn. Weary and sore from all the work he'd done the day before, he was relieved when Duane showed up to help with the chores. Their load was made even lighter when several neighbors came a short while later to lend a hand with the milking machines.

By the time everything was done and the men had gone back home to their families, Sam's stomach was growling for breakfast. He made his way to the house, crunching across the snow on the lawn, feeling hungry and cold but also ready for the joyful chaos of the day. It was Christmas, after all, even if things were very different this year.

As he stepped inside, he was met with the sounds of clanking dishes and the smells of roasting turkey and pies and tarts baking in the oven. His mother and sisters and several other female relatives were weaving in and out of each other's way as they stirred and chopped and rolled out dough and did whatever else needed doing in the kitchen. The scene was a classic Danner Christmas morning, with two exceptions.

First was the fact that Daed was not part of it. Eventually they would help him down and get him settled comfortably in an easy chair in the living room, but for now he was still in bed. Instead of hovering on the fringes and pretending to read the paper while snitching bites of this and that, he was upstairs with his mouth wired shut, his face still terribly swollen, and his mind somewhat dulled by pills for the pain.

The second difference this year was the way Mamm kept shushing people, making them keep it down in case Daed was trying to sleep. Sam had a feeling the noise probably wasn't bothering him nearly as much as the smells were. All these delicious aromas, yet the only thing his father could consume right now was liquid through a straw. The heady fragrance of the Christmas baking alone was probably driving him up the wall.

"There's oatmeal in the pot on the back right burner," Mamm said to Sam with a quick glance over her shoulder as she whisked something around in a giant bowl. "You'll have to serve it up yourself though."

"That's okay. Thanks, Mamm."

Getting through that room was like trying to cross Lincoln Highway in a buggy, but somehow he managed to reach the cabinet for a bowl, then the drawer for a spoon, and then the stove for his food without bumping into anyone. He served himself a big heap of steaming oatmeal with raisins, only to realize that he'd have to head into the fray one more time to retrieve a little milk and some brown sugar.

Finally he settled at the far end of the dinner table, said a silent grace, and dug in with gusto. After a while his focus shifted from the bowl in front of him to the people around him. Not for the first time he watched in fascination how well the ladies worked together, flowing seamlessly from task to task. At one point his Mamm was stirring beans in a pot, sprinkling cheese on potatoes, and reminding the men who were coming inside to wipe their boots on the rug, all the while bouncing one of her grandbabies on her hip.

Every year it was tradition that a large group of family members, friends, and neighbors assembled at the Danner farm for a big meal on Christmas Day, a meal that all the women pitched in to make. It was a time of great fun and food and fellowship, Sam's favorite day of the year. The problem was, not only was Daed still in a bad way, but also someone was missing, someone who should've been here and wasn't.

Andy.

Sam halfheartedly spooned more oatmeal into his mouth, telling himself that maybe it was time to follow Nellie's example and truly turn the whole matter over to God. At this point what other choice did he have?

⌀⌀⌀

Family gift time was midafternoon, and Sam was pleased with his present, a pair of good leather work gloves. With all the extra jobs he'd be taking on around the farm for the next month or so, they would definitely come in handy.

Gift giving was followed by devotions, a time not just of reading the Bible but also telling the little ones the story of Jesus's birth. By midafternoon there were plenty of children among the group, mostly Sam's nieces and nephews and neighbors' kids. Since Daed wasn't able to speak, the reading of the Christmas story had fallen to Duane, who lacked Daed's flair but did the best he could.

The Umbles arrived shortly before dinner, as always, bringing with them the dishes they had prepared over at their house. Just a few things needed to be finished, like heating the casseroles and chopping tomatoes for the salad, and then the table would be completely set, and the meal could begin.

Before then, however, Sam knew there was one thing he needed to do.

As soon as Wayne came in the door, Sam led him to the side room off the kitchen where they could speak privately. There, Sam apologized, saying how sorry he was for having been such a crummy friend lately.

"It's okay," Wayne replied, his expression earnest. "I'll always forgive you, no matter what."

"Yeah?"

"Yeah."

Warmth surging in his heart, Sam gave Wayne a light punch on the shoulder and said simply, "Thanks, buddy."

⌒⊶⟡⊷⌒

Nellie stood at the Danners' stove, watching Wayne and Sam emerge from the next room as she slowly stirred a pot of caramel. Seeing the happy, easy way they had with each other warmed her heart. Wayne had seemed lonely the last few weeks, ever since Sam had gotten busy with some job and stopped spending time with him. Wayne hadn't even come to the ice cream parlor last Friday for his free treat, because what was the use of enjoying it without his best friend, he'd said. Now it looked like the boys were together again, the rift fully mended, and she had a feeling Sam must have apologized. That was the kind of kid he was.

Returning her attention to the bronze liquid, Nellie gave it one more stir before turning off the flame and lifting the pan from the stovetop. She carried it over to the freshly-baked Bundt cake waiting on the counter and drizzled the caramel on top. As she did, a familiar ache began to grow inside her. This had always been one of Andy's favorite desserts. But as Wayne said, what was the use of enjoying it without her best friend? Dinner at the Danners' had always been one of her favorite parts of Christmas. Now she found herself wishing she was anywhere but here. For a moment she even considered slipping out and going home, but she knew that wouldn't be right. Her actions had already caused this whole family so much pain. The least she could do now was share this day with them, thereby showing how much she accepted and appreciated their grace.

Once the cake was done, Nellie set it with the other desserts and then began to help with the rest of the food. As she carried dishes and platters back and forth to the main table, her eyes kept going to Andy's father, who sat quietly in a chair in the corner, watching the activity around him and trying not to let on how much pain he was obviously in.

Nellie paused in her work to pour him a fresh glass of water, add a straw, and carry it over to him.

"You doing okay, Glen?" she asked softly, and he nodded in reply.

When she gave him his drink, he held her hand a moment longer and patted it, as if to say thank you. Nellie had to blink back tears. This man should have been her father-in-law. She loved him like one. She loved the whole family.

Most of all, she loved Andy.

Nellie turned away before he could see her tears, telling herself to think of something—anything—lest she completely fall apart.

⌒⌒⌒

Sam couldn't believe how much he had eaten. Even an hour after the meal was done, his stomach still felt near to bursting, like the cows must feel prior to milking time.

It didn't help that poor Daed hadn't been able to eat a thing. He'd just stared at all the food longingly as he sipped chicken broth through a straw. Watching him, Sam had felt a pang of guilt so deep and strong that it was a physical ache. He didn't know how he would ever tell his Daed about the stupid thing he had done, how the man's misery was all his fault.

Once the dishes were finished and all the food had been put away, it was game time. Over the years Mamm had accumulated a closet full of board games, and the younger ones raced to it now and began debating which game they most wanted to play.

Watching them, it struck Sam suddenly how old he felt, almost as if he belonged more with the grownups in the room than with the children. Even Wayne seemed a little young to him now, especially at that moment as he was over in the corner engaged in a spitball war with his ten-year-old cousin.

Gazing around the room, Sam's eyes landed on Nellie, who was standing in the kitchen near the other women but staring off in the distance, her mind apparently a million miles away. As if sensing his gaze, she seemed to come back to attention, and then she turned and looked at him.

Their eyes met and held for a long moment, and it was almost as if they each knew what the other was thinking. As lovely as this day had been, as warm and wonderful as these people were, none of it could make up for the one who was missing, the one who was so far away.

Just then a knock came at the door, and for a moment Sam's heart leaped to his throat. Nellie seemed to have the same thought, because she immediately stepped toward it and swung it open.

To Sam's deep disappointment and no doubt hers as well, the person at the door wasn't Andy, there to surprise them after all. Instead it was a woman, an Englisch woman, though not until she turned did Sam realize that it was, of all people, Vincent's friend Gloria.

Sam rose and began to move toward the door, seeing as he got closer that she wasn't alone. Beside her on the threshold stood Vincent.

"Hello," he said, "we're looking for Sam Danner. Is he here?"

"I sure am," Sam replied, coming over to join them.

"There you are," he cried, grinning widely. "Merry Christmas."

"Merry Christmas to you too," Sam said, accepting a hug from Gloria and a pat on the head from Vincent.

Confused but pleased, he invited the couple inside, wildly curious why they had come. Before he could ask, however, Nellie offered them coffee, and someone else tried to take their coats, and then they both were being herded toward the dessert table.

"We just stopped by for a minute," Vincent said. "We really can't stay."

Grinning, Sam rescued the pair from the throng and led them to the side room, where things weren't quite so chaotic.

"What are you guys doing here?" he asked as they stepped inside and he pulled the door shut behind them. Only then did he notice they were quite dressed up, with Vincent in a coat and tie and Gloria wearing a red suit with a sparkly Christmas tree pin on the lapel.

"Are you on a date or something?" Sam asked, looking from one to the other.

Vincent and Gloria shared a glance, shy smiles on both of their faces.

"We're on our way to church actually," Gloria replied. "A Christmas evening hymn sing."

Sam nodded sagely. It was a date all right.

"Anyway," Vincent said, looking a bit chagrined, "I've been feeling bad ever since you called me from the hospital. I wanted to apologize for how I acted. Considering your situation, I should've been more supportive. Instead, I was thinking only of myself. I'm so sorry."

Sam felt a small bit of his stockpile of guilt fall away. He hadn't realized how strongly Vincent's reaction had affected him. "It's okay," he said, exhaling with relief.

It struck him how far Vincent had come, from the man who couldn't even apologize to his own son to the one who stood here now, easily asking for forgiveness. That thought was replaced by another, more urgent one: Sam still had someone he needed to ask for forgiveness—his own father.

Sam's mind reeled. What could he possibly say, how could he ever apologize for the carelessness that led to such tragedy? That's the thought that was pounding in his mind when he realized Vincent was talking again, something about a Christmas present.

"What?" Sam asked, blinking. He forced himself to focus.

"I said I brought you a Christmas present."

Sam's eyes widened. "You didn't have to do that."

"I know, but I wanted to," Vincent replied. "Though you'll have to help me bring it in. It's kind of heavy."

"Sure," Sam replied, wondering what it was. Then he realized it must be the Amish-made rocking chair, the one he'd put up the flier for at the creamery. While Sam had no use for it himself, his heart was warmed knowing the man had thought of him—and that now Sam would have a Christmas gift for Mamm after all.

Growing excited at the thought, Sam led his two guests back into the main part of the house and over to the coat rack. He quickly pulled on his jacket and was looking around for his shoes when he spotted his father's work boots tucked neatly against the wall. His smile faded as a fresh wave of remorse washed over him.

Sam knew he had to do this right now, had to admit his wrong-doing before another minute passed.

Spotting his mother in the crowded room, he waved her over and introduced her to Vincent and Gloria, to buy himself some time. Then as the three adults greeted each other and began to chat, he excused himself and walked toward his father's chair over in the corner, his heart pounding in his chest like a horse trotting across a busy intersection. Fortunately, so much else was going on that no one seemed to be looking his way.

Except for Daed, who was watching intently as Sam approached.

Swallowing hard, tears filling his eyes, Sam knelt beside the chair. "It was my fault," he blurted softly, his face burning with shame, his throat thick. He looked down as he continued. "The accident with Gerty. I'm the one who left the gate unlatched. I was in a hurry, and I didn't pay attention and—"

"Sh," Daed replied, cutting Sam off before he could even finish.

Then his hand was on Sam's chin, lifting the boy's face, forcing him to meet his gaze.

Even though Daed could not speak, he could still communicate with his expressions, with his gestures, with his eyes. And what he was saying now took Sam's breath away.

I know, my son. And I've already forgiven you.

*A*ndy hovered beside the car, rubbing his hands together to keep them warm. He sure wished they would hurry up. Their scheme had been for Vincent and Gloria to go in and get Sam and come right back out again, ostensibly to unload a large and heavy Christmas present. Out here, away from prying eyes, the two brothers could share a relatively private reunion—after which Andy would send Sam back inside to retrieve Nellie for the same. Only after he had connected with the two of them would Andy go into the house to greet his parents and siblings and everyone else.

That was the plan, but why was it taking so long? He was practically shaking by now—though whether from the cold or the excitement he wasn't sure. Trying to relax, he forced himself to focus on his surroundings. The big farmhouse that had been his home for most of his life. The workshop beside the barn, where he'd first learned the craft of carpentry. The wide, snow-covered pasture that practically glowed in the light of the full moon.

Looking up at that moon, he saw that its glow drowned out all but the brightest stars. The very first Christmas, God had used a star to guide the three wise men to the Christ child. And though it was known as the Star of Bethlehem, Andy preferred to think of it as the star of the whole world. Placed there in the sky to herald the divine unfolding of God's plan, it had been a star of hope, a star of love.

A star of grace.

Andy's thoughts were interrupted by the sound he'd been waiting for, the opening of the back door. Gloria emerged first, followed by Vincent, who was talking to Sam, saying something about how he should've thought to bring a handcart or a dolly with him, as that would've made this easier.

Sam seemed to have no inkling whatsoever about what actually awaited him out here. His eyes were on Vincent's as they moved into the moonlight, and Andy's breath caught in his throat. His little brother wasn't so little anymore. In just six months, he had shot up like a cornstalk. But it wasn't only his height that seemed different. It was the way he carried himself—like a young man.

Andy could feel the grin spreading across his face as he waited, watching the three draw closer. Finally, when they had nearly reached the car, he stepped from the shadows.

"En frehlicher Grischtdaag, Boova," he said softly. Merry Christmas, little brother.

The astonished look on Sam's face was worth every one of the thousand-plus miles he had traveled to get here—and then some.

"I do believe the boy is speechless," Vincent chuckled, beaming with joy.

All Andy could do was pull Sam into a giant bear hug. When they stepped apart again, it didn't really surprise him to see that the kid was crying. They all were.

"I've only been gone six months," Andy said, brushing the tears from his face and giving his brother a broad grin. "How on earth did you do enough growing for a couple of years?"

Sam smiled shyly and ducked his head, mumbling, "I don't know. Just at that age, I guess."

Andy laughed and reached out to put the kid in a mock choke hold, bending his elbow around his neck to pull him close, then tugging his hat down lower on his forehead. He'd missed this guy so much. Only now did he realize *how* much.

Releasing Sam, Andy looked at Vincent and Gloria, who stood off to the side, watching and smiling and dabbing at their eyes as well. He'd already thanked them a number of times, starting when the travel agent contacted him Wednesday afternoon and said there were some people in her office who would like to speak with him about "this train ticket situation."

Earlier that same day, Andy had been so relieved when Sam called and told him the trip was a no-go. But as soon as they'd hung up and Andy absorbed the fact that he was off the hook, something began to shift inside of him. Relief turned to disappointment, then to frustration, then to out-and-out sorrow. At that point he still hadn't known what he was going to do about Nellie, but he realized that he didn't *want* to be off the hook, especially now that Daed was hurt and unable to handle the dairy for the time being. Andy was needed at home far more than he was in Mississippi.

By the time he got that call a few hours later from the agent, who passed the phone over to Vincent Cook, Andy had just about decided to borrow the money from Ivan and pay for the ticket himself. Instead Vincent informed him that he would like to cover the cost and that he and his friend Gloria could even pick up Andy from the train station on Christmas Day if he wanted and drive him home as well.

He had thanked the man profusely, accepting his offer but insisting it be a loan, not a gift.

"No need," Vincent replied. "Thanks to your little brother, I was able to sell a valuable piece of furniture today, an old rocking chair. I was just going to throw it out, but wouldn't you know, because of him, I ended up getting five hundred dollars for it."

Andy's heart had soared, and he accepted the man's generous gift with humility. He'd had less than twelve hours to speak with Ivan and pack his things and tell his landlady and arrange for a ride to the station and get some sleep. But he'd managed to do it all, catching the train out of Hattiesburg the next morning.

It had taken until noon today—more than twenty-five hours—to reach Philadelphia, where he'd transferred to a different train and continued for one more hour to Lancaster. Once there, he'd been weary and dirty but also oddly elated. Falling in step with the crowd that poured onto the platform, he headed up the long flight of stairs and spotted an older couple at the top watching expectantly as passengers filed by.

"Vincent? Gloria?" he said when he finally reached them.

They were so excited to see him that the woman actually gave him a hug even though they had never met. He thanked them both again, this time in person.

The one thing he hadn't yet thanked them for was the conversation that took place during the next half hour on the drive home from the station. For some reason the three of them had slid fairly quickly past the niceties of casual conversation and talked of deeper matters instead. Vincent was saying how fond he was of Sam and how hard Sam had worked, and then he started trying to explain how, in the end, the boy had helped him find forgiveness for someone he loved who'd done a terrible thing but was truly sorry for it.

That was when Andy realized who Vincent Cook was and why he looked so familiar. His son had been the drunk driver in that horrible buggy crash a few years ago. The man was talking about Vince Cook Junior and telling how, thanks to Sam, he had decided to forgive him for what he'd done and to reconcile with him.

They had gone on to lighter topics after that, Gloria chatting in the easy way some women had when conversation lulled, but Andy was only half listening. Inside his mind it was as if an explosion was going off, a giant blast of understanding and insight. Andy hadn't kept Nellie at bay all these months because he didn't *trust* her, he realized, even though that was what he'd been telling himself.

He'd kept Nellie at bay because he had never really *forgiven* her.

He'd said he had, and he'd prayed a prayer or two using the words, but the truth was, he had never truly forgiven. Though his hurt and anger and pain had been justifiable, he'd never fully surrendered them to the Lord.

It was high time he did.

There in the car, as they turned onto Danner Road, Andy prayed silently, finally forgiving Nellie in his heart. When he saw her in person, he would ask for *her* forgiveness of him. God willing, they could move on together from there.

"Is she here?" Andy asked Sam, who knew instantly whom he meant.

Sam nodded.

"You want to get her and send her out? I'm excited to see Mamm and Daed and the rest of the family, but I need to talk to Nellie alone first."

Sam's face clouded. "Are you going to be mean and make her cry?"

Andy threw back his head and laughed. "I might make her cry," he said, "but hopefully they'll be tears of joy."

With a huge smile Sam took off for the house, and Vincent and Gloria seized the moment to bid Andy farewell, saying they needed to get to church. Andy took his bags from the trunk. Then after another flurry of thanks and handshakes, the two drove off. Andy watched them go, and just as he was turning back toward the house, the kitchen door swung open, and Nellie Umble emerged.

The sight of her took his breath away. Even in the semidarkness, he could see that she was more beautiful than ever. Her delicate features. Her willowy figure. Her natural grace.

She moved swiftly toward him, but as she came closer, he realized she hadn't even stopped to put on a jacket.

"Are you crazy?" he cried, dropping his bags and quickly undoing the front of his own coat. "It's freezing out here."

"I don't care," she laughed, coming to a stop when they were face to face at last.

Andy opened his coat wide and wrapped Nellie inside it, wrapped her in his arms and held her tight. They stayed that way for a long, long time, his heart overflowing as he smelled the familiar scent of her hair, heard the distant laughter of his loved ones, felt the sweet softness, the *rightness* of this woman who'd loved him enough to wait for him, who'd believed all along that eventually he would come home.

Just a short while ago, when Vincent turned his car into the driveway, Andy had thought he was home.

But only now, he realized, was he truly home.

Home in North Star.

Home in Nellie's arms.

Epilogue

~~~~~~~

by Katie Ganshert

One year later

> ## ANNOUNCEMENT
>
> **Where:** North Star Community Center
> **What:** Food Stand and Auction Block
> **Why:** Raise funds to update the Amish Birthing Center
> **When:** December 10, 2016, from 1–5 p.m.

The infant's mewling filtered into the kitchen, where Rebekah stood cleaning the birthing equipment with a brush. Before the cry could turn into a wail, the sound stopped. Her assistant, Roseanna—a natural-born baby whisperer—no doubt had something to do with the sudden quiet.

Outside, flecks of white began to fall. Rebekah glanced out the window and noticed a familiar truck idling in the driveway. Oh dear, was it noon already? Originally she'd planned on going to the community center with Savilla to help set up, but then an expectant mother arrived a week earlier than anticipated. If Rebekah had learned anything over her many years as a midwife, it was the art of flexibility. Babies rarely came on schedule.

She had used her emergency cell phone to call Roseanna, asking her to come quickly. Rebekah didn't trust her shaking hands to safely deliver a Bobbeli any longer. Not on her own, with the tremor in her hands so pronounced. But she couldn't bring herself to leave—not on the cusp of a new arrival. So she stayed and assisted her assistant. Funny how the roles had shifted over time.

Rebekah pulled the suture scissors from the cleaning solution, made quick work of placing the equipment inside the sterilizer machine, and peeked down the hallway. Roseanna was just stepping out of the room, closing the door behind her to give the parents and their newborn some privacy.

"How's everyone doing?" Rebekah whispered.

"The baby is nursing. I expect they'll be ready to leave in a few hours." Roseanna smiled knowingly. She was young but astute. She knew full well how difficult it was for Rebekah to let go. This would be the first time since opening the birthing center that she'd leave with a new mother under her roof. "I promise, Rebekah, all will be well. Now you'd better hurry, or you'll miss the entire event. From what I've heard, it's going to be a grand one."

Rebekah returned the young woman's smile. As sad as she was to pass on her life's work, she had no worries about the one she was passing it to. Roseanna would do wonderfully, especially with all the updates this fund-raiser promised to provide. She fastened her winter cape in place and tied on her bonnet, then stepped out into the wintry air.

Chase Wellington climbed out of his truck and opened the passenger-side door. "Delivering a baby and hosting a fund-raiser, both in a single day? I think someone needs to buy you a superhero cape for Christmas."

Rebekah laughed. Hosting was a bit of an embellishment, considering she'd barely lifted a finger to help. In large part all the funds raised would be thanks to the gentleman holding her door open. As soon as

Chase had found out how much work the birthing center needed—a new roof, updated bathrooms, a better generator—he'd contacted all four of the babies she delivered twenty-six years ago, and together they planned the event.

Chase finally wrote his article too—the one he'd wanted to write last year when he first showed up on her porch—and advertised the event in the *North Star Tribune*. From the sound of things, the entire town planned on attending. Which meant they might have enough money left over to purchase some extras—like birthing balls and stools, better baby scales, and new fetal monitoring equipment. Should Roseanna ever find herself in the same predicament Rebekah had all those years ago, she would at least be fully prepared.

She pulled the seat belt across her lap as Chase slid behind the wheel. It sure had been a pleasure getting to know him over the past year. "So tell me, Mr. Wellington. Have you proposed to Elle yet?"

He reached inside his pocket and pulled out a ring. "I'm thinking I will on Christmas."

Rebekah grinned. The two had been carrying on a long-distance relationship for a year now. Elle returned to North Star often, and Chase had flown to Peaks more than a few times. "If you're waiting until Christmas, why do you have it with you now?"

"You never know when a romantic moment might arise," he said with a wink.

The two of them talked easily as they drove over the covered bridge, past the twinkling lights in the park. When they arrived, several horses and buggies were already parked in front of the community center. Inside was a bustle of activity. Men worked together setting up tables, Andy Danner and his little brother, Sam, among them. Sam had always been a naturally happy kid, but ever since his brother moved back to North Star and Nellie became his sister-in-law, Rebekah wasn't sure he'd stopped smiling.

Nearby, John Lantz unfolded chairs with his son-in-law. It'd been quite a year for the Lantz family. Not only had Elle shown up on their doorstep—the spitting image of her mother—she and Chase had surprised everyone by finding Ruth. It had caused quite a stir in the community, and while many thought it would have been better left alone, Rebekah couldn't agree. Relationships were slowly mending, and that was always a good thing.

Off to her left, Kore Detweiler worked alongside Jesse Yoder and Eden Hochstetler, organizing items for the auction. Jesse and Eden arrived a couple of days ago to help with the event. As they were engaged, not yet married, Eden was staying with her Aunt Suzanna, and Jesse was staying with some cousins. They planned to attend church tomorrow before returning to Sugarcreek on Monday.

Savilla's and Kore's friends Jacob and Esther King, along with Nathaniel, their ten-month-old son, were here too.

Kore spotted Rebekah and Chase and waved them over. "Good day for an auction," he said, shaking Chase's hand. "Savvy and I finally read your article. We both thought it was well done."

"Thank you," Chase said.

As the two men struck up a conversation, Rebekah took in her surroundings. Baskets of food, handmade furniture, birdhouses, quilts, wall hangings, crafts, at least a dozen beautiful poinsettias donated by the local nursery. Each item was carefully labeled and ready for auction. Emotion welled in Rebekah's throat. It was touching to see so many people coming together to help her.

Savilla walked toward them with two cornhusk dolls in each hand, a look of pure excitement on her face. "What do you think?"

"I think you all outdid yourselves."

"Glad you like them." Kore wrapped his arm around Savilla's waist and kissed her temple. "There are a lot more of those waiting to go on the auction block." He chuckled, smiling at his wife. "She's had me helping make dolls for this event since we were married. After all you've done for our community, it was the least we could do."

The sight of the two of them together, happily married now for a little more than a month, warmed Rebekah's heart straight through. She was well acquainted with the burden Savilla had carried for so long. Watching that burden lift—watching Kore help his new wife see a future filled with hope—was every bit as amazing as watching a new mother cradle her baby for the first time. Someday, in God's timing, the two would make wonderful parents. Whenever she prayed for them, she imagined that they would become parents to at least two orphaned newborns and a few toddlers or preschoolers over the next decade or so, and their home would overflow with love for a lifetime.

Rebekah glanced across the room, where Elle helped her parents— Mitchell and Vanessa McAllister—set out desserts, doughnuts, funnel cake, coffee, an array of sandwiches, and a couple of donation jars with money already tucked inside. The three of them were living proof that families were made in a variety of ways. Rebekah trusted that Kore and Savilla would experience the same joy Mitchell and Vanessa experienced in Elle.

As final preparations were made, Rebekah joined in where she could. And then, with five minutes to go and Sam Danner itching to open the doors, they gathered for a moment of silent prayer. Rebekah folded her hands, her heart filling with thanksgiving. God had answered her prayers that wintry night long ago when four babies entered the world by her hand, healthy and whole. She'd prayed then that no matter where life took them, these four would know the Lord. And here they were—Eden, Savilla, Elle, and Andy—their heads bowed along with hers, helping her raise money for the very birthing center that cradled their beginning.

Emotion knotted her throat all over again. Who was she that God would be so generous to her? This gift He gave of bringing little miracles into the world. Thanksgiving mingled with expectation. Another Christmas was coming. A celebration of the ultimate miracle. A baby in a manger. Light in the darkness. An everlasting reminder that no matter what lay ahead, hope had already come.

About the Authors

Award-winning author KATIE GANSHERT graduated from the University of Wisconsin–Madison with a degree in education and worked as a fifth-grade teacher for several years before staying home to write full-time. She lives with her family in the Midwest, where she was born and raised. When she's not busy penning novels or spending time with her people, she enjoys drinking coffee with friends, reading great literature, and eating copious amounts of dark chocolate. Visit her website at http://katieganshert.com.

AMANDA FLOWER, a three-time Agatha Award–nominated mystery author, started her writing career as a sixth grader when she read a story she wrote to her class and had them in stitches with her description of being stuck on the top of a Ferris wheel. She knew at that moment she'd found her calling of making people laugh with her words. She also writes mysteries as national best-selling author Isabella Alan. In addition to being an author, Amanda is an academic librarian for a small college near Cleveland. Visit her website at www.amandaflower.com/.

CINDY WOODSMALL is a *New York Times* and CBA bestselling author who has written seventeen works of fiction and one work of nonfiction. Her connection with the Amish community has been widely featured in national media outlets. Cindy has received numerous honors for her writing, and the *Wall Street Journal* listed her as one of the three most popular authors of Amish fiction. When not writing, reading, or watching movies, Cindy can be found enjoying her family, especially her three young grandchildren. Visit her website at www.cindy woodsmall.com/.

MINDY STARNS CLARK is the best-selling author of more than twenty-five books, both fiction and nonfiction, including *A Penny for Your Thoughts, Whispers of the Bayou,* and the number-one-ranked *The Amish Midwife* with Leslie Gould. Mindy has received numerous honors, including two Christy Awards, an Inspirational Reader's Choice Award, and *RT Book Reviews Magazine*'s Career Achievement Award. Mindy and her husband live near Valley Forge, Pennsylvania, and have two grown daughters. Visit her website at www.mindystarnsclark.com.

EMILY CLARK is currently an MFA Creative Writing candidate at the University of North Carolina–Wilmington, where she was awarded a merit-based writing fellowship. She was also the recipient of Eastern University's Thyra Ferre Bjorn Creative Writing Award, which is given to the graduating senior "with the greatest writing potential." As an undergraduate, she worked on the school paper and was a tutor in the school's writing lab. Emily is the daughter of best-selling author Mindy Starns Clark and has helped with many of her books. *Amish Christmas at North Star* is their first published cowritten work.

Meet the *Women of* Lancaster County

Open your heart to these fascinating young women
as they explore their roots, connect with family,
and discover true love.

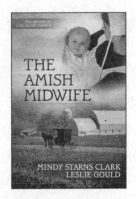

The Amish
Midwife

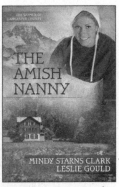

The Amish
Nanny

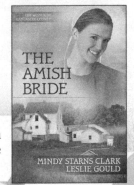

The Amish
Bride

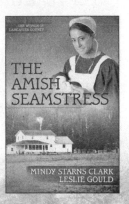

The Amish
Seamstress